MW00989719

SOFT CORE

SOFT CORE

A NOVEL

Brittany Newell

FARRAR, STRAUS AND GIROUX
New York

Farrar, Straus and Giroux
120 Broadway, New York 10271

Library of Congress Cataloging-in-Publication Data
Names: Newell, Brittany, 1994– author.
Title: Soft core : a novel / Brittany Newell.
Description: First edition. | New York : Farrar, Straus and
   Giroux, 2025. |
Identifiers: LCCN 2024034089 | ISBN 9780374613891 (hardcover)
Subjects: LCSH: Psychological fiction. | LCGFT: Novels.
Classification: LCC PS3614.E582 S64 2025 | DDC 813/.6—
   dc23/eng/20240726
LC record available at https://lccn.loc.gov/2024034089

Designed by Abby Kagan

Our books may be purchased in bulk for promotional, educational, or business
use. Please contact your local bookseller or the Macmillan Corporate and
Premium Sales Department at 1-800-221-7945, extension 5442, or by email at
MacmillanSpecialMarkets@macmillan.com.

www.fsgbooks.com
Follow us on social media at @fsgbooks

1   3   5   7   9   10   8   6   4   2

To all the sweet piggies

A body always moving between identities is as evasive as that of a saint, or of a masochist who is never where others expect her to be found.

—KARMEN MACKENDRICK, *Failing Desire*

I think now, after studying the history of sex, we should try to understand the history of friendship, or friendships. That history is very, very important.   —MICHEL FOUCAULT

CONTENTS

Simon Says

I.

I had been stripping for three weeks before I met Simon. A lot had happened in those three weeks: I changed my stage name (from Daisy to Baby), lost a hundred-dollar bill in the bathroom, developed ketchup-hued bruises on my ass cheeks and thighs, got locked out of the Victorian I shared with my ex-boyfriend, Dino.

Ruth! Dino shouted, coming to the door. *Is that you?*

No, I shouted back, *it's Baby.* My arms hurt from carrying my three pairs of shoes.

I don't know a Baby, he sighed, but I could hear him fiddling with the locks. Finally, he let me in and I collapsed on the couch, his dogs swirling around us. Dino eyed me. *Good night or bad?*

I dropped my bag to the floor and money spilled out, along with balled-up burger wrappers and wrecked lipsticks. *It's relative*, I said, burrowing into the couch.

Dino was on his way out. He was a ketamine dealer who

worked even weirder hours than me. We'd broken up at the start of the summer and now it was fall. *You smell like a Vegas casino*, he said. *Try to get some sleep, love.*

He wasn't wrong: ever since I'd started dancing, I couldn't shake the smell of the club from my hair. The other girls didn't seem to have this problem, they drifted around in clouds of patchouli and Victoria's Secret Love Spell, edged with tequila and jojoba oil. I, on the other hand, reeked of cigarettes, hotel sheets, cramped male sweat. I smelled like an airport bar, the tang of the lonely with hours to kill. I smelled like someone's deadbeat dad.

The only thing that half masked the smell of the club was the smell of the french fries I ate in my car. Dancing made me ravenous; no one had warned me about that. They'd warned me about shitty dudes who try not to pay and the inconvenience of getting your period onstage, but not the radical, tectonic hunger I felt when the club closed at 3:00 a.m. Once I'd cashed out, I'd head straight to McDonald's. I paid all in ones and winked at the fidgety senior working the drive-thru. It would take me an hour or more to stop flirting with everyone, to stop being Baby and return to Just Me, Ruth in her clogs and thick socks. Ruth didn't flirt. Ruth was a chick with bad dreams and blisters, requesting extra pickles with her Happy Meal, regretting her master's degree.

I would eat until my tummy hurt, then drive straight home, urgent as a man whose wife was giving birth. That's how I thought of myself, swerving past cars as the sky turned grapefruit: *I gotta be there! Get outta my way!* Though what I was so eager to return to is difficult to say. My life at that point, twenty-seven, semi-single, was hazy and bland. It felt loose, like favorite panties with the elastic stretched out. It was somehow both chaotic and boring, full of glitter and TV. I was either in a rush or staring at the ceiling, thinking of boys I used to kiss. Did they still remember me?

The night I met Simon was a slow one. There were eleven girls on; Nikki and Gemini were the only dancers to break $300, while the rest of us wiggled to Drake for fistfuls of ones. My sole dance that night had been with a coked-up ex-Mormon who confessed in a whisper to being bisexual.

Have you ever been with a man? I asked, playing with my hair.

He looked alarmed. *Of course not!*

Making my rounds in the club, I resisted the urge to dislodge my wedgie. At work I often felt like a fish in a giant aquarium, floating from the stage to the bar and back again. The room was shaped like a horseshoe, with the stage at its center. I paced in my clear plastic Pleasers and a Barbie-pink bikini cut high in the hips. I wore the top upside down to bolster the illusion of breasts on my frame. *Cute*, I'd been called. *Approachable. Sporty.* I looked like an exclamation point and I tried to make that work for me. My breasts were the size of Hostess cupcakes. My ass had the slight curve of a lowercase *b*; the swirly club lights hid the hieroglyphic stretch marks across my hips and inner thighs. Men seemed most impressed by my waist-length hair; it had the look of a dare (*how low can you go . . .*), both wholesome and disarming, the color of whole wheat bread. The real reason for its extravagant length was my fundamental shyness; I liked having something to take the heat off the rest of me, a built-in conversation starter.

A man materialized by the bar, nursing a seltzer. It was 11:45 p.m., neither early nor late by club time. He wore a rust-colored sweatshirt and baggy pants, which didn't mean he wasn't rich. Rich men lived by different rules. He waved me over, scooped me up, and put me on his knee. He looked like my middle school math teacher.

Hey, baby, he said. He sounded unconvincing.

Funny, I said, *because that's my name.*

He acted like he hadn't heard me. *I'm Simon. How'd ya like to make some money?*

Up close, he was clean. Clean as a baby. His clothing was ratty, but the squares of skin I could see—his wrists, his throat—gleamed. His body reminded me of a bar of Dove soap. He needed a haircut. I smiled in a way I hoped was beguiling. *Money is nice.*

He gave me his card, which was actually an envelope on which he'd written a phone number. I folded it up and tried to fit it in the strap of my shoe. I'd seen seasoned strippers keep their money there, but mine always seemed to fall out (chuckling businessmen helped me gather it up, patting me on the rump and calling me klutzy; once I dropped my money bag and a drunk dad called me butterface until the bartender gently corrected him: *I think you mean butterfingers . . .*).

Call me, Simon said, emptying his glass. *I've got a gig for you.* He sounded congested. I felt disappointed until I noticed the hundred he'd slipped under his glass.

My sleep schedule was totally fucked by the club. It had never been consistent, but now it was doomed. I would get home at 4:00 a.m., fizzy and erect as a trick birthday candle. Since the breakup I'd been staying in Dino's guest bedroom. It had an en suite bathroom and Murphy bed. Counting my ones hopped me up even more. I would empty my money bag and make stacks of bills, big fat beautiful stacks like sub sandwiches. I did the thing from the movies where I covered my bed in dollars and fell backward into them like autumn leaves. I got a bill in my mouth and it tasted like ass, reminding me of something the house mom, Cookie, had said on my first night at the club: *There's nothing in this world more dirty than money.* She was eating Cup O' Noodles, sitting on her exercise ball in a somehow magisterial way. While we changed in and out of neon bikinis, she always wore the same Juicy Couture sweatsuit and butt-toning sneakers. She had a little desk in the corner covered with inspirational quotes she'd printed off the internet.

Name one thing, she'd said, *more dirty than money.*

Men? joked Dallas. She had infamous black hair that fell to her knees, longer even than mine. When she went upside down on the pole, her hair unfurled beneath her and pooled on the stage. I didn't feel envy; I felt, as we all did, a soft awe.

Cookie didn't laugh. She slurped up her noodles with grave, weathered eyes. *No*, she said. *Wrong answer.*

It was a trip to be constantly surrounded by beautiful women. I'd had many jobs before stripping: bartender, waitress, overpaid babysitter, Red Bull promoter, test subject at UCSF (they filmed me while I slept for a month and I still don't know why). None had required me to be in the company of innumerable babes—quite the opposite, really. I felt lucky each time I walked into the locker room, shy and alert as a foreign exchange student. It wasn't that I felt attracted to the other dancers—that would have been easier to process—but that I felt unworthy. I had no illusions about my status with men: I was fresh meat, a 7/10 at my finest, the friend of a friend of a friend. The most marketable thing about me was that I was new and white. Our club had a bleak reputation for keeping the roster of dancers 75 percent white. *That's why I've never been there before*, Dino chuckled. I was hired immediately and given good shifts because the manager owed Dino a favor.

One night, the couple I used to babysit for came into the club. I'd always suspected the Hensons were swingers. When I worked for them as a dead-eyed high school senior, they would come home around dawn and compulsively flirt with me, chatting until the coke burned off. I'd be scraping myself off the sectional where I'd fallen asleep watching TiVo, and they'd be blocking the doorway with big, flashy grins. They held each other in the way of prom couples: the man behind the woman with his arms around her waist.

Did you have fun with the twins tonight? they would ask me. I'd say the twins were asleep. *Good*, they'd say, *but did you have FUN? We want you to have FUN!* They wouldn't let me leave until I said that I did. Then they would walk me to my car and rub my shoulders while I tried to find my keys. Mr. Henson wore those running shoes that outline your toes. *Loosen up*, they'd say in eerie unison. *Life's short, yanno?*

When I saw them at the club, there was none of that friendliness. They locked eyes with me from across the room and froze. The woman wore a gold lamé dress so tight I could see the egg-sized bulge of her pubic bone. After a beat, I waved; they waved back. They were being led into a VIP room with Veronique. She waved too, a bit aggressively. *Have fun*, I mouthed to the trio, then kept bouncing to mashups.

Did I feel a flash of jealousy that they had chosen Veronique over me? I'd always thought they had a thing for me, a teeny crush born of convenience. Still, I couldn't blame them. I'd pick Veronique for a private dance too. She had cushy breasts like those teddy bears you win at the fair. She smelled like crème brûlée.

I called Simon the following afternoon. I'd slept late, then dragged myself to 7-Eleven for a jumbo iced coffee and a pack of white powdered donuts, which I ate in bed with chopsticks (a trick I'd learned from a Korean YouTuber to avoid sticky fingers) until I couldn't procrastinate any longer.

He picked up after the first ring. *Howdy*, he said.

Howdy.

Long night?

I feigned a laugh. *Yup.*

I have certain tastes, he said. I had to hand it to him: he got right to the point. *You might call them kinky.*

That's good, I said dumbly.

Is this something you cater to?

Sure. I felt like I was being honest. At that point in my life, most things seemed kinky, kinky here meaning specific, hushed, and charged with weird light. I'd already had my fair share of foot dudes at the club. They were well regarded by most dancers, paying for VIP rooms just to rub our feet; we got to take off our Pleasers and shoot the shit for an hour. The ones I'd encountered had been mousy, demure, cowed by the weight of desire. They wore their fantasies like girdles, an everyday secret. It must have felt good to finally exhale, alone in a room with a beautiful girl. That was our job at the club, or so it seemed to me then: to make men feel OK about whatever moved them. Big nipples, knee socks, monkeyish toes— if it makes you feel good, I'm your girl. Take a load off, settle in. What could Simon possibly want, I reasoned, that would shock me?

When things were slow on the floor, I liked to duck into the locker room and study the clipboard. To me it was like poetry, this ever-changing list of all the girls on that night, including those who had flaked. Angelina, Kitty, Buttercup. I tried to memorize them all. When I was a child at playdates and we saw a pretty girl on TV, we would shout, *I'm her!* It was a race to claim the best girl for yourself, your future ghost, your big-tittied analogue. Picking a name felt similar to me, an act of intrapersonal voodoo, earnest and raw. Who could make the whole world bend to her? Scarlet, Candy, Foxy, Grace?

One night I asked Arabella how she came by her name. She was scraping the bottom of her boots with scissors. She didn't look up. *It was my stepmother's name.* She was naked from the waist up, her breasts resting on her knees as she examined her work.

Oh, I said. *That's sweet.*

Sweet? Arabella snorted. *Fuck that stupid fucking bitch.* She spritzed the hacked-up bottom of her boot with hairspray. *I just wanted a name that started with* A. *If shit is alphabetical, I wanna be on top.*

What Simon said he wanted was a favor here and there. Really, they weren't favors. The word made me laugh, as if I were giving him a ride or lending him a sweater. We agreed on $800 a month, sent to me automatically through PayPal. He'd come to the club every now and again; whenever I saw him, he'd give me my instructions.

The night of the first favor was a busy one. Some big soccer game was playing, Mexico vs. Croatia. Men divided their attention between the women onstage and the TVs over the bar. Just because it was packed didn't mean we'd make money. On busy nights it was easy for dudes to melt into the crowd, feigning innocence when we singled them out and purred for a tip. *I'm just here to drink* was a familiar phrase. *I'm just out with my guys. I don't have any cash on me. I just wanna drink in peace, OK?*

Experienced dancers knew what to say. They could sweetly shame a college boy into, at the very least, subscribing to their OnlyFans. *This is no ordinary bar,* they'd say with a wink. They'd indicate their breasts, foaming out of a bustier. *Do you like what you see? Yes? Then show me!*

I envied their skill. I didn't know how to be sassy yet endearing, lovably firm. When rejected by guests, I just walked away. I was scared that if I opened my mouth, I might end up shouting. There was a very small yet ferocious girl inside me that was prone to throwing drinks in men's faces. Dino had seen her, though I tried my best to keep her under wraps.

When Simon waved me over, I felt a flash of relief. At least I knew he liked me. He was sitting at the bar and drinking a beer from a tall, frosted glass.

Howdy, he said. I could never get a read on Simon's inebriation, if he was totally plastered or just sat there drinking for something to do. It was rare that he would finish a drink but sometimes he bungled his words, betraying internal confusion. He smiled and pushed his glass toward me.

No, thanks, I said. *I don't really like beer.* Actually, I loved it, but I didn't want to be bloated in my little lace set. After work I often drank a Corona with lime in my bed, letting my tummy slope over the waistband of my terry cloth shorts.

He smiled. *Me either.* He ran a finger around the glass's rim. *But I think you should take this. I think you should go to the ladies' room.* I can't remember if he told me directly or somehow implied it, but it finally dawned on me: he wanted me to piss in his glass.

I picked it up and hurried to the most remote bathroom. Then I locked myself in a stall, dumped the beer in the toilet, and squatted. I closed my eyes and thought of sprinklers, tsunamis, big bruised-up peaches splattering juice. Finally, a modest stream came out. I managed to fill up a third of the glass, then diluted the rest with tap water. I washed my hands thoroughly and returned to the bar, where Simon appeared to be studying the innermost seam of his jeans.

He didn't look up as I placed the glass on the bar top. I sat down beside him and felt a bit shy, as if I'd written him a poem and was waiting for him to review it.

Well, I said. I folded my hands in my lap. *There you go.*

There was long fizzy pause in which we avoided eye contact; then he reached out and downed the whole thing in one go. I could hear the cartoonish *glug* as he swallowed. When at last he looked up, his eyes were glassy, wide.

Delicious, he whispered. His usual zip-lipped machismo was gone; he looked like a little boy on his birthday. *Thank you so much.*

I was glad for the club lights as they hid my blush. *No problem. There's more where that came from.*

He licked his lips. *Really?*

Well . . . no. I didn't think I could pee for at least one more hour. *Not now.*

He nodded. *That's OK.* Now that I'd fulfilled his favor, I felt some distance between us. He wasn't cold or mean, exactly, but it seemed like he wanted to be left alone. I could relate; in my early twenties I was the type to get high solo, to withdraw from the after-party spangled out in some underfurnished living room and tuck myself into a stranger's empty bed. I wanted to swaddle myself in good vibes, hoard them, and I feared that mindless socializing would somehow pollute my high.

I'm gonna go powder my nose, I said, sliding off my stool.

He nodded. *Sounds good.* He studied the grain of the bar, hands folded in front of him. The bartender swept past and grabbed the now-empty glass. We both said nothing as she walked away, dunked it in the sink.

The rest of the night was a blur. All I remember is dancing for an older couple who asked to take me home (*We could eat you right up!*) and, later, a man passing out on the toilet with his pants still buckled. Management found him an hour after closing; they thought, at first, that he was dead.

Things the other dancers told me: There was a girl named Horsie who named herself after the drug. There was a girl named Penny who never made shit. There were two girls called Unique who got in a fistfight over the name. There were the identical twins named Molly and Holly, Lola and Lila. There was a girl who had her regulars call her Trash Bag. There was a girl named Patience who was so very beautiful, so beloved by all men, that no one dared use that name ever since.

The summer I started dancing, the Olympics were on. Dino and I would watch them together in the late afternoons, hiding out from the heat in the living room. He would order pizza from Domino's—olives, peppers, extra cheese—and save the crusts for me. I dipped them in ranch and tried not to drip on the couch. For a lifelong drug dealer, he was surprisingly fastidious. It was one of the things that had made dating him hard: he was all about order, whereas I felt most comfortable in a state of mild scatter. He had a key bowl in the foyer where he actually put his keys, a fridge full of rainbow farmers' market vegetables. One of our biggest fights had revolved around me putting a Diet Coke in the crisper. I can still hear his voice: *Jesus, Ruthie. This is why I don't fuck with white girls. The world is your motherfucking oyster, isn't it?*

I didn't tell Dino about Simon. I wasn't worried he'd be jealous. In the last months of our relationship, sex stopped being important to us. We'd become so fused that intercourse felt redundant. Our love affair pivoted on a shared taste for self-negation. We loved to get freakishly high and melt into the sofa, not moving for days, more blanket than body. We would mash our foreheads together, hold hands so hard our fingers tingled, a eunuch's idea of hot sex. We kissed like twins and showed love by taking turns getting the mail.

Some people thought Dino was slimy, they distrusted his charm, but they didn't see what I saw: Yes, he owned nun-chucks, yes, I was forbidden from being alone with his friends, but he also loved Miyazaki movies and Dolly Parton. Despite his dark appetites, he was a softie who cross-dressed. He wore leopard-print satin around the house, Agent Provoca-teur lingerie under his gym clothes. This always struck me as more of an art project than a fetish, but then, I was used to it. His K was good, he never cut it. He used to be a chef of local renown and knew everyone. He kissed his rescue doggies on the lips and named them after nineties supermodels: Linda was a hell-raiser, Cindy was chunky, Naomi, the favorite, slept in his arms every night.

When Dino made house calls, I liked to ride with him. It was fun to drive around the city together, watching the bars empty, parking out by the beach and waiting for his regulars to call. His clientele was mainly young men with money, fresh out of college, reeking of Axe. They called women babes (as in, *I got a babe waiting upstairs*) and spent thousands of dollars on weekend-long music festivals. I think they were intimidated by Dino's size, his ropy forearms and throat tattoos (MAGDALENA, for his mom). If they ever noticed me in the passenger seat, they never let on. If he'd caught them

looking, Dino might've smiled and said, *Don't be shy, man.*
Ask my lady her star sign.

He would double-park outside some tech bro's loft and tell
me to look out for cops. I leaned the seat back as far as it
would go and held Naomi in my lap. All the windows were
down and I could smell the night air, forever autumnal in San
Francisco. On these nights I felt happy. I wanted for nothing.
I had my man and my city, two odd, salty beauties. I knew
what would happen when Dino got back in the car: We would
speed down the Great Highway, blasting *Jesus Christ Super-
star* and singing along, then park in the driveway and make
out for a bit before going inside and getting ready for bed. I
would wear one of his XXL T-shirts and he would wear a
100 percent silk negligee, green to bring out his eyes.

The second favor was less flashy but no less impactful. Simon
asked to see inside my mouth.

We were sitting at the bar, ignoring our drinks, when a
look of misty consternation came over him.

Do you mind . . . he sputtered, looked down.

Spit it out, I said, not unkindly.

He couldn't help but smile. *No,* he murmured, *you.*

Me, what?

You spit.

I shrugged and began to summon saliva to the front of my
mouth. To do so, I imagined I was sucking a Lemonhead.
Simon watched me intently, breathing slow. He leaned closer
and said, *Let me see.*

I couldn't speak without losing the saliva I'd conjured, so I tilted my head to communicate uncertainty.

He smiled and said it again. *Let me see.*

Balancing my hands on my thighs, I puckered my lips into the shape of a bowl and opened my mouth.

Perfect, he whispered. *Now swallow.*

I did so with a melodramatic gulp. If I'd had an Adam's apple, it would have bobbed.

Oh god, Simon said. *Oh my god.* He looked winded and wowed, like he'd spent the day at a museum. *I wish that was me in there. I wish you could swallow me whole.*

But you're too big.

He nodded sadly. *I know.* Though half-naked women jiggled all around us, we spoke to each other like children, blunt and believing. Somehow I knew what he meant: he wanted to be the size of a grape, of a gumball, something you're warned your whole life not to choke on. He wanted to slide down my throat, disappear into darkness. I imagined my belly like a room with the blinds drawn on a summer day. He wanted to enter that room and lie down. It was a desire both pure and absurd.

I think the reason I didn't tell Dino about Simon is because I didn't know how to explain it to him. It felt taxing to put our entanglement into words. I didn't want him to worry. The truth is, I felt great. I felt purposeful, driven. Here was someone who needed me, who appreciated my work. Simon was a satisfied customer. Unlike with my other regulars—a traveling salesman too large to fit on one barstool, a widower who told me young pussy should taste like cream soda—it felt good to make him happy.

That autumn, Simon came and went as he pleased, sometimes showing up fifteen minutes before closing. I got the impression that he knew the manager. That's why he never got dinged for violating the dress code with his soiled hoodies and infamous flip-flops. He drifted in, ordered a beer he didn't finish, tipped Sadie the bartender handsomely, and waited for me to be free.

I never got a hypersexual vibe from Simon. Our first encounter, when he sat me on his lap and called me baby, was our most flirtatious. After that, his dudely act seemed to soften. He was not a cowboy, but a cow. Big brown eyes, staring at nothing . . . Either sad or content, hard to tell.

I didn't think of what we did together as especially sexual either. Sure, he got off, but in a muted, private way. Whatever he gained from these favors was his business and he didn't need to spray me with it. Over the course of our arrangement I pissed in his beer; spat in his face; stepped on his toes; put my socks in his mouth; gave him my dirty panties in a Ziploc bag; pinched his belly fat until he cried uncle; called him many, many names. He alternated between wanting to be a good boy and a bad boy, praised and torn down. I called him ugly, pitiful, unlovable, rank. I got creative and called him reprehensible, lugubrious, toady, a serf. I told him about my wild sexual exploits (which, of course, I made up), stressing how irresistible I was to the captain of the UC Berkeley swim team, a freckled twenty-one-year-old beefcake I named Rocky.

For the mind games, we sat at the bar; for the more physical stuff, Simon paid for a private room where I was free to abuse him. It was nothing major: I spanked him, pulled his hair, gave him titty-twisters. Once he asked for a used tampon. Another time he reserved a VIP room for two hours and told me to sit there and ignore him. That was a wonderful night. I watched TikTok on my phone and pretended to text Rocky while Simon trembled and sighed in a corner.

He never got hard, which I liked; he never called me sexy or pretty or cute. I never had to dance for him or take off my clothes. The closest we came to that type of exchange was one night when he asked me to slap him. I was standing in front of him, leaning down, wearing new heels I'd failed to break in. I slipped on the beery floor; he put a hand out to steady me and grazed my breast in the process. There was a long, hot pause before he snatched his hand away.

I'm sorry, he mumbled, looking down.

I stepped back. *It's fine.*

We could hear the bass from the main room, the sound of girls laughing. Someone called out, *No faaaair!* in a high-pitched voice. I wracked my brain for something to say.

Finally, Simon stood up. *Thirsty?*

Absolutely, I lied.

He almost ran to the door, held open the curtain. *Let's get you a Shirley Temple.*

I recited the list to myself on the drive back to Dino's: Jezebel, Brandy, Kitty, Veronique, Natalie, Harmony, Arabella, Dior,

Gemini, Roxie, Fiona, Elite, Saskia, Gigi, Delaney, Mary-jane, AJ, Paris, Dallas, London, Raven, Lola, Lana, Lux.

It was hard, at first, to know what to do with my money. Dino was no help. He clipped coupons and tracked his monthly expenses on a password-protected spreadsheet. His one indulgence, as far as I could tell, was high-quality ice cream. He'd scold me if I bought quilted toilet paper for the house (*You can feel the difference!* I bellowed) but would easily drop $11 on a pint of hand-churned gelato.

It's the little things in life, he'd say with a mouthful of pistachio. *You want?* He revealed his age in the flavors he liked: rum raisin, black walnut. I, on the other hand, liked flavors with *swirl* or *chunk* in the name, anything with crushed-up candy bars.

You have the palate of a twelve-year-old boy, Dino sighed, watching me microwave dinosaur-shaped chicken nuggets.

Why do you know so much about twelve-year-old boys?

He rolled his eyes. *Hardy-har. I'm seriously worried about your iron intake, Ruthie!*

I reached for the half-empty bottle of ranch. *I'll suck pennies.*

He couldn't help but laugh. *That's sick.*

I tried different ways to spend my money—online gambling, shopping sprees—but it all felt a bit forced. I didn't want or need more clothes; the only places I ever went, besides the club, were Trader Joe's and the YMCA pool. I didn't need knee-high boots or complicated athleisurewear to shop for chips. My one sartorial outlet was the lingerie I wore for work, the virginal teddies and psychedelic bikinis, schoolgirl skirts and short-lived stockings. There was a boutique in Daly City called Candyland where Dino and I would shop for lingerie together, Dino walking slowly as if in a botanical garden. Using my stripper cash to buy more stripper clothes felt like a mean joke, a glittery ouroboros. So I washed my old stockings in the kitchen sink and filled a coffee tin to the brim with balled ones.

Cookie suggested I go to the Korean spa during the day. To my surprise, the only people there at 2:30 p.m. on a Tuesday were other strippers and a smattering of spaced-out grannies. Gigi saw me and gave me a hug, our bodies misted and slick as supermarket produce. She was the club's biggest earner, though you wouldn't know it here. *Hey, Baby*, she said. She looked sleepy and small. *Ready for that TLC?*

Uh-huh. We soaked together in the hot tub until it was time for her full-body scrub. She walked away with her hair in a frazzle.

I wandered upstairs and lay down in the clay room. It was a pink-lit closet filled knee-deep with clay balls. They were smooth and hot and the size of billiard balls. It reminded me of the children's ball pit at McDonald's; did those still exist? You were supposed to wear your panties, but I was alone, so I took mine off and hid them in a corner. It felt amazing to roll around in all those hot little balls. I buried myself as deep as I could. For a moment, I thought of Simon. Was this something he would like? Then an employee came in and chastised me for not wearing panties; I was told, very sweetly, that I'd need to leave.

———

There were all the different nouns, lifted from their humdrum meanings: Daisy, Opal, Lyric, Karma, Olive, Poppy, Destiny, Sapphire, August, Serenity, Diva, Faith, Rosemary, Crystal, Angel, Diamond, Fawn, Savannah, Princess, Fate.

My favorite dancer was a girl named Harmony. She liked to bake and brought us gluten-free treats in Tupperware containers. *Harmony wants us thick!* we cried, mouths full of coffee cake. Though she'd been dancing forever, she wasn't part of any clique. She had a wide, dimpled ass and, I swear to God, the most beautiful pussy I've ever seen. I kept looking, discreetly, for someone to rival her, but none held a candle to our Harmony's.

Before I started dancing, I rarely thought of my body in any great detail. It was only during sex that I found any reason to savor it. Its robust capacity for pleasure was something to be celebrated, like a nation's exports. At all other times I was fond of my body like you'd be fond of a favorite mug—I liked it enough to use it every day but not enough to talk about it.

Sometimes my body betrayed me. I'd awake to discover that my favorite jeans were too tight in the ass. Then, two days later, they'd fit like a dream. My body was a friendly ghost, causing trouble just because. I dealt with it as one must deal with a poltergeist; I didn't take its hijinks personally and tried to ignore what it did after dark. That's when I went out, got horny and stupid. That's when I sucked dick in big-box parking lots and told strangers that I needed them.

What a trip it was, then, to enter a profession where fielding comments about every inch of my body was part of the job. Nothing was off-limits. I got used to being told I was both too skinny and too fat, far from thick but not quite waifish. What was more surprising were the things men *did* like about me. They liked my toes; they liked my lack of a waist; they liked the freckles spread across my shoulders and chest, which I'd never had occasion to notice.

You look like this girl I used to know, one man told me. *She had big brown eyes. They reminded me of my childhood dog's eyes.* He blinked, suddenly maudlin. *RIP Lambchop. What a good girl.*

We toasted to Lambchop and he gave me a twenty.

When we first started dating I kept a list of Dino's favorite foods on my phone. Cottage cheese with black pepper, the tortillas that stretched. This was how I knew that I loved him. I'd never before had occasion to wonder what a man ate in a day. With Dino, it was different. I needed to know what he put in his mouth and how much it pleased him. I wanted the world to be to his liking, a party I'd thrown just for him. Finger foods and fizzy drinks, everything glossy and kind. He was so beautiful it made me nervous. Suddenly my passwords related to him: 0505 to unlock my phone, the day of our first kiss. Once I took a picture when he wasn't looking, when his lips were slack and soft, his hands the size of catcher's mitts. He was wearing an eyelet blouse that made me think of Greece. I looked at it often, feeling my heart tauten. I wanted the weather to always be clement, the sun on his bared wrists.

Simon and I had a good thing going. That was undeniable. I didn't tell the other girls about it, but I'd overheard them talking about similar arrangements. I didn't think about Simon the way I thought about other dudes at the club, with an ever-shifting mix of appreciation, pity, and disgust. He was just Simon, this strange man I knew. Half uncle, half stray dog I put out a dish for. Yes, there was fondness there. You don't see someone every other Friday night without developing a connection. I guess when someone drinks your piss, you feel like they know you a little.

Still, I couldn't have predicted the last favor he'd ask me.

It was a day shift, which I rarely worked, thanks to Dino's connections. Simon sat at his usual spot at the bar, notdrinking a Bud Light. He looked the same as always: grubby clothes, shifty eyes, unwashed hair. Upon my request, he'd started growing out his mustache. It made him look even more likely to jack your car.

Hey there, I said, slinking up.

Hi.

I was just thinking of you.

Really?

Mm-hm. It was true. I'd just finished a private dance for a fidgety frat boy no older than twenty-two. As soon as we were alone in the VIP room, he turned around and bent over. Frothing out from his jeans was a lacy pink thong. *So literal*, I thought. Why did all the sissies like the same things? Always frilly, always pink. Barbie Dreamhouse bullshit. Why couldn't they be sleek like Dino or quiet like Simon? It would be more realistically girlish to display yourself shyly, with a hint of remorse. Dino seemed to understand this with his ocher and seafoam, his classic black satin.

Cute, I told the boy.

They make me feel pretty, he said in a forced high-pitched voice. *Pretty like you!*

It was then that I thought, *Where is Simon?*

At the bar, he smiled into his drink. *That makes me happy to hear*, he said.

Well, it's the truth.

His face darkened. *Too happy, in fact.*

What?

He ignored me. I waved my hand at Sadie to order a seltzer and waited for him to speak. It wasn't abnormal for Simon to get tongue-tied around me.

At last he opened his mouth. *I have another favor to ask you.*

OK, I said, playing along.

I want you to delete me.

I put a hand on his shoulder and said, *Come again?* I thought perhaps he'd said, *Feed me.*

You heard me, he said. *I want you to delete me. Forget all about me.*

Simon, I said. *Did I do something wrong?*

He shook his head. *Quite the contrary.*

I thought perhaps he was kidding, trying to goof around. *Well, OK . . .* I played with my hair, batted my lashes. *But won't you miss me?*

When he looked up, his eyes were hard. *That's the whole fucking point.* I'd never heard him use this tone before; it revealed his age, the specter of children or wives he'd chastised in the very same way.

Fine, I snapped. *You're the boss.* But I just stood there, arms crossed. I felt tingly with rage. I thought about throwing a drink in his face, but that's the problem with masochists— they like it rough. Instead I just forced myself to smile and play with my hair, the armor of girlhood, my eternal security blanket, until he stood up.

When he put a fifty on the bar, I knew he meant business. He kept his eyes on the floor as he zipped up his coat, a shapeless parka the color of gravestones. If I saw him from behind on the bus, I'd never recognize him. He moved toward the door, hands in his pockets, unrushed. As I watched him go, I was suddenly seven years old: I was standing outside my school at the end of the day, waiting to be picked up. Car after car drove past, their headlights making gold lines on the blacktop, until the group dwindled down to just me and one other kid. When his mother finally came, she rolled down her window and looked at me sadly.

Where's your mom, honey? she asked.

I didn't answer the mother; instead, I sat down on the curb. I was terrified of her next question: *Where is your daddy?* I wouldn't know how to answer her. As I watched them drive away, my mouth tasted like blood. It became clear to me then, at seven years old: other people lived in orbs of warmth that I was quietly exempt from. They had dinner and dogs, but I had the night.

Keep the change, Simon called from the doorway. I blinked, confused, until I realized he was talking to Sadie. I overheard her chatting with Gigi later that night as she broke down the bar: *Never underestimate the quiet ones. They always have money. So true*, Gigi said, raising her glass. *Here's to them.*

At dinner one night I asked Dino what his stripper name would be. He pondered, setting down his beer to think. Finally he tapped my knee. *Diana*, he said. *Because I love her so.* He meant, of course, the princess.

I could never sleep after a shift. I'd crawl into bed with my phone and get lost online. I liked Quora, a website exclusively used by old people and tweens. Users uploaded questions for other users to answer.

> *What's the worst thing you've done for money?*
> *Which celebrities are infamously bad kissers?*
> *Do you have any memories from inside the womb?*

I read until I heard Dino's dogs waking up. They circled the living room and whined for their breakfast. His voice was often the last thing I heard before drifting off.

Come on, little girlies, he sang. In private he spoke to them so tenderly. Sometimes I found myself missing that tone. It reminded me of when we first met. I was twenty-five, still in the habit of drinking three coffees a day. I was riding the bus to the SFSU library when he plunked down beside me and smiled. I remember his rings, one for each finger. He seemed expansive, full of light. Like a shoplifter with a microwave under his jacket, that's how full of light he was. He sat with his fingers fanned out on each thigh. As we rode the hills of San Francisco, his body didn't budge. Burdened with bags and books, I envied his poise. He was irrefutably beautiful, a big-boned angel in cowboy boots. At last he said, *Going somewhere?*

I stammered, *Library.* Every day I sat in the stacks and pretended to write.

He smiled. *I like a girl who reads. You know why?*

I tried to smile back. *Why?*

Cuz glasses are sexy.

Now I lay in this man's guest room and listened to him putz around, barefoot and blurry-eyed, in the rude hours of morning. His thighs would have goose bumps, bared in his nightgown. *You're telling Daddy that you're hungry*, he sang. *Daddy's on it, don't you fret. Daddy loves his little girls.*

I looked down: I had goose bumps too. I fell asleep with my phone in my hand.

Simon's payments kept coming, every month on the dot, but I never saw him at the club again. I would sometimes see men shaped like him at the bar and my heart would leap. But no, it was just some other lonely fool, another man studying his beer. Secretly I missed Simon. We were twinned in a deep, mysterious way, like two people who survive the same plane crash. Loneliness was our destiny; unlike the men at the bar and the women onstage, we didn't try to deny it. We were each other's child bride, linked by something more lasting than lust.

The only person I told was Cookie. It was a packed night and we were alone in the locker room. By then I'd been dancing for almost two months. I'd seen every color of bruise on my thighs, made more money than I ever thought possible, and been called names I'd only ever heard on TV. That night I'd spilled cranberry juice on my teddy and rushed to Cookie for a new outfit. My stage set was in a few minutes; I could see my name on the list.

This is the one! Cookie said, combing through her crate of clothes. She pulled out a long-sleeved black bodysuit made of wet-looking material. *This will make you look bossy. Boss bitch! Boom!*

It wasn't something I would normally wear, but Cookie was right: it made me seem powerful. I wriggled into it and grew three inches.

Cookie slapped me on the ass. *Baby's not a baby tonight!*

I smiled. *Simon would like this.*

Qué?

I told her about our arrangement, the piss in the beer, the recurring payments. She nodded as I spoke, unfazed. You couldn't shake Cookie. Gigi once described her as Strip Club Santa: generous, jolly, nocturnal.

Plus that bitch keeps track of who's naughty and nice, Gigi had whispered. *It's best to stay on her good side.*

When I finished talking, Cookie stood behind me and ran her fingers through my hair. I became unrecognizable as she yanked it into different braids. We were quiet as she worked. Finally she looked in the mirror, speaking not to me but to my reflection.

Isn't it funny? she said. *Sometimes shit feels so good it's unbearable.*

I nodded, not really following.

These men! she sighed. *They think we're the only ones who show ourselves. But of course they think that. If not, they'd kill us!*

Hm?

She laughed merrily, then grabbed me by the elbow and pulled me out of the chair. *Just playing!* she cried. *Now go make a bag.*

OK, I said, feeling a bit unsteady. What girl was I tonight? What did men think of her, what did she keep in her purse? Pressed flowers and love letters; sticks of beef jerky and ChapSticks without caps . . .

As if reading my mind, Cookie pinched me and said, *Good girl. You got this, OK?*

OK, I said, then walked onto the floor.

I remember, early on, watching Dino sleep. I had just moved into his place. We were watching a movie and he'd fallen asleep. He was physically incapable of watching a film start to finish. He was curled up on the couch, his knees to his chest, his cheek on his knees. His long dark hair coiled down his shins. He was wearing a nightgown, filmy white. It was softer than his usual looks, less vixeny, more coquettish. One sleeve had slipped off his shoulder, revealing a square of bare skin. His lips looked like plums. Naomi, as always, was huddled up next to him. Over them both was a blanket, fuzzy and blue.

The blanket was what did me in. I looked at them both and started to cry.

I was shocked by my tears. The sight of him sleeping was somehow grotesque. Though the lamps were orange and the heater on high, I felt a sliding sense of terror, acute as if I'd heard a door creak open. I had to get up and go to the kitchen, wiping my eyes on a dish towel. I'd never before been in love with a man, so I couldn't identify what was happening to me, why my heart felt so full it could burst. These are the things we don't know when we're young. Asleep on the couch with one brown shoulder bared—I saw him, suddenly, as a breakable thing. In his waking life, he was so big and so bright. He was sexy and brave and a little bit bossy. He always said, *Thank you, driver!* when he got off the bus. When he was younger he lived with the drummer of Deafheaven and an aging drag queen named Kate's Bush. He dealt at the Attic and blew off steam at the Stud. He wept when the men's suit superstore on Mission went under. To me, he was San Francisco embodied, misty, bookish, and debased. But now, in the lamplight, I saw that he too could be shattered. Like a game or a favorite earring, he could easily be lost.

After a few months at the club I began to notice a change in my body. My belly stayed soft but underneath the flesh was a wall of muscle. I could feel it contracting when I wrapped myself around the pole. As a newbie stripper I could still only manage the most basic tricks. My legs and arms ached when I limped offstage. *Use your core*, Dallas advised. She punched me, lightly, in the gut. *It's all about that core.* Sometimes at work I stood in the bathroom, touching my belly. I was so used to softness that even this small amount of hardness intrigued me. I liked that it was something only I knew about, a change in my body that the men couldn't discern. They still saw me as a fleshy thing, a bouncy ball, all juice and pulp. They knew nothing of my secret strength. They knew nothing of my hard core.

Out to dinner with Dino for his thirty-seventh birthday, I remembered the name of the couple I babysat for in high school. We were at his favorite restaurant in all of San Francisco: the Cheesecake Factory at Union Square. When he was a cook, he headed kitchens with Michelin stars, yet he still waxed poetic about the Cheesecake Factory's crab rangoon. He downloaded the menu online to decide in advance which cheesecake he wanted. This, from the man I once swore I would die for. Watching him ask for four olives with his martini still made my heart ache.

Cheers, he said, raising his glass. *Another year closer to death.*

We sat on the deck and ordered like tourists in love: calamari, crab cakes, steak cooked rare, french fries in a wire cone. We'd dressed up for the occasion, him with his Prince-tight trousers and vetiver cologne, me in a black velvet bustier that looked almost normal when paired with blue jeans. Since I started dancing I had forgotten how to look nice without also looking slutty. The night felt festive, as if we hadn't seen each other in a long time. We got tipsy and accidentally flirted. We were conspiratorial as sisters, touching our foreheads together to gossip, but there was an edge beneath the chumminess, a summery recklessness. We were retracing old patterns, hot grooves of feeling we'd retired. He read my palm and didn't give my hand back, absentmindedly tracing its lines. It felt OK because it wouldn't last. We'd shrug off this evening, its weight; until then, we romped and shimmered, letting other tables envy us, the loudness of young love.

I couldn't remember the last time we'd gone out to dinner. I was too tired, Dino too busy. On my days off, I liked to lounge around in my boxers. I would wake up at noon, then walk to the YMCA pool, where I wore myself out doing laps with the grannies. We were all required to wear a swim cap and goggles. I liked this unbecoming costume, how sexless I became. It was relaxing, somehow, to surrender to irrelevance after a weekend spent arching my back.

I would swim until my belly ached, then trot home. I'd take a bath and listen to a podcast on economics or murder. Usually Dino would cook for me, vast Dominican feasts; we played chess while we digested. We always walked the dogs together after dinner, talking about everything but work. If he was doing his drug runs that night, he'd kiss me on the forehead and leave me on the couch, surrounded by the girls.

Be good, he'd say, taking his keys from their bowl and clipping them to his belt. A bit of burgundy lace peeking out from his waistband.

Or what? I'd ask, laughing, but he was already gone.

II.

One of my earliest memories is of a porch in July. I still see it clearly: a pitcher of lemonade, shoes by the door, the red-and-white tablecloth printed with chickens. When I touched it, it felt waxy, wet. When I looked up, there were flowers hanging over the banister, frothy and white. I remember somebody naming them. *Jasmine*, he said. He was tall and all-knowing, with hands as big as frying pans. He wore a sweater and smelled good. He pointed high above my head. *That one's called jasmine.*

In retrospect, this should have been my dancer name. It's pretty, delicate. But I couldn't really pull it off. I didn't possess the abundant femininity it implied. My body suggested something more like Jean. I went with Baby because the bartenders called me that. Of course, they called everyone baby, honey, babe; it wasn't just me. But when I heard it that second or third night at work, I felt hailed. I liked the idea of it, the touch of perversity: a baby was pure but also driven by hunger. You called someone baby when you detangled their hair but also when you fucked them (*Turn around for me, baby*). How many men in my life had called me baby, gifted me this name? Too many to count—from bored taxi drivers to boys who made moussaka for me, strangers and lovers and strangers who became, by dint of will, lovers. I still had some of their underwear, tossed in with mine, which I wore on the second (and worst) day of my period; the crinkled white briefs barely made me think of their owner and yet I still kept them, year after year, move after move, long after far more important things (diaries, checks) had been lost. I didn't remember their full names but I remembered their voices, husky and hushed, sexily dehydrated, whispering *baby* in myriad beds.

It was only a matter of time before one such man saw me at the club. Charlie: an ex, of sorts. A man whose cum had dried in my hair (I didn't notice until after we'd gone out for drinks, in the taxi ride home, as I held my face in my hands), whose mother was named Shirley and sent him butter cookies in a big blue tin. We'd eaten them in his living room while his wife was in Vermont, visiting a sick cousin (or was she a surgeon, away at a conference?); he made us English breakfast tea to dunk our cookies in. We laughed at the prospect of staying up all night.

I'm not supposed to drink caffeine after four, he declared. He was the type of man who wore a white T-shirt under his button-down; when he wanted to relax, he took off the button-down but left on the T-shirt, his sly nudity. He only slept three hours a night and practiced intermittent fasting;

he smelled like Christmas trees even in summer, courtesy of an egregiously expensive cologne.

I saw him, on and off, for three holiday seasons—three tins of cookies. He was a cross between a client and a boyfriend. My friend Mazzy called him my sugar daddy, and it's true that he gave me envelopes of cash each night we met up, but the amount was different every time. He didn't like the words allowance or sugar baby; to him, I was a project. I was his poor little match girl, buying off-brand soap and instant coffee. My poverty amused him. At the time I was finishing school in my meandering way, wed to my thesis on surveillance, ghosts, and reality TV (some working titles included "If You Got It, Haunt It" or "The Spectacle of Paternity: What Maury Didn't Know"). In the summers we drifted apart—he traveled with his family, I went back to Marin and worked as a waitress—but come winter, for whatever reason, we would reconnect over coffee in some dank café of his choosing (reflective of his dire attempts to be hip), then over cocktails, then over tea and the best coke I'd ever had in the condo he kept for work downtown.

I hated his condo: it felt so tragically masculine, devoid of warmth or homey charms. It was on the top floor of the Four Seasons Hotel. Everything in it was shiny: the floors, the stainless-steel kitchen, the satin sheets on his California king, the brand-new pool table. The pantries were half-heartedly stocked with protein bars, ramen, various supplements. The amount of supplements he took betrayed his age. On a good day (and he had quite a few) he could pass for thirty-five. The fact of the matter is that he was tall; tall men get the world on a platter; they stay fuckable long after anyone else and they know it. He had dark hair, a puggish nose, and an average-sized dick. He was, in his own words, remarkably well preserved.

They're gonna study me after I die, he said proudly. We were puttering around in the bathroom, cleaning up after sex. *They're gonna put my dead body in the Smithsonian. Will you go visit me there?*

Depends, I said. I was sitting on the toilet and looking at my phone, letting my pussy drip-dry. *Will you buy my plane ticket to D.C.?*

He stooped to kiss me on the forehead. *First class*, he said. *I promise.*

Sometimes we went to his real house in Pacific Heights, where we fucked on the sectional and watched trash TV. (I considered this research.) He was always very careful to lay a towel down on the couch; as soon as we finished, he put it in the wash. We would sleep in one of the guest rooms, sur-rounded by fake flowers and pillows stiff from disuse. At night, as he slept his three hours, I got out of bed to comb through his wife's closet. The usual suspects: angora sweaters, Ann Taylor shifts, a jewelry tree. She had a tray full of expen-sive perfumes. If he ever smelled her scent on me, he never let on. Perhaps, to his sleep-addled mind, this was what *all* fe-males smelled like, our chemical makeup, an olfactory dowry of roses and musk. Or maybe his nose was too stuffed up by the coke.

His wife's underwear drawer depressed me: an even split between comfy beige biggies and black bra-and-panty sets, as if she'd read and remembered that black panties mean sex. Her favorite color seemed to be ecru. All the wives of men

I've ever dallied with have had a penchant for ecru. It's like they were colluding with their obsolescence, making nonexistence trendy. My tits were bigger than hers, which was saying something, as I really only wore bras to give men something to do. When Charlie slowed down to undo the clasp, we had to look at each other. We paused and breathed. Sometimes this felt better than whatever followed.

Waiting tables in Marin, I often fantasized about his family coming in for dinner. The shabby-chic Italian joint where I worked every summer was right up his alley: expensive but not snooty, with little round tables and red candles melted into empty wine bottles. The place was called Adrianna. During the course of our stop-and-start affair, we often ended up at bars and restaurants named after women—Celia's by the Beach, Tosca Café, a Tenderloin dive called Jonell's where he swore he got roofied. Whether this was by mistake or design, I can't say, but it felt like a message, a sly warning that the world was full of women. He may have picked me tonight, but I was no match for this Jonell, lest she saunter in. I had to stay ready, pert and clean; I had to guard my youth fiercely, like a car parked on the street with a handwritten sign—NO VALUABLES INSIDE. Youth made my general aimlessness cute; without it, I was just a bad investment.

This is how the fantasy went. I would recognize his family as soon as they entered the restaurant: his stooped shoulders, her muted lambswool (eggshell, peach, that damned ecru), the daughter with her blond braids and somehow melancholic poise. She was three years younger than me, ninety-nine pounds, and wanted to be a ballerina. *Duh*, I thought when he told me, wielding the brochure for *The Nutcracker. Of course.*

It was the dream of all thin white girls. Of course I would serve them. I would march over in my nice black skirt and uniform T-shirt (a plate of spaghetti spelling out: THAT's AMORE!) and shout hello. Of course I would study his wife as she debated between the Chianti and the Merlot; she might flick her kind, sleepy eyes at me to ask if the mussels were good.

Yes, I would say, nodding like a doggy. *They're delicious. So salty and fresh. Irresistible.*

I wouldn't question the daughter's order: plain spaghetti with no sauce, no butter, no oil. What was her name again? She reeked of Emma or Alice. I would pocket the exorbitant tip that he left and clear the table in a studied rush. Then, in the privacy of the dish pit, I would eat from his wife's plate. I would pick up each shell and suck where she'd sucked, slide my tongue into the hollows that hers had missed. I wanted all the juices, all the salt. I would hold the bowl with both hands and drink her broth to feel stronger. Then I'd throw the little cup for his espresso on the floor, watch it shatter, and pretend that I had dropped it.

Looking back on this fantasy, something occurs to me. It wasn't his wife I envied most, sleepy in slacks, but his taciturn daughter. She was bored, taut, and concupiscent. She wore white and no bra. Her braids skimmed her nipples. He'd shown me her school picture; I can still see her now. Using a fork and a spoon to twirl her pasta (who taught her that?), staring out the open door. She was the luckiest girl in the whole wide world and she didn't even care. She wore her hair up in a bun, her neck cool and pale as a halved pear.

———

For all my torrid fantasies, Charlie and his family never came into Adrianna or any of the other places I worked. He kept his distance, I kept mine. It was during the annual pause in our affair that I met Dino.

Dino, in fact, is the reason I stopped seeing Charlie. Once Dino entered my life, I focused all my energy on him: the things that once mattered to me, like friends or school, became background noise. I didn't need anything other than what he gave to me; he was my nightlife, my superstore, all the books in the world. I wrote this in my journal after our first date: *He kisses like he's famous but doesn't want me to know.* The most pressing questions became what to wear on the days he came over, what to have in the kitchen to make him for lunch. He was a big man with big appetites. At twenty-five I knew enough to know that my silly little body was far from enough. This was not self-deprecation, just brute fact. Thus I had to always be prepared for him, my pantry well stocked, deli meats and sliced cheeses and sour pickles on hand. He'd told me, when we first met, that he worked at Zuni Café, which was partially true. He'd cooked there for many years before becoming a full-time drug dealer. I filled my fridge with his favorite brand of beer. In no time, it became my favorite too.

It was late May. Charlie and his family were packing for Greece. Dino and I had met that blazing morning on the bus; we got drinks later that same night at an underground tiki bar in the middle of Chinatown. I'd spent the day doodling in my planner, recalling his musk, too besotted to study or do anything useful. By the time of our date I hadn't had dinner and felt dangerously light-headed, like everything was bathed in light, not starlight or lamplight, but the rotating red light of an ambulance. Watching his linebacker frame pick up two mai tais and carry them, so delicately, back to our table, I felt certain that this man could turn my life upside down. Just as easily as he played with his little paper umbrella, that's how he could play with me.

I wasn't dressed for a date. I'd come straight from the library, where the only person I could possibly try to impress was the melancholic TA who arrived every day at 8:30 a.m. and bogarted all the books on paranormal activity. He and I battled over the seats by the window. I showed up to the bar in jeans and clogs, my unwashed hair shoveled into a clip. I stuffed my backpack, heavy with books, under the table and tried not to topple it as I crossed and recrossed my legs.

Dino, by contrast, looked dashing. His wet hair was slicked back, shiny and ridged like birthday cake frosting. He wore a silk blouse printed with seventies paisley, crimson and gold, with cream-colored trousers and pointy-toed boots. One wrist drooped with bangles, the other was bare. He smelled like gasoline and apple cider. When he went to the bathroom, I sat on his stool and inhaled. He excited me even in absentia. I was back in my seat before he returned, drying his hands on the ass of his pants and smiling in a kind, wily way.

After our drink we made out in the park, next to a group of elders line-dancing to a dusty boom box. We faced away and got freaky. To the tune of Cher, he stuck his head under my T-shirt and gnawed on my nipples. Kids called us names from the playground. We didn't care. It was after dark and the laws of the city had shifted. As soon as night fell, parks became the province of the raw and depraved. Lovebirds and junkies ruled in peace, each party ignoring the other's fumblings, the misbuttoned shirts and fucked-up hair. We would return the park to the children at dawn. Dino turned and waved his arms over his head. *I'm a vampire!* he yelled, causing the kids to scatter. The elders, unbothered, kept grooving. They danced in their many sweaters while Dino and I frotted with our pants and shoes on.

Later, he called me a car. *Till next time*, he said, holding open the door. That night I fell asleep with all the lights on, my belly remembering his. I slept crunched to the left as if to make space for his bulk. I farted in my sleep and whispered groggily, *My bad.*

I didn't sleep with a man until my twenty-third birthday. In college I made out with strangers at parties but lacked the fortitude to see things through. I couldn't stomach the infinite hours that led into fucking—the movies illegally downloaded and barely watched, the pointless walks around campus repeating ourselves. The buildup was so boring that I didn't believe in the payoff. Was sex good enough to justify watching three episodes of *Curb Your Enthusiasm* on a dude's fold-out couch, fumbling with his bong? Whenever a boy suggested we go back to his room, I asked, *To do what?* I wanted a promise, a sexual coupon. When he couldn't give me a straight answer, I took myself home.

The first dude I fucked was a line cook at Adrianna with enviably long lashes who was silent throughout the entire ordeal. When he came, he made a sound like, *Oh!*, as if he'd accidentally bumped into me. I can't remember his name, just the fact that he tasted like chopped garlic and kept his lava lamp on. I watched orange and magenta blobs of light disfigure his bare belly. I would learn that most men, in fact, taste like chopped garlic. It's so common that I've wondered if it's something on my end, a chemical reaction caused by my spit—if I went slower, perhaps, would it taste more like pasta sauce, something simmered and braised?

After the line cook, I went on a spree. I began my weekends on Thursday and slept with a different man every night. They were easy to find if you lowered your standards. Suddenly I had a hobby, a task to master, to fill the drab hours between dinner and sleep. I didn't have to feel lonely with the taste of them in my mouth, nor did I have to open up. Mazzy put it succinctly: *You've found something that you're good at.*

She would know; she was a prodigious slut. I suppose you could say that my slutdom was modeled on hers, that her exploits laid the groundwork for my tardy attempts to be free. She had a winning combination of spunk and entitlement, plus a figure her mother called zaftig. She was forever marked by being the first student at her private all-girls school to need a real bra. We met at a CPR training course when we were sixteen. She was wearing beige overalls that were positively obscene. She would go on to blow the father of the family she babysat for.

We did it in his Tesla, she told me as we cruised the streets of Marin. In high school these things were points of pride rather than inchoate traumas. *And then again in the pool house.*

So much of our friendship took place in a car going nowhere. Somehow it was easier to be honest while driving around, our eyes on the road instead of each other. I would watch the little solar-powered flower on her dashboard dance while I spoke about my loneliness, my mom's decline, the rumors I'd heard regarding my father's death. Mazzy was the only person I talked to about him. She knew everything, which wasn't much: the letter he'd left on the fridge, the toxicology report, the gory news articles my mom did a poor job of hiding. Though I dared not turn to see her face, I could feel her concentration, her bracelets sliding up and down her arms as she palmed the steering wheel and said only, *Hmm*.

Around midnight Mazzy would drop me off at home, where my mom would be asleep in the kitchen. She never wondered where I was. How could she? Half the time she slept sitting upright with her sneakers still tied. I took them off and washed the dishes. If I was hungry, I ate the untouched TV dinner she'd abandoned on the counter or finished her sherry, hating the taste. On weekends I slept over at Mazzy's big house in the hills, where we ate microwaved garlic knots and watched Pornhub for research in her canopied bed. I knew for a fact that her mother did laundry two to three times a week. Her house smelled like Fruit Roll-Ups. They had two fridges, one in the kitchen with a designated cheese drawer and one in the garage just for drinks.

If I couldn't stay at Mazzy's, I babysat for the Hensons. The peace I felt in other people's homes was almost otherworldly; I gazed upon things like air fresheners or fruit bowls, wowed by their beauty. I can remember to this day how clean and thick the Hensons' towels were. I disagreed with Virginia Woolf: I didn't need a room of my own but nocturnal access to someone else's. Even a double shift at Adrianna was preferable to being at home. My house felt haunted, gummy, grim. We barely ate, yet there were crumbs everywhere. My mother took day-long baths and didn't dry herself off; she just put her pajamas back on, leaving the tub full of water. Worse yet, she never turned the lights on. She said she did this to save money, but in truth I don't think she noticed the passage of time from daylight to darkness; it was all the same to her. On my rare nights off I walked around the neighborhood and waited for Mazzy to be free. It would be inaccurate to say that I snuck out when really I just put my shoes on and left through the front door. If my mom was awake, supine on the sofa, she'd blink at me and say, *Get milk.*

As I got older, I realized that Charlie must've liked this about me: my newness to the world of men, my half-concealed wonder. I was so young. He was in it not for my expertise but for my shyness. All I had to guide me then, at twenty-three, were Mazzy's stories of public sex with venture capitalists, relayed in a hungover rasp when she FaceTimed from bed. In her world, sex was a sitcom and she was the celebrity guest star. Of course I pretended to be in the know, but privately men mystified me. When push came to shove and we were finally naked, I was constantly shocked by their tenderness. I expected the brutality, the bloodied sheets and blocked calls, how they gripped my hip bones like handlebars, but not the moment when Z placed a hand on my belly and said with a sigh, *This is my favorite thing.*

I hoarded every moment of male sweetness, of cattish grace, to dwell upon later, like a nonbeliever tallying her encounters with God. After a while, I had to repent: I was wrong about men. They too liked to be safe and warm. They had blankets and nicknames, candy stashes in their desks. The line cook kept his lava lamp on because he was scared of the dark. Charlie would stand in front of the mirror with his face in his hands. *Rate me*, he'd beg. I gave him an eight but he didn't believe me. *I'm a six*, he said sadly. *I know what I know. I am a six.*

I never could have guessed that the next time I'd see him would be at the club, in part because I didn't think strippers were his thing. He was the type to wake up at dawn and go windsurfing in the bay before heading to the office. He liked superfoods and mountain air, North Face and Blue Moon. He spent his Saturdays riding to Stinson and back, blowing off steam at a German beer hall in Fairfax called Brats, Brews & Bikes. *I'm a regular*, he bragged. *They know me too well.*

And now here he was, lingering by the red velvet curtain, looking both boyish and heartbreakingly old as he fiddled with his wallet. It had been one week since Simon had ditched me, if that's what you could call it. I felt a flash of anger, like Charlie had hidden something from me, pretended to be someone he wasn't. Then I felt stupid: of course he had. I registered the group of men he was with. They were swarming the ATM, loudly ignoring the girls as they prepped for debauchery. First they needed singles, then they needed booze. Only once they felt nice and juiced-up would they finally turn toward us.

Every girl noticed them. This group screamed money,

four-digit shit. They had the energy of businessmen who kept it together all day, the shape-shifting mania of dudes in suits. Sometimes this energy scared me; sometimes it aroused me, the way that reading about natural disasters or serial killers could make my pussy tingle. Feeling close but not too close to death—that was sex appeal. I sat at the bar and sipped on a seltzer. I wouldn't approach him. This time he'd have to come to me.

He remembered that I wore maroon.

Hey, kiddo, he said, tapping me on the shoulder. *That's not your color.*

I turned to him, seltzer in hand. My money bag dangled lifelessly off one wrist. I was wearing a leopard-print one-piece with furry black trim. I pretended to be defensive, but in truth I was moved. *Well,* I said. *Things change.*

Evidently.

He was referencing our first real date, the belted maroon leather trench coat I'd worn to a wine bar over an hour from my apartment. On my way there I'd gotten caught in the fog and needed a jacket; I found it at Out of the Closet for $12. When I wore it, I felt long and mean, a seasoned slut, a girl who'd stuff her dirty panties in her pocket and power-walk to catch the bus. Charlie loved it. *So dramatic,* he said, tugging on the belt. *And that color! How rare. You look like a spy.*

Over the course of our affair, *maroon* became a code word of sorts, a stand-in for devotion. *Are you feeling maroon?* I might text him after a long day with no contact. He would write me back promptly: *Maroon on my mind.* He would tell me when and where to meet him for dinner, then add: *I have a reservation for two under Mr. Maroon.* It was the closest he came to saying he loved me. *I have a craving*, he would text me at two or three in the morning, when he'd been drinking alone, the one person still up in his household. *Only maroon will do.*

Now he stood before me, shifting his weight. In a twist of events, I was calm and he was nervous. This was my house and he came toting encyclopedias; after years of upselling my body to him, it was finally his turn to pitch. I raised my eyebrows as if to say: *Tell me what you have for me.*

You look good, kid, he said, fixing his eyes on my face. He refused to look at my tits; having a teenage daughter had trained him well. *You look really good.*

Thank you, I said, oozing forward. I wanted him to look at my tits. I wanted him to smell my sweat, the Creamsicle flavor of my drugstore lip gloss. My outfit had a cutout exposing my midriff; I wanted his eyes to land there, to remember the plains that, cowboy-esque, he had wandered. Also like a cowboy, he liked to sing when he drank. I knew who he was. I saw his real life, his tax bracket and death wish, I knew what it meant. I'd seen him weep at karaoke. He loved and hated me for this.

I nodded to the men behind him. They were sitting by the stage. *What's the occasion?*

Oh. He smacked his forehead as if he'd forgotten. *Benny's retirement. The whole firm is here. Batty ole Benny.* He said the name as if I would know who that was. Another pause followed.

Can I . . . buy you a drink? he asked. He was holding a glass of brown liquid. I knew what it was. His drink of choice was Angel's Envy with ice, a name I found poetic and jarring.

I shook my head. *I'm OK.*

He looked wounded. I remembered that look, how his eyebrows bunched up. He was over forty years old and he looked like I'd stolen his cookies.

How's the family? I asked.

Good, he said. *Good. Sophia just graduated. Dual major from Vassar, art history and English. Still dancing, as always.*

Oh. Of course that was the daughter's name. I pictured her in her dorm room: fairy lights, bunny slippers. Her long blond arms coated in an anorexic fuzz. The dining-hall mugs she washed out in the shower. She didn't yet know about longing, the shapes it made your body take. Only poverty could teach her, be it material or romantic. I smiled at Charlie; he smiled back.

Well, I purred, standing. *Let me know if she's looking for a summer job. I can put in a word.* I kissed his cheek. *Nice to see you,* I said, already walking away. I had my sights set on Benny, his bills in the air. *Give the family my love.*

I felt certain that this was the last time I'd see him. Oh, how wrong I'd be.

All of my love affairs have revolved around drugs. The substances varied, but the fact that we met to lie down in dark rooms and get blasted stayed constant. That was my type, I'd quickly discover: thirsty, supine.

I can close my eyes and remember them all, sorted according to their drug of choice, all those different little baggies. Dusty liked downers. He lived in a yellow Victorian in the leafy part of the Mission; his roommates were yuppies who took pity on him. On our very first date he shot me up with Dilaudid while *Dirty Dancing* played on the TV. The walls of his room were papered with vintage *Playboy* centerfolds, betraying his fetish for tan lines. These dewy-eyed coeds and aspiring actresses looked down on us kindly as we fumbled around. High off my ass, I thought of them as our angels. Their nipples looked weird to me—lost in translation, between this world and that, between his bedroom and heaven, like a scan gone awry.

I met Dusty at, where else, a bar. He was a wannabe rock star shocked by his sudden decline. He'd always been given a lot, free drinks and girls' numbers; and while he still received the perks of being tall and tattooed, his bounty had dwindled. Drugs shut him up, made him tender and pliant. We got loaded with our shoes still on and drooled into each other's mouths. Fuzzy-headed and many-fingered, we unspooled on his bed. He knew what he liked: squishy things and nonbeing. When I spotted him money. When I brought him Parliaments and beer. When I sucked his dick until we both fell asleep, commercials playing on TV.

After our affair, I never craved H again. I liked it because I liked being with him, merging under the covers. He called me Toothy Ruthie. *Pretty baby*, he'd croak. *You're so young and happy and full of light.* He reminded me of a stray dog: mangy, dumb, and good to hold.

Rafi liked ecstasy. We took it together at parties but also out in the world. We ran errands while high. We got lost in Costco, hands balled into fists. I sat on a pile of twenty-pound bags of rice; he leaned over me, kissing me, as blended families wheeled past. He lived in a literal closet in a house full of acrobats. *I'm a genius,* he told me. *Do you believe me?* I did.

There was a bartender named Jax who liked to drink. He drank so much he tasted inhuman, like pencil erasers and steel. Mazzy detested him. His texts always came after midnight, when I knew he was blackout. I was a cross between a booty call and a suicide hotline. Still, I replied. He was so much nicer over text than in person. He sent me kissy emojis, memes of puppies in baskets, links to Joan Armatrading songs. We never sexted, just exchanged inspirational quotes. *Be Gentle with Yourself, for You Are a Child of the Earth* . . . Who knows how he'd saved my number in his phone? Needy Ho, Long Hair. Always Texts Back. A string of emojis I'd be too afraid to decode.

Charlie, unsurprisingly for a lawyer, liked blow. Uppers were never my thing. Still, I took what was offered. I didn't want to feel left out—a desire that has underpinned most of my big life decisions. I wasn't easygoing, as some lovers claimed; I was just lonely. If the people I was with were melting, who was I to remain solid?

Charlie and I only did coke when we were at his condo downtown. We went to bars his coworkers recommended, purple-hued joints where we jerked around to house music and left $20 cocktails with poetical names (Heavenly Bodies, The Cruelest Month) on top of the toilet. He liked to dance, but more than that, he loved to sing. When he was properly sauced he'd take us to Japanese karaoke bars where he hogged the mike. It was the only time I ever saw him come undone. Even in sex, he was tidy. He popped a Viagra and told me to go wash my hands. When he came, he made the soft grunt of somebody sliding into the bath. *Awhh.* Afterward, he shook my hand. *Pleasure doing business with ya*, he'd say, his idea of a joke. We showered and bullied ourselves into sleep. Charlie hated sleeping.

Sometimes I caught him wiping powder from his nose in the mornings, just before leaving for work. He declined my offers of coffee and toast. I didn't judge him; I knew he was busy. Besides, if he fell asleep during a meeting, he might have to stop seeing me on Tuesdays and Wednesdays. How would I pass my weekday evenings then? I didn't love the bars he and I went to, but at least they were full. They were somewhere other than my room. I left them with bruises and new smells in my hair, the narcotic tang of cigarettes and Aperol . . . So long as he stayed on top of his shit, a little blow was fine by me.

And then there was Dino, with his grade-A ketamine. Our two-year romance. The kicked-off shoes. The roses in the wallpaper, sliding down the wall. K-hole conversations with angels and demons and post office workers. Daylight creeping under blackout curtains. Trapdoors opened in the carpet (*whoosh*). Kate Bush on the stereo, Cocteau Twins, Slowdive, anything swoopy and round with girls' screams. How time felt like a pack of cards, shuffled in that Vegas way. The hours swooped and gooped around us like fallen ice-cream cones.

We kissed and became millionaires. I rearranged my teeth to speak: *You are my Lotto ticket.* A stick of incense burns forever, stuck into an orange.

I flip through them when I'm lonely or sad, these snapshots of our love affair. It felt famous and rare. Yes, it fell apart. Our relationship petered out like a song from a car driving by— there's a term for that, I think, the eerie warpage of sound as it swells and dies. The Doppler Effect, like the title of a noir novel. The ending was far less eventful. Nothing major or tragic; I just bowed out. I guess you could say I got spooked, by the demands of his love, by the encroaching finale. The electric days had come and gone, that period of grace and squalor. His body didn't cease to amaze me, those long, easeful limbs, but it stopped seeming real after a while. I came to feel like I was watching a movie of him. As with any movie, my attention strayed. When he touched me, I felt far away. *What's up?* he asked, eyes dark with fear. Cheesy phrases occurred to me: *I wanna be free*; *I'm afraid of your love.* They were too embarrassing to say aloud; instead I shook my head and shrugged, the cruelest act of all.

When it finally ended, we didn't fight. Instead we sat at the kitchen table in the dark for five nights in June, talking in low voices, too sad to get up and turn on the light. We poured cups of coffee that cooled. Each night we repeated ourselves. *Ruthie,* he begged, *don't shut me out. I don't wanna throw this away. Tell me, what's wrong? Did I do something bad? Please, let me in.*

Again and again, I told him I couldn't. As if I'd been in a car crash, he had to accept my body's new limitations. I couldn't open my heart any more than I already had. I told him I wanted to (*Dino, I'm trying!*), but in truth, I was tired. Being loved by him put me on edge. I kept waiting for the camera crew to pop out of the bushes and shout, *Surprise! You really fell for it, didn't you?* Then Dino would take off his skin-suit and slink into the gutter with my Social Security card. This was where my mind wandered when he ate my pussy for hours. I wondered how defective he would have to be to choose me as his partner. Was he masochistic or dense? I'd told him, in the beginning, that I'd never had a real boy-friend before. He took this as a compliment instead of a red flag. He was, no doubt, my first true love. That's partly why I had to quit; I wasn't ready for the nonstop feast, the five courses of kisses. I craved the safety of loneliness, cool and plain—that, at least, was something I knew.

On our fifth night at the kitchen table, as he wept into his coffee cup and I rubbed his shoulders, I wanted to say, *You did good, though.* He'd gotten more out of me than anyone else. He'd fucked me until I'd cried, big rainbow tears making lines on my belly. He'd cracked me open, reached inside, touched the apex of my heart—and now I felt depleted. It was beside the point if I still loved him. That was like asking an expat if she ever felt homesick. I really meant it when I said it wasn't his fault.

The very first time he took me home, I was amazed by his place. *You live here all alone?* His house was in the outer Mission, sandwiched by a pupuseria and a 24/7 laundromat. It was like a house from a fairy tale: light-filled windows, hardwood floors, a working laundry chute. The curtains were gauzy and he called the fridge an icebox. The yard was filled with sour grass, the outside painted powder-blue. *How can you afford this?*

Well, he said, *I'm old and I've lived here forever. Selling drugs helps.* He paused, fondling the banister. *Have you ever dated a drug dealer?*

My heart swelled. *We're dating?* The rest of the afternoon was spent draped on the sofa, sampling his wares. When at last we came to, we ate pizza and chopped salad in a place with red vinyl booths. He drank a pitcher of beer and watched the game over my head. At the yellow-lit bodega next door he waved his hands at the candy counter. *Anything you want is yours.* Our fingers stank of love.

The breakup was amicable. We vowed to still be friends, etc. I moved into the guest room and paid for the internet. We still split the grocery bill, still played chess in the evenings. We had the TV shows we watched alone and the TV shows we watched together, an inviolable distinction. In a way it was easier to enjoy him now that I wasn't so afraid of being hurt. I was an anxious lover but a very good friend. Once I started stripping, he helped me pick out my work outfits and didn't get jealous. It stung, in fact, how impartial he was. I'd trot out in my Pleasers and stand in front of the TV; he'd sit there, examining me. He'd tell me turn around, bend over, lift up my hair. He took his job seriously. He might stand behind me and untwist a strap.

Pretty, he'd say, rubbing the fabric. He touched my hair. *Did you use a new conditioner?* Sometimes I felt a familiar tingle as he straightened my hem. Sometimes I felt myself dripping, willing to go backward, to blow up our home. Then he'd sigh and say, *But does pink REALLY go with red?* He didn't see me; he saw what he was supposed to see, what I'd asked him to see, a body for sale. *G-strings give you the illusion of a waist.* He smiled encouragingly, a hand on my shoulder. *If I were you, I'd stay away from white. And don't forget your baby wipes.*

After our first date in Chinatown, I couldn't wait to tell Mazzy about Dino, how he was The One. I called her the next day until she picked up. I'd just gotten home from the library and made myself a pauper's dinner: fried rice with mayonnaise, a bit of dried dill on top. Everything tasted good to me then. I ate it out of the pot while sitting on the fire escape, watching the fog roll in. Half the city was hot lilac, the other shushed and gray. I sat with my bare legs dangling over traffic, playing chicken with my slippers. If I could keep Mazzy on the phone with me, my bedroom wouldn't seem so empty and soon enough I'd be asleep.

Dino sounds fab, she said. *Ten out of ten.*

I could hear that she was in the bath. At the time she was living in Bernal Heights, working remotely as the social media manager for a reproductive health start-up called Babe Alert. As I understood it, they were designing an app that would "disrupt contraception." Every day the app would send you your fertility score along with a new sex position. One of her duties was to come up with names for these positions— the Windswept Moors, the Vegas Buffet. When we weren't together, she was either taking Zoom calls in the bath with her camera turned off or reading trashy paperback novels about doomed love affairs.

But what about Charlie? she said.

What about him?

Well . . . what will he think? The sound of Epsom salts being poured. *I can't imagine he'll like it, some new dude swooping in.*

Fuck Charlie, I said, surprising us both. *Who cares what he wants?*

Oh, Mazzy said. *I didn't realize you felt that way.*

I do.

What did he do?

What?

What did he do to make you so mad?

I stared at the fog; it was picking up steam. *He doesn't love me enough.*

Babe! I could feel Mazzy's sympathy, hot and fast. *Don't say that. You really think he doesn't love you?*

No, I said firmly. *I know he does.*

Oh . . .

Just not enough. I scooched to the edge of the fire escape. I thought of him driving his daughter to dance class, her shoulders bared in a leotard. Maybe they'd stop for smoothies. All the men in the parking lot would turn to watch her walk past and he would feel a sense of pride not unyoked from the erotic. *He didn't choose me over everything else.*

Mazzy took a sip of her drink. *Is that what you want? For him to choose you, like, over his family?*

No, I said. *But it would have been nice. To know that he would.*

Right.

It would've been nice to be someone's top pick.

There was a pause. I pictured Mazzy turning the water off, setting her book aside. Finally, she sighed. *What a bastard*, she said, though I knew she was acting for my sake. *What a total dickhole.*

I know. The fog was so close now. I could smell it and taste it, that barely-there tang. It smelled of concrete and kisses blown out of cars. It reminded me of something Charlie had told me: *The best pussy tastes like nothing.* I'd been too scared to ask if he included mine in that camp. Now I'd never know.

So what are you going to tell Charlie? Mazzy asked. She knew when to calm me, when to speak soft.

Nothing, I said. *Nothing at all.* I closed my eyes to receive the fog's full fist, right in the kisser. Bull's-eye.

III.

The day that Dino disappeared began like any other.

It was early October. The days were balmy, the nights quick and bitter. The shifting seasons made my nose run. I was on the second day of my period but I still went to work. I wore black to look less bloated. I danced for a man with one arm; I suppose that was noteworthy. He tipped me OK. I chatted with Sadie for the last half hour before clocking out early. I left with $500, stopping at Wendy's for two baked potatoes and a Frosty I ate in the car.

By the time I got back to Dino's, it was around 2:30 a.m. I was wearing my maroon leather coat, the one that Charlie so loved. I didn't notice anything off at first; I was too cranky and tired to play girl-detective. The dogs were quieter than usual, that's true. They always barked when I came home, stopping only once they recognized me. Tonight, they swarmed me as I entered, but instead of barking, they just looked at me. Their eyes were yellow in the dark. I realize now that they were scared.

Dino wasn't in the living room, tidy and dim. The remote was lined up with the edge of the coffee table. The TV was off, humming slightly as if recently used. A light was on in the kitchen, just over the stove. The last time I saw Dino, he was drinking coffee at the kitchen table, reading an old *Vogue*. Now the kitchen was empty, his mug in the drying rack. I'd bought it for him two Christmases ago—I ♥ DADDY in melty red letters. I could smell his last meal: mashed plantains, garlic rice, some sort of stewed beef. I wondered if he was doing a drug run. Sometimes he got drinks with his friends, anonymous men I wasn't allowed to meet. *You wouldn't like them*, he'd tell me, putting on his most macho outfit (leather pants with turquoise cowboy boots). *The vibe's a bit . . . rough.*

To be honest, I was glad he was out. I was too beat to chat. I wanted to shower and take off my makeup, which was exactly what I did. I could hear the dogs in the hallway, their toenails on hardwood. They gathered solemnly outside the bathroom, noses pressed to the door, a raspy choir. *Quit begging*, I called out, soap in my eyes. *I don't have any treats.* They stayed where they were, leaning up against the door such that when I finally opened it, they all came tumbling in.

We marched single-file to my bedroom and piled into bed. Naomi, the princess, wormed under the covers to sleep in the curve of my neck. She had four eyelashes total. Dino had warned me about Chihuahuas: *They're not very evolved*, he said. *They don't understand consent.* Cindy and Linda, the soft-eyed pit bulls, took up residence at the foot of the bed. I looked at my phone for an hour before falling asleep.

The last questions that I read on Quora:

> *What is a horror movie based on real life?*
> *Did Marilyn Monroe have poor hygiene?*
> *Are twins really telepathic?*
> *Should we trust the CIA?*

I was awakened the next morning by Naomi's sardine breath. The girls needed to go out. I left them in the yard while I went upstairs to check on Dino. *D?* I asked, nudging the door open. *Knock, knock?* His bedroom was empty, which gave me a start. He hadn't spent the night anywhere else in the two years I'd known him. He was a creature of comfort, his flashiness balanced by his self-control. He was wedded to his skincare routine, all the little vials lined up on the windowsill, plus his drawer of lingerie worn only at home. If he wanted to fuck some girl, he'd probably do it at her place and leave before nightfall, giving himself enough time to take a hot bath and walk the dogs with me before bed. Even after a night out with his mysterious friends, Dino always dragged himself home.

It was a trip to step inside his room, which I'd avoided since the breakup. It smelled just like I remembered from the early days of our courtship. He burned this medicinal incense that came in little cones, not sticks; the sweet, woody smell of it mingled with that of his drugstore-brand dandruff shampoo and the Italian soap he used to hand-wash his lingerie, plus an underlying scrim of a thirty-seven-year-old dude—chopped garlic and decay. The décor hadn't changed much either: the crushed-velvet bedspread (turmeric-colored; I called it yellow, he called it orange), the little dish for his rings, the framed picture of La Virgen de Guadalupe over his bed. I tried not to think about what we did on that bed and then again on that floor (which he promptly swept afterward). It was dangerous to remember, it made my heart hurt. Those days were roped off, long ago.

His drying rack was set up by the window, with nothing on it but a handkerchief. I walked over and grabbed it, baby-blue silk printed with gold Orthodox crosses. I'd never dared to mess with his stuff before, never so much as used a dash of his hazelnut creamer without asking first. Something was off; I could feel it in my spine, a grim tingle. We may not have been dating but we were still bound; how much of the other did we breathe in all day long? I looked out the window at the dogs in the yard, making merry figure eights. My heart knocked in my chest. There was a sprig of dried rosemary on his bedside table, plus a girl's hair elastic. I pocketed these before rushing downstairs. I called the dogs in and fed them, then went to the pool. I swam until I saw Orthodox crosses, gold against the pool's cool blue.

Time passed.

For the first twenty-four hours, I tried to stay calm. I suppose I was in shock. I couldn't sleep or eat or watch TV. I texted him, of course. I left him increasingly frantic voicemails. Then I felt guilty and sent him pictures of the girls, wrapped up in blankets like little burritos. *We miss you!* I wrote, adopting their voices. *We hope Daddy has a good vacation (even though we wish that we could come). Don't you think we look good in bikinis too?! We hope you bring home LOTS of BONES for us to eat. Big wet sloppy kisses.* The fantasy, I suppose, was that he went off to the beach for some me-time, maybe back to Santo Domingo to deal with family. Somewhere nice and warm and tropical, the opposite of this fog-wrapped Victorian on the edge of the Mission, a space heater in every room.

I thought about calling someone, but who? I didn't know how to reach his friends or even who they were. Dino was a grown-ass man, ten years older than me. He'd led a long, tangled life. He could come and go as he pleased; we were spiritually enmeshed but not technically dating. He was free to elope or go off on a bender, though as far as I knew he only did drugs at home.

Moreover, this was not the first time he'd dropped off the radar. Due to the nature of his work, he'd occasionally disappear for hours on end. He called these, half joking, his work trips. On these mornings he'd dress out of character—black jeans, black sweater, nothing too flashy—and kiss me on the forehead. He didn't seem stressed out or rushed.

Later, skater, he'd say. *Watch the girls for me, will ya?*

He'd fill a thermos with green tea and bring a duffel bag full of smaller duffel bags. I knew not to ask where he was going or for how long he'd be gone. If I did, he just smiled and affected a Tony Soprano accent. *I gotta meet a guy about a thing.* Or: *I have a business meeting in the city.*

We live in a city, I'd say.

He'd wink. *Different city.*

Sometimes he was gone for twelve hours straight. If I called, it went straight to voicemail. When at last he came home, he'd head straight for the shower, leaving his boring black clothes in a heap on the floor. Then he'd float into the kitchen in his favorite bottle-green negligee and black fur-trimmed mules. *Ruthie*, he'd sigh, *I'm famished*. These were the rare nights I cooked for us. Later he'd pass out on the sofa, his negligee ridden up to reveal the pale parts of his thighs. As I remembered this, my heart ached.

Every time the thought of calling 911 crossed my mind, I shooed it away. *Stupid white girl*, I scolded myself. The truth was, I didn't know the depth of the shit he was into; all I'd seen was the ketamine and his tech-bro clients, but I knew he had shoeboxes under the bed, legal pads full of numbers and code names I couldn't decipher. There were the nights when he let me do drug runs with him; there were the nights when he made me stay home.

If something ever happens to me, he'd mused one afternoon in the car, *take care of the girlies and don't call the cops. Just sit tight and be cool. Promise?*

I promise. We were in the drive-thru at Jollibee on a lush spring day. *But what's gonna happen?*

Nothing, he said. He was smiling, untouchable. *I'll be OK.* He made the sign of the cross. *Cross my heart and hope to die.* We ordered supersized fries and ate them in the parking lot, sitting on the sun-warmed hood of his car.

At the end of the second day, I wrote on my hand in blue ballpoint: *BE COOL*. I knew that I couldn't escape my bad feelings. All I could do was move with them and through them; it was like going to the club with a cold. I focused all my energy on the dogs, who followed me from room to room. I couldn't tell if they knew nothing or everything about

Dino's whereabouts. I fed them, bathed them like prophets, carried them in my sweater as I paced the house. I kept the place spotless, the way Dino would like. I honored the agreement to not watch our TV shows without him there too. All the while I longed for him in a mute, scary way; I felt like a little girl lost in the mall, not wanting to show anyone that she was afraid.

He'll be back, I told myself each night before bed. He wouldn't leave for no reason. He has something that he needs to do, but eventually he'll come back for us. He has a plan. He always does. I told myself I'd wait a week; if I hadn't heard anything by then, I'd have to do something, though what, I didn't know.

When my Wednesday shift at the club came around, I kissed the girls goodbye and promised not to be too long. I knew they hated being left alone, even more so than me. I told them I needed to make money to buy them bikinis for our upcoming trip to the DR. I, in fact, packed only bikinis to wear to the club, smoothie-orange and sunshine-yellow: further bolstering this beachy fantasy, I guess, as if that might bring Dino back to us or give me some new insight into where and why he'd gone. I worked every single night that week just for something to do. If I was going to pace in circles, I might as well do it in stockings for money, giving men an opportunity to say, *Why so blue?*

The Friday after Dino's disappearance, Emeline showed up at the club.

I didn't usually keep track of the new girls. They neither

interested nor threatened me. My regulars were loyal, committed to the Plain Jane fantasies I unwittingly fulfilled. The more beautiful a new girl, the less relevant she was to me and my ilk. One regular would buy my used underwear, but only full-coverage panties printed with cherries and kittens (I bought them in bulk from the kids' section at Target); another called me *little lady*. He liked to sit crisscross-applesauce on the floor of a VIP room and play with my hair; sometimes he asked for my help with a crossword. A hot girl didn't scare me—or so I thought then.

I can't forget the night I first saw her. I was doing the rounds, trying not to cross my arms. When the club was less than full, you felt the full force of the AC. I did my best to keep my body language open, friendly, but I was shivering in my minidress. I wore Day-Glo mesh with my favorite shoes: six-inch Pleasers with a plastic goldfish in the platform. Dino had picked them out when I first started dancing. *So camp!* he'd exclaimed. *How exquisitely stupid!* He told me they could be my trademark, as if irony and flair were what drew men to me rather than my cheerful passivity and tween hips. Wearing them made me feel closer to him. I was scanning the room when Emeline walked onstage.

What I noticed immediately was her long blond hair; it had the sheen of buttered toast. She stood with one hand on the pole, one hip cocked. Her eyes were blank, lips loose. She didn't do any pole tricks, barely looked at the crowd. She didn't act flirty or sultry or brash; nor did she act timid, the knock-kneed Bambi shtick. She moved as if she were alone, undressing in her bedroom. Her underwear was simple, a white satin bra with matching thong, a thin gold necklace

with the letter *E*. For the entirety of my life I've been jealous
of girls with thin gold necklaces; they always seem to have it
all, a beauty that invites and never frightens. I stood there
watching her, rapt as a client. There was a touch of teenage
arrogance to her gestures, the belief that death did not apply,
mixed with an almost genteel grace. I could picture her crossing the floor with a book on her head. I could picture her
flashing the gardener just for fun. She was soft-spoken, churl-
ish, sleepy, raw. Like the sticker I'd put on my childhood
notebook: 90% ANGEL.

She swung her hips in lazy circles, eyes fixed on the floor.
Her café-latte-colored nipples faced in opposite directions, a
trait I'd always found sexy. Her belly ring twinkled in the
stage lights; from time to time, she toyed with it. Her forehead
was frosted with sweat. From where I stood by the stage, I
could see the silvery stretch marks on her ass cheeks and
thighs. Somehow they looked sexy too, hickeys left by aliens.

She was so thoroughly, overwhelmingly girlish that it almost hurt to behold her. The men, of course, ate it up. This
wasn't theater; it was realism. Our clients wanted what they
couldn't have: a girl alone, unmarked by men, a girl freed
from their need and persuasion, their projections of who she
should be. Like smoke, their longing made our hair smell
funny. Perhaps that's why they loved the girl-on-girl shows;
they wanted pussy in its purest form, a slicked pink infinity
sign. It was something they constantly whined about. *I want
someone genuine!* they'd cry, knocking over their beer. *No
bullshit! Are you the real deal?*

Oh yes, we lied, making our ponytails bob. *But of course!*

As she rocked her body back and forth, her breasts

addressing both sides of the room, she did something that surprised me—she sang along to her song, softly, under her breath. *Loneliness is such a sad affair* . . . I wondered if I was the only person close enough to the stage to hear her. It made me think of high school, cruising around with Mazzy at night, car windows rolled down, speakers blasting. Joy Division, ABBA, Lana Del Rey. We sang until our throats hurt. Sometimes there were other girls too, girls I'd lost touch with, girls Mazzy knew, Sophias and Hannahs and Kates. All their different bedrooms, all their different smells, their jewelry and shampoo, somehow contained by Emeline moving her hips in figure eights.

The man behind me waved a twenty in the air. He reeked of whiskey and mothballs. He wore steel-tipped cowboy boots. To no one in particular, he said: *Now, there's a thoroughbred.*

For the rest of the weekend I took note of how the other girls treated her. There was a distance, a studied chill. Cookie was nice to her, but girls like Gigi and Dallas, who'd taken me under their wing, shared their Love Spell and super-strength tampons with me, turned away from Emeline. Like, they literally turned their bodies away when she entered the locker room. I watched Sadie refill Emeline's drink (vodka soda with lime), then mutter to herself: *Rich bitch.*

It's true, that's how she came across. Milky and clean-cut, oozing privilege. She was self-possessed in a way that was somehow off-putting. She kept her headphones on when she entered the club. Her dance outfits were simple but expensive: she only wore lingerie, never microkinis or slingshots, favor-

ing neutral shades like bone, fawn, tan, cream. She brought a
book to read when it was slow and always left her purse out
on the counter, her slippers tucked under her chair. While
most girls came to work wearing some combination of pajamas and clubwear, she showed up in tailored slacks and cropped
sweaters, her belly button blazing, long hair held back with a
clip. She made turtlenecks look lewd. Mazzy would've rolled
her eyes at her style. Somehow it was both slouchy and slutty,
evoking blow jobs in a pile of leaves. I could hear her calling it
art history ho or *the spit-and-never-swallow*.

More troublingly, she never sat around naked or half-
naked like the rest of us. When doing her makeup or counting her money, she always donned a full-length robe. It had
an Old Hollywood look, champagne-colored with feathered
trim; when she sat down, it frothed over the sides of her chair
and spiraled behind her on the floor. Her sleeves and hem
leaked feathers everywhere. You'd find them stuck to your
blush or travel-sized toothpaste tubes. I'd gotten home and
found a white feather in the strap of my backup shoes, the
ones buried deep at the bottom of my bag. On someone else
the robe would have looked cute. *Miss Diva*, we might've
hooted. On Emeline, it was a message to us all: *I'm different
from the likes of you.*

It would be too easy to say that the other girls didn't like
her because she was pretty. There were, in my opinion, far
prettier girls than her at our club: Dallas with her royal hair,
Harmony's pastoral ass. A girl we all called Sexy Lexie with
her Tempur-Pedic lips. There were other leggy blondes—
Kimmy, Skye, Lana—who catered to men with cheerleader
fantasies. Besides, being pretty didn't mean you'd make

money. The big earners were girls like Gigi, who knew how to deploy their looks, the stretched breasts and frizzy hair; Gigi had a preternatural ability to know exactly what a man wanted before he knew it himself. Perhaps her secret was having no tattoos, no piercings, not even a toe ring. Her boxy frame contained all female shades: barfly, bride, bambina, bimbo. She went from pencil-wielding sex therapist to hitchhiking teen over the course of an hour; all she had to do was tuck her hair behind her ears and suddenly she transformed.

No, it was something else about Emeline, something harder to pinpoint, that had girls on edge. Dallas put it best. She'd done an In-N-Out run and brought us back milkshakes. She sipped on hers darkly and gazed at the new girl, who sat reading her book and drinking expensive bottled water. No one had offered to buy her a milkshake. Her robe drooped on the floor, molting all over the linoleum.

That chick wigs me out, Dallas said, not bothering to lower her voice. The assembled girls nodded. *I think she's here for shits and giggles.*

For all that so-called life experience.

Maybe she lost a bet.

Or her boyfriend thinks it's hot.

No! Dallas slammed her milkshake on the counter. Tonight she wore a fishnet body stocking that made her breasts look mythical. *You know what it is? I think she's writing about us.*

Really? Like, for school or something?

Yeah. Dallas sat up. *She's gathering data. Her vibe is, like, totally anthropological.*

We bobbed our heads. Gigi raised her finger in the air. *I read an article like that in* Time *magazine once. This college girl went undercover at a strip club in Vegas for, like, maybe two months. She wrote about how degrading it was, how her relationship with men would forever be ruined.*

Everyone groaned; Gigi continued. *She wrote about giving her first-ever lap dance and said that his semi-hard cock felt like a baby's fist.*

What?

I'm serious. I remember that line, a baby's fist in her back. She said that she hid in the bathroom and cried all night long. She claimed to donate her tips to women's shelters, but it was later discovered she went to Miami and got her boobs done.

Jesus Christ.

I bet she got baby oil all over the pole.

Plus, she chose the dumbest stage name of all time.

What? Jesus Christ.

Gigi raised her eyebrows. *Bubbles.*

Everyone booed. *Look at her,* murmured Dallas, bringing the attention back to Emeline. She hadn't moved, absorbed in her book. *You know what else I think?*

Tell us.

She pretends to drink vodka, but I bet it's just lemonade.

We studied her, mulling that over, before finally dispersing to get dressed.

It was because of her robe that Emeline had to move lockers. Her original locker was next to Brandy. Brandy was a tempestuous lifer who spoke often of the heyday we missed, a hellfire nineties Frisco full of poets and whores. *You shoulda been there,* she hollered, daubing Erase Paste on her banged-up knees. *The city was vibrational. Freaks in the streets! I ate anything I wanted, then fucked off the calories at Power Exchange.* In the early 2000s she worked at a peep show called the Lusty Lady, where she had an act involving nylon ropes and hard-boiled eggs. She called it Picnic Panic. *What did I do?* she cackled. *I got tied up and made egg salad. Help! The ants will eat me alive!*

She had cropped brick-red hair and cartoonishly huge breasts; everyone spoke of her multiple clit piercings and rumored rib removal. Her regulars, a motley crew of fetishists, never strayed from her and, according to Brandy, included a Kennedy. They were always leaving her gifts, purplish liqueurs and heart-shaped boxes of cherry cordials. The liqueurs she shared with us but the candies she hoarded, saving the boxes for god knows what and stacking them up in her locker.

According to Brandy, Emeline's robe (or, more specifically, her feathers) was a safety violation. *They're fackin' everywhere*, she whined to Cookie. *They get stuck to my gawddamn rhinestones. I don't wanna breathe that garbage in. It's a hazard to my health.*

Cookie stirred her ramen. *So what do you want me to do?*

Brandy stamped her feet; unlike the younger girls, she wore more conservative heels. *Fackin' something! New girls have no respect these days. When I was her age, I was living in a squat with five other chicks. We sucked dick for peanuts. And do you know how many of them are alive to this day? Do you?* She didn't wait for an answer. *One! That's me!*

Are you sure? Cookie asked with a smile.

Oh, I'm sure. Brandy threw her hands up in disgust. *What I'm trying to say is that goddamn girl needs to learn the rules.*

What rules?

Brandy sighed. She cradled her head in her hands and defeatedly hit her vape. *The rules of the goddamn game.*

Cookie eventually agreed to move Emeline. As luck would have it, she gave her the locker right next to mine.

I walked in that Friday to find her sitting at the makeup counter, flipping through her book (*Kissing in Manhattan*). She had excellent posture. She wore black slacks, black boots, and an oversized white button-down that was preposterously sexy despite showing almost no skin. She looked like she was headed to a day job in publishing. What did I know? Maybe that was what she did outside of the club. Maybe the rumors were true and she was writing a book about us, a zingy exposé.

She stood up when she saw me. Her belly ring sparkled in between the gaps of her shirt, a charm in the shape of the Playboy Bunny. *Hi*, she said. She set her book down and smiled. She wore thin gold bracelets on one wrist, that thin gold necklace with the letter *E* at her throat. Her teeth were prettily crooked. *Looks like we're neighbors now.*

I nodded. *Looks like it.*

She watched me as I opened my locker. I felt self-conscious in my sexless puffer, scored from a yard sale in the outermost Avenues. Meanwhile, she always showed up to work in a floor-length suede coat, the color of caramel. I thought she would turn away when I began to undress, but she continued to watch me with something like a smile.

When I was down to my skivvies she finally spoke. *You look familiar*, she said. She played with her belly ring, twirling the gem-encrusted bunny around and around.

I do?

Uh-huh. She cocked her head, freely examining my body. *Did you grow up in the city?*

No.

It's so odd, she said. *You look exactly like this girl I used to know. You're . . . what's the word? A dead ringer.*

Oh. Our lockers were in the corner. It was quiet over here in a way that I usually liked. Though at least twenty girls were on the roster that night, it felt like Emeline and I were alone. I didn't know what to say. *What was she like?*

Who?

The girl I remind you of.

Oh. Emeline shrugged. *A ravenous cock-slut.* She turned to face the mirror, running her fingers through her hair. It was glossy and yellow, the color of pencils. *You know the type. She could never get enough.*

I opened my mouth but said nothing.

She looked at me in the mirror. *That color looks pretty on you.* Her voice was sincere.

Thank you, I said. I felt grimy and small, unsure of what to do with my hands.

What would you call that?

What? I looked down at my microkini, my belly poking out.

That color.

Oh. Purple?

I would say fuchsia. She bit her lip. *Or maybe magenta.*

Yeah.

She smiled at me. *I bet you do really well here.*

I felt myself blushing. *I do OK.*

If I were a rich dude, I would totally book you.

Oh, I said. *Thanks.*

You're welcome! she said. She picked up her brush. *I totally get it. The thing that you're doing. The hair, the eyes. I'm into it.*

Good, I said. I flapped my hands. *That's good.*

She began brushing her hair and fell silent. She seemed entranced by her reflection, by the grave task at hand. I sat down beside her to touch up my makeup, relieved by the quiet. We didn't speak for the rest of the night. She disappeared on the floor and I got lost in my work. I danced for a dude who said he was tripping on mescaline and then for a bighearted virgin named Hanky. When I returned to my locker at 2:30 a.m., Emeline had already gone home for the night. Her shit was packed up, her corner clean. All she'd left behind was her name on a locker (EMELINE!!! ☺) and some strands of blond hair, stuck to the wall like cooked spaghetti, plus a feather on my chair.

I didn't realize how much I depended on Dino to feed me until he was gone. After just a few days on my own I was losing weight. He was an excellent cook, the kind who was never satisfied with his creations. Our meals were usually a fusion of different cuisines, betraying his stints at various restaurants. He'd sulk at the dinner table while I dug in for seconds, thirds. *Bravo!* I'd cry. *This katsu is so crispy. These collard greens are divine.*

He'd shake his head somberly. *Don't pity me.* I'd pile leftover pepper steak into Tupperware containers while he'd suck on a Popsicle and claim he was full.

Now that I was alone in his house, my diet disintegrated.

I fed the dogs royally while subsisting on saltines and off-brand peanut butter. When I felt dizzy, I scrambled some eggs and threw in a few basil leaves from the plant on the counter. After the club I still hit up McDonald's, bringing home twenty-piece nuggets to feed to the girls. I started to worry when, Day Five, my G-strings fit baggy; I had to hike them up over my hip bones and safety-pin them into place, praying my clients were too horny to notice. If they felt a little prick during a lap dance, I hoped they wrote it off as static electricity or yet one more female mystery.

I hated eating because I hated eating alone. I kept the television on at all hours: I couldn't eat without distraction, the fuzzy approximation of a dinner date. I didn't feel hungry without Dino to prompt me, the smell of stewed chicken and crushed garlic filling the rooms. It had been one of my principal pleasures, to be lying in bed on my day off and find myself lured into the kitchen at 5:30 p.m. by the smell of food cooking. Dino would be standing over the stove, his apron askew, a look of pure concentration and despair on his face.

Ruth! he would wail. *I screwed the pooch.*

I would wash the dishes while he finished cooking, speaking to him softly about insignificant things. In the evenings we dined off Goodwill china in the orange-lit dining room. I put my phone in a cup and we listened to music, gay Italo-disco or throaty female love songs, depending on the weather.

I had no reason to enter the dining room now. Instead, I skittered between the kitchen and living room, often falling asleep on the sofa in front of the TV. After five days alone I was doing everything from the sofa: checking my phone, eating crackers, doing my makeup for work. My dirty pajamas piled up on the ottoman, while my dance bag, stuffed with bikinis and stockings, lay on the floor. The dogs were attracted to it, the baked-in smell of harried bodies. I'd pop to the kitchen and return to discover Naomi nestled inside it, her little head resting on a bunched-up G-string.

At night I found myself calling his phone just to hear his voicemail message. *Hi, you've reached Dino, soooo sorry I'm out . . .*

Are you? I bellowed, upsetting the dogs. Though I did my best to stay calm, a bad thing was brewing inside me. I made the mistake of watching an old horror movie called *Possession*, in which a psycho babe falls in love with a tentacled demon. She houses him in her gorgeous West Berlin apartment, where he fuses with the walls, goops on the bed, and kills all her suitors. I wasn't quite as manic as she, but I identified with her devotion, her love-shaped lunacy. Was this why I decided, after seven days passed, to keep waiting before I involved anyone else? I told myself this was an act of faith, that I was trusting in Dino to finish his business and find his way home, but perhaps I was prompted by something less pure. I'd been jilted in a way I didn't know possible. I wanted to keep this between us as ex-lovers. I was too embarrassed to admit to authorities that the man I had loved, in a rainbow of ways, might have just walked away. Yes, I had hurt him and he had hurt me, but I never imagined he'd throw in the towel. We needed each other like kids need their teddy bears, those grubby archangels left in hotel rooms and trains. I couldn't shake the feeling he was trying to tell me something. Was this whole thing a prank, an inverted valentine? I vowed to find out. It didn't feel random. After all, he loved theatrics. If this was a game to him, I'd play along too. I refused to be the loser.

On the seventh day the stink of the living room got to me. My dance bag reeked of rubber, bubble gum, and pussy. I lugged it into the bathroom and hand-washed all my outfits. Then I hung them to dry, draping them over the backs of the dining room chairs. This was the first time I'd entered the dining room since Dino went away. It felt big and empty, aggressively quiet. The curtains were drawn; who had closed them? I couldn't remember. If I shut my eyes, I could smell the cooked garlic. I could see Dino chewing, slow and stern. I could see him feeding a drumstick to Naomi and whispering, *Don't tell*.

Girls at work were always disappearing. It was just the nature of the industry: here today, gone tomorrow. They got burnt out, finished school, found God, settled down, moved to L.A. or Vegas where the money was better, became lawyers or porn stars or stay-at-home moms. Holly moved back to Alaska to finally get clean; Mystique fell in love with a basketball star and moved into his penthouse; Rory switched to camming and made thousands a month. No one had spoken to Lulu in ages, but last they heard, she was driving from San Francisco to Florida in a refurbished school bus. Once a girl hit the road, rumors were all we had left.

The disappearances weren't personal. No one planned to dance forever, or if she did, she kept it to herself. The job was too hard on the body and soul, it ruined your knees and circadian clock, it made sex for free seem pointless. The money was good, but money was slippery. A clean break was often the easiest way out. Just text Cookie, and it's over with. Goodbyes could be so messy, when, really, what was the point of all that boo-hooing? We were holograms flirting with holograms. My friendships at the club were real, but I wasn't. The real Ruthie was far away, snoozing in her fuzzy socks. Or so I told myself.

Every month there was at least one girl who quit the club for love. *Joshie doesn't want me to dance anymore*, she might say, a little smug, a little sad, as she cleaned out her locker. *He says I should get my real estate license. He'll support me until I get back on my feet.*

Other girls weren't so lucky. I remember hearing about a dancer named Natalie. I don't know if that was her real name or dancer name. She left before I started. She'd told Cookie she was planning to move in with her boyfriend. Three months later, her body was found under a bridge. The last person to see her alive, according to the news article that Cookie passed around, was a homeless man named Chaz. He and Natalie had been drinking together, something he said they did often; he went to go buy more booze and returned to find her dead body, partially covered by leaves. The police cleared and released Chaz in under twenty-four hours. Her boyfriend declined to comment. No one knew anything else.

I danced with her for years, said Gigi, *and never once heard her mention a boyfriend. Is that a coincidence?*

For a while, Natalie was all we could talk about. Did the boyfriend know about Chaz? Why wouldn't he talk to police? Before she died, I'd heard very little about her. She was OK-looking, nothing special; she liked to get hammered, she had small boobs, she and Sadie had long-standing beef. Now she was our patron saint, at least for a few weeks. The article hadn't mentioned her career as a stripper; it referred to her, simply, as "a South San Francisco bartender." Perhaps the mystery of her death appealed to us because of its involvement with multiple men. There was something important about men and sex in that article, but it was too faint, too garbled, to see. As sex workers, we were tuned in to it, it made our teeth buzz—the warning. Danger was an elemental part of our job, even if we never got hurt. We coexisted with the potential of masculine wrath, like asbestos in the walls. Natalie had succumbed to it, though how or why, we'd never know. It only felt right to drink to her, at least until we moved on and forgot. Even Sadie drank to her.

Fuck that lying small-tit bitch, she mumbled, raising her glass. *May she rest in peace.*

Did the possibility of foul play ever cross my mind?

Yes and no. I knew Dino was a drug dealer with his finger in many pies. I knew there were men in his life who might be called shady, who went by many names. I knew he kept secrets from me, as all lovers do. Still, as I paced the house, I felt certain he'd left of his own accord, no nefarious parties or threats of violence involved. I felt in my gut that if he was in trouble, I would know. Call me superstitious, but I was bound to this man, in ways that had previously scared me away. Exes or not, we still had that link, like a ring you keep after the breakup. Maybe the thought of Dino in danger was too much to bear; maybe I blocked it out, refused to entertain it. In truth, I believed that my body would tell me if he was unwell. It told me the night my father died. I was seven years old. Out of the blue I started to vomit. I didn't wake my mother. I took one of the big steel mixing bowls and slept with my arms wrapped around it, waking up every hour to puke. The next day, they found my father's car. They had to drag the river before they found his body too. Perhaps this is why I didn't panic after Dino went away. I was gutted but calm. I knew what it felt like to lose something major. I wasn't shocked by loss itself but rather by how swiftly it had come for us, like fog on a warm day.

The first red flag with Emeline was when she asked to borrow my panties.

By then Dino had been gone for a little over two weeks. His silk handkerchief lived in my dance bag, jumbled up with my crimper and lip-plumper and mommy-sized packet of baby wipes. Nobody knew he was gone, especially not at the club. It was easy for me to act normal at work; after all, I wasn't Ruth there. My ex-boyfriend wasn't MIA, because I had no exes; Baby dated everyone and no one, she loved chilled vodka and the color pink, she lived to just have fun. I didn't bring my troubles to work with me; I left them outside in the parking lot, like a dog in a car. It felt good to get out of the house and become someone else for a night. The men at the club did it too, though they wouldn't admit it. Under the swirly pink lights we became simpler versions of ourselves, bonding over basketball and watermelon shots. We didn't feel lonely and we didn't feel scorned. We became agents of a desire unyoked from our traumas, as if that could ever exist. I didn't have to worry about anyone taking my elbow and saying, *What's the matter, honey? You haven't been yourself lately . . .* because, frankly, they wouldn't know.

I was braiding my hair when Emeline rushed up to me, seemingly out of nowhere. *Do you have a spare black G-string I could borrow?* she asked, her face flushed. She was wearing a sheer negligee that barely covered her ass, naked from the waist down. *I've got stage in five minutes and I forgot to bring mine.*

Shit, I said. *Yes, of course.* I didn't think to question why she'd come to me instead of Cookie. It was Cookie's job to help us out: she had Listerine, Benadryl, Summer's Eve, Wet Ones, 5-Hour Energy, infinite bobby pins, tampons of every size, concealer of every shade, stacks and stacks and stacks of clothes. Instead, I dug into my bag and fished out my panties, which I kept in a Ziploc bag with my name written across it in Sharpie.

They're clean, I assured her. *I've actually never worn these before. They're my emergency pair.*

Bless you! said Emeline, wrapping her arms around me. As she pulled me close, I could feel, rather than see, her bare pussy. It bonked into my belly, making me feel small. *You're an angel.*

No worries. She smelled of strawberries, not strawberry-scented products but the wet red fruit.

Jesus, she moaned into my neck, *I'm so fucking dumb.*

It happens to everyone.

No, she said, pulling back and staring at me. Her eyes were grass-colored. Her face reminded me of a Renaissance painting of a maiden: pale, round, hopeful. It even had the faint greasy sheen of oil paints. *I'm so pissed at myself.*

It's fine, I said. I tried to back out of her embrace, but she held me too tight.

Fuck me, right? she said. *Fuck me for being such a dumb stupid cunt.*

Emeline, I said, trying to smile. *It's OK.*

At last she released me. She wriggled into the panties and fluffed up her hair. The G-string, plain black Spandex, made her legs look like superhighways. *Thanks a million*, she said, bounding toward the door. *I owe you, OK?*

Forget it, I said, turning back to the mirror.

No! she cried, nearly shouting. The other girls stopped to watch her. Dallas rolled her eyes, already annoyed by Emeline's antics. *I won't forget this, Baby. I owe you.* Then she strode out of the locker room and onto the floor, where she'd melt everyone's hearts with her performance of nudity, gentle and bored. She'd play with her hair and look at her feet, cup her breasts idly, spread her ass cheeks apart while dreaming of June. She was your babysitter and also your concubine. As I finished getting ready, I could hear the song that she danced to: "Goodbye Horses" by Q Lazzarus.

Sometimes I get this strange feeling. It happens most often when summer fades into fall. I'll be walking down the street and the chill will excite me. It's an erotic feeling, edged in sorrow. I'll breathe deeply, as deep as I possibly can, filling my lungs with the smell of decay. Burning leaves, rained-on metal, etc. My heart rises up in my throat, where it bobs like an apple. I feel a sense of loss so deep it touches my pussy. It stretches, in fact, from my pussy to my throat, like the doctor saying, *Now go AHHH.* It is a sadness so intense that my body processes it as arousal, a feeling I know I can handle. I look at the city, the rosemary bushes outlined in shadow, the clear blue sky with cum-stain clouds, and feel so full-up with longing that I want to cry. That's the harshest kind of desire: the kind with no object, just a wide arc of want. It's operatic and raw. Do I think of my father? Of Dino? If only. I started feeling this feeling long before Dino disappeared and would in fact keep encountering it, every so often, for the rest of my young adult life.

It lasts for, at most, a minute. Then, as if waking from a trance, I feel normal again. Everything fits back into place. I carry on with my walk to the big Asian market to get kimchi, cream cheese, frozen peas. It's Manila Oriental Market, but everyone just calls it MOM. Dino used to joke about getting the logo tattooed on his arm. I take my things home in my backpack; I defrost the peas and make dinner. But as soon as it's ready, I find I can't eat. I let the food cool, left out on the counter. It stays there until the next morning, next night. I lose hours standing at the sink, looking at the moon.

It didn't concern me, not at first, that Emeline never gave my panties back, nor that she wore them almost every night after that. They were black and went with everything. I couldn't prove that the ones she wore religiously were mine. We all had a pair just like that in our bags. The second red flag was both more and less alarming—when she stole my scent.

In our world, we studied sex appeal and sold it back to glands in suits. Our clients were not men so much as a cluster of sensory organs, perky and damp. Perfume was important and a bit controversial. There were some girls who didn't wear any at all, claiming that men preferred their natural scent. According to Gigi: *You don't want to smell like a stripper. More importantly, HE doesn't want to smell like a stripper when he goes home to the wifey.* A fair point. She used Bath & Body Works lotion with a preppy lemonade smell.

There were, on the other hand, girls who swore by their perfume. They felt naked without it. Dallas rotated her fragrances based on her menstrual cycle, claiming it had to do with pheromones. *When I'm ovulating*, she said, *my glands respond best to something smoky and warm.* Cookie kept a few communal perfumes on hand (Obsession, Alien, Prada Candy Kiss) plus a medley of Victoria's Secret body sprays (Dream Angels Forever, Love Spell) that I hadn't seen or smelled since high school. One dancer, Delaney, wore a popular coconut sunscreen for kids. *It's such a familiar smell*, she said. *It reminds men of summer.* I had to agree; one whiff of her brought me, with a jolt, back to childhood, to chlorine and wet hair and french fries in a paper boat. Sometimes it made me sad to smell her. I thought of who I was back then, how different I was now. I'd lost and gained in equal measure since the days of playing chicken in Mazzy's pool and falling asleep in the car wearing wet swimsuit bottoms. My sadness had nothing to do with being a stripper; rather, I felt like my younger self would be sad to discover that I lived all alone. I had so few people to love now. Not even Mazzy called me back these days.

At every club there were the zealots, the dancers who fiercely guarded the names of their signature scent. If you asked one of these girls what she wore, she'd smile coyly and say, *Nothing!* Or: *It's just Secret deodorant.* Secret indeed. To copy her scent would be blasphemy, tantamount to chatting up one of her regulars. Arabella, for example, smelled exactly like canned mandarin oranges. It was so distinct that you had to wonder if she literally daubed her wrists with juice from the can. When asked about it, she shrugged. *It's just me.*

I was far from an aficionado when it came to my scent. I used a perfume that Dino had gifted me years ago, before I started dancing. It was called Soft Core and came in a heart-shaped bottle; it smelled, to me, of licorice and orchids, leather and plums, borrowed cigarettes, a zigzaggy purple mix. It was sexy in the way that a poem or a sweater can be sexy. I applied it every night before dancing, just one spritz on my neck and belly. It was more of a ritual than anything else. Sometimes men would comment on it, but only when we were alone in a private room, insulated from the other girls' haze. *Ooh, you smell good. You smell different.* One guy said, *You smell like a library in ancient Egypt.* I liked that image. Still, no matter how hard I tried, I always left the club smelling like everyone else, a psychedelic mixture of gardenia, musk, and marshmallow fluff, plus hair spray and cigarettes.

I probably wouldn't have noticed if Emeline hadn't said something. It was a dark Friday night in October. The three-week mark of Dino's disappearance was approaching. We were getting ready in our corner, chatting in undertones. By then we had a nice rapport. The other girls were still suspicious of her, but proximity had softened me. I thought she was nice, if a bit narcissistic. She struck me as the sort of girl who was handicapped by her beauty. She thought the world was a sweepstakes, a series of favors and pranks. She told me a story about going to Jack in the Box and asking for ketchup for her fries. The drive-thru worker gave her an XL soda cup filled to the brim with sauce packets.

Not just ketchup, she said. *BBQ sauce, honey mustard, ranch too!* She shrugged. *I had to throw most of them away anyway.* She regarded scarcity the way she regarded bright colors or synthetic fibers: not her thing.

It wasn't just that she was pretty, but how—hearty, blond, bountiful. Round-hipped in white blouses. She looked like amber waves of grain, like prize roses and all-you-can-eat. Her legs were an infrastructural feat, something you drive for miles to see. It was patriotic to want to fuck her. If she were to go missing, every news station in America would jump on the story. They'd flash her headshot every hour, on the hour. Posters would list her height, weight, cup size, star sign. Men would call the tip line just to heavy-breathe. After a week she'd be found in a Vegas motel, wearing only a men's button-down that she'd tied at the waist. The mayor would give her a key to the city. She might get her face on a stamp.

We weren't friends, but we were friendly. We kept our conversation light, club gossip and TV. She did more talking than me. She might show me a hairstyle that was trending on TikTok, then prop her phone up on the counter and try to emulate it. She liked to ask me what I'd eaten that day, then recite her own meals—boiled chicken, butternut squash. She would describe each food item in exacting detail, as if it were important that I could picture them clearly. Fortunately for both of us, I found this mildly interesting, in the semi-detached way of cruising the web.

There were the occasional nights when she said nothing to me. She wasn't angry so much as distracted, stewing in opaque emotions. I couldn't name these feelings, but I could smell them: burnt coffee, old lipstick. She'd brush her hair for twenty minutes, staring into space. I assumed her blue moods were brought on by men. What else could quell a beauty queen? On these nights I didn't try to chat. I listened to music and ignored her. Her dark spells never lasted long. The next night she'd be perky again, asking if I'd tried that Korean BBQ place on Balboa. *Believe me*, she said, *it's to die for.*

On the night in question, she was wearing her robe and curling her hair. Feathers flecked the countertop. Her street clothes were scattered on the floor at our feet: long suede coat, high-waisted jeans, gauzy off-shoulder blouse. Her blouses were forever falling off her shoulders, intentionally or not, a sultry accident that made me feel close to her. I wore yellow terry-cloth shorts and a T-shirt reading FREE BRITNEY. Suddenly she turned to me and held out her wrist.

I almost forgot! she said. *Like it?*

Like what?

She waggled her wrist at me. When I said nothing, she leaned forward and brought her neck to my nose. *Come on*, she said. *Smell familiar?*

Oh. Sure. To me she smelled like figs, tobacco, sweat, black tea. She smelled like the shadowy back of a knee. I didn't put two and two together.

She thunked into her chair and smiled. *Did you know that the manufacturer of Soft Core went out of business in 1999? The only way to get a bottle now is through resellers online. Like, fa-natics who collect the stuff.* She cupped her hands to her nose and breathed deeply. *It's so worth it, though, isn't it? God, it's delicious. Like . . . sex in a graveyard.*

Totally. My brain was a flickering light bulb, spooky and dumb. *That's so weird. Did someone give you a bottle?*

I wish! she said. She held her purse in her lap. *I got it for myself. An early birthday present. It wasn't easy to find, but I managed.* She giggled. *I'm a little obsessive.*

How did you know what it's called?

She smiled. *I looked at yours, Baby. It's always out on the counter.* She started digging around in her purse. *It was killing me! I HAD to know. I used to wear Byredo's Slow Dance, some-times Santal 33, but I'm SO over them now.* Finally she unearthed a Ziploc bag full of apple slices, blithely munching. *Want one?*

No, thank you.

You know what they say. She waved the bag in the air. My name was written in thick black ink on the front. *An apple a day keeps the perverts away.* She noticed me staring at the baggie and said with a wink, *Oh yeah! I forgot I got this from you. Waste not, want not!* She stood up suddenly, feeling her phone buzz. *I gotta take this call. Sorry!* She hustled away, leaving a trail of faded purple behind her. The Ziploc baggie of apples lay slumped on the counter, my name illegible from this angle.

I picked up her discarded blouse and pressed it to my nose. Her body reacted to the perfume's chemicals so differently than mine; this, I think, offended me the most. On her, Soft Core smelled like mail-order flowers on a dirty king bed. It smelled like cashmere stained with female juice—moody,

mystic, animal. A dash of salt, a touch of violence. It transformed her blank blond beauty into something more pris-
matic, lushly queer or queerly lush. It mixed divinely with her
faint BO, peppery and private. On me it smelled like my
twenty-sixth birthday, Dino eating crumb cake and drinking
cheap wine. We'd stayed in and gotten wasted. We fucked
under the dining room table. He gave me the perfume wrapped
in aluminum foil with a pink satin ribbon. *Sorry*, he'd said. *I
couldn't find wrapping paper.* He tied the ribbon around his
throat. *Do I look like a French prostitute?* I'd said yes.

That was a bad night for me. After my encounter with Emeline, I wasn't in the mood to dance. My regular flaked. My
period came early. A group of seven businessmen rejected me,
one after the other. *No offense, honey*, the ringleader said, *but
I'd prefer someone more womanly. Got any friends?*

Nope, I murmured, remembering to smile. *None at all.* I
reached out to straighten his collar, play with his tie. *Hey, is it
snowing?*

In San Francisco? he grunted. *Of course not. Why?*

Oh . . . I flicked a pile of dandruff off his collar. It swirled
in the air, illuminated by club lights. Time stopped as the
eight of us looked at it. *Silly me.*

Watching Emeline spritz her long neck with Soft Core, her
breasts moving as she laughed at me: this was the start of my
undoing, the moment I started to fray. I tried so hard to be
cool, to keep it together in Dino's absence. I wanted so badly

to be brave. Fluorescent lights flickering, girls chatting in the background. The smell of our perfume mixed with somebody's vape, a hint of gasoline. Like lipstick left on overnight, I began to crack.

I remember driving with Mazzy one summer night in Marin. She'd picked me up from my closing shift at Adrianna. We were maybe eighteen. She was wearing jean cutoffs and a silk scarf as a halter top, tied precariously around her breasts. The scarf was yellow with pink roses. As we zipped under streetlights you could make out the shape of her nipples through the fabric, also the size and color of roses.

I was talking about someone who had a crush on me, a busboy I no longer remember.

Damn, Ruth, she said. *I'm so glad I'm not in love with you.*

I choked on my soda, surprised. *Why?*

She started to laugh. *You know why!*

No, I said, *I don't.*

You don't believe in happy endings.

I raised my eyebrows.

Come on, she said. *You know what I mean.* She swallowed, hesitating just a bit. *What happened to your mom won't necessarily happen to you, you know.*

Are you saying I have Daddy issues?

Her cheeks pinked. *Well* . . .

I don't have Daddy issues, Maz. I slapped my thigh for emphasis. *I just have issues with everyone else.*

There was a long, dense pause before we burst into laughter.

Fuck, I moaned, *I can't believe I just said that.*

I want that on a T-shirt! Mazzy laughed so hard she zig-zagged down the residential street, upsetting the bins left out for garbage day.

We continued to drive. This was what happened most nights, our teen summers spent driving in circles. Maybe we went to the one bar we knew wouldn't card us, a crusty fisherman's dive in Sausalito called Smithy's. There, we drank the drinks we assumed older women would order (screwdrivers, martinis) and gave the evil eye to prowling men. If one of them approached us, his shirt stiff with salt and his face baked by hard living, we told him we'd come from a funeral.

Please excuse us, Mazzy would say. *We're grieving.*

It worked like a charm. *Sorry,* the man would mumble before slinking away. It was hard to keep our faces straight. One night, after being rebuffed in this fashion, a man gave the bartender $50 and said in a voice loud enough for us to hear, *This is for the twisted sisters.* We got so drunk on Tito's we started to dance to the jukebox, a Bruce Springsteen ballad we pretended to know.

This is what he would've wanted! we cried. *RIP!* The assembled men watched us with fond disdain. We were visitors from another world. Every single one of them could've been our father. In another setting they might have tipped us. *Oh, how he loved to dance.*

At the club, men said crazy things to me. I was proposed to more or less monthly. Most of these compliments blew through me, generic love-drunk spluttering, an elastic sort of worship that fit any chick. It was rare that a comment hit home.

One night, quite early on, a man said that I reminded him of an Egon Schiele painting. I went home and googled whoever that was. His paintings of girls, spindly and ghoulish, reminded me of my days in Dusty's bedroom, spangled on the hardwood floor. I related to that druggy languor, a hypersexual disorientation whereby a kiss was also a hoax. I especially liked one painting of a girl on her knees with her ass in the air, her skirt bunched to her chin. I was so taken with this image that I ordered an $80 coffee-table book of Egon Schiele's stable of babes.

Another night, I was stopped by a woman arm in arm with her husband. She was achingly beautiful, with heaps of black braids. *I'd KILL for your breasts*, she said in a clipped Caribbean accent. Her husband, standing beside her, nodded. *She would*, he echoed, *she definitely would*. They didn't take me up on a dance, but they still made me feel blessed.

Then there was the man who made me want to quit on the spot. He had come with a bachelor party, hanging back from the group and staring at me. I figured he was an easy mark. I sauntered up and asked if he was having fun.

Sure, he said nasally. *You could say that*. His body was diligently muscled, but his bearing was dweeby. He wore a Dropbox T-shirt and a seersucker blazer. San Francisco was full of dudes like him, under-socialized overachievers who treated the gym like a second job. He'd probably concocted an algorithm to produce thicker thighs. Of course he wore an Apple Watch. I'd bet a million dollars he was drinking a vodka soda to cut down on calories.

I leaned in. *How about something a little more private? We could go to the back . . .*

He stared at me, his voice plain and clear. *Why would I have ground beef,* he said, *when I can get rib eye at home?*

I don't know, I said. I tried to stay calm, though my stomach lurched. *Maybe because you're hungry right now?*

He let out a laugh. *Sorry,* he said. *I had a snack before I got here.* He made the gesture of jerking off, one quick wrenching motion. I noticed his gold wedding band. *Better value.*

Of course. Disgust and embarrassment bubbled inside me. I turned away for a moment, not wanting him to see me shake. Then I stood up straight and forced a smile.

Well, I said, *have fun.*

Later I'd see Arabella dancing on his lap, her ponytail grazing the floor. He had that same dead look in his eyes. He kept his stupid blazer on. I guess he must've gotten hungry.

The night Emeline stole my perfume, I came home from the club and couldn't find Naomi. The pit bulls and I roamed the house, calling her name. It had started to get dark so early and the halls were thick with shadow. *Babyface?* I called out, heart thumping. Panic rose in my chest. *Miss Princess-pants? Queen Stinky?*

At last the girls and I found her in Dino's bedroom. She'd fallen asleep on his pillow. She looked up at me boredly and batted her four eyelashes as if to say, *Oh, you again.*

I entered the room gingerly. I didn't want to disturb the traces of Dino, the exact way he'd left things. To be more precise, I didn't want to get in trouble should he suddenly come home, tanned from vacation, and find his shit messed with—his cowboy boots in the wrong order, the rug not aligned with the floorboards. He'd groused at me once for replacing the lilies on his desk with pink roses.

I was trying to surprise you, I mumbled, dumb and deflated.

He softened, slinging an arm around my shoulders. *You know I hate surprises, girl.*

When I reached his bed, however, something inside me cracked. The bedspread was so big and soft. It was like a prairie of tall grass, begging to be disturbed. I pulled back the covers and slithered inside, displacing Naomi, who wheezed and rearranged herself in the crook of my elbow. Cindy and Linda hopped up, panting with illicit glee. When Dino was here they were never allowed in his bed. They had to sleep on the floor on big pillows. Now everything was topsy-turvy. It was quiet anarchy. We wormed down under the covers as far as we could. We dug tunnels to China. We wrote letters to inmates. Mainly, we just thought of Daddy. The sheets smelled so strongly of him, it was like burying our faces in his belly. All of my anger fizzed into nothing; I was left with a broad blue longing. I held the dogs close to my body and cried. We missed him equally.

From then on I conducted all my business from Dino's bed. His bed replaced the sofa as the family HQ. I dragged the TV upstairs and set it up in his room with the help of two extension cords. When eating my breakfasts of graham crackers and crystallized coffee, I held a plate under my chin to catch the crumbs. I didn't want to sully my office, his shrine. I wanted to preserve the smell of him for as long as I could. It was precious and scant; it was my job to protect it.

I thought that by minimizing my movements, I could trap the smell like a butterfly. During the afternoons I lay as still as humanly possible, the dogs splayed beside me, TV on. The vibe was flophouse meets Pompeii, forgotten cups of to-go coffee arrayed across the floor.

Let's play a game, I'd say to the girls. They wouldn't look up at me. *FREEZE! Whoever moves first loses. Whoever moves first is a rotten egg.*

Somehow I lost every time.

October dwindled; Halloween approached. I'd heard mixed reviews from the other girls about working that night. Lots of youngsters, lots of drinking. General bedlam, which didn't lend well to tips. The cover was lowered to allow for big groups. Sometimes girls came in wearing slutty outfits, which added to the mayhem. Paying customers couldn't tell the French maids and naughty nurses apart, who was working and who was there just for kicks. A fight almost always broke out between two guys dressed like Thor. The DJ played "Monster Mash" one too many times.

To make matters worse, the week leading up to Halloween was a hot one. In San Francisco we had to wait until Labor Day for the fog to burn off and the beaches to emerge. Instead of falling leaves, we got heat waves and an eleventh-hour sense of fun. The air smelled salty and lush, plumped up by the odor of dead flowers and BBQs. The city became tropical; we slithered into short-lived shorts and took buses to the beach, where we bumped into people we hadn't seen since last fall. It was the time for novels, spliffs, hard seltzers. We were heady and reckless, sharing the feeling of having tricked time, of being the lucky ones, partying hard before the incoming chill. Bureaucrats called in sick to drop acid, while teens kissed in a fury. When I was still single, a train-hopping acquaintance ate my pussy at the beach in a sandy little cove barely shielded by rocks. I found it hard to focus, though I appreciated his effort. He wore a cowboy hat that he decorously removed before parting my legs. On the walk back up from the beach, he interlaced his fingers with mine.

If we are going to hold hands, he said, *we have to do it right.* Hours later, he blocked my number.

When the forest towns up north caught fire, the sky over the city turned eerie pumpkin-orange. *Boo*, it said. Ash filled the air, dirtied our windowsills. We were told to stay inside, though the balmy weather beckoned. Younger people flocked to parks, where they endeavored to get tan despite the bad taste in their mouths. When we looked out the window, our eyes filled with tears that we couldn't control, a city of jilted lovers. We stocked up on bottled water, N95 masks, ice-cream cones, dirty magazines. After a few smoky days, the winds would change in our favor. The city was dreamy and steamy once more. We swarmed the beaches as if nothing had happened, high-fiving strangers in the surf.

Once I started dancing, I came to dread the warm weather. The heat made our clients snappy, crass. They demanded more and more. Perhaps the sight of so much flesh for free, on the bus and in the streets as girls excavated sundresses, amplified their hunger. The nicer the weather, the more our clients pushed boundaries. They wanted something big, extreme, to match the city's peppy nihilism.

In the end, I went to work on Halloween because I had nothing better to do. In years past Dino and I had wandered the streets of the Castro. I didn't want to celebrate without him, nor did I want to stay home. After four weeks on my own, the house had started to turn on me. I'd tried so hard to keep the darkness at bay, but somehow it snuck in. While tucked in bed, I would hear footsteps downstairs, the shower turning on and off. I'd look at the dogs to see if they heard it too. They sniffled, unfazed. *Thanks a lot*, I would whisper, then turn up the TV to drown out the noise.

I took a nap, drank a Red Bull, and got ready for work. On the way to the club I stopped by the Dollar Tree and found a pair of white bunny ears. I bought a bag of cotton balls to mash into a tail and pin to my ass, plus a jumbo bag of Halloween candies that I finished on the drive.

The night started out well. The locker room felt festive, rowdy. Girls drank champagne out of plastic flutes, dropping candy corn in their glasses, while Harmony passed out vegan cupcakes. There were kitties, cowgirls, sailors, devils. Delaney was the St. Pauli Girl, Arabella was Cleopatra, Veronique was Uma Thurman from *Kill Bill*, and Brandy was dressed, somewhat inexplicably, as the green M&M.

Everyone knows she's a sex symbol, she bellowed defensively, zipping up her white go-go boots.

Dallas stole the show as Catwoman in a black latex jumpsuit. She had a single-tail whip that she expertly flicked around the locker room. *God*, she cried, *I pray that I get to use this on some loser tonight!*

Ask and you shall receive, said Cookie, a pregnant nun.

When I made my way to my locker, Emeline wasn't there. This didn't surprise me. I assumed she had somewhere better to be. If not at a party, she was probably at home. She was the type of girl who could stay in and not feel embarrassed about it. *Self-care night!* I could hear her chirp. The thought of her eating pizza and watching *Hocus Pocus* in bed made me feel sleepy and jealous. Perhaps this was why I accepted a glass of champagne from Gigi, though I rarely drank at work. She was dressed perfectly as a cheerleader, looking anywhere from seventeen to thirty-five in her little red pleated skirt. Instead of a money bag, she carried a plastic Halloween pumpkin.

No money, no honey, she said by way of a toast. We clinked glasses and drank.

Things started to get dotty around 11:00 p.m. I walked out of a private dance with a dreadlocked pirate and found the club packed. You could barely hear the music over the din of men's voices. The girls onstage looked they like were levitating over the crowd. I elbowed my way to the bar, where I didn't recognize the bartender. She wore a pink satin corset and a towering wig of white curls. Her eyes were pinwheeling and her shoulders concaved. Of course it was Sadie. She'd powdered her face and drawn a tiny black mole on her cheekbone as slutty Marie Antoinette; you could tell by the jerkiness of her movements that she was on speed. Sadie went through peaks and valleys of partying. She'd been on and off every stimulant you could name. When other girls needed a pick-me-up, they went to Sadie for pills. She gave them out cheap and didn't judge, she carried Narcan in her purse.

I couldn't blame her for wanting to get high tonight; really, how else could she keep up with the rush? Already the line for the bar was five dudes deep.

When she saw me, her face lit up. *Baby!* she hollered. *Get your tush over here!* She reached over the counter and dragged me toward her. I crashed into a few men and muttered my apologies, but they were too drunk to care. *Drink this, little baby.* She handed me a glass of neon-green liquid, then raised her own. Our drinks appeared to glow in the dark. *This will blast your night open. Bottoms up!*

We clinked glasses and I downed it. Big mistake. My eyes started to water and I wanted to howl. I had never tasted anything so vile before. The first word that came to mind was Satanic.

What, I gasped, *the fuck is that?*

Sadie was laughing, her white curls vibrating. *You've never had absinthe before? Poor baby.* I could never tell if she was saying my name or just calling me baby. *Happy Halloween, kiddo. Watch out for ghosts.* Then she was galloping off to the other end of the bar, where a gaggle of men dressed as the Village People was waving money in the air. *I'm coming!* she barked. *And not in the good way!*

I turned and scanned the room, looking for my next mark. At first all I felt was a mild buzz, enhancing my champagne high. My eyes landed on a group of men in cheap wigs. Great, I thought. Time-wasters. There were five of them, laughing and drinking beer. Most of them wore jeans and sneakers; only one man was in full drag. He wore a long bottle-green slip with a slit up one thigh. Under that he wore sheer black thigh-high stockings and black fur-trimmed mules.

When he turned, I felt the room contract. Had I been holding a drink, I would've dropped it in shock. I recognized that slip, that thigh. *100 percent silk*, Dino had bragged, rubbing the dress against my cheek. *Total glamour.* We were still in love then. Those were the days spent playing dress-up for hours, closing the curtains to block out the sun. We took K and collapsed on the sofa, still wearing our party clothes. This was our party, the soft bacchanal of two lovers dressing and undressing ad infinitum. I remember him placing his foot on the bed frame to roll down his stockings, I remember his thigh all rippled with muscle. It reminded me of the turkey legs you get at the Renaissance Faire, crispy and golden. I knelt on the floor and pretended to gnaw on his tendon. He tasted salty and plastic. He patted my head like a happy dog owner.

I like that dress a lot, I'd told him, still kneeling on the floor. *That slit is so whorish.*

Really? He was pleased.

Really, I said. *You look like a Carmen. Or even a Daphne.*

Daphne? He clutched his throat in mock horror. *Give me a fucking break.*

Now I watched Dino laugh with this group of strange men. My body reacted, as it always did, to his body, to that loud, lambent flesh. Despite his laughter, he moved with liquid intention, never forgetting himself. My pussy spasmed accordingly. What was he doing here, a place he'd made a point to avoid? Moreover, who were these men? Were they the so-called rough crowd I was forbidden from meeting, his shady business associates? They didn't look so rough to me, standing around in their *Pulp Fiction* bobs and glossy Marilyn waves. If you took off their wigs they would look like any other group of dudes at a strip club, waiting to be approached. Though they only spoke to each other, I could tell their feelers were out. Even Dino bore an air of expectancy, like he was waiting for someone to compliment him. He held a beer in his hand like a single red rose. His wig looked expensive compared to the others', thick chestnut waves that touched his shoulders. Though my hair was longer, it was a similar hue.

I pushed through the crowd toward their table. I had to say something. What, I didn't yet know. *What happened to you? What happened to us?* Or something like, *The dogs are OK. I'm taking care of the house.* If I was brave: *Do you miss me?* I didn't know if I'd feel angry or happy or scared once I reached him. I just knew that I had to touch him, grab him by the wrist, and say, if nothing else, *Hello.*

But before I could get there, Emeline appeared in their circle. She looked radiant and breakable in white lace lingerie, her only costume the bridal veil she wore over her face. She said something and they all burst into laughter. My face got hot. Dino clapped his hands as he laughed, a habit I'd forgotten, causing one spaghetti strap to fall off his shoulder. I watched Emeline reach out and right it. She didn't move her hand from his shoulder. She rested it there, smiling in an experimental way as if to say, *You like this?* Then she leaned forward to whisper in his ear, her breasts drooping out of her bra to touch the bare skin above his neckline. I felt light-headed as she took his hand. A man dressed like Elvis blocked my path with his body.

I've got a carrot for you, little bunny! he slurred.

I elbowed him out of my way. My heart was a rice cooker; at any moment it might boil over. Dino and Emeline were walking toward the VIP rooms, hand in hand like honeymooners. They smiled at each other like they couldn't believe their good luck. *You really want ME?* I tried to move faster but knew it was futile. I was swimming in place. I looked back at his group of friends, but they too had dispersed. The room was full of strangers now, horny dudes in polyester clothes they'd throw away tomorrow. It was a sea of vampires, monsters, and bad liars. The Elvis caught up to me and grabbed my arm.

You're a feisty one, aren't you? he said. *I can handle that.*

Can you? For the first time, I stopped moving. Suddenly everything seemed so pointless. This wasn't a place of celebration, it was a place of slow death. Men would do anything to feel less alone; why couldn't they be like women, humming through the pain, too shy to ask for mercy?

Elvis nodded, patting the wallet-shaped bulge in his pocket. *Be vewy, vewy quiet.*

What?

It's wabbit season and I'm hunting wabbits.

I looked into his small, dark eyes. I made the shape of a gun with my fingers and held it to my temple. *You got me*, I said.

What?

I pulled the trigger. *Kaboom.*

He looked confused. *So are you gonna try to sell me a lap dance or what?*

No, I said, backing away. *We're done here.*

Stuck-up bitch, I heard him shout. *No tits!*

I fought my way back to the bar and leaned up against it, feeling woozy and numb. My limbs were heavy and I couldn't focus my eyes. My heart was scraped clean, like a plate after dinner. I felt, in a way, like I'd just been fucked hard, that frothy exhaustion. Sadie saw me and poured me a Coke with no ice like I liked.

Chin up, baby, she said, sliding it toward me. *The night is still young.*

That's what they want you to think.

Who's they? She tucked a twenty into her corset.

I shrugged, voice cold. *Dunno.*

I kept my eyes peeled but I didn't see Dino again that night.

I stayed at the bar until the room stopped spinning, then gave a lap dance to a man dressed as a bottle of ketchup. He told me, as I writhed, that his wife was dressed as a bottle of mustard.

What does that make you? he asked, attempting to be flirty.

A pickle, I said. I kept shaking my ass. *That makes me a pickle.*

He started to laugh. *I like you*, he said.

No, I said. *You like pickles.*

He nodded, considering this. *I like pickles a lot.*

You see? I said. *I told you so.*

I left the club with $300, a dismal sum for a Friday night. On the way out, I bumped into Emeline. She was alone. She had on her suede coat and jeans but still wore her veil. Even in a plain white T-shirt she looked famous. We stood in the now-empty main room, the floor dotted with garbage and puddles of booze.

Baby! she cried. *Good night?*

I glared at her. *Not really.*

Me either. As she spoke, she played with the hem of her veil. *I got stuck with one dude for my whole fucking shift. He kept extending the booking.*

Oh, I said. *Really.*

She nodded. *Uh-huh. He was awful. This big fat techie covered in moles. He told me he heads the AI division at Google, but who really knows?*

Oh.

Total creep. He kept saying he liked me because I looked like his wife when they first got together. He wouldn't stop talking about how she "let herself go." She leaned forward, lifting her veil. *He even had moles on his fingers,* she whispered. *Big black moles.*

How dreadful, I said. I looked into her eyes, the color of Heineken bottles, and felt empty. I believed her because it was all I could do. I just wanted to be home in bed with the dogs, staring at my phone. I didn't want to investigate my intolerable feeling of feminine failure, especially when she was around. *At least you made good money.*

That's true, she said. *At least there's that.*

Well. I looked around. *I'm leaving.*

Me too, she said. *I gotta cash out.* She grabbed my arm suddenly, pulling me close. I was surprised to smell vodka on her breath, buried under the purple smell of our shared perfume. *Be safe tonight. There's a lotta weirdos out there.*

I will, I said. *I'll be OK.*

She smiled in a sheepish way and released me. *Sorry.*

It's OK, I said. I was surprised to find that I meant it. *I know what you mean.*

I got in my car and cranked up the heat. It felt good to cruise. The streets were empty at this hour; I didn't see anyone walking, no other cars on the road. All the trick-or-treaters had gone to bed. I turned up the radio; Delilah was playing old love songs. She'd been coaching broken hearts for as long as I could remember. My mom loved Delilah. I can remember her shushing me to listen to Delilah's advice. We were driving home from school one afternoon. This was in the good days, when she still left the house. Sometimes, if we got home and a good song was playing, we'd loop around the block to keep listening. Few things in life were constant, but you could depend on Delilah to tell you the time. I liked the way she spoke of God like an understanding friend.

I have a memory of my mother, aimlessly driving, drumming her hands on the steering wheel. She wears her hair in a bun held in place by a pencil. She's the only person I've ever met who does this. She's picked me up late from school once again. At this point she's stopped giving excuses for why. Now she's singing along to the song on the radio. *The first time ever I kissed your mouth . . .*

I'm shocked to discover she knows about love. I must be nine years old. At this point my father has been dead (or "gone away," as we said) for two years. Up until now I'd assumed that love was something set aside for me, a muggy world of affect from which she, as my mother, was barred. It was nothing personal. She belonged to a world of grown-up things like cars and work, while I belonged to a secret underworld of romance and desire. Now I'm forced to reconsider her, this prettyish woman in sweatpants, her grave-colored hair. Wisps of it frame her thin face. She's lost so much weight. She catches me staring and smiles.

I love this song, she says. *Roberta Flack. I used to listen to it all the time.*

You don't listen to it anymore?

She shrugs. *Not really. Why would I?*

The memory stops there.

After that night I started seeing him everywhere.

First I saw him on the bus, sitting in the seats reserved for the elderly. He was wearing a long leather coat belted at the waist, reading a *Hustler* magazine. *Dino!* I screamed, lurching toward him. When he looked up at me, he became someone else. He hadn't shaved for days. *Sorry,* he said with a definite lisp, *can I help you?* My heart rose and fell like a pop star. I got off at the next stop.

Next I saw him on the beach, two blankets over. He was lying down with a girl. They had a cooler full of beers, big deli sandwiches wrapped in white paper, a carton of figs. I stayed very still and watched them without turning my head. They were both asleep, legs tangled. The girl had short black hair. Dino didn't like short hair. He liked feminine women, as they were more fun to play dress-up with. He liked glamour, excess. I wasn't glamorous, but I was submissive, undeniably feminine in the ways that I bent. I had the marks of men all over me in a way he found sexy or maybe endearing. I picture a pie with latticework crust; that was my heart, all marked up by men. The girl wore a wedding band. When she turned in her sleep I ran into the surf. My belly snaked with rage, though a part of me felt relieved—he looked well. I swam until my teeth were chattering. By the time I returned to my blanket, Dino and the woman were gone. They'd left behind a pile of stems from their figs, which I buried in a ceremonial fashion. *How dare he*, I whispered, testing out rage. It felt good. *Who the fuck does he think he is?*

I saw him at Trader Joe's on multiple occasions, anytime I gathered the strength to put pants on and go. He was in the produce aisle squeezing melons with a judicious expression. He was wearing reading glasses and studying the backs of granola bars. He held them up to the light like paperbacks. Of course I saw him in the freezer section, hunting for ice cream. But that wasn't like Dino. Dino went to the rich-person grocery stores to get his gelato; he liked freaky flavors like buttermilk and black sesame.

I stood behind him in line, examining the contents of his little red basket. Trail mix, lettuce, frozen steaks . . . what could prove it was him? I knew he liked English muffins. I knew he liked Mexican beer. He ate cottage cheese at least once a day. I studied the back of the person in front of me: broad shoulders, blue jeans, oiled hair, a cleanly shaved nape. I've always loved the backs of men's necks. There's something disarming about that naked patch, the shimmering tendons, a perfect juncture of hard and soft. In the early days of our love I would sneak up on Dino and kiss him right there. The back of his neck was the size of a kiss, of a postage stamp. He'd smile and say, *Howdy*, reaching back to pin me in place. Remembering this, I felt dizzy with longing. I wanted to do that to the person in front of me, to see what he would say.

I stood up on tiptoe, but before I could touch him, the cashier waved him over. He hurried away, revealing a nose that could never be Dino's. I abandoned my basket of dog treats and corn chips, a single tomato, and rushed out the door.

Did I think that I was going crazy? Yes and no. I ran in a world where everyone was someone else. We were always changing our names and cutting our hair. I knew three separate Angels but not one Anne, I'd met no fewer than one thousand Johns. In our smoky world of make-believe, how could I possibly know who was who? It was rude to question someone's wig, their slipshod disguise or fake accent. The rules of the game were constantly changing, but one thing stayed true: fantasy trumps flesh. Our job was to roll with the punches, to play along too. Sadness was unbecoming. Our permissiveness bordered on saintly. If you told me your name was Clint Eastwood or Cocksucker, I would smile and say, *Cool*.

The next time we worked together, Emeline gave me a present.

For you! she cried. We were standing by our lockers. She wore white linen pants with a white linen crop top; she looked like an ad for a beachside resort. *Since you've been so sweet to me. I'd be lost here without you.*

Oh, I said. *That's really OK.*

Come on, Emeline said, pushing it into my hands. It was a sparkly pink gift bag stuffed with pink tissue paper. I reached inside and pulled out a bundle, also wrapped in tissue. As I ran my thumb under the tape, I was struck with an intense sense of foreboding, as if I were being pranked. When the tissue fell away and my fingers touched the gift, I thought, at first, that it was an animal. I recoiled and dropped it, making a weird sound with my mouth. Spooled out on the floor, I finally understood that it was a wig.

It's human hair! Emeline said proudly, scooping it up as if nothing had happened. She held the wig out and finger-combed it with her French-tip nails. It was the color of butter, of sunshine, of kid's birthday cake. *Really nice quality. I don't wanna brag, but, like, it cost a lot. Do you like it?*

I stared at her, feeling foggy. Her generosity made no sense to me; I waited for the barbs. *It's . . . beautiful.*

Right? She held it out to me like a baby I was supposed to want to cradle. *Touch her,* she demanded. *Feel how soft she is.*

I did as she told me. *Wow.*

Soft, huh?

Yeah. I swallowed. *Soft.*

You wanna know what I named her?

I wanted to ask, *What the fuck do you want from me?* Instead I said, *Sure.*

She paused for emphasis. *Diana.* She clapped her hands to her heart. *Oh my god, you're gonna look SO sexy tonight! Diana will make you SO much money! I promise she will.*

You think so? I asked. I reached for my lipstick just for something to do. I tried to focus on my reflection, the wan girl staring back at me. Her real hair the color of hamburger buns, of dirt roads going nowhere.

Emeline smiled. *Trust me. I know so.* She dropped the wig

in my lap. It had the weight of a kitten and made my legs itch. It was the exact same color as her hair.

Tonight's gonna be a good night, she sang. She returned to her seat and started brushing her own hair, which shone like a lamp. *I can feel it coming in the air tonight.* She made kissy faces in the mirror, spraying feathers on the countertop. *Tonight's gonna be one for the books.*

When she wasn't looking, I slid the wig in my locker. I piled my backpack and old Pleasers boxes on top of it. I was afraid to acknowledge it, as if it might come alive. It would stay at the bottom of my locker for weeks, gathering a layer of sweet-smelling dust.

I saw Dino on the streets, playing the sitar and collecting money in a paper cup.

I saw him in Chinatown, eating shrimp-and-chive dumplings; I saw him at Sixteenth and Mission, quietly shooting up. I saw him all the way down at Fisherman's Wharf, spying on the sea lions in a hat that said I ESCAPED ALCATRAZ. I saw him leaving an SRO next to the strip club, carrying a plastic bag full of plastic bags.

I saw him brokering deals, steaming milk, walking dogs. I saw him getting into limousines, dressed sharply in black. I waved, but he was too engrossed in his Bluetooth to notice. Once I saw him driving a Muni bus, the 33. He looked good in the uniform. At a hairpin turn the bus got stuck. He got out to reattach the bus to its cables, which sizzled above him. I wanted to call out, *Be careful!* Instead I kept walking.

I learned the hard way not to approach him; the few times I had, he looked angry or scared. *Back off, lady!* he yelled. *I got pepper spray!* That wasn't the Dino I knew. The Dino I knew would be happy to see me. The Dino I knew brought me love letters and smoothies. Though I longed for him daily, I vowed to let him come to me. I was learning the rules of his game as I went.

I started walking a lot. When I couldn't bear the quiet of the house any longer, I put on two sweatshirts and went for a walk. Sometimes I brought the girls with me. Sometimes I applied lipstick, grenadine-red, as if I were meeting someone. Was I actively looking for Dino? I can't say. All I knew was that he was everywhere, and if I walked for long enough, eventually I'd see him, as a doorman or lawyer, as a waiter on a smoke break, as the man accosting passersby with his clipboard. I signed the form without listening to him explain what it was for. I put down my stripper name: *Baby Blue.* I so rarely had occasion to use the last name. I winked at the man, who'd spontaneously grown a mustache, and said, *Keep fighting the good fight!* When he didn't embrace me or say sorry for leaving, I kept walking.

If I was hungry, I bought little steamed tacos from the ladies on the curb. They reached deep into their baskets and undid layer after layer of dish towel, a complicated system I admired. I tipped them 100 percent. On my walks I gave money to anyone who asked. A man who was definitely not Dino smiled at me from beneath his soggy blanket and said, *Marry me.*

I smiled back in a way that was meant to be gentle. *I don't believe in marriage.*

The fog determined how long I would walk for. It followed me home like a man; I crossed the street but it caught up. I'd be dripping wet by the time I walked through the door. One gray night I sat naked in Dino's bed, drip-drying and eating the last of his cottage cheese, when I saw him on TV. I changed the channel and there he was on the screen, smiling like a maniac. He held a bottle of aspirin in one hand and said, *For the boo-boos kisses just can't fix.* He wore an argyle sweater and penny loafers.

For the first time in weeks, I turned off the TV. I drew a bath and took a Xanax from the little stash in Dino's desk. He kept them in a purple-and-gold Fabergé egg. I listened to music and tried to relax, but I couldn't shake the feeling that I wasn't alone.

Hello? I called out. *Who's there?* No one answered. Was I losing it? I didn't really feel like I had much to lose. The dogs lay on the bath mat, dreaming. I took another pill.

I told myself I was seeing things. I was overworked, underslept. I was very possibly having a mental breakdown. Still, my heart fluttered whenever I glimpsed him, on a billboard or the bus. They may have been hallucinations, but they kept me company. They felt real, and that's what matters. In this way he was my private dancer, making me believe.

I was strict with myself: Whenever I saw him out and about, I no longer approached him. I was sane enough to know I might have the wrong guy. Moreover, I couldn't bear to be wrong—to hug a stunt double, to goose a ghost. I would die of disappointment. *All right*, I wanted to cry, *you win! I*

miss you. I need you. My heart is a carton of milk with your face
on the side. Happy now? Come home.

Maybe my work was partly to blame. I'd been method-
acting as a dream girl, and now I couldn't touch back down to
earth. I'd become untethered from the real world, where
people go missing every single day and there are few happy
endings. I'd dallied for too long in fantasies that were not
even my own, like falling asleep in a hot tub. Yes, I was crazy,
but so was true love. It was crazy for Dino to have loved me
in the first place. I had to believe we'd meet again, that Dino
would come home to me. If not, I'd never leave my bed. I'd
fall down a manhole in my new strappy shoes. I'd let the pi-
geons of Union Square eat me alive. *Save me, save me!* Who
would come?

In the early days of our love affair, we walked a lot too. We
walked from Russian Hill to Lands End, from Marshall's
Beach to Chinatown, from bar to bar to bar. We went to cafés
at the tops of hills so steep they had stairs cut into the sidewalk. We sat on the steps of Grace Cathedral, looking down
at the city, the lacy Victorians and SROs blanched in light,
the fire escapes draped with blouses and bedsheets and strips
of dried meat. I remembered my love for this city with Dino.
Together we visited the kissing spots of Frisco, the secret gar-
dens and blue bars where old men watched us smooch. One
man offered us $100 to have sex in front of him. *No, thank*
you, we told him, but in truth we were flattered. We drank
tequila-pineapples and continued to kiss, my bare thighs

stuck to the vinyl stool. It was so much fun to fall in love. On hot days we rode our bikes to China Beach, stopping at little Russian delis for herring. We picked through the big bins of imported candy, choosing the ones with the strangest wrappers. I still have one today—black-and-white checkerboard. I'd put it in my special-things box, alongside a drink token from Aunt Charlie's Lounge and a scrunched-up bar napkin on which Charlie had written his home address and the words *BE DISCRETE.*

After a day at the beach, we would bike back to his place. The light was swollen, amber, casting ghoulish shadows on the hot concrete. Cruising past mansions with their geometric lawns, our bodies browned and warm to the touch, I felt so happy I could die. I felt bright and full and chosen. I thought: Remember this. Remember the BBQ smell in the air, my gingham bikini. Remember Dino swerving to grab a fistful of rosemary. How he rubbed it on his pressure points, then tucked it behind one ear.

I remember the first time I had an orgasm during a lap dance.

It happened suddenly, randomly, like a sneeze. I didn't make any sounds, but my belly erupted, a molten bouquet. My client had no clue. I said nothing and kept grooving. I remember the song that was playing: "Closer" by Nine Inch Nails.

I wasn't attracted to the man I was dancing for. Quite the opposite, really. He was meaty and sweaty, with minimal neck. I believe his name was Sergei. He had gigantic thighs, which perhaps can account for my arousal on a physical level. There was a lot of terrain to rub against. Also, he was wearing corduroy pants, a soft nubby brown.

He was the taciturn type, a grunter and pointer. There was also a language barrier; the length and price of our dance was negotiated mainly through hand gestures. *Do you wanna have fun?* I repeated, twirling my hair, and he nodded, yes, yes. All of this was fine by me.

It was only midway through the dance that he said anything. In a soft, raspy voice he whispered, *Need me.* I wasn't sure if I heard him right but he said it again. *Need me. Need me.* It was less of a command and more of a plea, a doggish lament. It felt so out of place, like a flower dropped from his pocket. The pathos of it touched my cunt, figuratively speaking. He said it three or four more times. Shortly thereafter, I came.

As soon as the dance was over, I scurried away. I could've hustled him for more money, but I needed space. I hid in the bathroom and stared at myself in the mirror. My belly muscles ached. I felt shock and shame but mostly confusion. Even with someone I loved, I never came that quickly. Dino used to keep a carpetbag of vibrators under his bed to get me off, the Rabbit and the Magic Wand and a 1970s back massager he found at an estate sale. I'd never, ever come just from bumping and grinding before. Did not being in love somehow help? I splashed water on my face, baby-wiped my pussy, and went back on the floor. I avoided Sergei for the rest of the night. His mournful eyes followed me around like a stench.

A few months later, I overheard other dancers discussing the phenomenon of accidental arousal. From what I could gather, it was a very rare though not unprecedented event whose causes were hotly debated. A group of girls got into it, huddled around a Golden Boy pizza.

It's about being worshipped. I mean, IF the guy is good-looking. Sometimes it's hot to be hot.

No wayyyyyy. Nuh-uh! I could care less about him. I don't even SEE him. It's purely mechanical. It's like humping a pillow.

I think it's the wrongness of it. Like, the grosser the dude, the better for me.

Really?

Yup. I can't explain why.

That's twisted, sweetie.

What is there to explain? They're getting theirs, we're getting ours. We're all fuckin' animals at the end of the day.

It's good for you to orgasm at least twice a day. That's what my wellness coach told me.

I'll only come if someone's watching. Preferably, his wife.

October passed; suddenly it was November, and Dino still hadn't come home. The heat wave subsided, making way for a grim autumn that befitted my mental state. One gray Friday night I took an Uber to work. I don't know what compelled me, as nothing was wrong with my car and I hadn't been drinking, but before I knew what was happening I was sitting in the back of a stranger's SUV. A plastic bowl of hard candies was balanced on the console with a handwritten sign that said EAT ME.

Don't mind if I do, I whispered to no one. I'd begun talking to myself more and more.

The radio played softly, the Manhattans, Marvin Gaye. The driver was bathed in blue shadow, his skin and his hair and his jacket all the same color. I sat behind him, examining his shoulders. He wore a torn denim shirt with the collar popped. When he spoke, I felt a familiar tingle.

How's your night going so far?

Good, I said carefully. I didn't want to spook him. I needed to get a good look to confirm what I felt in my gut: it was Dino, of course, in a shoddy disguise. We'd been playing tag for days now. It only made sense that he'd raise the stakes of our game. The driver didn't smell like Dino, but I blamed it on the brand-new car. *How about you?*

Eh, he said, waving one hand in the air. He wasn't wearing his usual rings, but his body radiated heat in the way Dino's did. *Could be better. D'ya mind if I vent?*

Not at all, I said, leaning forward. I was trying to look at his nose. Dino's nose could be seen from outer space. He hated how big it was, but I wanted to worship it, grab on to it like a tire swing hung over a lake. It was one of the things I thought about most in my long lonely nights in his bed. *Go ahead.*

So I've got this girl, he said. He spoke with his hands. *We've been together for a while, but things aren't going so great.*

I froze. *Is that so?*

He nodded, drumming his fingers on the steering wheel. *Don't get me wrong. Sometimes it's groovy. She's easy to be with. But other times I feel . . . restless. Like nothing is wrong but it doesn't feel right. It doesn't feel like it used to.*

In the early days of spit and wonder?

He grunted. *Exactly. At the start, it was wild. Everything*

felt good. Then she started to, like, pull away. She's quite a bit younger than me, so maybe that's it. When we met, she was—
Twenty-five?

He whistled. *How did you know?*

I forced a smile. *Good guess.*

He nodded in time to the music. Neither of us was looking at the road. I didn't care if we crashed. I would do anything to keep him talking, talking.

What else? I asked.

Well . . . The back of his head looked sheepish. *I don't want to be mean, but she can be kind of . . . cold.*

Oh?

It's not like she's depressed. It's . . . something else. She goes offline. I hug her, but she acts like I'm a goddamn ghost. Or maybe she's the ghost. My arms go right through her.

She's there but she's not really there.

Nailed it.

I sat on my hands to keep them from shaking. *Do you love her?*

He thought about this, rubbing his jaw. *I know that I used to.* He kept rubbing. *Now I'm not sure that I can.* He chuckled. *Can a guy love a ghost?*

I think so, I said. *But he has to like being scared.*

That's funny! he cried. When he turned around to look at me, I was shocked to discover that he had a mustache. Dino couldn't grow a mustache; he could barely grow chest hair, he shaved his face once a fortnight. This stranger was grinning. *You're a very good listener.*

Thank you, I whispered. Everything had shifted. I hated

him now. I felt like I'd hugged the wrong man from behind. I would tip him, but I hated him. I wanted to get out of the car and walk the rest of the way. I'd hitch a ride from the first car that stopped for me, serial killer or no.

So wuddya think? he said. *You're a woman.*

I am.

What's your take?

I looked out the window. *Maybe she's scared.*

He looked affronted. *Of what? I'm a good guy.*

Sure, I said, *but maybe she's scared of being let down. Maybe bad things have happened to her. Maybe there's something rotten inside her and she's sparing you from it. Maybe she's scared you won't like her as much once you find these bad things. Maybe she knows she'll lose you eventually so why waste your time?* I took a deep breath. *Just a guess.*

Huh, he said, stroking his beard. *But she hasn't lost me. I'm right here.*

Are you sure?

He frowned. *I think so.*

We listened to music for the rest of the journey, the driver occasionally singing along. He had a velvety baritone that also disqualified him for the lead role of Dino. I basked in my feelings of disappointment and loss. As soon as we pulled into the parking lot, I grabbed my shit and jumped out. He rolled down his window and called out, *Hey!*

He waited until I turned around. *Thanks for the therapy session.*

No problem, I muttered. I fumbled for something clever to say, to mask my disdain. I'd learned never to let a man know what you really think of him. *The first one's on me.*

I listened to his soft laughter, then the rumble of his engine as he sped away, back to wherever the fuck he came from, never to be seen again.

I met Dino in May and graduated in June. Two summers later I'd start stripping. Harried men would tell me their life stories; they'd put their hands on my thigh and say, *Thank you so much.* I often felt like a therapist, like a professional. I didn't have a corner office, but I had the sticky zebra-print cushions in the VIP rooms. I didn't have tailored suits, but I was sometimes paid extra to wear nylon stockings. I wore my hair up, I wore my hair down. Clients liked me because I didn't judge. I understood the imperative to feel good or else. If I were to encounter them in the outside world, I'd smile and keep walking. Confidentiality was important in my line of work. Their secrets, gory or boring, were safe with me. I kept them with me like hickeys hidden under a scarf. I kept them with me like cigarette burns.

I remember this: Walking down the street with a man in late summer. I am twenty-three or twenty-six. I don't remember who he was. Dino and I used to go for long walks, crisscrossing the city, outfoxing the fog. Was it him? I can't say. It could have been anyone, the lovers too cheap to pay for the bus, the strangers met in taquerias I'd never go to again. I don't know if he was sweet or pushy, drunk or high, only that the man stopped suddenly, one hand raised. He took a deep breath and sighed.

Jasmine, he said, tilting his head back. *Do you smell that?*

I do, I said, though I hadn't. I was too drunk or horny or cold to notice the dense opal smell in the air.

The man smiled. He put his hands on his hips. I remember this part clearly, as men so rarely have occasion to acknowledge their hips. He said, *Jasmine smells like sex to me.*

Oh?

He nodded. *As a kid I would smell it and feel weird. I didn't understand what was happening. When I started fucking, I got it. I understood what the smell, like, activated in me.*

Lust? I guessed. *Desire? Longing?*

Close. I thought he would kiss me, but he started to walk fast. I hurried after him, hurt that he'd missed a golden opportunity to pull me to him, lift my blouse, call me worthless or chosen, whatever his flavor. Instead he looked into the yards of the houses we passed and said, *Lonely. That's what jasmine made me feel. Because if I could stop to smell it in the air, I probably wasn't fucking someone.*

The memory cuts out there. I don't know if we went back to his place, though I'd guess that we did. Telling you about it now, I just remembered something new: his jeans. He wore tight blue jeans with a hole in the crotch where his cock had rubbed the fabric thin. I remember the hole but not the cock. When I close my eyes, I can see him walking uphill, a few hundred feet in front of me. The wind is picking up. I want him to squeeze me until I see spots. The sky is woozy and purple, like the insides of flowers. The fog is coming in hot.

When Dallas told me about the dungeon, I thought she was joking.

What's so funny? she asked. *They're always looking for new girls.*

We were leaning on the bar, waiting for men to come in. Turns out Cookie had told her about my arrangement with Simon. I was still getting his payments, every month on the first.

Really? I said.

Uh-huh. Are you interested? She gave me a phone number and told me to tell the headmistress that Miss Dallas sent me. *You may never come back to the club after this.*

Why not?

She smiled. *It's a whole different ball game. Domming can be a little addictive.* She paused. *You'll have to change your name, though. Miss Baby won't fly.*

I nodded, feeling unexpectedly protective of Baby, this silly girl I'd created, so earnest and fey. *OK . . .*

Got any backups?

I'd have to think about it.

Dallas nodded. *Don't force it.* She stood up, making eye contact with a new dude. She furtively adjusted her breasts. *I don't know about you, but I don't wanna do this forever. Do you?*

Before I could reply, she was gone. I could hear her high, soft laughter from across the room, so different from how she laughed with me. I didn't know how to answer her question. I didn't think about forever. I was focused on the here and now, on feeding the dogs and going to work, on sitting tight and being cool, waiting for my Dino. I had to admit, there was peace in my loneliness. I'd worked fear and sorrow into my daily routine and now I felt attached to them.

Still, Dallas's words stayed with me as I circled the floor.

I thought of Simon, all our little games. One night I asked what he'd been up to and he had said, very casually, *I just came from a dungeon.*

I thought he was being sarcastic. *Is that so?* I'd cooed. *And what happened there?*

I got what was coming to me, he'd said, eyes bright. *I got what I deserved.*

The next morning, I walked to the 7-Eleven for my usual coffee and donuts. On the way back, I called the number Dallas had given me and made an appointment. I was told to go to a particular Starbucks, then call that same number once there to get the dungeon's real address. This was described to me as a standard safety precaution. When asked my name, I said, *Sunday.* I don't know where it came from, but it made me feel tingly.

Lovely, said the voice on the phone. She had a lifelong smoker's gravel and said her name was Hugo. I pictured her sitting in an armchair, puffing on a cigar. *We'll see you then, Miss Sunday.*

Angel's Envy

IV.

Let's call it Dream House.

Dungeon conjures up the wrong image. Close your eyes and revise it: a pea-green four-bedroom in a quiet cul-de-sac, toeing the border between Berkeley and Richmond. Bought in the eighties when this neighborhood was still working-class: pit bulls in scrubby yards, cars on blocks. Today the house could go for a million. The place is dated, paint flaking in spots, but the yard is well loved. Picture a garden full of roses, a girl in a kimono picking cherry tomatoes, another lying on a towel reading the Marquis de Sade. If the towel is white, it came from the Medical Room. If the towel is green, it came from the Student Dorm. There are always cars parked nearby, never directly in front, men coming and going with guarded expressions. They know that if the American flag is hung off the porch, Dream House is open for business.

Sometimes the men bring bottles of wine. Sometimes they bring standard-sized envelopes stuffed with twenties, forgetting that their business address is printed on the front. Most will call themselves Michael or John. They are every-one: teachers, lawyers, junkies, techies, bodybuilders, gentle-men, bisexuals, creeps, the underemployed, the clinically depressed, the barely legal, the newly betrothed, fathers, brothers, lovers, losers, always someone's son. They come in Porsches and beat-up sedans, they come in Ubers from the city that cost them a fortune, the lucky few get a ride from their wife.

Some men will be flashy and some will be coy. Some will act like they hate me, while others beg to kiss the space be-tween my toes. To some I really am a deity. The old sex work cliché will prove true here too: many of my clients just want to talk. They want to talk about their gang-bang fantasy, their unfinished novellas. They want to talk about ponytails and being pimped out. They speak of relationship woes and new medications with weird side effects. They speak of dry mouth, speckly vision, unexpected weight gain. One man told me, during a session, that it was his fortieth birthday.

You know what I regret most from my youth? he asked, lying back on the bed. *Not fucking more women.* He flapped his hands despairingly. *Now it's too late.*

As an ex-slut, his comment gave me pause. Had I been bettering myself during my ho era? Not decreasing my value but stockpiling experience? This thought made me feel ten-derly toward my younger self, that skittish girl beholden to her appetites, chasing any smidge of warmth. Men's bodies were the best blankets. It seemed smarter, in the long run, to have more warmth than less, to hoard this animal currency that never went out of style. The forty-year-old man on the bed—pudgy, salt-and-pepper hair—looked suddenly cold to me, as if parts of his body had never been touched. He needed me to share my heat, to coax his body into shapes he had forgotten he could make. Studying him, I felt generous and overly qualified, a beacon in hot(!) pink.

The training period at Dream House was minimal. Most of what I was taught revolved around hygiene. *Always wear gloves when changing the sheets*, Hugo told me. *Always put your stockings in a lingerie bag before washing them. Otherwise they'll run.*

For the first two weeks, I shadowed Miss Ophelia. I was instructed to stand in the corner during her sessions, watching her work. This was an added bonus for her clients, many of whom had exhibitionist fantasies. They locked eyes with me and made melodramatic noises as she flogged them. In between sessions Ophelia would show me how to sanitize dildos, sort whips, fold towels. There were so many towels, color-coded and washed into nubbly stiffness. After two weeks, if Hugo approved, my name would be added to the roster of dominatrices on the Dream House website and men could book BDSM sessions with me.

But how will I know what to do? I asked, panicked. Ophelia and I were putting away toys. *What if I get booked to, like, tie someone up?*

She shrugged. *It's kind of sink-or-swim around here.*

What's the craziest thing you've had to do?

She smiled gently. *I don't HAVE to do anything.*

OK, I said, chastened. *But you know what I mean.*

She thought about it for a moment, pensively tapping a Magic Wand against her thigh. *I used to see this dude with a*

belly button fetish, she said. *He'd stick his finger in my belly but-*
ton and swirl it around. One time he put lipstick on it and pre-
tended it was telling jokes. Like, "What's the difference between a
chickpea and a lentil . . . ?"

I would learn from Ophelia that Dream House had a
spotty reputation in the Bay Area kink scene. It was considered the budget dungeon, dingier and cheaper than the well-
appointed Victorians near Lake Merritt or Folsom Street. It
was either busy or dead. When I started working there, it was
$200 a session, up from last year's $175. Regulars would call
the unlisted number to complain of the price hike.

Wankers, said Hugo. *Ignore them.*

There was one particular wanker who called almost daily
to ask if any Mistresses catered to adult babies. Most girls
knew to hang up on him right away, but if you said yes, he'd
ask if any Mistresses catered to poopy diapers. If you said yes,
he asked if any Mistresses catered to big, wet, stinky, messy,
yucky poo-poo wee-wee uh-oh in his little widdle piddy
pants. And if you didn't, for some reason, hang up right then,
he'd switch back to his regular voice and ask, *Well? Does*
anyone do that? This is a serious inquiry. I'm looking for someone
who can clean my yucky poopy woopy panty-wanties . . . and on
and on.

The worst thing is, said Ophelia, *that's not even his kink.*

How do you know?

Most adult babies are sweet. Nonconfrontational, you know?
This dude gets off on wasting our time. He wants you to feel em-
barrassed. She flipped off the rotary phone. *What a freak.*

Next to the phone was a leather-bound notebook frilled
with multicolor Post-its. This was referred to as the file. After

every session, girls were required to write down the name and birthday of their client, plus a general summary of the experience. The idea was to keep track of our clients' tastes and habits, weeding out the men who didn't play by the rules.

When I was bored between sessions and waiting for the phones to ring, I studied the file. It read like a dream journal, the hastily jotted entries like freaky haikus. Some were fanciful, some were curt, some I couldn't decode. I read it and time-traveled through twenty-plus years of kink at Dream House, so many different men with so many different desires who all looked the same in my mind's eye.

Easy cross-dress scene, we played dress-up & did BJ lessons on dildos, client expressed interest in breastfeeding 4 future sesh, very sweet & tipped well! —Miss Angelica

We role-played as therapist and patient . . . he's in love with his mother, needs hypnosis to snap out of it, ends up worshipping me, etc etc . . . client was respectful & chill (& kinda hot), he has a thing for black tights & pencil skirts . . . A+ sesh!! —Miss Justine

Not good match. Too grabby. G/S, JOI. Boundary-pusher, NOT recommended 4 new girls. Do NOT book me w/ him again —Miss Valentina

Client very shy & nervous, handed me "letter from wife" that said he was a bad boy & needed a beating, eventually he relaxed, responded well to thuddy pain—PLZ NOTE: HAD BIGGEST BALLS IVE EVER SEEN, like medical

condition??!??! Literal watermelons. He seemed not to mind
or be restricted by them . . . other than that, pretty average
sesh —Miss Amazon

What made the entries all the more amusing was the neutrality with which they were dispatched. The secrets of men
scribbled out like grocery lists. Their fantasies, their flaws, the
failures of their bodies . . . relayed with no more passion than
a school nurse's note.

After my first week of working as a professional dominatrix,
my clients began to bleed together. The latex-lovers and
cross-dressers and masochists, the sissies and piss-drinkers
and self-described brats—they all got mixed up into one
gnarly soup. My sessions didn't become less interesting, but
they did lose their shock value. After a month I could gaze
upon the fuzzy butthole of a lawyer bent over my knee and
barely register disgust. If I was lucky, I'd enter a flow state; if
not, I got bored and pushed on. I got used to grown men not
wiping well or at all. Ophelia would call this their Hershey's
Kiss.

When I look back on my time at Dream House, a handful
of sessions stand out to me, but I know there are so many I'm
missing. Perhaps if Dino had been around, I'd remember
more of them now. I would've loved to come home and tell
him all about my day, saving up potent details—the bubble-
gum texture of a sub's cock in a cage, the aquatic cuteness of
a micropenis, how all cucks wore too much cologne, how
fisting someone's asshole felt like trying to find a wedding

ring that's been baked into lasagna. As it was, I had no one to shock. The dogs didn't care. Poopy buttholes couldn't faze them.

Did I feel simpatico with the clients whose names and birthdays I can still recite to this day, Pledge of Allegiance–style? Tim, 10/10/75. Pasqual, 6/9/69. The oldest client I can remember was born in 1939; he wanted to be kicked in the balls. Who knows. All I know, in fact, is this: Men are dying to be let in on the secret pleasures of girlhood. They feel cheated out of ease and glamour, friend-kisses and hushed gossip. Heterosexuality is defined by a longing for wholeness. Terror undergirds desire. Most straight men long to suck a dick, if only to know how.

I saw a man with a human furniture fetish. He asked to be my dance floor. I played Donna Summer over the speakers and boogied on him for an hour straight. We both had a wonderful time.

I saw a man with tremendous BO. Terry, 12/6/70. It filled the foyer as soon as he entered. Ophelia told me to put Vicks VapoRub under my nose. *It's an old hooker trick*, she said. *If he asks, just say you have a cold.* I ran to the bathroom and looked in the medicine cabinet, but all I could find was Tiger Balm. I smeared too much on my upper lip and spent the next hour in agony. When I spoke, tears filled my eyes. Terry, bound and gagged, pretended not to notice.

I had a well-to-do client with a cigarette fetish. He brought nice wine for us to drink. I immobilized him with Saran Wrap and shotgunned smoke into his mouth. I ashed my cigarette in his wine and made him chug it. I put two, three, four lit cigarettes in his mouth all at once. He got so light-headed that he had to lie down. *How do you feel?* I asked, masking my panic. He flashed me a peace sign and murmured, *Out of this world.*

I saw an obese cross-dresser who told me he slept in his double-D breastplate every single night. He wore it under his Notre Dame T-shirt. He wanted me to pee on him, but I just couldn't do it, despite drinking two Diet Cokes in a row. He tipped me OK, but I could tell he felt cheated.

There was a regular at Dream House named Junior. Everyone had sessioned with Junior. He didn't care which girl he saw, he'd take whoever was free. A session with him was always the same. He would bring you a pair of high-waisted granny panties, brand-new with the tag. You would put them on, then he'd sling you King Kong–style over one shoulder. With his free hand he would jerk his dick until he came. This took about six minutes. The rest of the hour was spent chatting, sitting crisscross on the floor. He lived in the Tenderloin with his elderly parents and worked as a janitor at a middle school. He was infamous for taking extremely long showers. Hugo disliked him for this reason alone; the rest of us found him disarming and sweet.

There was a man who claimed to be a composer for Broadway musicals. He was visiting San Francisco for work and had a cannibal fetish. He booked me for a double with Miss Buffy in which we pretended to be the queens of an all-girl island. We tied him up and pounded his flesh with our fists to tenderize him. *Mmmmm*, we said. *Man-burger. Man-bun.* We made squirrelly little munching sounds as we nibbled his digits. Suddenly he began to sing. He had Sondheim's repertoire memorized. *Isn't it rich?* he warbled. *Isn't it queer?* Eventually we joined in. *Send in the clowns!*

I remember a session with a man who looked like Jeff Goldblum. As per his request, I wore seven-inch Pleasers. He threw himself at my feet. *Please, Goddess,* he cried. *May I please be permitted to touch your perfect right foot?* I said yes, and his body started to shake. In slow motion he reached out and dragged his pointer finger down the length of my heel. *Oh god,* he moaned. He cradled my foot in his hands, exactly like you'd hold a baby bird, and I was surprised to find my body responding. His extreme gentleness aroused me. It was so pure it was almost violent. He pressed his lips to the bottom of my shoe and whispered, *This is the seat of your power, your divine feminine grace.* Then he began to cry, his tears collecting between my toes. *Thank you, Goddess. I know I am not worthy to experience such bliss. I will never forget this moment.* He clutched at my hem like a peasant. I extended my left foot and snarled, *Go on.*

By mid-November I'd established a new routine. I worked at the strip club Thursday, Friday, Saturday, and went to the dungeon Monday and Wednesday. I felt less bereft with only two days off. These days were spent mostly sleeping. When I woke up around 3:00 p.m., I took the girls out. We walked all over the neighborhood, making eye contact with everyone. When we got home, I tended to the chores I'd put off: laundry, emails. The hours fizzled away, leaving nothing behind them. My work was the only thing keeping me sane, as it gave me people to talk to and a reason to bathe. I made myself go to bed around 10:30 p.m. by taking two Xanax and a tablespoon of kratom in pineapple juice. To no one, I called this my nightcap. If I really couldn't sleep, I took two more Xanax and put on *Sex and the City*. This almost always worked.

At the dungeon I started my shift at 10:00 a.m. and got off at 3:00 p.m., a schedule that felt remarkably civilized. It had been ages since I'd worked a job with daylight hours. Not that there was much daylight to be found at the dungeon. The many windows were covered with heavy-duty blackout drapes.

Soundproof too, said Hugo. *So the neighbors can't hear screaming.*

Hugo had greasy gray hair that she kept in two braids and often smelled of Windex. She wore men's Hawaiian shirts, cargo shorts, and plastic flip-flops. In her breast pocket there was always a fresh pack of Newports and a lighter with a cat on it. I wondered how men felt when they first came to the dungeon and she answered the door, ushering them in and offering them a Diet Coke from the mini-fridge in the foyer. She looked like someone's hippie grandma, driving off in her Prius to do the weekly Costco run. When she got back, everyone rushed to unload the car. We carried in giant packs of paper towels, fabric softener, disposable gloves, rubbing alcohol, toilet paper, tampons, Jergens baby oil, jumbo bottles of half-and-half, tortillas, clementines, prepackaged biscotti, so many cans of Diet Coke. To passersby, we must have looked like preppers, stockpiling for the end with a womanish eye.

While the rest of the dungeon was meticulously organized with little handwritten labels (BUTT PLUGS ETC, WATERPROOF

SHEETS), the kitchen tended toward entropy. The fruit bowl on the counter was always full of slightly rotten stone fruits gathered from the garden. There were boxes of takeout in the fridge marked with the initials of girls who no longer worked there, ancient pieces of cheesecake and coagulated pad thai. Every week Hugo boiled two dozen eggs, then put them back in a carton marked: EAT ME!!!! I was too shy to take one, though Ophelia assured me they were communal.

Help yourself to whatever, she said, refilling her mug. It said YOU'RE NOBODY UNTIL YOU'VE BEEN IGNORED BY A CAT. *God knows there's more than enough.*

I was only ever brave enough to microwave a few tortillas and eat them with room-temperature butter. Hugo had a habit of drifting through the kitchen, scanning the overfull counters, and then drifting out. She made me feel like I'd done something wrong, but I didn't know what. Was she mad that I wasn't eating enough fruit, leaving it to blacken? When I touched one of the plums my finger went straight through it in a way that felt lewd. I always made sure to unload the dishwasher and rinse out my mug. I favored a simple white one that read THIS TOO SHALL PASS. When the laundry dinged, I sprang off the couch to help sort it. I folded sissy panty after sissy panty, some the size of picnic blankets, and stacked them in a wire basket. Hugo was silent except to point out my mistakes.

We fold towels hamburger-style, she snapped. *Not hot-dog.* She seemed to have two emotions: happy and not. Sometimes she led me into the garden and pointed out her tea roses, her crabapples, her gargantuan plums. We would stand in a patch of sunlight, warming our shoulders. Other times she stared through me when I asked how she was. *Hurting*, she said once, in response to my question. *Everything hurts.*

Oh no, I said, *why?*

She turned around and left the room. *Do you think I know?*

My coffee consumption doubled while working at Dream House. I drank it while waiting for the phones to ring. If the laundry was sorted and you didn't have a session, there wasn't much to do except wait. In between sessions girls lounged in the common area, combing through the costume closet or drinking coffee on the porch. The closet was a prodigious mix of pin-up, tween, and business casual, Frederick's of Hollywood and Limited Too and Ann Taylor and Guess, culled from East Bay thrift stores over the last twenty years. We took turns manning the phone, a mint-green rotary with a long curly cord that reminded me of childhood. When a client called, we picked up and said, *Hello?* Nothing more, nothing less. If the man on the other end asked who it was, we were always to say, *Lorraine.*

I liked doing phone duty. I would sink into the faux-leather couch and stare at the handwritten charts on the wall. They denoted a complicated system of boundaries—Deja did strap-on but not fisting, Amazon did brown showers with a $300 deposit, everyone but Pandora was down for couples. Alongside these charts was a patchwork of sticky notes, accrued as the weeks went by: *Valentina has asthma so no smoking scenes; Don't book Ophelia with John, 6/23/53; Buffy has pierced nipples now, plz mention when booking; Alejandro is still 86'd!!!*

Sometimes the phone rang incessantly; sometimes it didn't

ring at all. During my first week at the dungeon, I was booked five times in a day. The next time I went in, I wasn't booked at all and spent the day doing crosswords in the garden. Some girls, like Xenia, never had a slow day. She'd flit in and out of the common area, pausing just long enough to drop her cash in the safe. Just as soon as she dumped her soiled outfit in the hamper and picked out a new miniskirt, the doorbell would be ringing for her next appointment. She favored knee socks, hot pink, pigtails with scrunchies, a barely legal pixie shtick. I only spoke to her once, on a blustery Monday when she came in early.

I'm gonna take a shower, she announced.

I was sitting on the sofa, drinking my first coffee of the day. I was shocked to see her civilian clothes. She wore ripped jeans covered in chains, a safety pin through one eyebrow, and a T-shirt that said SICK PUPPY. Her usually blond hair was gummed to her scalp, the color of nothing. She reminded me of the girls from my high school who went to raves and got fingered.

The water at my squat is out so I haven't bathed in days, she said. She stripped off her clothes and left them in a pile on the oatmeal-colored carpet. She wore torn men's briefs as underwear. *Will you tell me if anyone calls?*

OK, I said, trying not to stare at the Canada-shaped birthmark on her belly. It was the color and texture of a hot-water bottle. I had to wonder if it was part of her appeal, the secret to her success. Or was it the barely-there boobs? The crusted rings in her ears? She looked like a track star, a child of divorce, with a wringable waist and pale symmetrical scars down one thigh.

What's your name again? she asked, hovering in the doorway. She rested one foot against the inside of her other leg, flamingo-style. It was hard to imagine her hurting a fly, though I knew she was frequently booked for corporal torture scenes. She was the only girl on the schedule who did needles and blood play.

Sunday, I said.

She smiled. *I like that. My cat's name is Tuesday.*

Wow, I said dumbly. Was I in love with this girl? That was how I was acting, moony and shy. She probably had a can of spray paint in her messenger bag. Our East Bay romance: dumpster-diving for Trader Joe's flowers and tagging our initials on underpasses. Before I could decipher my feelings, she'd danced out of the room. I heard the upstairs shower turn on, her little voice singing. To my surprise, I recognized the lyrics: *Some velvet morning when I'm straight . . .*

The morning passed slowly. I only had one appointment booked. A man named John (of course) called to book Valentina for a golden shower at 5:30 p.m. *Can you please ask her to refrain from drinking any coffee beforehand?* he asked. He sounded nervous, as though he were speaking to an authority figure. *I don't like when I can, um, taste it.*

No problem.

Does she smoke?

Nope.

Excellent. He exhaled. *Nice and clean.*

Valentina was a heavily tattooed lesbian who worked part-time as a 911 operator. She was frequently booked for face-sitting and smothering scenes due to her tremendous rear end.

I scraped myself off the couch and reheated my coffee. Though Hugo was out, I felt the need to stay busy. I gathered the lingerie from the clothesline outside, put away the dildos on the drying rack, then sat at the kitchen table practicing my knots. Ophelia was due to come in around noon, though she was always fifteen minutes late. She bounced between her boyfriend's place in West Oakland and her parents' house in Daly City. It took her over two hours to get here by bus.

I liked when Ophelia and I worked together. We got along well. She was a kind and patient teacher when it came to BDSM. She smelled like vetiver and wore tatty clothes, wrecked dresses, holey T-shirts. With her liquid gaze and yogi posture, she seemed somehow both older and younger than twenty-eight. She had a drowsy sort of sex appeal, moving through a room as if unsure of its solidity, gently touching doorframes and table corners, still submerged in her dreams. She was thoughtful and regal with moments of bravado. She wore black leather chaps while doing sudoku, fingering her lips as she thought. *Hush*, she muttered to no one. *I'm thinking.* One client said she had the lips of a vampire. Next to her, I felt dull-edged and childish. If she was opium, I was baby aspirin. Men were forever trying to guess her ethnicity; she weathered each guess with a gentle smile, revealing only to me, as we sat eating cheesy toast, that her father was Armenian and mother was third-generation Daly City Filipina.

Dudes call me Cleopatra. She sighed. *Their semi-exotic goddess. One time, I got Cher.*

When Hugo was out, we sat at the kitchen table with the

porch door ajar. We dug through the costume closet, trying on outfits. It gave me a quiet thrill to sit close to Ophelia, ignoring the other girls as they uploaded selfies to OnlyFans or read magazines. Everyone was nice enough, but I wanted my ties to Ophelia to be known. On particularly slow days she would cook us a big breakfast (scrambled eggs, beans, tortillas wrapped in a dish towel) and we ate with our hands, using tortillas as vessels. Did I always fall in love with whoever fed me? Was my devotion so easily won?

We killed time telling stories. Though she was barely a year older than me, she'd been around the block. When she was twenty-four, she had a sugar daddy so old and so famous he made her sign an NDA. They never had sex; they met up once a month at a hotel in Mountain View, where he stripped down to his socks and asked her to examine his penis.

His cock was actually pretty big, she explained, *but he wanted me to say it was tiny. A teensy-weensy wiener. His itty-bitty clitty.* She would bring little objects to hold up to his dick for comparison: golf pencils, ChapSticks, baby carrots, etc. He paid her rent on a walk-up in the sunniest part of the Mission for four dreamy years, until his stepchildren put him in an assisted living facility and seized control of his funds.

That was kinda my gateway into domming, she said. She wore a peach-colored corset she'd fished from the closet and tights with no panties. I wondered if Hugo would be mad at her for sitting on the kitchen chair bare-bummed. The rule of thumb was to always put a towel down. *For years after college, I did regular escorting. I could live well in San Francisco with just three johns a month. That's how much I charged per hour.* She smiled wistfully. *I leaned into the starving-artist shtick. My johns ate it up. One sent me Harry & David gift baskets every single week. He wanted to make sure I ate.* She chuckled. *You can only eat so many pears.*

She still did escorting every now and again, but her boyfriend, a painter of mild renown named Lorenzo, was against it. He sold twenty-foot nudes with glow-in-the-dark nipples. *He can handle me crushing some dude's balls for two hours,* she sighed, *but not me sucking dick for ten minutes. Is he weird or am I?*

I shrugged. This was something the other girls at the club spoke about. They bemoaned jealous boyfriends, guys who pretended to be chill until suddenly they weren't. It was always a gamble, when dating someone new, to disclose your real job. The dude either freaked out or got way too into it. He might ask if you liked it, you know, *reallyyyy* liked it, for which there was no safe answer. It was not uncommon for someone's drunk baby daddy to show up at the club in a rage. Security handled these run-ins with bored nonchalance, telling the offender to take it easy as they steered him into the parking lot. *Don't worry, man,* they said, thumping him on the back. *We got this. Chill out.* Meanwhile, the gay dancers nibbled on the snacks their girlfriends had packed them and made sympathetic faces.

Dino had never gotten weird about me wanting to strip. When I first told him I was thinking of auditioning, he acted like I was applying to grad school.

Good for you, Ruthie! he said. *I think that will be good for you.* We were sitting in the Costco food court, balancing mammoth pizza slices on stained paper plates.

Really? I had expected some pushback.

Totally, he said, dabbing his lips. The fluorescent lights made him look old but in a sexy way, like I was interviewing a famous Latin American poet. He'd seen and done it all, as evidenced by his eye bags and silvery hairs. *It'll get you out of the house.*

I get out of the house.

Sure, he said. *I meant, it'll get you out of your shell.* He elbowed me. *And out of your granny panties.*

Rude! I threw my balled-up napkin in his face. He used his paper plate as a shield, grease running down the sleeves of his sweater. He took it off as soon as we got home, putzing around in a satin slip for the rest of the night. I remember the color of it: teal, a color that nobody wears.

I remember a session with a very shy man. He wore baggy clothes covered in paint and looked down at his feet. He was silent as he gave me $200 in cash and signed the consent form, silent as we walked upstairs and entered the Red Room. The Red Room consisted of a four-poster bed hung with red velvet scraps and a vanity table, a cheap attempt at a boudoir scene. It was the smallest and least popular room, but I liked its melodrama. I closed the door and he turned to me suddenly, guiding my hands to his throat.

Do it, he said. He had a faint accent.

I pulled my hands back. *Do what?*

You know. His voice was library-soft.

I can't actually choke you. I tried to sound firm. *Breath-play is against the rules.*

For the first time since he'd arrived, he smiled. *I know*, he said. *It's just pretend.*

He took my left hand and placed it over his mouth. *Please?* he whimpered. I applied mild pressure and his eyes widened with pleasure. I made him sit on the edge of the bed and placed my other hand on his throat, gingerly squeezing as if testing an avocado's ripeness. I was scared to do more. Already I felt like I was pushing it, though who would tattle? He stared up at me like a doggy, blank and trusting. When I pulled my hands away, he said, *May I kiss you?*

No, I said. *That's against the rules too.*

But . . . He sounded so sad. *Can't we just pretend?*

Who was in charge here? I was both annoyed and endeared by him. I wanted, very badly, for him to have a good time. I sat on the bed next to him and offered my cheek. *Here.* He leaned in and kissed the air an inch above my cheekbone.

Good, I said. His expression was so earnest, his hands in his lap. *That's a good boy.* Air-kissing reminded me of Mazzy, as it was something she loved to do when drunk and pretending to be French, nearly falling off her barstool to pepper me with them. The air around my head would smell like her, her smoky perfume and wino breath. Men would turn to watch. Suddenly I missed her with an intensity that scared me, that rivaled even my longing for Dino's return.

Again, I told the man, attempting to regain my authority, though I felt, in that moment, like a little girl. We were having a tea party with imaginary cups. Would we soon be playing Doctor, I'll-show-you-mine-if-you-show-me-yours? I offered him my other cheek. He dutifully swooped in, his lips making the teeniest squelch by my ear.

Again, I said. *Again*. *Again*. We were like society ladies greeting each other, stuck on an infinite loop.

At last he stood up. *Thank you*, he said. He was trembling. *Thank you, Mistress.*

You're welcome, I said, though I didn't know what for. That's not true: I can guess what I gave him. A pleasure too pure to name, something childish yet dire. A stray crumb from another world; the frizzed outline of the divine.

When our session was over, I walked him to the door. He looked the same as he did when he arrived, pale and pencil-shaped, as if nothing significant had happened between us. He stood in the doorway and handed me two fifty-dollar bills.

Thank you, I said. The door was open, which was also against the house rules. Any neighbor could see me in my fishnet shirt and plastic miniskirt. All I could think to say by way of farewell was *Take it easy*.

He nodded, turning. His expression was unreadable. *You too.*

I wrote in the file that I'd love to see him for another session. He never called the dungeon again.

I spent a lot of my time as a domme answering emails. The Dream House website had our emails listed under our head-shots, all of which were taken with flash on Hugo's digital camera in the hallway upstairs. Seventy-five percent of the emails I got were pure nonsense. Strangers wrote rambling, lurid, incomprehensible messages.

I wish to live inside your tummy

You are beautiful & very rich

Hi hi hi hi hi hi hi hi hello

*I wish you were a Giant Woman stomping around saying
FEE FI FOO FUM!!!!*

One man wrote his entire message in the subject line, the body of the email blank but for his automatic sign-off—*Be Well.* Another man emailed me at least once a week to ask if I was Leslie from Fresno. *Or the greater Fresno area??* Men sent blurry pictures of their dicks, taken while sitting on the toilet, their dirty gray underwear pooled at their feet. Their email addresses never failed to amuse me: pregnantlover1986@ gmail.com, platform.addict@protonmail.com, slave4uuuuu@ hotmail.com, year_of_the_cuck@yahoo.com, accounting@ rosehillcrematorium.com.

I was sitting on the sofa at Dream House one Monday, sifting through my inbox. Hugo liked to blast the heat, so I was stripped down to just a tank top and hot pants. All I had on the schedule was a 1:00 p.m. session with Mike, 7/14/77, for over-the-knee spanking. He was remarkably easy to please, needing no role-play or dirty talk, just pure impact, to get into sub space. He chided me if I tried to check in on him. *Shhh!* he'd say, very much like a sullen child. *I'm trying to focus!* One time I put on a murder mystery podcast to play in the background while I spanked him for forty-five minutes.

He didn't seem to notice or care. My hands came away sore. Ophelia had told me that wearing two pairs of rubber gloves would ease the pain, but all that seemed to do was make my palms sweaty.

I opened my first unread email. The subject line looked promisingly concise: *Inquiry into Session.* The email address was nobody.is.home@protonmail.com.

Dear Miss Sunday,

I hope this message finds you well. Please forgive me for addressing you without your permission. I understand completely if you wish to stop reading. If, by some chance, you are kind enough to go on, I have a rather specific request for a session with you.

Out of respect for your time, I will be frank. I wish to end my life. I am seeking a Mistress to help push me over the edge, both literally and figuratively.

There are many shapes that this arrangement could possibly take. I am open to all of them. Would you be willing to discuss the details of a session with me? Or do you find my desire repulsive? No wrong answers, of course.

Again, please forgive me for wasting your time. You are a beautiful woman to whom I feel myself drawn. Your face relayed a certain grace. Perhaps I just wanted to share my daydreams with you.

Your humble servant,

X

I put my phone down. I was suddenly scared that Hugo would look over my shoulder, though I could hear her puttering about in the garden. My tummy felt squiggly, like the time I walked in on Valentina masturbating in the Red Room.

Excuse me! she'd shouted, waving her Hitachi at me. *I'm on my five-minute break!*

I showed the email to Ophelia as soon as she got in. *Oof,* she said, leaning against the kitchen sink. She wore a figure-hugging halter dress that looked like it was made of fabric scraps. *That's hardcore.*

In a bad way?

The coffeemaker rattled. *Totally.* She poured her coffee into a mug that read TELL YOUR CAT I SAY HI. *I once had a dude call to ask if I'd beat him unconscious and then break his finger. Preferably the little finger, he said. He swore he'd sign a contract to prove the whole thing was his idea. I hung up immediately.* She shook her head as if to dispel the thought of him. *Your guy is the same. I don't know any domme who'd agree to something like that.*

So what should I tell him?

To get bent.

Really?

She shrugged. *Honestly, this guy is full of shit. He has no real plans to off himself. Dudes just like to fuck with you. They want the attention.* She touched my shoulder. *He'll be fine.*

I wasn't so sure. While Ophelia was in a session, I opened my email and drafted a reply. As I typed, I could hear scuffles and thuds from the Torture Chamber upstairs. The Torture Chamber was the room where the more aggressive sessions took place, the canings and electrocutions. I couldn't make out any words, but I could hear a man's grunts, followed by the cartoonish smack of a paddle on flesh. You'd know it any-where, that Looney Tunes *thwap*. I got up and sat on the porch to concentrate as I wrote.

Hello,
Thank you for the kind words.
I must admit I've never encountered this fetish before. Part of me wants to tell you to drop it and find a new hobby. But I know that would be pointless . . . Fantasies don't just go away, as I'm sure you are aware.
I am not willing, at this time, to session with you. I am willing, however, to hear a bit more. Perhaps I don't un-derstand exactly what you're proposing. I'd be willing to educate myself on this particular longing. Is that a better word for it than fetish? I'd be lying if I said I wasn't a little bit curious. But we all know what curiosity did to the cat . . .
Best,
Miss Sunday

I pressed send and pocketed my phone, then went back inside to get ready for Mike. I dug through the costume closet until I found something I liked, jeggings and a fuzzy pink tube top. Most girls favored a whips-and-chains look (think Joan Jett meets Elvira, vampiric groupies) but I leaned into the sweet-but-psycho vibe, invoking high school mean girls, suburban secrets, torture in the rec room. Baby's breath, baby blue, I'll beat you cuz I'm bored, etc. It wasn't like Mike cared what I wore anyway; he was too blissed out to notice.

I threw on some Mary Janes and readied our room. I chose

the Student Dorm because it was the simplest in terms of décor, the easiest to overlay with whatever world he got lost in. I disinfected the rubber twin mattress, put on clean sheets, and laid out three towels: one for me to sit on, one for me to spread over my lap, and one more for him to clean up with in case he self-released. Then I burned some sage, dimmed the little Hello Kitty lamp on the nightstand, and waited for him to arrive.

I'd had three sessions with Mike so far and he was always the same: punctual, brusque, and spaced-out. The file warned of his mysterious skin condition, a rash that appeared on different parts of his body at different times of the year. He refused to name it but swore it wasn't contagious; he'd allegedly shown Hugo a doctor's note long, long ago. Different girls' entries charted its evolution over the years: Miss Iris wrote that it wasn't too bad (*hardly noticeable*), while Miss Valentina warned that it'd spread to his asshole (*watch out for runaways!*) and had a weird medicinal smell (*not bad, just WEIRD*). During our first session the rash was so pronounced that little snowflakes of skin spiraled off with each blow. I understood then what Valentina had meant by runaways. After our session, I'd had to vacuum them up, all the little white flecks in a heap on the floor. I wasn't supposed to, but I opened the windows to let in a breeze. The room smelled of lunch meat and drugstore deodorant. I'd do bad things for a breeze.

In a way, I admired his insouciance. He was comfortable in any and all states of decay. He seemed to accept his body as mercurial and imperfect. Then again, he wasn't the one sweeping up butt flakes. He got to play baby, googoo-gaga-ing softly. Who knows what he dreamed of while I whaled on him? This time around, his rash was under control, just some pink splotches on his calves and thighs. I forgot to put on music, so the hour dragged. I closed my eyes and thought of Clue. What a strange board game, centered around the chummy recitation of all the ways one can die. A wrench in the rose garden, borrowed drugs in the ballroom, erotic asphyxiation in the walk-in closet, a plastic Chinese take-out bag in the 2000 Ford Explorer . . . Working at the dungeon was like playing this game in real time, trying to guess the flavor of a stranger's death wish. As always, Mike was quiet, eyes scrunched shut as if trying to remember a joke. I can only assume he enjoyed himself. When his time was up he didn't tip and left without saying goodbye.

I didn't check my phone until I was driving back to the Mission later that day. It was 4:30 p.m., the light heavy and gold. The cars on the bridge cast long shadows on the water. I felt unmoored, anxious, as I always did at this hour. The shadows seemed to spell things out, cryptic ditties on the concrete: *Sayonara, Mama tried* . . . By the time I got home, it would be totally dark out. Fucking daylight savings time, the sad girl's frenemy. I tried to stay busy after my shifts at the dungeon. I did laps in the supermarket, loitered at Sephora . . . anything to keep the doom at bay. I needed someone to perform normalcy for, even if that someone was a TikTok-famous teenager working at the mall. I didn't have the energy anymore to fuck someone new, so I distracted myself from intrusive thoughts with perfume samples and soft pretzels.

My phone lit up as I was crossing the Bay Bridge: a new

email. I abandoned my errands and drove straight home with
a strange sense of urgency. Then I sat in the driveway with my
headlights on. I could hear Cindy and Linda zinging around
the living room, celebrating my return. Naomi was presum-
ably asleep on the ottoman, playing hard-to-get. I cranked
the car's heater and opened the email.

Dear Miss Sunday,

*I cannot express the joy your message brought me. To be
recognized by a Mistress as beautiful as you—it is beyond
my wildest dreams.*

*I understand your reservations completely. Over the
years, I have contacted many different Dominas; not one
has humored my request as gracefully as you. Most chose to
ignore me—again, I don't blame them. I know my desire is
deviant, shameful. And yet, every few months, I feel compelled to reach out . . . Please add "poor impulse control" to
my long list of flaws.*

*You said that you would be willing to learn more about
my particular longing. A perfect word, Mistress. "Fetish"
implies a fixed object of desire, whereas my longing for "It"
is fluid, shifty, tricky to encapsulate . . .*

By way of explanation, I have a little story.

*Once upon a time, I went to a party. The house was
full of people I didn't know. I wandered upstairs and found
one of the bedrooms unlocked. Everyone had piled their
coats on the bed. I closed the door and buried myself in the
pile. I stayed like this for the rest of the night. It excited me
to hear the party downstairs, carrying on without me. At
one point a girl came in to grab her coat. I played dead*

while she dug through the heap; she didn't notice me. God,
how I loved that. I suppose it was a little like being buried
alive . . . I started to wonder how long I could stay there
without being found. I thought about lying there for weeks,
months, years . . . until everyone moved out and the house
was sold and the new owners moved in and found my
corpse gummed to the mattress.

These are the types of thoughts that excite me.

Does this make any sense? Forgive me, Mistress, if I've
bored or offended you. I'm not used to company.

Yours,

X

I went inside and greeted the girls. I walked them, showered, and made a semi-healthy dinner of chicken strips and
frozen peas. I put on comfy clothes and tried to read in Dino's
bed, a months-old *New Yorker* I'd filched from the free clinic,
but I couldn't focus. I found myself thinking of the last time
I'd been to a party. It felt like lifetimes ago; who was that girl?
I'd chewed up someone's Adderall and gotten blisters from
dancing in my new strappy shoes. It was Mazzy's going-away
party; Babe Alert was opening a satellite office in Santa
Monica and she would be heading the social media team.
That night we wore matching velvet scrunchies and drank
fernet to feel fancy. The party was at a bar with streamers on
the ceiling, causing everyone to stoop. It was a place called the
Makeout Room, which was constantly alternating between
being cool and uncool. The crowd was a mix of dozy Stanford
grads from her start-up and sexy sluts she'd met at bars. The

barflies danced to disco, while the techies stood in quiet clumps.

This will always make me think of you, Mazzy wailed, tugging on my scrunchie until I yelped in pain. *If I'm not wearing it in my hair, I swear I'll wear it on my wrist. I'll never take it off and neither should you. Promise?*

I promised; forty-eight hours later, I lost it in some bartender's garden apartment. It got caught in my sleeves when I took off my sweater. Or perhaps I hung it on the doorknob when I used his grim shower . . . I doubted Mazzy still had hers. She was probably sucking well-connected cock in the Hollywood Hills, in a glass house with a view. I hadn't heard from her in ages, not since she sent me an e-card proclaiming *YOU ARE THE CEO OF YOUR OWN LIFE* in sparkly red letters. I hadn't done a good job keeping in touch; once I got with Dino, I totally dropped off. I committed the cardinal sin of putting dicks before chicks, and now I had neither, just three dogs and a house full of holes.

I grabbed my computer from the nightstand and opened my email. Naomi grumbled in protest, roused by my typing.

There's so much to say, I wrote, *but what should I call you?*

Their reply was almost instantaneous. It came so quickly I felt spooked.

Me? it read. *I'm nobody. Nobody at all.*

The first time Ophelia crashed at my place, she and Lorenzo were beefing. Apparently he'd gotten drinks with one of his figure models, who also happened to be an ex-flame. Ophelia only found out because the girl tagged him in a photo on Instagram with the caption: *an artist and his muse.*

I can't even look at him right now, she said. *I can't even bear to smell his shampoo.*

She was planning to trek to her parents' place in Daly City.

I have a car, I said. *Just stay with me.* She could sleep at mine, then take BART to the dungeon the next morning.

She widened her eyes. *Are you sure I'm not putting you out? Not at all.*

You're a lifesaver, babe!

It's really no problem. We were standing in the garden, shouldering our bags. Hers was a black leather duffel with a pair of silver handcuffs attached to the zipper. They jangled as we walked toward my car. *Besides,* I said, *I could use the company.*

I immediately regretted saying this, but she didn't seem put off. She folded her body into the passenger seat and toyed with the heater. She was wearing black knee-high boots and a long lace dress that was somehow both skanky and prairie. She looked at me with a bright smile. *Slumber party?*

I smiled back. *For sure.*

She had a magic ability to immediately acclimate to any situation. She fiddled with the radio, eventually settling on an R&B station. As we whizzed over the bridge she stuck her head out the window. Her black hair flared around her face, the sleeves of her dress ballooned. When she sat back down, she looked like she'd been mugged. *God,* she sighed, *that feels so GOOD. Sometimes you just need a little bit of melodrama.*

We made it home by twilight. She strolled through the

house with her hands on her hips. *This is your house?* she cried. *It's fucking palatial! You live here alone?*

It's complicated.

Oh?

It belongs to my ex.

Gotcha, she said, making an X with her arms as if to ward off bad luck. *No further questions.*

The dogs took a shine to her, trailing behind us as we continued our tour. I showed her to the guest room, where she dropped her bags on the bed and threw open a window. *This is the type of place where you could be happy*, she said to no one in particular, peering down at the scrubby backyard. She turned to me. *This feels like the type of place where you could write a novel.*

Really?

Mm-hm. She smoothed her hands over the bed, which I prayed wasn't too dirty. Every time I got my period, I bled on the sheets. I'd tried every menstrual product on the market and still it happened in the night, little rust-colored splotches. The dogs would sniff at them idly, detecting a vague animality. Washing the sheets just turned the stains brown. Should Ophelia happen upon one, I wanted to shout, *It's not poop!!!* Watching her, I felt an almost crushing need to be a good host.

I'll start dinner, I said, hand on the door. *You have a bath and relax. I'll call you when it's ready, OK?*

She turned to me. Her eyes were bright, as if I'd just told a joke. Her body was frank, her tits level with mine. A shadow passed between us, followed by a moon. Summer went out the window and the bedroom became autumnal, crisp and electric. Something was cooking. She didn't know what exactly, and neither did I, a pre-rain sizzle in the air. Her hair shone as if wet. Her gaze was curious, inviting, seeking out the shape of our entanglement. The dogs paused to look up at us. They could feel it too, this novel need for heat.

Finally she smiled. It was like turnips pushing up out of the earth. *Sounds fab*, she said. *I'm ssssstarving.* She stood on one leg to unzip her boot, then the other. She placed them neatly at the foot of the bed. *Let me know if you need any help, OK?*

OK.

She was taking her dress off. I resisted the urge to study her tattoos, the spiky black flowers wreathing her hips. The dogs glanced at me, then followed her into the bathroom. I could hear their nails on the tiles as they arrayed themselves around the tub. I knew from experience they'd watch her bathe, asking questions with their eyes. *Who are you? What's happening?* No answer sufficed.

That November I found the first note. It was tucked into the slats of my locker at the strip club. The location made me think of high school, leaving valentines for your crush. I unfolded the note with a smile, assuming it was from Cookie or Dallas. On cheap notebook paper, in curly red letters, someone had written:

see ya

I stared at it, waiting for the punch line to hit. When it didn't, I balled up the note and threw it away. I didn't feel scared, not really. Imagine sitting in a movie theater. You know that sound at the start of a movie, the throbby crescendo that widens and widens until it becomes a thick gush? It was sort of like that, like I was sitting in a warm musty theater, with strangers all around me, munching in the dark.

I found the next note at the bottom of my money bag. It said the same thing, only now with more force: *see ya!* I couldn't tell if this was meant as a threat or a farewell, an ominous fact (*I can see you*) or a plucky sayonara (*see u later, alligator*). After that, I began finding the notes every time I worked at the club—two under the leg of my chair in the locker room, two more scrunched into my locker, one inside my eye shadow palette, pressed into a midnight blue I never used. They all said the same thing in the same curly writing: *see ya!*

The strangest note was the one I found stuck to my Pleaser. I was taking my shoes off at the end of my shift and there it was, flagging from my heel like a scrap of toilet paper. In red cursive:

miss you

I threw it in the trash before anyone could see. I grabbed my bags and left, not even pausing to say bye to Cookie. I didn't go to McDonald's; I'd lost my appetite. I went straight home and buried myself in Dino's bed, the girls clustered around me like sentinels. They seemed to sense that something was wrong. Naomi fell asleep with her head on my chest, her chin positioned between my breasts like a pendant. Cindy and Linda blinked at me solemnly. *Things are going south,* they seemed to say. *You're falling apart. Don't worry about us. No matter what happens, we'll be OK.* I had to look at my phone for an hour and a half before falling asleep. On Quora: *Do cheating husbands love their wives? Do animals feel pain?*

We sit in his bed, eating a movie-theater box of peanut M&M's. I'm twenty-five, he's thirty-four. It's the beginning of everything. He turns on the light; he's bare-chested, wet-haired.

They taste better this way, he explains. *I like to see which color I'm eating.*

Which one is your favorite?

Blue.

I pick through my handful and give him my blues. Dino gives me his reds. When we kiss, our tongues turn purple.

This is a memory I cherish. I carry it with me like a pocketknife. I carry it with me like a postcard that I need to send but I don't have any stamps.

Before long, Nobody was emailing me two to three times a day.

Please understand me, they wrote, *I do not wish to burden you. You don't need to worry about me: I know myself well enough to know that I'm not strong enough to really do "It," at least not on my own. What I seek is a compatriot in darkness. A witness to my ruin. Or, if I am very lucky, a nurse to pull the plug.*

Why don't you just block that guy? Ophelia asked, glancing over my shoulder at my phone. We were sitting on the sofa at Dino's, sharing a packet of sour straws, Himalayan clay masks smeared on our faces. She was spending the night once again.

I shrugged. *I'm probably their only friend. What if blocking them pushes them over the edge?*

You can't think like that, babe. He's not your responsibility.

I know . . .

She petted my hair. *Don't let him get too attached. Who knows what he really wants?*

I thought about this. *I think they want someone to talk to.*

She smiled sadly. *That's all?*

The real reason I felt close to Nobody, I think, is because they reminded me of Simon. I still hadn't heard from Simon, despite his monthly payments. They both shared the same attitude, gloomy and demure, like Victorian poets. They both thought I was interesting. Maybe they were old college roommates. Onetime lovers? Anything seemed possible. Maybe Nobody lived alone in the desert, a Joshua Tree hoarder with an autoimmune disease. Or maybe they were a celebrity, bored in Dubai, dictating these emails to an intern. Ophelia seemed certain that Nobody was a white cis dude, but I couldn't be sure.

I waited until I was alone to reply to their messages. I needed to focus. When I wrote to Nobody, I felt like I was back in school, bent over my laptop, swirled up in ideas.

It's not that I find your fantasy sick, I wrote, *but that I do not feel comfortable engaging with it. It seems like an oxymoron to me: If one's fantasy is suicide, then how can anyone else join in? Even suicide pacts are notoriously one-sided. I think of suicide as twinned*

*with solitude, dark rooms, basements, roofs. But perhaps that's
misguided. Maybe suicide is more expansive than that. In which
case, a collaboration could seem fruitful.*

*But for you to have a witness changes the whole act, shifts the
onus onto the observer. When there is someone who can answer
suicide's central question—WHY WHY WHY?—then the poetic
potential of the fantasy is lost. The WHY WHY WHY must be
preserved in order for the suicidal fantasy to remain attractive.
Suicide, the mystery girl. Suicide, the one who got away. I can hear
the widows sighing: If only I knew why he did this, if only I'd
known and gotten home sooner . . . The mystery is part of it, the
tremulous WHY! To make our object of desire concrete or know-
able would be to kill the vibe (ha ha).*

Nobody always replied to my emails within the hour, sug-
gesting a great deal of free time on their end. Something like
a friendship was forming; I suppose, in my own twisted way,
I felt like their celebrity crush. They started to refer to their
suicidal fantasy as S.

I've thought about S for as long as I can remember, they wrote.
*As a teenager, I would stand on the train platform and fantasize
about jumping. I would get so excited that my vision would blur.
Then I would step back from the edge, suddenly terrified of falling
onto the tracks. S could not be accidental; that wouldn't be sexy
at all! To jump was erotic; to fall was just sad. How's that for
fucked up?*

After dinner, a new one:

*For the longest time, my fantasy of S was not rooted in any
embodied experience. I didn't care HOW I did it. I didn't care if a
train ripped me open or I OD'd on pills or I leapt from the Golden*

Gate Bridge. What mattered was the thought of it. What's more taboo? These days people speak freely of their various fantasies: incest, torture, furries, whatever. But to say that you fantasize about killing yourself—that turns the notion of pleasure inside out. It troubles even the most seasoned kinkster. To desire the undesirable, that's a part of what makes S so hot. But there's so much more . . .

Typing on my phone in the bath, I wrote back:

On the topic of S, the line between reality and fantasy is so blurred. As an abstract fantasy, I must admit it draws me in, as I'd guess it does for many people. Sylvia Plath, Ian Curtis, Marilyn Monroe, so many sexy suicides. But as a reality, I recoil. In BDSM we see this line constantly crossed. Do my subs really want to fuck Mommy or do they just want to imagine it? I'm sure I look nothing like her! This is what we negotiate in the BDSM game: the boundary between This World and That, between horror and heaven, between the real and the dreamed, between grace and gore. With S, how can you play at something SO serious? At what point does it become TOO real?

I sent that email, washed my hair, and sent another.

If I am perceived to have helped you do S, then is it really S at all? Does it then become murder or some dangerous love affair? A sex game gone wrong? I say this just for argument's sake, as I have zero intentions of indulging your fantasy.

Nobody replied minutes later:

To the kind and wise Miss Sunday,

I do not deserve your words, your mind! I deserve nothing and yet I have so much. My privilege is egregious. The tragedy of S is that it is one-sided; I can't make a deal with the Devil, exchange X for Z, tit for tat, an Angel for little old me. Sometimes I think that you are an Angel, a pen pal from another realm. Does this make me feel excited about one day meeting you up there? It's never been heaven I long for but death. But now I have someone to show me around up there. A celestial tour guide, if you will. Things are looking up . . .

I stared at my phone; my brain had turned off for the night. This would happen to me when I was writing my thesis. Come twilight, I went dumb. I forgot the definition of ontology but remembered the names of the Housewives of Beverly Hills. I didn't know how to interpret the last lines of Nobody's message so I turned off my phone and drained the tub. I stood naked on the tiled floor, toweling my hair. Moonlight slanted in. The dogs were with Ophelia, balanced three on one thigh as she sat cross-legged on the floor. After work we'd done a hatha flow and then cooked a vegan taco casserole. I washed dishes, she dried. Now she was Skyping with a sub who wanted to be called racial slurs. He was a Hong Kong–based businessman but said he was open to all epithets—except, he wrote, the N-word. *Anything else is A-OK!* As I walked down the hallway, I could hear the purr of her voice through the closed guest-room door. I heard her laughter, soft and mean. I heard the sub say, *Please, Goddess, may I suck my dick? I've been practicing for you.* Then I closed the door to Dino's room and put on a podcast about murder.

After that first sleepover, Ophelia didn't leave. We went to the dungeon together. We drove back to Dino's when our shifts ended at three. Once or twice a week she stayed at Lorenzo's or had dinner with her parents; all other nights were spent in the Outer Mission with me. When she was gone, she kept her bags in the guest room. The bed was neatly made, her toiletries (mineral sunscreen, salt-stick deodorant, glossy Aesop serums) lined up on the nightstand. It was her room now; I stayed in Dino's. The girls went back and forth each night, depending on their moods.

Having her around made me think of that Frank Sinatra song. How does it go? *It was a very good year for city girls who lived up the stair* . . . She reminded me, at times, of Mazzy, a Mazzy who meditated and preferred microdosing to coke. They both needed men while also finding them tiresome. They both liked to dance and be looked at while doing so. They both touched their necks when they spoke, a habit I found entrancing. They both yanked me from my grief.

On cold nights Ophelia and I shared a bed. It was the most practical option—Dino's Victorian was impossible to heat. We slept in leggings and sweatshirts, Costco wool socks, the dogs draped across our middles. We needed as much body heat as possible. A nighttime ritual was formed: after dinner I would send my emails to Nobody, wash my face, brush my teeth, then come sliding into the guest room, soundless in thick socks.

Welcome, she'd say, patting the bed. She put aside whatever book she was reading. *I warmed it up for ya.*

We watched TV on her laptop and talked about love. She vented about Lorenzo: He was controlling, petty, secretive, mean. He kept nudes from ex-girlfriends because he said they inspired him. He wore a beanie even when it wasn't cold. In the mornings, he didn't talk. If she spoke to him before noon, she'd be punished.

Do you love him? I asked.

She looked startled. *Of course.*

What do you love about him?

She thought about this. *He's a very lovable person when he wants to be.* She paused, thumbing her lips. *He looks sexy when he's stressed.*

She told me Hugo used to be a semi-famous pro domme in the nineties, back when the kink scene in SF was huge.

You'd never believe it, but she was a mega-babe.

What?

Oh yeah. Cross my heart and hope to die. She was the queen of hardcore. Everyone at the Armory was afraid of her.

I slept better with Ophelia next to me. My dreams felt less jagged, turning pearly and blue. I dreamt of talking dogs and bodies of water, gigantic undulating plains of something similar to grass. In the mornings, I let the dogs out while she made us coffee. Sometimes she read my tarot, the cards balanced on the comforter. She organized her schedule around my shifts at the strip club; on the nights that I danced, she went on sugar dates with techies at mood-lit bistros, many of which Dino had cooked in.

He's calling me an Uber now, she'd say, gussied up in black latex. We tried to leave the house at the same time in the evenings. Despite her yogic leanings, she preferred heat, glamour, action. Perhaps she too was afraid of staying home at night, subject to the shadows in rarely used drawers. She knew not to tempt fate by sitting alone as the TV went snowy and the dogs barked at ghosts. *What was this kid's name again? Wally, Walter?* She consulted her phone. *Walt. He's a textbook cuck. Wants me to cut up his steak for him and step on his toes during dinner.* All she had to do to get ready was put on red lipstick; her soft, puffy mouth did the work. *Easy-peasy. He's twenty-five and richer than I'll ever be. You better believe we're getting two tiramisus!*

Have fun, I said. We stood together in the driveway, arms crossed against the gloom. She towered over me in stiletto boots. She looked like an anime figure, spiky and long. *Be safe, OK?*

OK, she said, laughing. She bent and kissed me on the cheek, her ponytail blowing sideways. *You're the boss, applesauce.*

Of course I had a list of suspects regarding the notes. It could be one of the other girls, pulling a prank, a belated form of hazing. It could be a client, sneaking into the locker room after hours. It wasn't uncommon for dancers to have stalkers, diehard regulars whose loyalty tipped into obsession. Dallas had several, something she attributed to being half-Japanese.

They can't get the submissive Asian fantasy out of their heads, she sighed. *They all want to propose to me and make me their good little wife.*

But wouldn't security see someone creeping around? There were cameras everywhere. Or Cookie would catch him and hit him with a hair dryer. Still, it wasn't entirely impossible for a client to dash in and out . . .

I wondered if it was one of the club managers, trying to intimidate me. But why would he do that? I made good money for the club; I kept to myself, I never caused problems. Whoever it was clearly knew my work schedule. This wasn't difficult information to come by, as it was posted on the club website in flashing pink letters. SEE WHICH OF OUR BEAUTIES ARE ON TONIGHT . . . followed by a horrible picture of me bending over as if tying my shoe. I wore a baby-doll dress and looked prepubescent, which was probably the point. My pig-tails were cinched with little white pom-poms. Forget me, ghostly Ruth with her checkered sexual past; who would want to scare *her*, this fawnlike girl in too-high heels, smiling cheesily? Poor Baby. While I was driving home from work one night, a dark thought occurred to me. I wasn't woman enough to inspire obsession from men, nor was I child enough to merit their protection. I was neither siren nor waif. I floated somewhere in between salvation and a hard pass. I was afraid that if I told the manager someone was leaving me notes, he'd sigh and say, *As if.*

Emeline was the only person I told. She caught me one Friday as I plucked yet one more scrap from my locker (*see ya!*).

What's that? she asked, smiling. She wore a new plum-colored lipstick that made her look royal.

Nothing. I stuffed the note in my pocket and turned away.

Come on! She poked me in the ribs. *Tell me, Baby, what's the joke?*

There's no joke, I said shortly. *It's just a dumb note.*

A note from who?

No one. It's nothing.

Her face fell. *Oh*, she said. *I get it now.*

What?

She sighed. *If you and the other girls are gonna talk shit about me, will you please not do it in front of me? Thanks.*

Emeline, I said. *You've got it all wrong.*

It's OK, she said, strangely calm. *I know everyone hates me.*

Emeline, I repeated. *That's not what this is.*

She looked unconvinced. *Then what is it?*

I did my best to explain. She listened like a kid being told a ghost story, sitting on her hands, eyes round. *Oh shit*, she said. She actually whistled. *That's freaky! Now I wish it WAS just the other girls talking shit about me.*

I know, I said. *Me too.*

Are you gonna tell Cookie?

Why would I? It's not like she can do anything about it.

Emeline frowned. *I guess that's true.* She rolled up the sleeves of her robe, causing feathers to fly. *Well, I'll be on the lookout for anything weird.*

Thanks, I said wearily.

Do you think it's someone you know?

I shrugged. *Maybe.*

I don't mean to sound rude, but do you have any enemies?

I pursed my lips. *Not that I know of.*

What about crazy exes? She giggled. *I used to have one in college. He hacked into my email. I had to switch dorms because of him.*

I thought about this. None of my love affairs had ended abruptly. They just petered out. We stopped hanging out as much, got busy, changed numbers. We both understood the stakes of our affair, a not-insignificant intimacy that nonetheless foregrounded its own demise. After things ended, we'd still check in every now and again, sending each other memes to say, *Thinking of you.* The only conflict I could imagine might've revolved around borrowed T-shirts never returned, a manageable casualty of sleeping around.

But was it possible I was wrong? That one of my ex-flames was livid and bitter, seeking revenge via carrier pigeon? I seriously doubted it. Dusty was a junkie, Rafi lived with his parents, Jax never loved me, Charlie had his real life, Dino was gone. If I had to peg one of them as the vengeful type, I guess I'd pick Charlie. But he was too busy to waste his time on me. He had his law firm, his coke habit, his darling Sophia. He was probably biking around Mount Tamalpais right now, thinking fondly of the grad student he'd dry-fucked last night. Did she tell him about her thesis while he refilled her glass? Did he serenade her at karaoke with "Forever Young"? For however real our connection had been, I was but a blip in his memory now. I was one of many grad students with unresolved Daddy issues and he was one of many OK-looking men doing everything in his power to finally feel free. We were both replaceable by design.

I tuned back into Emeline. *Nope*, I said. *Can't think of one.*

Damn, she said. *What a mystery.*

I'll say.

So what are you gonna do?

Nothing.

She looked genuinely worried. *Well, if there's anything I can do for you, just ask me, OK?*

I felt oddly moved by her offer. *OK.* I glanced at the clock on the wall. *We better get moving. I have stage in ten minutes.*

She nodded, then took both of my hands in hers. Her eyes were wide and wet like a dog's. *Just so you know*, she said, *I believe you, Baby.*

Later, onstage, I would remember her words with a shiver. Why did she say that? Of course she believed me. There was no reason not to. I was telling the truth. I felt suddenly antsy, my vision blurred. I rushed through the rest of my stage set, receiving $5 in ones and a piece of gum as a tip.

After that night, I started saving the notes. Though it felt somehow unlucky to do so, I kept them in a Ziploc bag in my locker. Across the front of the bag in black Sharpie I wrote: *EVIDENCE*. Of what, I didn't know. I had faith that, sooner or later, I'd find out. It was like Cookie said whenever somebody's money bag went missing.

Sit tight, she'd tell the victim calmly. *The truth always comes out in the wash.*

I was walking to my car when Emeline caught up to me. She still wore her plum-colored lipstick, her suede coat draped over her shoulders. I hadn't seen her since our conversation about the notes hours earlier; she'd had back-to-back bookings with a VIP rumored to be Jake from State Farm.

Hey, she said, touching my elbow.

I turned around. *Hey.*

She smiled, almost shy. *Are you hungry?*

I was starving, but I shrugged. *I could eat.*

Good, she said, *I'm ravenous.* She pointed to her car, a freshly washed Prius. *Do you wanna, like, get food with me?*

Oh. I blinked, struck by the notion of seeing Emeline outside the club. Who would she be in the regular world? Would she stop for red lights, put cream in her coffee? Would this mean we were friends?

It's on me, she said. Her voice got soft, pleading.

OK, I found myself saying, *why not?* We were drifting toward her car. She opened the passenger door for me like a chivalrous date. I slid in and surveyed the scene: paperback books in the backseat, air freshener in the scent Summer Breeze, a plastic Starbucks thermos with a plummy kiss mark on the lid. She didn't turn the radio on, which surprised me. *Buckle up!* she said. *Let's bounce.*

That was how I found myself sitting opposite Emeline in a greasy red booth, both of us shivering under the diner's fluorescent lights. As with most 24/7 establishments, the Silvercrest was home to a rotating cast of chatty winos, junkies in sandals, and insomniacs pondering their fifth cup of joe. A heroic waitress zinged between all of us, her sleepy smile like a lighthouse beam. She didn't need a notepad, she remembered everything. Her name tag said LORI. She reminded me of Cookie, in that nothing could faze her. When she found someone nodding off in the unisex bathroom, she nudged him awake and said gently, *Not here, honey.* She escorted the man out the door, then delivered two slices of lemon meringue pie to a juiced-up couple in the corner. I watched them feed each other bites of pie, giggling like chosen fools. They poured mini bottles of whiskey into their coffee mugs, their legs tangled together under the table.

Look at you lovebirds, Lori sighed, hands on her hips. *Isn't that precious?*

How different was she, really, from us girls at the club? She was the late-late shepherd of broken hearts, enabler of appetites, a cushy female presence to distract us from decay. If she was good at her job, she remembered her regulars' names.

She didn't get naked, but we watched her ass just as hungrily, tracking her movement from table to table. Come to me, we thought, increasingly desperate. It's my turn now. See me. Come back. It was her job to feed us, an angel in stretch pants. The difference was that the strip club was dark and the diner was bright, alarmingly so. At last, she approached me and Emeline.

Howdy, ladies, she said. She wore a tight white T-shirt barely able to contain her waist-length breasts. *What can I getcha?*

Emeline ordered a cheeseburger and fries; I got the soup of the day, broccoli cheddar. After Lori hustled away, Emeline leaned in. *I'll probably get the cheesecake too.*

Oh?

She nodded, unusually peppy. *It's good here. I've had it before.*

As she ate, it gave me sick pleasure to notice the acne scars on her cheeks and jaw, wee moony dents usually covered by makeup. Tonight she wore a short white polo dress, white sneakers, white socks, her hair in a high ponytail. She looked like a country club queen.

I'm really glad you're here, she said, dissecting her burger to remove the tomato. *It's nice to have someone to talk to.* Outside of the club, she seemed to relax. Her icy posture thawed. She licked her fingers and spoke earnestly, in one bright babble, her emotions like bangles decorating her wrists. At times she looked at me a beat too long, waiting for me to look back.

No problem, I said. My soup was too hot.

Sometimes I hate going home after work, she sighed. *Do you know what I mean?*

Nope, I lied. Of course I did. *What's wrong with home?*

Oh, nothing, really, she said. *I live with my dad.* She spoke with her mouth full but still looked sexy. *After I graduated, I traveled for a little. Italy, France. Then I moved in with my dad, you know, to save money. He doesn't know that I do this.* She nodded to her stripper bag. *He thinks I have a bartender boyfriend and that's why I stay out so late.*

Would he care?

She doused her french fries in ketchup, a noteworthy amount. *I dunno. He's never been strict with me. When I quit ballet, my mom, like, wanted to disown me. She's . . .* She scrounged for the right word. *A lot. She told me my eating disorder was totally normal, that the women in our family have been cursed with "childbearing hips."* She rolled her eyes. *Does that sound normal to you?*

I shook my head. *No.*

Anyways. She played with her fries. *My mom had a shit fit but my dad backed me up. He just wants me to be happy. That's all he cares about. Still . . . I don't want him to know.* She bit her lip. *Not yet, at least.*

I nodded. *Makes sense.*

That's why I hate going home. I feel . . . guilty, I guess? I know he's still up and I don't wanna lie, you know, if he asks where I've been.

Where do you live?

Pac Heights. She giggled. *I know, it's so bougie. Don't judge me.*

I felt a prickling on the back of my skull. *Your dad stays up late?*

She nodded. *Oh yeah. Total insomniac. He watches TV until, like, three a.m., then gets up at dawn to go swimming. He's crazy.*

I set down my spoon. *Where did you say you went to college again?*

Vassar. It's in upstate New York.

I nodded, or at least I think I did. *I know where it is.* The room began to throb. *And your mom? Where is she?*

Emeline flubbed her lips like a horse. *Santa Barbara. She's living in our beach house, at least for now. She and my dad are getting divorced.*

Oh no, I mouthed. I felt like an actor forgetting my lines; my appetite had vanished and my ears had started to ring. *Do you know why?*

She shrugged. *They weren't happy. They never were, really. She accused my dad of some crazy shit, but I don't believe her. I guess you could say I'm a Daddy's girl. God, is that awful?*

No, I said softly, sitting on my hands to stop them from shaking. *No, it's not.*

As Emeline continued to pick at her burger and blab about summer camp (*the first place I felt happy, like, actually happy*), I remembered two things. The first memory took place in their Pacific Heights mansion. As Charlie got his usual three hours of sleep, I tiptoed between floors. One night, instead of exploring his wife's closet, I crept into his daughter's room. She was away at college, studying novels. I remember how my bare feet felt on the thick white carpet: like I was walking on sheet cake. I circulated the room, touching things I didn't even know I'd been deprived of. She had a four-poster bed cluttered with stuffed bunnies, only bunnies. Her bedspread was shiny lilac satin; when I lay upon it, I almost slid off. I noted the glow-in-the-dark stars stuck to the ceiling. I had those too in my childhood room. I said so aloud, to the audience of bunnies: *I had those too.*

On the bedside table was a mirror-backed brush, clotted with her hair. I picked it up and brushed out my own hair, which had gotten knotted during sex. I was hot with a feeling I couldn't name then. Now it seems obvious: I was jealous, achingly so. There was so much to want that I didn't know where to start. If there was a fire, what item here would I save? What would make me feel whole? At last I crept back to the guest room where Charlie was sleeping and threw myself on him. He awoke to me scrounging around in his boxers. *Slow down,* he chuckled. *What's the occasion?* But he quickly gave in.

Next the diner blurred and became Charlie's condo downtown, the air-conditioned site of so much mediocre sex and earnest conversation. I remember the ATM in the liquor store across the street; that was where Charlie took out cash to give me, still warm from the machine, plus tallboys to drink. We were lying in his king bed, naked, surfing TV channels.

Stop! I said. An episode of *The Bachelor* was on. *Can we watch this?*

The Bachelor was one of my mom's very few hobbies. She had startlingly strong opinions about which girls were worthy and which girls were scum. We used to watch it together on school nights, sharing a blanket; sometimes she even made popcorn, the first thing she'd eaten all day. It was the most animated I ever saw her, pointing at the screen and hissing,

Fucking gold-digger! or daubing her eyes and sighing, *How ROMANTIC.* She was partial to wholesome girls from midwestern states. She couldn't remember the name of my high school, but she remembered every contestant's age, hometown, job. She remembered which ones wore a bra and which ones needed, in her words, "a reality check."

Really? said Charlie. *You like this shit?*

Yeah.

He laughed, stroking my hair. *Sometimes you remind me so much of my daughter.* He froze. *Fuck,* he said. *Did I make it weird?*

I smiled, snuggling into his armpit. *No,* I said. *Don't worry.* The memory gets patchy there, though I do know he gave me $400 in cash, tucked inside a greeting card that read *GET WELL SOON.* I still have it in my special-things box, a glittery pink card with a cartoon of a bunny using a carrot as a crutch. Inside, it read: *SOME BUNNY LOVES YOU.*

Sorry, he'd said, laughing. *It's all they had left at the store.*

Now, in the diner, as the fluorescent lights played up her scars and the odor of cooking oil cut through her perfume, I studied the girl to whom all these things had first belonged. The lilac bed, the lying man. She had no idea that I'd sullied them both, my longing like an automated sprinkler wetting everything in its path. She thought of me, preposterously, as a friend. She was chatty and relaxed as she dug into her cheesecake.

Want some? she asked, extending a fork. *It's good, I promise.*

I shook my head no. Watching her dab her lips with a napkin, I knew I couldn't tell her what I knew about her dad. I didn't care enough about her to upend her life. Beneath the brash beauty was something fragile, imminently snappable. Don't get me wrong: part of me wanted to snap her, to crush her like a pretzel on a barroom floor. But right then, with my heart in my throat and my stomach in knots, I didn't feel up to the task. I looked around for Lori, gesturing for the check.

Damn, I said, feigning a yawn. *I'm fading.*

Oh, totally, she said. She pulled out her money bag and left three twenties on the table. *Of course, of course. Sorry for blabbering. You're so easy to talk to. I swear, it's like we've met before.* She actually blushed, two peachy splotches high on her cheekbones. *Sorry*, she said, *did I make it weird?*

It's fine. I stood up, stuffing my hands in my pockets. I needed fresh air, the welcome violence of night. *Thanks for dinner. This was . . . fun.*

She threw her arms around me, enveloping me in the smell of dried violets and fryer grease. *The pleasure's all mine!*

I followed her out of the diner, into the parking lot. She still walked like a ballerina. She had a body that a man could fall in love with from behind, both swannish and fertile, that inquiring neck. I trailed behind, taking her in. The long blond ponytail coiling down her back, those famous child-bearing hips, the little bobby socks. This was the body Charlie hugged daily. This was the body he tucked in at night. She looked like a Sophia; it was obvious now. Charlie used to tell me he'd never missed a single recital of hers. *I'll rearrange an entire workday if I have to*, he'd bragged. *That's what I live for, seeing Soph dance.*

She gave me a ride back to the club. As we were pulling into the parking lot, I turned to her. Of all the things eating at me, this topped the list. *Emeline*, I said, *what made you start stripping?*

Oh! She smiled self-consciously. As she spoke, she looked at herself in the rearview mirror. *A couple things, really. After I got back from Europe, I worked at this swanky art gallery. I just sat at a desk. I barely lasted the year.*

Why?

I was suicidally bored!

Oh.

Her voice deepened; she held her chin in her hand. *When I was little, we would walk past the strip clubs in North Beach to get to my dad's favorite restaurant. He'd, like, put his hand over my eyes, but I could still see the posters, you know, by the door.* She sighed. *They mesmerized me. I wanted to be like those girls. Whatever they did, I wanted to do it too.*

I knew the restaurant she was talking about; Charlie and I had eaten there before. It was dim and somber, the walls covered with oil paintings of the Italian countryside. He'd urged me to get the veal even though I'd wanted cheese pizza.

She played with her ponytail. *Maybe this is vain*, she said, *but after a year of sitting at that fucking desk, I just wanted to be looked at.* She chewed her lip. *Does that make any sense?*

Sure.

I missed having an audience. She shrugged. *It's the ballerina in me. Desperate for praise. When I'm at the club, it almost feels like a game: How many men will fall in love with me this time?* She rolled her eyes. *Tacky, I know, but I love being chosen. God, it feels so fucking good.* She idled her car; we were here. *That's my long-winded way of saying I'm an attention whore.*

I zipped my coat. *Aren't we all.*

She turned to face me in the dark. *And what about you?*

I felt myself freeze. *What about me?*

What do your parents think of you dancing?

The question stumped me; I'd never had occasion to wonder. *Well,* I said, *my dad is dead and my mom might as well be, so it's not much of a problem.*

I'd tried to be flippant, but my voice sounded harsh. Emeline stared at me, stunned. *I'm joking,* I said quickly. *About my mom, that is. She's alive and well. She's just . . . depressed.* I hated that word. It was too tidy, contained. It didn't conjure up a bathtub of slimy gray water or the wet spots she'd leave on the couch. She'd lie in one spot for so long that the cushions were permanently discolored. A better term for her condition would've been off the grid, despite the fact that she lived in a Mill Valley bungalow with cable TV and AC.

Oh, whispered Emeline, *that's so sad.*

Yes, I thought, surprising myself, it is sad, isn't it?

Has she always been that way?

I shrugged. After my father's death she'd managed to keep things together until I was fourteen. Little things were always off: she slept more than other mothers and gave me absurd amounts of cash to use for school lunch. Still, she drove me to class and usually remembered to wear pants in the winter; we watched TV at nighttime in peaceable quiet. Then, as soon as I was old enough to fend for myself, she let herself go. She'd stayed afloat just long enough to teach me how to forge her signature and shop for soup. Her condition reached its nadir when I was a senior in high school. That was the era of the marathon bath, of mold in the carpets and ketchup packets for dinner. I never caught her eating them, but I'd find hundreds of empty packets in the trash can, drops of blood or ketchup on the tiled floor. I made sure to bring more home for her whenever I ate out.

I could never bring myself to tell anyone my mother was depressed. It wasn't that I doubted the gravity of her condition, but that it didn't seem to tally with the mopey waifs in black velvet, the other depressed girls I knew. I thought often of the girl who lived down the street. She only ate apples and wore long sleeves in the summer to hide the scars on her arms. Her sadness felt sharp, driven, surgical, whereas my mother's was smeary, matted, willy-nilly, something she'd dragged home one night. It had none of the neighbor girl's perverse clarity. After I left home, she found new distractions. She played tense, day-long games of online Scrabble with Romanian teenagers and read *Star Trek* fan fiction. If I were to tell her I stripped, she'd probably whisper, *It's a good time to invest in coal, but you didn't hear it from me.*

I couldn't think of a way to convey this to Emeline, so I just waved my hands. *Lucky me. I have no one to let down.*

Emeline smiled weakly. *I guess that's true.*

I gathered my things and slid out the door. *Thanks for the ride, Emeline.*

Anytime. She seemed suddenly spent. Her big fluffy bed awaited, her fan base of bunnies, her ceiling of stars. Charlie would be asleep on the couch, fully dressed. His drink would be sweating on the coffee table, Angel's Envy with melted ice. *Text me when you're home, OK?*

OK, I said, but I just sat in my car, alone in the parking lot, collecting myself. My heart was still pounding, my mouth oddly dry. It occurred to me that Emeline was twenty-four, roughly the same age I was when Charlie and I got together. It was crazy how much could happen to a girl in three years. Compared to her, I felt ancient, weighed down with stories that didn't end well.

I found an old bottle of Gatorade in the backseat and chugged it. I turned on the radio, skimming through stations until I found a song that I recognized. *I'm a fool to do your dirty work* . . . Just as I was about to leave, I saw a man on the opposite end of the parking lot. He was on all fours, crawling into the bushes.

Hello? I shouted, starting the car. *Who's there?*

But when I flashed my brights, there was no one. Mine was the only car in the lot. The club was dark, anonymous, looking like a bank or a school. You'd never know what went on in there. Maybe people took night classes; maybe people gave blood. I locked all the doors and hightailed it home. The roads were wet, glossy, though it hadn't rained.

Though Ophelia stayed with me most every night, I chose not to tell her about the notes. I didn't want to sully our sleepover vibes. We had fun together, nothing but fun. We took baths and swapped sweaters. We drank tequila out of coffee mugs and coffee out of cereal bowls because it made us feel European. Our nights were stupid, blurred and bright.

I still saw Dino in the usual places: bus stops, banks, bodegas. Ophelia and I would be in the supermarket, buying ingredients for the gumbo she wanted to make me, and Dino would be bagging our groceries. *Evening, ladies*, he'd purr. I'd give Ophelia my card and tell her I needed some air, then flee the store. My entire body would be trembling. I'd crouch behind my car until I saw her wheeling the cart across the parking lot, humming to herself, alone.

I couldn't bear the thought of the two of them meeting. It filled me with guilt, as if I'd betrayed him. Had I? Yes, she was living rent-free in Dino's windswept Victorian, rearranging his knickknacks and seducing his dogs. She was clean and polite, but she liked to get comfy in a way that would irritate Dino, unfurling her limbs over every possible surface. She ate his Kewpie mayonnaise, his farmers' market pickles. She kept the windows open, letting in a welcome breeze. Her presence made the house less eerie, the rooms ballooned with light. If before the place was spindly and old, Ophelia fattened it up. She put flowers in Mason jars and shooed out the ghosts. It was a consensual exorcism.

I guess I felt guilty because I'd found someone to love. *That was quick, wasn't it?* I imagined the neighbors snarling. *The body's still warm and she's on to the next.* They'd write me up on Nextdoor for unseemly behavior. *It's not what you think!* I wanted to scream. *Dino's OK! He's just working stuff out. I saw him last week at the Castro Street Fair!* Ophelia cooked for me and kept me company; she did her impression of Hugo and I peed my pants laughing. Somehow I knew this was breaking the rules of Dino's long, obtuse game. I still pined for him nightly, dreamt of his forearms and garlic BO, the cold touch of his silver rings. I wasn't being unfaithful, but my faith had lost focus. Ophelia distracted me from longing, that 24/7

Vegas throb. She stoppered my ache, at least for the evening.
I was still going crazy, but now I had reason to hide it and,
sometimes, forget. We blasted Lana Del Rey on the drive to
the dungeon and drank Coke Zeros with lime. My wake became a pizza party, and for this I was ashamed.

One night she and I lay side by side in the guest room.
She'd covered the bed with a new blanket, soft brown-and-
white cowhide. *Lorenzo bought it in Milan*, she told me, *but
he'll never notice it's gone.* We were watching *Showgirls* for the
umpteenth time on her laptop.

At some point, she turned to me. *Can I tell you something?*
Sure.
It's kind of embarrassing.
I tried to relax my face. *Hit me*, I said. *I won't judge.*
I know, she said. She looked at her hands. *I started to go by
Ophelia when I turned twenty-one. At first it was my escort
name, but then it kinda stuck.*
Oh, I said. *That figures.*
Do you wanna know my birth name?
For some reason, my heart quickened. *It's not important*, I
said.
But do you want to know?
OK.
She didn't look at me. *Nancy.* She let that sink in. *I'm the
last person ever in the whole world named Nancy. What were my
parents thinking? They named me after my grandma, that fucking
bitch.*
Me too, I said. *That's how they got Ruth.*
Ruth, she said. She held it in her mouth like a Life Saver.
Ruth.

Boring, right?

No, she said, rolling toward me. She wore black tights with nothing underneath. *It's pretty. Pretty like a church.*

When we kissed, it was anticlimactic. We had been sharing a bed for almost two weeks; all signs pointed to sex. I let my loneliness propel me. She was feeling deep feelings and I didn't want to be left out. I wanted her halo to warm me, her belly to bounce off. So I lifted my shirt. Her body was so soft and warm it almost felt like a trap. Was this why men went crazy? For a moment I could understand their lunacy. I too would forget all my manners when confronted with something so inconceivably plush. I had a taste and now I wanted more; a sample would not fill me up. I wanted all of her body, all of her in me, like those collapsible tents that you carry in bags or those specialty dishes of meat filled with meat. I wanted to eat my own tail, form an infinite loop, just so that she could drink from me. She smelled like apricots, a smell I'd forgotten. Apricots, I thought. Apricots! Her dark hair made the pillows look damp. Her mouth was like a Slurpee: endless, red, and wet.

Later, as she slept, I got out of bed to let the dogs out. I sat on the doorstep and watched them scuttle about, pissing single-file and digging up the flower beds. What a beautiful term, flower beds. I felt peaceful and sore. It seemed to me then, in my floaty postcoital daze, that the number one evil in the world was loneliness. It drove people to do terrible things. It was the reason strip clubs existed, to abate male longing and its grim consequences. How lucky for men! To know that every city in America had a long list of places, some seedy, some luxe, some playing hip-hop and some playing jazz, where any man could go to feel less alone. Yes, he had to pay to enter. But of course—we were feeding him.

A woman's touch, Cookie might say. *That's what they come for.*

I thought of it differently. I sold men distractions, the fleshly equivalent of a TV on at night. A murmur to deny the void, the fuzzy specter of amour. They wanted woman-shaped outlines to fill with their lust, a series of jiggly vases and jars. We weren't The One but we were around. They spoke about our holes in varying tones and yet they were the gaping ones, desperate to be stuffed. What a terrible verb, to stuff. I remember one client yanking me close to whisper, *I would stuff you like a Christmas ham.* His breath was thick with booze.

I stood up and smiled, playing with my hair. *I'm Jewish*, I lied.

What?

What? I swung my hair over my face so that he disappeared. *I didn't say anything. Did you?*

One Friday night when we were sixteen, Mazzy and I watched porn on her laptop. This was one of our rituals. We ate baked potatoes with everything on them and looked up a new genre of porn. This particular video was shot with a handheld camera, starring amateur actors barely older than us. The title was *Kaylee Gets Spit-Roasted in Casino Bathroom.* The genre, I suppose, was Public Sex. I still remember the clip to this day.

It starts with a girl being fucked in the back of a car. She is little and blond. One man fucks her from behind while another face-fucks her. Her chunky female friend sits in the passenger seat, looking at her phone, unmoved. A third man stands outside the car and films, occasionally turning around to reveal the deserted parking lot.

Shit, we hear him whisper. *I thought I heard someone.*

Then it's back to the girl being plowed, her shorts at her ankles. There's a sudden flurry when the men hear a car coming. They throw a beach towel over Kaylee and shut the doors. Still in a sex daze, she crawls forward to kiss her chunky friend, who appears to perk up briefly.

Then the video cuts to a bathroom stall inside the casino. Kaylee is lying on the baby-changing table while the men fuck her from both sides. Her chunky friend is gone; this worried me. The cameraman chuckles and says, *Atta girl.* Kaylee looks drunk, her eyes wide and glassy, but when the men instruct her to turn over, she snaps out of it and says in a normal voice, *No problemo.*

Under the video people left comments. Most were basic variations of *She's so naughty* and *I'm horny.* One comment, however, stayed with me. Someone with the username Markie-duh-Sod wrote: *I can't believe that's someone's daughter.*

Later that night, while Mazzy slept next to me, I opened her laptop and rewatched the video on mute. I reread Markie-duh-Sod's comment, mouthing the words to myself. I studied Kaylee's spit-covered face. Who was this girl? Maybe she really was no one's daughter, a medical mystery. A porno angel, offering her body to the teledigital void. Maybe she was a regular chick who had a job and played with dogs and liked it rough. She could be all of the above: divine femme and graveyard-shift waitress. I wrote a comment replying to Markie-duh-Sod, typing softly so as not to wake Mazzy: *Every girl is someone's daughter, fucking DUH.*

Then I closed the laptop and tried to sleep, my body curled in a ball.

I really started to panic when I found a note stuck to my windshield, pinned down by the wiper. I'd just gotten off work at the club one particularly frigid night. This note was different from the others. Scribbled in red ink on a piece of notebook paper that had been folded over many times, it said:

be good

I whirled around, scanning the near-empty parking lot. It was 3:30 a.m. *Who the fuck are you?* I screamed. I ripped the note into pieces and threw them up in the air, unfun confetti. *Fuck you!* I bellowed, turning in circles and addressing the parked cars. *Fuck you fuck you fuck you! Just tell me what you fucking want. I can't do this anymore.*

I waited for an answer. The parking lot was still. I could hear the muted throb of the bass from the club, the wind dragging fast-food wrappers across the concrete. I squatted on the ground and buried my face in my hands. I was crying, but no tears came out. My shoulders convulsed, spit filled my mouth. My acrylics dug into my scalp, but I didn't notice the blood until it mixed with my spit. *Time-out!* I wanted to beg. *Give me a break! What's so fucking funny?*

Suddenly one of the bouncers stood over me. *Hey, honey,* he said, kneeling down. *You OK?*

I don't know. A string of spit extended from my lip to my wrist.

Come on, he said. He helped me up, gallantly ignoring the fluids all over my face. He was seven feet tall with beautiful eyes.

You have beautiful eyes, I said, craning my neck to look up at him.

Thank you, he said. His smile was shy.

I placed a hand on his arm. He wore a long black overcoat and leather gloves as part of his uniform. It was cold out, but I didn't feel it. *Do you want to get a drink with me?*

He shook his head, eyes soft. *Sorry, honey. I'm still on the clock.*

Well, when do you get off?

He smiled and just shook his head. It was then that I realized he was a little afraid of me, this jittery chick with blood in her teeth. He might've seen me talking to myself as I walked to and from the club every night. His kindness made it even worse.

OK, I said, forcing a smile. I fumbled with my keys and slid into the car. Not even sex could save me now. I felt like a magician whose trapdoor had failed to open. *No problemo. I get it.*

He waited until I started the engine, then waved and walked back to his post by the door.

I drove through San Francisco in a widow's daze. The heat was on high and yet I was shivering. I drove up and down the famous hills. I went down Lombard Street for the first time ever. I drove by the piers, by the opera house, by the onion-domed Orthodox church in the Avenues, by the old husk of the Stud. I drove halfway to San Bruno before turning around. I drove to Alamo Square and got out. At this hour the park was populated by winos, anorexics, high-end dog walkers. A smattering of lovers sat on benches, drinking and talking low. I hoped, for their sake, they'd get lucky tonight. I waved to a pair of them, two kids younger than me with multiple hoops through their noses. They wore identical outfits: baggy Dickies, white wifebeaters, bomber jackets, work boots. What I could see of their bare skin was colored by tattoos. Reflexively, they waved back.

Good morning, I said. Did I look old to them? At twenty-two, twenty-three, they looked like children to me. Children in their fathers' jackets.

Good morning, they said. One of them wore rings on each finger, but I knew it wasn't Dino. He had never been a morning person.

I returned to my car and drove home. Ophelia was at Lorenzo's, making up for the millionth time. I didn't even try to sleep. I put on water for coffee and began to make breakfast. Scrambled eggs, vegan sausage, sweet plantains, toast. I fried up a whole packet of turkey bacon for the girls, who shadowed me as I cooked. They wagged their tails in unison, not believing their luck. To them it must have felt like a very special day. Who knows? Maybe it was.

I was excited to meet Nobody. Like a gold miner awaiting his mail-order bride, I was eager to see them in the flesh, to behold my spooky friend.

At first I'd suggested we meet at a café fifteen minutes from Dino's. Close enough to be convenient for me, far enough that they probably couldn't figure out where I lived.

Not to be demanding but I'd prefer, if possible, to meet you outside, they wrote. *Enclosed spaces make me nervous.*

How about a park? I wrote.

A park would be just fine.

We settled on 11:00 a.m. at Lafayette Park. It was a bit of a drive for me but the setting felt cinematic, two people meeting on a bench in the middle of the workday. Steep hills, the smell of fireplaces, doormen pretending not to watch us . . . I told Nobody to wear red so I could easily spot them.

I'll have no trouble finding you, Miss Sunday, they wrote with uncharacteristic cheer. *I'd know you anywhere.*

I labored over my outfit that morning, a little bit jittery. It was Tuesday, my day off. Ophelia was still asleep after a rocky night with Lorenzo. They'd gone to a porno-themed bar on Polk Street, where they made out on waterbeds and drank Long Island iced teas. *Everything was groovy,* she moaned to me later. They only started to fight on the drive back to Oakland. He accused her of flirting with the bartender by tipping him $5 and ejected her from his car just before merging onto the Bay Bridge. She found her way to Powerhouse, where she got beer-drunk and befriended the local leather daddies, finally arriving at Dino's at dawn.

Why didn't you call me! I'd cried when she appeared in the doorway. Her ponytail was disheveled, her red lipstick licked off. *I would've come gotten you.*

No, no, she'd said. She started taking her clothes off: snakeskin pants, old black leotard, her favorite boots. She looked like Buffy the Vampire Slayer. *I got an Uber.*

YOU called an Uber? I'd never once known Ophelia to call her own car. It was always included in the price of a date.

She smiled. *Well, the bartender got it. Such a cool dude, single dad.* Her expression turned sheepish. Standing in her stocking feet and little black panties, she looked suddenly young. There were bite marks on her belly and neck. *Can we sit together and watch* Sex and the City *for a little? Or are you too sleepy?*

No, I'd said, pulling the sheets back. *That's exactly what I want to do.*

Now she was passed out, her body diagonal across the queen bed. Her bite marks were pale pink in the morning light, the shape and color of tomato slices. I was glad she was sleeping so I didn't have to tell her about my date with Nobody. I knew she would worry.

Bring pepper spray, she would say. *Or better yet, a pocket-knife. Text me your location. Do you want me to come and watch from the car? You never know when one of these dudes will snap.*

A part of me wondered if she was right. Maybe I was naïve. Maybe Nobody was dangerous and this was a trap. They were mentally unstable, which they freely admitted. They wrote once:

> *Psychologists have never helped me. They refuse to acknowl-*
> *edge the erotic component of my longing for S. They prescribe*
> *Lithium, they ask about a family history of depression, they*

*recommend CBD tinctures. What they can't fathom is that
S has nothing to do with my mood. It's not some weepy cry
for help. When I think about S, I'm not sad; I'm excited!*
*I've been 5150'd innumerable times. The nurses at a
certain Berkeley clinic know me by name. They know I prefer tapioca to chocolate,* Days of Our Lives *to* General
Hospital. *I think of my months in the hospital with fondness. I know what to pack: shoes with no laces, sweats with
no drawstring. It's the perfect place to sit and dream of
S . . . If ever I stop writing, you can assume that's where I
am. Playing solitaire by the window in hospital pajamas,
thinking of my Mistress . . .*

I settled on a short plaid skirt, black tights, and a sweater
of Ophelia's, soft black cashmere with tattered sleeves. I
wanted to look nice but not too nice, as if I always looked this
adorable and today was no different from any other day. I
wanted to look like a girl who read novels, who drank wine
and slept well. I spritzed my wrists with Soft Core, found my
maroon leather coat in the back of the closet, and hurried out
the door.

I got to our meeting spot early: second bench from the left.
I sat there drinking McDonald's coffee and watching the fog
subsume Marin. I wondered if I should've gotten something
for Nobody. It was hard to imagine them eating McMuffins.
They seemed austere, an oatmeal-with-no-raisins type. It was
a gray, damp day, and the park was almost empty but for a
smattering of elders on their morning walks. They nodded
to me and I nodded to them. They looked like they liked
oatmeal too.

I didn't start to worry until ten minutes after our agreed-upon meeting time. Maybe parking was difficult. Maybe there was traffic on the bridge. I tried not to jump to conclusions. My coffee cooled; my gloveless fingers ached. Thirty minutes in, I had to accept that I'd been stood up. I looked at my phone and, lo and behold, had three new messages from Nobody.

At 10:58 a.m.:

Miss Sunday,
You look lovely today. More lovely than I can possibly say.
O my heart, be still!
X

At 11:05 a.m.:

Miss Sunday,
I am here. In a way. Can't move. Can't type. Forgive me,
Miss. I'm trying. Please please.
X

And at 11:25 a.m.:

Miss Sunday,
I can barely bring myself to write to you.
  I do not expect nor deserve your forgiveness. Your time
is precious and I wasted it. For this, I deserve the ultimate
punishment. Death would be too swift.
  Please believe me when I say that I was looking for-
ward to our date. Oh, what an understatement! I got my

only suit dry-cleaned, so pathetic, I know. As if that might make a difference in how repulsive you find me. Of course I sabotaged this date. How stupid of me, to think I could do this. To think I was capable of enduring such bliss.

There's something wrong with me; this much is clear. I want you to know: this is not some sick game. I never meant to keep you waiting. I wanted to come, I wanted to bask in your light. Part of me thinks I still might, though I know that you've moved on by now and probably want nothing more to do with me. Block my email! Who can blame you? The trash must be thrown out. Perhaps they'll find me tomorrow morning, frozen to the second park bench from the left. Death by exposure. Death by embarrassment. Wouldn't that be fitting?

X

I looked over my shoulder, feeling my skin prickle. At the top of the park was a playground. Bored nannies clustered by the entrance to smoke while toddlers defied death on the slides. I scanned the bushes, then the cars across the street. Was Nobody in that Mercedes, that Tesla? A teen girl and her pug walked by; I gave them both a long, hard look. Then I grabbed my coffee and began to run, not daring to look behind me. I ran past my car, looping the park twice. I wanted to throw them off. The smoking nannies gave me wary looks. I had the mad urge to ask for a drag, but instead I kept running.

Crossing the street toward my car, I felt someone behind me. I could practically feel their hot breath on my neck. I whirled around and, of course, there was Dino. He wore a long floral dress and a knitted shawl around his shoulders but the nose was unmistakable.

Dino? I bellowed, flapping my hands. *Are you Nobody?* My stomach lurched. *Are you fucking kidding me?*

Pardon? He fumbled with his cane, suddenly becoming a shell-shocked granny.

I waved the figure away. It can't be him! It can't be!

I jumped in my car and sped down the hill. I took the squiggly route home, wasting time. I felt freaked and embarrassed and something pricklier, stickier. I felt how I'd felt in the strip club parking lot, when the bouncer backed away from me—like I was something untouchable. I thought I knew Nobody; we talked every night. Now I was forced to face the music: I didn't know this person. They were one more thing I'd gotten wrong, one more omission, one more chatty ghost. I felt jilted, as if we'd been on a date; a better word might've been orphaned. Not even this morbid sliver of a person wanted to see me, this wraith with no other commitments or plans. Who was the bigger loser, them or me? I'd played myself by forgetting the golden rule: everybody goes away in the end, even those who were barely there to begin with.

I turned on the radio, seeking distraction, but nothing was on. Literally nothing, though I flicked between stations. All I could get was a low static sound, a man's heavy breathing. We'd gotten a few of those prank calls when I was a kid, neighborhood boys calling our landline to pant into the phone. My mom would stay on the line, though I begged her to hang up. *It's a joke,* I moaned, but she ignored me. She clutched the phone with both hands, her eyes wide. There were days when this was the first time she'd moved from the couch.

Hello? she'd cry. *Hello? Who's there?* She'd stay on the phone until the boys got bored and hung up. Afterward she looked so crushed. She'd turn to me with a solemn expression and say, *I wonder who that was.*

Hours later, in the bath, I opened my email.

I was calm in a numb, sleepy way, like when you've cried yourself inside out. I'd spent the day at home with Ophelia. We'd donned baggy T-shirts and cleaned out the fridge, scoured the bathrooms. Instead of washing our T-shirts after we were done, we threw them away. We literally walked to the bins in the yard and took them off there, skittering back inside and squealing from the cold. We put green beans in the Crock-Pot, her Armenian grandmother's recipe. When she asked where I'd been that morning, I said I went for a drive.

That's nice, she said, dousing her beans with Tabasco. *It's good to take time for yourself.*

Now, after dinner, there was nothing from Nobody. This worried me. They would have usually written to me at least twice by now. I reread their emails from earlier, trying to think of what to say. Finally, I typed:

I forbid you from killing yourself.

I trashed this and wrote:

I'll be so pissed if you kill yourself.

Then I threw my phone across the room. It landed behind the sink with a thud. I soaked in the bath until the in-betweens of my fingers got pruney, then met Ophelia downstairs. She'd just completed a Blogilates workout. *Never too early to target flabby arms*, she said gaily. We walked the dogs around the block, incognito in hoodies. When she and I were together we dressed like teen boys; it was only for men we barely liked that we wore bracelets and lip liner, bras, body glitter. We watched *Sex and the City* until 1:30 a.m., eating bowl after bowl of her grandmother's beans and a tiramisu she'd brought home from a date.

I missed, of all things, Dino's stomach. He was a big man, broad-shouldered, forearms twined with muscle. The only soft part of him was that slight, sloping belly. When we watched TV together, I rested my head in his lap. I could hear his heart beat through his belly button as if through a hole in a wall.

Careful, he'd say. *You break it, you buy it.*

His tummy felt precious to me, this semiprivate site of nonresistance, exposed in rare glimpses when he petted the dogs or unloaded the dishwasher and his blouse came un-tucked. He leaned down and his belly bunched, like venetian blinds, over his belt. It made me feel close to him, this shared secret of softness. As a child I'd been indoctrinated by the internet to worship flat tummies. I did the viral thirty-day ab challenges alone in my room, then studied tabloid pics of Megan Fox in tube tops. Meanwhile, Dino rejected the school of the hard core.

Sex should be fleshy, he said. *Or maybe I mean, the best part of sex is the flesh. Am I being old-fashioned? Is that sexist somehow? I don't care.*

I came around. Love had so many edges; why not seek out the bready center? When he and I slept together, I hoarded his belly. It was warm and constant like a pet. I wanted to crawl inside it like a bounce house. Night after night, I placed my ear against his belly button and listened for the sea.

It was hard to understand why Ophelia stayed with Lorenzo. She could get strangers online to wire her money without leaving her bed. She knew things about medicinal herbs and noise music. She could use three whips at once, twirling them overhead like a ringmaster. Yet with Lorenzo, she was someone else—someone, frankly, more like me. She became antsy and passive. She threw out underwear he didn't like and lived in terror of keeping him waiting. She drafted her texts and read them aloud to me.

Am I being too harsh? she'd ask. *Do I sound like a bitch?* When waiting for him to text her back, she literally paced the room. It worried me; it reminded me of the first forty-eight hours after Dino went away, when I was glued to my phone. I recognized her helplessness. But anytime I tried to voice my concerns about Lorenzo, I felt her stiffen, pull away. *You don't know him,* she'd say. *It takes two to tango.*

I only met him once, when he swung by the dungeon to drop off Ophelia's laptop. He parked right in front of the house, which was against dungeon rules, and honked. When

Ophelia introduced us, he stuck out his hand and said, *Charmed.* He had the ruddy look of a man who drank too much milk as a boy. His body was toned but his face was bloated, his vintage Bad Brains T-shirt too tight. By way of goodbye, he pinched Ophelia's thigh and said, *Later.* As far as I was concerned, he was a wannabe art star with too much gel in his hair. I told her this later and she erupted with laughter.

Holy shit, she gasped. *What am I doing with that sad, sad man?*

But the next evening she was pacing again, distraught because he'd flaked on her to go to Benihana with his ex.

Am I being paranoid? she asked. *I don't wanna smother him.*

Have you met her before?

No, she said. *She lives between Barcelona and L.A. She's visiting.*

Oh, I said. *That's good. Where is she staying?*

Ophelia looked down. *At Lorenzo's.* She held up a hand to silence my squawk. *He has a futon in the living room!*

She only spoke to me about Lorenzo when the going got tough. When they kissed and made up, she was cagey. She bought new clothes from fancy boutiques and pretended they weren't new. *Oh, this old thing?* Eventually she tried to keep their dates from me. On the nights when I worked at the club we'd still leave the house at the same time, walking single-file through the yard.

Can I give you a ride? I'd ask.

She'd smile too quickly. *No, no.* She always wore flats when she was headed to his place. He didn't like her to be taller than him. *I'll manage.* This meant Lorenzo was picking her up.

Suit yourself, I said, starting the car. There was tension between us, an unfamiliar coldness. She knew I didn't trust Lorenzo, just like she didn't trust Nobody, but she also knew I'd never say so aloud. Our conversation became a game of chicken, each of us seeing how close the other would get to the truth. *Do you know when you'll be home?*

Nuh-uh. She was retouching her lipstick; he liked natural colors. *I'll text you, babe.* But she wouldn't. Sometimes I couldn't tell why exactly I was mad—because Lorenzo was an asshole and O deserved more, or because she was a hypocrite for staying with him, or because I couldn't bear the idea of her keeping secrets from me, or because she'd still be at his place when I finally got home and I'd have to watch TV alone.

Her shiftiness reminded me of when I was seeing Jax, the alcoholic bartender, and hiding it from Mazzy. *That guy's bad news,* Mazzy would tell me. She didn't beat around the bush. *He's totally using you.*

I know, I would say.

Do you think he's ever going to change?

No.

You don't REALLY think he loves you, right?

Right.

She softened her voice. *He barely even likes you, Ruthie.*

I know.

In truth, I liked him for using me. I liked him for being a tool. The cashier at his local bodega knew him better than I did. I couldn't explain why, but his cruelty felt cozy. It felt

good in the way of pressing down on a bruise, morbid curiosity meets bored masochism. My friends were operating under
the assumption that I deserved better, whereas Jax and I were
agreed on the topic of my disgrace. He fucked me when he
was lonely or depressed and didn't try to hide it. We didn't
waste time with movies or sushi. He used me like a rental car.
I always knew how the night would end. He would come in
squiggles on my chest, then let me shower first—how gallant.
It was a strangely peaceful pact and I was determined to keep
up my end of the deal by never wanting more.

So, in a way, I empathized with Ophelia, though her ca-
giness wounded me. I knew how exhausting it was to defend
your taste for debasement. As far as I was concerned, she deserved nothing but heaven. It was a fact as plain as day, as
uncontroversial as her being tall. I told her as much, drinking
coffee on the porch at Dream House.

I wish I could create the perfect man for you, I said. *Someone
on your level.*

Oh, Ruth, she said, smiling. *Stop.* She was the only person
these days who used my real name. Sometimes it sounded
odd to me, like an antiquated word. *You're making me blush.*

I mean it, I said, raising my voice. I was suddenly shouting.
*You're hot AND nice. Do you know how rare that is? To be both at
once?*

I'm not rare, she said, her voice changing slightly. *I'm really
pretty commonplace.* She stood up suddenly, reaching for my
mug. *More coffee?*

Sure. I watched her enter the kitchen, opening the porch
door with one bare foot. All my anger drained away. I only

wanted to hug her, finger-comb her hair. She was gone for a long time.

One morning, rooting through the kitchen in search of a can opener, I stumbled upon Dino's grocery list. I held it gingerly in both hands, an archaeological find. He'd put the date in the top left corner: the day before he disappeared. In pencil, he'd written:

> *Olive oil (good kind)*
> *Sesame oil*
> *Butter*
> *Check for tomatoes*
> *C.C.*

I held the paper up to the light, scanning it for clues. I felt breathless. What an intimate object. It exposed his optimism, his humble desires (ripe tomatoes, buttered bread). It seemed so innocent and hopeful, a diary entry. It made me think, somehow, of Pompeii: families' breakfasts on the table, their petrified routines. I read it again. What did this mean? Would someone who was planning to walk away from his life buy sesame oil? I didn't know. And what did C.C. stand for? Was it another message, a code? My stomach dropped: Was it someone's initials? Clarissa, Charlotte, Calliope . . .

Something like jealousy gripped me and I stuffed the list back in its drawer. I didn't want to look at it anymore, his curly handwriting with the undotted *i*'s. It reminded me of notes he'd written me in the early days of our love. Dumb little things on the backs of receipts: *To my favorite girl. I had a nice day with you.* He'd slip them in my textbooks or leave them on my pillow. One time he put a note in my sandwich, in between the lettuce and cheese. I spit it out and unfolded it: *You make me so happy.* I kept them all, though we never spoke of them. They were not the types of things you'd say aloud. They were, like birthday wishes or wet dreams, best kept to oneself.

One late November morning I met a client in the city. My failed meeting with Nobody had opened the floodgates and now I was agreeing to sessions I'd normally pass on. To be rejected by a ghost, was there anything more pathetic? A restlessness had started to build within me, a sense of dread I couldn't talk down. Without Nobody, I had no one to talk to. I found myself seeking edges when Ophelia wasn't around. Why take care when everything was shabby, rigged? I craved theatrics, anything to mirror the meltdown inside me, to affirm my sense of coming doom. I'd felt this way during my wild years too, until Dino had managed to calm me. When I missed him too much and O was off with Lorenzo, I spent hours on FetLife and other kink websites, entertaining pushy men with shitty grammar and profile pictures taken in the dark. Sometimes they paid me to rate their dicks over Skype (*a little too mushroomy, 4/10*); sometimes they sent videos of their blasted-open assholes and I got nothing in return.

This client's name was Rudolf. He messaged me on Fet-Life and gave me the address to his friend Micky's house. We met on the steps of a seafoam Victorian overlooking Dolores Park, where he leaned against the banister, completely nude but for a baseball hat worn backward.

Micky's very kind to me, he explained as he led me inside. He moved slowly and easily, like a tropical fish. *He's a fellow nudist, so he gets it. We met outside the Castro Theatre, you know, where all the nudists hang out. Maybe you've seen us? My place isn't big enough, so he lets me use his.*

For $300, I was going to pretend to kill him on tape. He showed me to a room filled to the rafters with trash. I couldn't possibly list all the things in that room. There was a baby grand piano snowed under with newspapers dating back to the AIDS crisis. A twin mattress stood against the wall, next to a filing cabinet stuffed with women's underwear. Panties frothed over the sides of each drawer like moss. Rudolf set up a camcorder on a pile of cookbooks and told me to stand in a clearing amid the mess.

Are you comfortable? Are you thirsty? he asked. *What a bad host I am!*

I nodded, and he dug through the trash until he found a Styrofoam cooler, the type that you'd take to the beach. He pulled out two bottles of water and handed me one. It was sticky, like a peach.

Thank you, I said. When he wasn't looking, I hid it behind the mattress.

We got right to work. He told me to don a Supergirl costume and throw him up against the wall, one hand on his throat, the other bending his arm behind his back. *That's good,* he said, reviewing the footage, *but this time do it meaner. This time really make me squeal. This time have a British accent. This time try a lisp.* He told me to be zesty, nasty, laid-back, bitchy, ditzy, surly, sleepy, French. He was committed to a vision far beyond my comprehension.

When at last he was satisfied, we set up the next scene. I took off the Supergirl costume and wore the clothes he'd asked me to come in—yoga pants, sports bra, dirty Converses. He sauntered into frame with his hands on his hips, bragging about fucking my boyfriend. *He's gay now,* he told me. His little dick jiggled. It looked like a chew toy. *I turned him gay. He wants my body-ody-ody!*

Fat chance, I said, then tackled him and wrestled him to the floor. I pretended to stomp on his throat with my sneaker. *My boyfriend wouldn't be caught dead with a loser like you,* I ad-libbed. As he thrashed on the floor, I noticed that he'd written FUCK THE PATRIARCHY on his ass in black Sharpie. DIRTY LIL WHITE BOY was tattooed on one thigh.

My boyfriend has impeccable taste, I went on. *He wouldn't even look at scum like you.*

Oh yeah? Rudolf simpered. *Are you suuuuure about that?*

I gently pressed my toe against his cheekbone. *Damn sure,* I said. *You've got no ass. My man LOVES ass.* I could tell by the light in his eyes that he liked this direction. We filmed three takes of this scene and then our hour was up.

Is it cool if I use your bathroom? I asked. I felt oddly energized by our pantomime of violence. The melodrama had gone straight to my head. Rudolf, meanwhile, seemed withdrawn. His demeanor had shifted as soon as my timer went off. His pep was gone, his manic hospitality; now he was surly, squatting on a pile of records by the window.

Whatever, he said, waving a hand toward the door. He glared out the window. *Go ahead.*

I walked down the hallway, peering into rooms equally full of trash. The house was dark and musty, reeking of baby powder. Through the gloom I could decipher the bones of a beautiful home: fireplaces stuffed with baby clothes, crown molding crisscrossed with cobwebs, grubby angels on the ceiling looking at nothing. At the end of the hallway was the kitchen. It was barren and blue-lit though it was not yet noon, the counters and shelves empty. I stepped inside and stifled a scream. An unidentifiable carcass was defrosting in the sink. It was knobby and bulky, swirled with blood. It looked primordial, demonic, oddly poetic, with streaks of purple and blue. It was all categories of thing: animal, mineral, vegetable, dream. I was torn between horror and a desire to get closer. I wondered if I could make out its face.

Suddenly Rudolf was behind me, looking bored. He'd changed into a new baseball hat, this one with rainbow stripes and a little propeller on top.

That's dinner, he said, standing with one hip cocked like a teenage girl. In the dim greasy light, his soft penis looked like a crustacean. Was everything in this house prehistoric, unpinned from space and time? *That's Micky.*

My stomach dropped. *What?*

That's Micky's. He shrugged. *He's into exotic meat these days.*

Oh.

Rudolf handed me a piece of paper. *Here,* he said. It was a coupon for rotisserie chicken at Mollie Stone's, buy one get one free. *For your troubles.* Then he strode to the sink, turned on the tap, and splashed his face with cold water. The basin immediately filled up, unable to drain because of the meat. Purplish liquid flooded the countertop. I mourned for the tile work.

Thank you, I murmured. I moved toward the door, afraid he might stop me. But he stayed where he was, drying his hands on his thighs as if he wore pants. The sink continued to flood, the swollen carcass bobbing like an apple in a children's game. *I'll see myself out.*

I ran down the hallway and into the street. I peed behind a parked car and wiped with the coupon, then threw it in the gutter. I glanced up at Micky's and saw the curtains flick shut. Someone was watching me. I walked through the park to Arizmendi and bought a cappuccino to calm myself down. I also bought a ham-and-cheese croissant but couldn't eat it. I wouldn't be able to eat meat again. The sight of it didn't bother me, but the taste was off. It tasted of kisses, frenzied male lips, a touch of baby powder.

I remember the last shower we took before officially breaking up. I'd spent the day moving my shit into the guest room. Dino knocked on the bathroom door while I was showering.

It's open, I shouted.

He sat on the lip of the tub, watching me.

Come on in, I said. *The water's warm.*

I don't know if I thought he really would, but he rose and removed his clothes. He folded them neatly on the closed toilet lid and stepped into the shower. He took the bar of soap from my hands and began soaping my back. He worked quietly, diligently.

I'll miss this, he said. He put the soap down.

I didn't turn to look at him. *Me too,* I confessed.

His voice was thick. *I'll miss you too.*

I'm not going anywhere.

He hugged me from behind, resting his chin on my shoulder. *It wasn't all bad, was it?*

Not at all! I cried, heart suddenly pounding. *Things just . . . got away from me.* I couldn't explain it any better.

He took a deep breath; I could feel his belly expanding against my spine. *If only we could fall in love all over again.* His voice was soft and, for one moment, happy.

I smiled. *That would be nice.*

Yes, he echoed, loosening his grip on my body. *That would be nice.*

I thought about kissing him, but before I could turn around, he'd stepped out of the tub. He left the bathroom bare-ass naked, dripping on the floor.

It hit me, suddenly, in the middle of the night. I sat up with a jolt. Cottage cheese. That's what it stood for, on Dino's grocery list. Cottage fucking cheese.

I stared at the ceiling and listened to the wind in the trees. I missed Dino. I missed who I was when he and I got together, that twenty-five-year-old fool. She'd never given a lap dance, she'd never had a mai tai. She believed in her thesis on cameras and ghosts. She seemed lighter and less damaged.

Or was that nostalgia speaking? Was I glossing over my slut-dom, all the traps I'd walked into at twenty-five, ditzy and ripe? That was my wild year; at twenty-seven, I felt tired. I felt like a widow living alone on a farm. Dino had tamed me, and sometimes I resented him for it. For the very first time, I wondered if he was gone for good. My faith spluttered, a cigarette smoked in the bed of a truck. I realized there might not be any winners in this weird little game. Loss opened in me like a Ziploc bag. I wanted to cry, but I was scared if I started, I'd never stop.

Ophelia lay next to me, sleeping. I wrapped my arms around her waist and buried my face in her hair. It was still wet from the shower and stuck to my cheeks. It smelled like coconut cream pie. Naomi wormed her way into the space between our bellies, wheezing softly. We stayed like this all night, not moving. For once, I didn't dream.

V.

One Sunday morning while Ophelia slept in, I found myself at church.

I went on a walk down Valencia Street and wandered inside, lured by the smell of incense and burnt coffee. A rail-thin man in a three-piece suit stood at the pulpit, shoulders bunched. The room was dim and shabby, poorly swept. Yellow paper streamers, the kind you get at party stores, were taped to the ceiling in loops. The pews were full of decked-out women and their docile babies. One hung off her mother's neck and stared at me, a bow taped to her head. I was one of the only white people present, lurid in my leggings.

If you've been impregnated by the Lord, the pastor cried, *then this is your spiritual C-section.*

I sat in the last row and fell into a trance. The pastor's words entered me, physically. I envisioned cartoons of angels and slutty devil costumes. I'd never been to a Baptist church before and it seemed so rock-and-roll. The ladies in front of me wailed and thrashed, waving babies like lighters. The pastor had us by the hair. He was my Master and I was his lamb. Or was God my Master? In any case, I was ready. I assumed the position and said bottoms up. He had the whole world in his big, hard hand.

When you call Jesus on the telephone, the pastor boomed, *He will NEVER ignore your call.*

The congregation moaned. A man jerked as if electro-cuted and hollered, *Praise be!*

When you call Jesus on the telephone, you will NEVER get disconnected.

The women in front of me stomped their feet. They wore big hats in primary colors. *Amen!*

Jesus NEVER puts you on hold. Jesus NEVER leaves you on read. The pastor paused, making us beg for it. I wanted to tug at the hem of his pants. *Jesus Christ will NEVER ghost you. Why? There's no such thing as a holy ghosting.*

The crowd erupted. *Hallelujah, hallelujah.* Thick arms seized me in a hug. When I resurfaced, an elderly woman in a purple pantsuit was smiling at me. *Peace be with you*, she said.

And also with you. The phrase fell from my mouth, per-fectly formed, like a tooth. Where did it come from? I felt both proud and alarmed. On the cushions of each pew were white paper fans; the old woman picked one up and gave it to me with a wink.

As soon as the service was over, I ran out the door. I was too scared to talk to anyone. I didn't want to break the spell, to become regular old Ruth again. At church I wasn't Baby or Miss Sunday but a girl I dimly knew: let's call her Ruthie. Wide-eyed and trembling, easy to spook and easy to please. She liked big men, tequila, and being cussed out. She pre-dated Dino and sometimes flared up in moments of surrender.

When I got home, I put the paper fan in my dance bag and forgot all about it until the next time I worked. I started using it at the club, carrying it around on the floor and fanning myself. Men seemed to like it, perceiving it as a joke or cheap stab at divadom.

You look like Cleopatra, one said. *May I fan you, my Queen?*

Another man stood with his hands on his hips, studying me. *Be still and know that I am with you.*

What?

He pointed to my hand. The phrase was embossed on the back of the fan in slanted gold letters: BE STILL AND KNOW THAT I AM WITH YOU. How had I missed that?

I immediately started to shake. I looked down at the fan, then back up at the man. It was Dino in a clip-on mustache. He looked like a detective in a children's film. He wore a herringbone coat and knee-high galoshes. I told him that I had to go and ran to the bathroom, where I sat on the toilet, dry-heaving. I didn't know what I was feeling, a confusion that was becoming familiar to me. I felt giddy but also rich with grief. I traced my fingers over the fan's raised gold letters. They felt like goose bumps on a thigh. I recited the phrase until it started to scare me. *Be still and know that I am with you.* This could be a proclamation of faith or paranoia. Was I ever alone? I looked under and over the stall: no one there. As children we'd tried to prank one another by squirming under bathroom stalls. I remember, once, crawling on the floor to scare Mazzy. I picked the wrong stall and found myself staring up at a mystery woman. She wore blue mittens with pom-poms, I remember them vividly. She wiped her pussy and ass with the mittens still on. I don't know if she saw me.

When I returned to the floor, the Dino-imposter was gone. The club was half-empty, the DJ playing nineties pop. I went to the bar and ordered a fernet and ginger ale from Sadie. *Mazel tov*, she said crabbily. When I lifted the glass, there was a note underneath it. In barely legible pencil on a pink cocktail napkin, it read: *take care*. It seemed like the note-writer was switching shit up. I glanced over at Sadie, who was arm-wrestling a lawyer on the far end of the bar, then rolled up the napkin and slid it into my garter. I'd add it to my baggie of evidence later. I downed my drink and scanned the room. If I didn't find a man right then, I would die. I needed someone to groove for, to mirror my wants. It was just like in real life, using sex to distract from the holes in my personage. The only difference here was that I always won. I always got paid and never got hurt in a significant way. Right? That was what I told myself as I sauntered up to a gentleman sitting alone.

Hey there, I purred. *I'm Baby.*

Baby, huh? He leaned forward, smiling like a cartoon wolf. *You look all grown up to me.*

I played with my hair. *I'm young at heart.*

Is that so?

I smiled, knowing that I had him now. *I may be young, but I know a thing or two about men.*

Ohhh really? He literally licked his lips. *Prove it.*

I hid my face behind my fan. *Game on.*

Later that same night, around 4:30 a.m., I got an email from Nobody.

It was the first one from them in over a week. After standing me up at the park, they'd gone quiet. I hated to admit it, but I missed them. When I saw their name in my inbox, my heart sparked. I opened the message immediately, standing naked in Dino's bedroom with one pair of lashes still on. The dogs were already in bed with Ophelia, everybody dreaming.

Dear Miss Sunday,
I saw something today that made me think of you. A paint-ing of a woman with a long, bare neck. Her eyes were brown and a little sad.
Please forgive me for writing. I know you do not want to hear from me but I couldn't help myself. Bad dog.
I pray that you are well.
xo

I wrote:

To Nobody,
Glad to hear you're still with us. I will admit, I was wor-ried . . . But then I realized that if you really did it (and you know what I mean by it), you'd at least leave me a parting note. It would be impolite not to. You are many things, some good, some bad, but impolite isn't one of them . . .
Sincerely,
Miss Sunday

With that, we resumed our correspondence, though more cautiously than before. Now we were shy. It was scary how much I'd come to depend on this stranger in just a few weeks. Walking the dogs, sharing a bed with Ophelia, driving to and from work with the radio on: these were the things that, just barely, held me together sans Dino. It hadn't felt good to lose one of my rocks. Our emails were sparser, slimmer, less grandiose. Perhaps our failed plans to meet up had driven home the point that both of us were really here. We had actual bodies with bruisable, touchable, feelable flesh. We wore sweaters when we felt a chill. Death may have been an abstract concept, but loneliness was real.

In the following week, we kept our emails to one each per day. Like lovers after a fight, we were gentle. We didn't make such lofty claims or pretend to philosophize. I acted less self-consciously dominant and they acted less nutty. At some point we exchanged phone numbers, "just in case something happens." Our relationship was revealed for what it had been all along: two solitary people passing the time. Every night that week I sat on the couch after dinner, proofreading my emails and drinking kratom in pineapple juice. Writing to Nobody felt like a hobby, a nourishing one, like crosswords or fermenting. Ophelia sighed when she saw me, returning home from a jog one chill Tuesday.

That suicide dude again?

We're just talking, I said.

I thought he got lost.

I shrugged, hiding my phone under my thigh. *They came back.*

She shook her hair from its ponytail. *So now he's totally in love with you.*

I hadn't considered that option. *No, it's not like that.* For some reason I lied, *They have a wife, you know.*

That's what they all say. She unlaced her sneakers, still standing in front of me. *You do know he's not really going to kill himself, right?*

I thought about this and realized I agreed. The actuality of suicide seemed beside the point. I didn't worry about them killing themselves; I worried about them losing interest in me, my emails suddenly bouncing. *I can handle it,* I told her. *Don't worry, OK?*

She sighed. *What do you see in this creep?*

They're my friend, I said curtly. I felt my cheeks flush. *Is that OK with you?*

Of course, she said, softening. *You can do whatever you want, babe.* She stepped closer and placed a hand on my thigh. *I just don't want you to get hurt.* She paused, mulling over her words. *I don't want you to settle.*

For what?

For whatever you get from this loser. You're a gorgeous girl, Ruthie.

I frowned, knowing this to be untrue. *Thank you.*

Don't waste your light on some internet stranger. She glanced at the clock. *D'ya wanna go out?*

I stared at her. *Out?*

Yes, out! She fluffed her hair. *To a bar. With men. And alcohol.*

I didn't know what to say. I'd forgotten this was an option, something I used to do nightly. The thought of meeting someone in a regular way—presenting myself as a wantable object, then waiting to be wanted—was exhausting. You put clothes on just to take them off. At this point in my decline I needed more hardcore distractions. I didn't think I could stomach the usual boy-girl chitchat. I didn't want to smooch and chill, I wanted to compare death wishes, I wanted to be perforated. I sought the company of broken hearts and wordy creeps. *I'm pretty beat, O. But don't let me stop you.*

She studied my face. She wasn't angry or hurt; she was worried. *You sure?*

I nodded, forcing a yawn. *I'd rather watch TV with you.*

OK, she said. Her eyes were flickery and grave. They made me feel sorry for her. *Let me just shower first.*

As she was turning to go, I grabbed her by the wrist. *You don't have to worry*, I said. *This person can't hurt me.*

Why not?

Because I've never seen them naked.

She let out a guffaw.

I'm serious, I said. *I don't know what they look like. They might be uglier than me. I can't be hurt by someone ugly. Not in a powerful, lasting way. Of course, they might be a dreamboat. A ten out of ten. But, statistically speaking, I'm probably safe. It's a risk that I'm willing to take.*

She smiled and shook her head, drifting out of the room. *Whatever you say, Ruth.*

Later that same night, while Ophelia paced in the yard and talked on the phone with the dogs at her feet, I opened my email. I was breaking the unspoken rules by messaging Nobody twice in a day. In my bed with the lights off, I wrote:

Dear Nobody,

I must admit, there's something I've been hiding from you. Not hiding, exactly, but withholding. I want to be honest with you, as you've been honest with me. Here it goes.

My dad might have been like you. This is to say, he might've killed himself. We still don't know for sure. This is what I do know: One night he drove his car off a bridge. He taped a note to the fridge, left our house around midnight, got in his car, and was found, days later, officially dead. The cause of death, I'd learn, was not drowning but blood loss.

My mom was told he'd been drinking. That's what everyone said. Why else would he lose control of his car? I have some memories of my dad drinking; he would sit on the couch and ask me to bring him a Heineken. Sometimes he let me taste the foam. I don't know if this is important or not.

I was 7 when he went away. That's how my mom described it; she could never actually admit that he died. When I was 18, she gave me a folder. She said, If you don't want to look, you don't have to. If you do, it's all there.

What was in the folder, you ask? There were newspaper clippings describing the accident. How the bumper separated from the rest of the car. How his body was found in the reeds, facedown. There was a toxicology report showing he hadn't been drinking. He had 1/1000th of the legal alcohol limit in his body at the time of his death, plus trace amounts of THC. The last thing in the folder was the note he'd taped to the fridge.

Now, I know what you're thinking. You're thinking this note is a clue, hard proof of my father's intention to die. His way of saying goodbye. In truth, it was pretty underwhelming. It was an index card on which he'd written: LOVE U. *It is important to stress that he wrote* U, *not* YOU. *What did this note prove? Only that he loved me, which is something I already knew.*

Of course there were rumors. They made their way back to me: My dad was a gambler who'd squandered my college fund. He'd been cheating on my mom with a twenty-something yoga teacher and knocked the girl up. He had no way out, he felt trapped. Other people truly believed his death was an accident. It was late at night and he'd nodded off at the wheel. Accidents happen. Right? He wasn't the suicidal type. People told me this over and over. There are times when I believe the stories. All of them make sense.

I don't remember much about him, but I know he wasn't sad. At least, not around me. Around me, he was happy. He was loud, hyperactive. That's all I know. Perhaps you can help me fill in the blanks. I don't expect you, of course, to solve the riddle of my father's death. That would be crazy. But maybe, through you, I can learn more about him. I can try to understand his intentions. I want to know what made S so appealing to him. Why choose S over us, over everything else? I don't blame him. Really, I don't. I just want to know, what did it feel like? To want something so badly? Yes, he loved us, but what else did he love? What type of person chooses death?

Perhaps you can help me. If not, that's OK. Not all mysteries get solved. Actually, most of them don't. My expectations are low. Sometimes it's best to let sleeping dogs lie . . .

    Yours,
    Ruth

Hours later, as I lay in bed staring at the ceiling, unable to sleep, I realized I'd committed the cardinal sex-work sin. I'd accidentally signed off with my legal name. Hugo and Ophelia would scold me, but a tiny part of me felt relieved. At this point, Nobody knew so much about me. If mailmen and Uber drivers could know my real name, why not Nobody? It didn't feel risky. There were probably hundreds of Ruths living in San Francisco proper. Knowing my first name didn't mean Nobody could find me, track me down in this seasick city of data and drugs. Right? I was an affable ghost, too shy to speak up when someone cut me in line. When I lay down in parks, I blended in with the daisies; dogs peed too close to my shoes. I was only visible when I took off my clothes in a dark room at night. Only then did I blaze like a Christmas tree on fire. Only then, in my stockings, was I easy to find.

I took two Xanax and tumbled to sleep. I dreamt that I was in my childhood home. I walked into the kitchen to find my mom eating cigarettes out of the box, as if they were French cookies. She saw me and said with a Halloween smile, *A moment on the lips, forever on the hips.* Then she kept eating, her lipstick rubbed off, watching jasmine pelt the window.

Blue Hour

VI.

There were many words for Emeline: stuck-up, princess, brat. I'd heard Dallas call her a poser, Brandi call her trust-fund scum, Cookie (ever the diplomat) call her green. Above all, she was clueless. She lived in her own world according to her own rules. It was a condition I alternately envied and pitied. It was only a matter of time before she got what was coming to her. You can't trip through life thinking everything's yours. Sooner or later, the bill must be paid.

When I walked into the locker room that Friday evening, I could tell something was off. It was too quiet, too still. The space heaters weren't plugged in and the room was glacial. The other girls ignored me, seemingly deep in contemplation of their zippers and pastes. Cookie was not at her desk, her Kindle left to charge.

Emeline was already there in our corner, reading her book (*Aliens & Anorexia*). She smiled and waved, sending feathers everywhere. *Hey, Baby*, she said. Her energy was downbeat, like she'd just been dumped. It was the first time I'd seen her since our late-night date at the diner. *How's it going?*

OK. You?

She shrugged. *I've been better.*

What's up?

Well . . . She looked around. *There's kind of a situation.*

Oh?

She motioned me closer. *Someone's been spreading rumors about me.*

Really? I set my bag down. *Like what?*

She lowered her voice. *Someone said I do extras. You know, like . . . special favors.*

Oh. I'd heard whispers of which girls sucked dick or gave handies, none of them confirmed. I suspected no one really did it, that it was just another male myth (like the one about us all having Daddy issues), but perhaps that was my naïveté. If the other girls did it, I commended their hustle.

That's not all, Emeline said. *They also say I've been stealing.*

Stealing what?

Other girls' tips, cash from the bar. Someone even said I've been stealing bottles of Grey Goose. She threw her hands in the air. *I only drink Tito's!*

Well, I said, *if they're not true, then who cares?*

I care, she said, *because someone told the managers and now I'm in trouble. Cookie's in the office right now. She says she believes me, but who really knows?* Emeline cradled her head in her hands. Under her robe she wore a cream-colored bra and French-cut thong. *Baby,* she said, her voice small. *You believe me, right? You've got my back?*

I thought about it. *I believe you.* She was too vain to do extras and too busy to steal tips. Every time she got on the floor she was hounded by men. I'd seen how much money she could make in a night. It would be a waste of her time to bother with anyone else's cash flow.

Good, she said. I was shocked to see her eyes fill with tears. *Thank you, Baby.*

For what?

For being my friend. Everyone here thinks I'm a total bitch. But I'm not! She wiped her eyes. *I'm a really good person.*

I know, I said, though I wasn't so sure. I barely knew her. I could speak more to her father's character than to hers. Did she stop to pet dogs in the street? Did she compost? I knew she liked cheesecake and *Swan Lake,* studied novels in college. I remember Charlie telling me that as a child she'd struggled with night terrors. I knew how men saw her and what they wanted to do to her, but whatever else was underneath that studied gloss was lost to me. I patted her awkwardly on the shoulder.

Don't worry, I said. *It will all be OK.*

She stared at me, toddleresque. *Do you promise?* she murmured. Her eyes were wet and round. She reached for my hand and squeezed it until my fingers started to hurt. *How do you know?*

I froze. What could I, of all people, possibly say? I was cruising the stages of grief. I carried a broken heart in my purse like a taser; I'd been doing it for so long I forgot it was weird. And yet, on the surface, my life seemed normal. She couldn't sense my decline, my divorce from reality. That's what freaked me out the most, my native ability to absorb any trauma like it was just one more step in my skin-care routine. Wake up at five, wash face, stare into void, moisturize. Death, or some perky variant, roomed with me. If someone like Emeline was looking to me for comfort, that could only mean we were doomed. I felt a flash of indignation, like she'd stolen my role; I was the one who should be crying and crawling into laps. Somehow I managed to keep my voice level.

Emeline, I said, edging away from her. *Everything will be fine.*

You mean it?

Yes. I pried her hand from mine. *Why don't you go outside and get some fresh air?* There was an alley off the locker room where girls went to smoke. *That always helps.*

OK, she said, nodding. *OK. I'll be back.*

She left her purse on the counter and drifted out the back door. As soon as she was out of sight, I pulled her bag toward me. It was surprisingly messy, full of Lärabars and scrunchies and CVS receipts, a few battered paperbacks. I dug through it until I found her bottle of Soft Core, the label nearly rubbed off. I spritzed the perfume all over my body—wrists, breast-bone, belly button, nape, behind the ears, behind the knees—then threw it on the floor. It shattered on the concrete, forming a heart-shaped lilac puddle.

Oops, I said loudly. Other girls turned to look. Gigi gave me a sympathetic smile, like, *Shit happens.* When I pushed the glass around with the toe of my shoe, the puddle retained its distinct heart shape. Another sign, I thought. I had all night to try to decode it.

I finished getting dressed and hurried onto the floor.

Cookie would handle the mess whenever she returned. If Emeline asked, I would tell her it was an accident. *Silly me, what a klutz!* I didn't see her until an hour later. I was leaving the lap-dance area as she was entering it with a man. She smiled when we passed each other. To her client, a midlife-crisis-cool-dad type, she stage-whispered, *There goes Baby. She's like a sister to me.* I couldn't tell if she wanted me to hear her or not.

Oh yeah? her dude said. Lesbian fantasies flashed in his eyes. He had a Celtic knot tattooed on one sagging bicep and a leather jacket that looked brand-new. *Does she like to be bad?*

No, she said firmly. *She's really, really nice.*

Then they entered their room and I was alone. I tried to sell a dance to a man who complained that my perfume was too strong.

Little word of advice, he said. *Tone that shit down.*

That's it! I cried, jumping up. *That's my problem! There it is! I could never put my finger on it, but now you've figured it out!* I pumped his hand like a politician. *Thank you so much for filling me in! How can I ever repay you?*

Jesus fucking Christ, he mumbled. *This place has gone downhill.*

Around midnight I returned to the locker room, winded. The crowd was heating up. I needed a break to drink seltzer and stare at my phone. As I limped to my corner, I was surprised to see Emeline back in her chair. She clutched her robe around her shoulders, her hair in two clumps, her shoulders concaved; from a distance, she looked almost common.

Hey, I said. I stepped over her heels, which had been kicked onto the floor. *What's up?* She never took breaks; she was either booked back-to-back or entrenched in conversation with her lovesick regulars.

She shrugged, eyes cloudy. *It's pointless,* she said. Her voice was thin, gloomy. *I can't hustle right now. I'm just not in the mood. Some finance bro wanted a three-hour VIP, but I told him I had period cramps.* She waved her hands in the air, causing her robe to fall open. Even she had a scrunched-up belly when she sat in a chair. This heartened me. *I bet all the other girls will be pissed to know I'm back here alone. You know, since I'm such a thief.*

Oh, I said, *that's still bothering you?*

She nodded. *Can't help it.* There were lines on her feet from where her shoes had dug into the flesh. *It's just so fucking . . .* She scrounged for the right word. *So fucking UNJUST.*

I said nothing, sipping my seltzer.

Of course this is the night I take an Uber to work, she moaned. *It was, like, forty-five dollars. After tip-out, I'll be in the negatives.* She heaved a sigh and checked her phone. *Fuck it,* she said. *Should I just leave now? Take the bus and go home? I just wanna chill and, like, hang with my dad.*

Her last words entered me; I turned toward her slowly, keeping my voice light. *Your dad's home?*

Uh-huh.

I studied her face, the fretful lines around her mouth. Though she tried to hide it, her hands were trembling. She looked pretty in a different way than usual, less sexy, more frail. Her eyes throbbed with upset. She was trying, and failing, to be brave. She was more sensitive than I'd realized; she was so easy to play. I set down my seltzer and opened my locker. *C'mon*, I said, making my voice low and honeyed. *Let's go.*

Now? She looked at me, baffled. *You wanna leave too?*

I shrugged. *I did good tonight.* This was a lie; I'd made $80 onstage and spent $85 on my outfit, a bubblegum-pink bikini with matching rhinestone thigh-highs that Dino had picked out forever ago. *Get dressed*, I said. *I'll take you home.*

Baby! she cried. *That's so sweet!* She smiled and rose, unfolding her legs, reasserting her dazzle. Her hair was suddenly bounteous. How could I forget that she was a heartbreaker? This made me feel less guilty about the plan I was cooking. She threw her arms around me and murmured into my neck, *You're a real one.*

It's nothing, I said, untangling from her embrace. *I'm tired tonight. We could both use a break.* I unpeeled my stockings. *Now hurry up and get dressed.*

Aye aye, Captain! she chirped. She stuffed her heels in her bag but kept her lingerie on, throwing a baggy men's sweater over her mostly nude body, which I had to admit was very glamorous. In the same spirit, I tugged my jeans over my bikini, powering through the instant wedgie. She fluffed up her hair. *Let's boogie.*

We exchanged our singles for big bills, tipped out Cookie and the bouncers, then ran to my car lest any club patrons see us out in the open. Once inside, I locked the doors.

Ugh! Emeline sighed, kicking off her loafers and sitting

crisscross in the passenger seat. *That feels GOOD.* She was suddenly revived, her green eyes gone neon. *Where to next, Baby?*

I thought you said home.

Her smile was sly. *I knooow,* she drawled, *but since we both have the night off . . . and it's Friday, after all . . . what if we went dancing?* Before I could reply, she yelped, *Just for a little—one hour, max—to blow off some steam—and then we'll go home! You can totally sleep over at mine, if you want. Pleeeeease!*

I felt a tickle of excitement—she was making this so easy. *Are you sure?*

Totally! She slapped me, lightly, on the arm. *It would be fun!*

I stared straight ahead. In the darkness she couldn't see me deliberating. *Will your dad mind?*

God, no, she said. *He's totally chill. He'll love you, I'm sure.*

I inhaled, exhaled. My heart was like an egg timer, jerking around in my chest. *OK,* I sighed. I turned toward Emeline and felt myself smile. *Did you have somewhere in mind?*

Hurray! she cried, a word I hadn't heard aloud in forever. *My friend's boyfriend DJs at this bar in the Mission. My other friend had an art show, so the place should be packed.* She held up her phone, which had a little Totoro charm dangling off it. *Let me MapQuest directions.*

You use MapQuest? I asked, genuinely shocked.

She giggled. *I know. Old habits die hard.*

Within ten minutes we'd found ourselves in a bar I'd never been to before. It was swanky, small, dim. The only light came from a modest disco ball, which flecked its light

on a hodgepodge of faces: art kids, normies, loners, hungry
dudes, a pleasantly mixed crowd. Emeline squealed and
jumped into the arms of the couple behind the DJ booth, two
pale people who looked somehow rich. Their clothes were
clean and understated, the girl had a European bob and no
boobs, while the boy, who was DJing, wore a massive gold
Buddha on a chain. They all hugged and gabbed as if they
hadn't seen one another in years. I floated to the bar, where I
ordered a beer from the statuesque bartender. Before I could
pay, Emeline appeared by my side.

Don't even think about it! she said, slapping $20 on the bar.
I'm treating you tonight.

O-em-gee, the bartender squealed. *Look who it is!*

Ohmigod, hi! Emeline leaned over the bar, her breasts
dangerously close to the limes, and embraced the bartender.
*Baby, this is Cassandra. We went to summer camp together, like,
forever ago.* She accepted the glass of wine that Cassandra
held out. *We reconnected after college. Turns out we had a few exes
in common.*

Cassandra giggled. *Small world.*

Emeline pointed to me. *Cass, this is my good friend Baby.
Don't let her pay for anything, K?* She downed her wine, linked
her arm through mine, and elbowed us back to the dance
floor.

I love this song, she cried, tilting her head back. The disco
ball made her blond hair snowy. *I really fucking love this song.*

I watched her as she danced, a compelling mix of rigor
and abandon. She wore white loafers, no pants, and a men's
cable-knit sweater, the color of half-and-half, frayed in the
shoulders, revealing patches of tan. It came down to her knees

and was somehow both clunky and ultra-erotic, something thrown on after getting railed. God, I thought, how did she do it? You couldn't try to be this hot, it was like perfect pitch, it simply had to come to you. Meanwhile, I wore dad jeans and a wifebeater yellowed with sweat. I'd balled up my puffer jacket and shoved it under a stool. I felt like Emeline's chaperone, gawky and dour. Still, I closed my eyes and swayed to the music, a reggaeton beat, until something happened. The more I danced, the more Emeline's ease seemed to rub off on me. Two drinks in, I felt blameless and carefree. I felt my old slut-self returning. I suddenly remembered why I loved bars, particularly bars full of men—you could disappear in a booth or blaze on the dance floor, you could modulate your solidity and flick between states over the course of the night, simultaneously nonexistent and showstopping, quiet and loud, both a ghost and an archangel. Tonight, of course, we were very much visible. We were two girls (sisters? friends?) cutting loose. I could feel men trying not to watch us, their eyes pinging off our shoulders, knees. But how could they resist? There is nothing more irresistible than two girls having fun.

A twenty-something with long black braids flashed us a peace sign. I thought of Ophelia. I felt a pinch of guilt picturing her at home all alone, the dogs in her lap, her face smeared with a clay mask. She was supposed to be taken out to dinner by a software engineer with a feeding fetish, but he bailed at the last minute. *Dammit!* she'd howled as we got ready earlier that evening, the house thick with setting spray. She wore an uncharacteristically dumpy dress. *We were supposed to go to all-you-can-eat sushi,* she cried. *I skipped lunch and went to the Goodwill to buy this damn muumuu! You know, to make room.*

He ended up offering to pay for her takeout; she promised to get extra inari for me. I pulled out my phone and texted her: *be home soon bb, crazy night at the club!*

She texted back almost immediately: *okey dokey! make a bag :)* Then she sent a selfie of her and Naomi, whiskers askew, in matching pink headbands: *girls night!!*

I put my phone in my pocket and stared at the ceiling, letting the disco ball discolor my throat. I shook out my hair and felt old urges resurfacing, the festive nihilism of my younger years. I wanted something bad to happen, something splashy and irreparable. I scanned the room for a dude I could die for, whose violence I might welcome. A few men smiled and nodded at me, sensing my flammability.

True to Emeline's word, however, we were only at the bar for an hour. I could've kept dancing, but she seemed to peak. One moment she was grooving, eyes closed in rapture, the next she looked beat. She looked at me and mouthed, *Fresh air?* I followed her through the crowd and out the door. The frosty night air was a blessing. We both gulped it down. *Whoo*, she said. Her face was slick with sweat, her blond hair almost brown. *I feel better.* Her eyes were starry, peaceful.

I blotted my face with my wifebeater. *Me too.*

A cluster of men was smoking on the sidewalk, eyeing us, laughing. They had paint-splattered pants and hip haircuts. Emeline noticed and rolled her eyes. *I think that's our cue to leave.*

Oh? My old slut-self would've waited until one or more of them came over. I would've decided which one I'd go for, then second-best, then third. I might've even bummed a smoke, pretend-shivering in the cold.

But Emeline was unbothered. *Let me just say my goodbyes.* We popped back inside, where the heat of bodies hit us like a force field. She flagged down the bartender while I unearthed my coat. *Cassandra!* she cried. *I'm gonna call it a night.*

The bartender blew her a kiss. *We need to catch up. Call me, OK?*

Absolutely! She waved to her friends in the DJ booth. *See ya!* she shouted. *Be good.*

Then she took me by the hand and dragged us into the night. It took me a moment to register her parting words, why they felt so familiar, so oddly sinister. We were halfway down the block when it hit me. I froze, the sidewalk suddenly swimmy. *Emeline*, I said, laboring to keep my voice steady, *what did you just say?*

She looked up from her phone. *Huh?*

What did you say to your friends?

I said bye.

No, I said, staring at her. Her eyes were round, merry. She had sweat on her chin. *You told them to be good.*

Did I? She giggled. *Yeah, I guess that was dumb.*

Why did you say that?

She cocked her head, eyes wide. *I don't know. Do you think it was rude?*

I said nothing, balling and unballing my fists. I thought of her purse, slumped on the counter at work, stuffed with makeup and books. Was there a notebook in there too, a handful of red pens? When I'd gone through her purse hours earlier, I'd found nothing of the sort. But maybe I hadn't looked hard enough. Maybe one could write a note in cranberry-colored lip liner on a cocktail napkin or an ATM receipt.

What's wrong? Emeline asked. Her eyes got rounder. *Did I do something bad?*

I took a deep breath; I could see my car at the end of the block. *Emeline,* I said, but I couldn't finish the sentence. I studied her face, hunting for clues, but even at this late hour she was bright and blank. She looked worried for me, as if I were the loony one. I didn't think she could be such a good actress; then again, I barely knew her. Gifting me the wig, stealing my perfume . . . What did she want from me? I leaned against a parking meter, hugging myself. San Francisco was sinking, I could feel it; it was a city of tricksters and frauds, dead ends and trapdoors, people who weren't who they said they were. The Victorians built on landfill were sliding into the sea, the buses all read NOT IN SERVICE. Emeline watched me, and I could see, in a small but real way, that she was afraid of me. Not because she thought I'd hurt her, but because she didn't understand what was happening. She'd never seen somebody snap.

Forget it, I muttered. I began to walk toward my car, digging around for my keys. *You're totally fine. I'm . . . tired, that's all. I'm fucking exhausted.*

She stood on the sidewalk, chewing her lips, trying to compute, before joining me in the car. *I get it,* she said softly. She slid into the passenger seat, choosing compassion. *I'm tired too. It's gonna feel sooooooo good to get into bed.* She strapped on her seat belt. *I'd kill for a hot shower.*

Same. I started the car, feeling jumpy. I looked in the

rearview mirror twice to make sure we weren't being followed. There was a lone man, several blocks down, with Dino's build. He had dark hair and a hooked nose. He started walking toward us, arms outstretched, a hunky Frankenstein; I did a U-turn against incoming traffic and fled into the night.

Emeline played Taylor Swift off her phone and gave me directions to Charlie's house in Pac Heights. I pretended not to recognize the streets as we got closer and closer. How long had it been since I'd taken these exits? When was the last time I'd walked down these sidewalks, my mouth tasting of gin? The houses seemed somehow smaller than the last time I'd come around. Perhaps I was less impressionable now, less easily wowed by money. Perhaps I was more sober tonight than I'd ever been with him.

Pull up here, Emeline said, pointing to the curb. *It's best to park on the street. My dad gets pissy if he's blocked in. My house is just down there.*

We got out of the car and walked in silence. Everything around us looked fake, the cars and trees and mailboxes, as if we'd wandered onto a movie set. I felt that if I flicked this rosemary bush, it would fall over, revealing itself to be papier-mâché. *Emeline*, I said, my voice ringing out across the cul-de-sac. I felt slovenly, brash, and lowered my voice to a whisper. Rich people liked muted things. *You asked your dad if I could sleep over, right?*

Don't worry, she said, *he won't care.* She was engrossed in her phone, walking slow. *Sorry*, she said, eyes on her screen, *I filmed a TikTok last night and it kinda blew up.*

I peeked at her phone. She was playing and replaying a video entitled *AUTUMN HAUL* in which she tried on different outfits in various shades of brown. Her hair was in a wet-looking ponytail and her lips were a charming shade of pink I'd come to know as "bitten."

Wow, I said dumbly. *You look pretty.*

She paused the video on a frame of her in a chocolate-brown athletic romper. *Thanks*, she said distractedly. *This company sent me their clothes, but they're not really my style. If you want them, they're yours. I've got a huge pile I've been meaning to donate.* She glanced up, put her phone down. *This is us!*

We stood in front of a gate, number six. It looked just as I remembered it, black wrought-iron with curlicues, somehow Parisian. Beyond the gate was the garden, full of apple trees and roses Charlie had nothing to do with. The gardeners came daily. I knew that in one corner of the yard was a trampoline he'd bought for his daughter when she was five. *Not that she ever used it*, he'd complained over a game of strip pool in his condo downtown. The yard smelled familiar: vegetal and crisp with a tang from the sea, which was mere blocks away. I felt giddy, untouchable; but before I could open the gate and walk in, Emeline's phone dinged.

Speak of the devil, she said. *He just texted me.*

Who? I lurched away from the gate.

My dad, silly.

Oh. My mouth went dry. *What'd he say?*

He said he'll be home in ten minutes. He went to get pizza.

She giggled, as if this were funny. *He's asking if I want any-thing.* She typed her reply, then looked up at me, waiting. *Well?* she said, staring. *What do you want?*

This question razed me. I opened and closed my mouth, making little grunty sounds. *N-nothing,* I finally stammered. I felt myself backing up, frantically patting my pockets as I searched for my phone. Just like that, my courage drained away. *I'm sorry,* I panted, *but I just now remembered I have a thing, like, an appointment tomorrow. It's really super-early, like seven a.m. Fuck, I'm so sorry. I can't believe I forgot.*

Emeline squinted at me. *You have . . . an appointment?*

I nodded. *Mm-hm, I have, um, a pap smear. The Kaiser on Geary, you know . . .* I slapped myself on the forehead. *God, I'm so stupid. I really should go. We'll do this some other time?*

Oh . . . OK, sure. Emeline looked too tired to be upset. It had been a long night. *Whatever you need, babe.* She blew me a weary kiss. *Get home safe, OK?* She unlatched the gate. *See you at work?*

Absolutely, I said, smiling like a maniac. *Tell your dad I say hi.*

I got in my car and drove ten times around the block, radio blasting. I drove until I felt certain that Charlie was home. When I pulled up in front of their house, I could see his Mercedes-Benz parked in the half-open garage. I could see slivers of light through the gate and the nightmarish shapes of the garden at night. I rolled down my windows and could swear I heard laughter, wafting out from the kitchen where they sat and ate pizza. When the kitchen lights flicked off and the house went black, I got out of my car. I walked through the gate and into the garden. The trampoline was exactly where I remembered it, off to the side, under the apple trees. I crawled through the netting and lay on my back. I looked up at the stars through the netting, trying to count my breaths. All my wily energy from the bar was gone. My old slut-self had curled up, become needy and confused. What was I thinking, coming back here? What was the point of this prank? I knew for a fact Charlie wanted nothing from me. What, then, did I want from him? Once again he had made me feel like a fool, this time without even trying.

When at last I got up and drove home, the sky was soft pink. There was a call-in preacher on the radio, wailing about the Rapture. *You better get ready!* he howled. *Get your ducks in a row! God sees ALL. He doesn't have time for hide-and-seek!* Though this was the usual time I'd clock out from the club, it seemed so much later. I prayed that Ophelia was asleep. I opened Dino's door quietly, tiptoeing like a burglar. I dared not turn on any lights. I was crouched in the hallway, digging through my dance bag in search of my phone, when my fingers touched something silky. I brought my hand to my face and inspected the thing: Dino's silk hanky, baby blue with gold crosses. My stomach lurched. When he first went away, this scarf was my talisman, my lock of his hair. Now it was no more than a napkin, crumpled, dingy, smelling of baby powder and Soft Core. How could I have done this? I felt a wave of longing so powerful that I opened my mouth. I made an animal sound like, *Urrrggghhhhhhh.* Then, without thinking, I stuffed the scarf in my mouth. It shut me up like a gag. I fell to the floor, head in my hands. I lay there for a long, long time. I repeated to myself: *You are not OK, you are not good.* The logic follows, if you are not good, then you must be bad. I felt bad to the bone. Eventually the dogs came down-stairs and circled me. They nudged with their noses. Naomi mounted my back and stood on my shoulders like a conquis-tador, conducting weather with her whiskers. She growled empathetically.

At last I rose, picked up my bag. I held Naomi under my arm like a purse. I fed the girls and refilled their bowls, then forced myself to drink a glass of water. I was reminded of something my mother had told me. It was right after my father died, when the house felt cavernous without him. We'd get into the car to go to school and my mother would auto-matically sit in the passenger seat, waiting for him to drive. I slept every night in one of his sweaters, though it smelled more like me than like him. One time I walked into the kit-chen to see if tonight was a night we'd eat dinner (it wasn't). My mother was standing at the kitchen sink, wearing paja-mas. This was back when at least her pajama sets matched. The water was on full blast and she was watching it run. *What are you doing?* I asked.

She saw me and smiled. *Water is good for you,* she said. *No matter what happens, remember to drink water. Even if you're not thirsty.* Then she put her head in the sink and drank from the faucet. She guzzled it down as if parched. When at last she was satisfied, she stood up and wiped her mouth with her sleeve. *Ahhhh,* she sighed. The water was still running. She turned and looked past me. *Your turn.*

Sometimes I forgot the name of my club. We dancers just called it work, as in, *See ya at work tonight!* When I heard a man say the name aloud, I got shivers. There was a pink neon sign over the entrance; I have a picture of it on my phone, taken at 3:30 a.m. after close, so I know I'm not making this up. It flashed: PARADISE LOST. That was my club, my sly little home just south of the city, though the place has long since shuttered and I've lost touch with all the girls. I heard that it became a gym and then a movie theater—places that, like strip clubs, dealt in bodies; air-conditioned tombs with flesh on display and a spectral promise of betterment.

Our club was known for dirt-cheap happy hour and a monthly swingers' night. The floor was always sticky; the VIP rooms stank of Lysol and the clove cigarettes Cookie not-so-secretly smoked. An industrial fog machine chugged in one corner, beheading the girls. There were nights when you only saw thighs, poking out from the fog. One time I found a tooth, a real human tooth, when I picked up my tips. Someone had thrown it onstage.

If I close my eyes, I can still see that sign, blinkering pink against the night sky. We had a reputation for the cheapest lap dances and sleepiest girls. *Why are they so SHY?* a disgruntled client wrote on Yelp. *Aren't THEY supposed to come to YOU? What happened to THE HUSTLE?* Perhaps the fog machine was partly to blame, as it made it hard for us to see. You had to walk slowly in your seven-inch heels, maneuvering the haze. After an hour or so, your eyes would adjust. You would see the men gathered around the horseshoe-shaped stage, hungry, gentle, and depraved. You felt yourself open, like a nocturnal flower. Only then did you let yourself be seen.

Dino was no saint. Even in his absence, I knew this. He was moody, controlling. He had always been secretive, about work and other things too. He refused to talk about his romantic past. In the early days of our love, I would blab about Charlie and Dusty, who hurt me and how, girlishly expecting reciprocity. I wanted us to dress each other's wounds. But when it was his turn to talk, he would affect a yawn and say, *Time for bed.*

Sometimes, late at night, I would walk into the kitchen to find him talking on the phone. When he saw me he'd hang up. *Who were you talking to?* I'd ask.

Why? He would smile and squeeze my waist. *Are you jealous?*

No, I'd say. *I'm just asking.*

Aren't I allowed to have a life of my own?

Of course, I'd say quickly. *It's not like that.*

He would kiss my hair. *You have nothing to worry about.*

I believed him.

There was only one ex-flame of Dino's that I knew anything about, a wannabe artist named Daria. She had fried hair and a tubular body. In pictures online her tummy stuck out like a toddler's. Her face reminded me of raisin bread, puffy white with dark flecks. Apparently she struggled with things like being on time and holding down jobs. She now lived with her parents after failing to make an art career happen. She and Dino met one summer long ago, had a fling, and haltingly kept in touch.

When Dino spoke about her, I felt nothing, no jealousy or threat. That's not quite true: I felt confused. It disturbed me, a little, that Dino had found this girl noteworthy. Everything I learned about her disappointed me. I'd thought of Dino as someone with exquisite taste. Had I been duped? Moreover, who or what would I see in my bed once the clouds of love parted? After that adrenal glow had run its course? I feared that I'd find, in either Dino or myself, an equal to this dumpy chick. For this, I hated her. I wished, paradoxically, that his ex was sexy or cool, if only to confirm the grandiose devotion I felt for my man. Kissing Dino made me feel like a winner, and I couldn't bear any proof to the contrary. Stubby Daria with her scrunched-up face and broken dreams was proof of something common in him, something that didn't sit right.

Mazzy put it best. We were holed up at the Geary Club one weekday evening, drinking martinis. Mazzy was stalking her current lover's ex-girlfriend online, a self-professed yoga priestess named Clementine. *Ugh!* she shrieked, throwing her phone on the table. *I can't believe this basic bitch and I have a dick in common!*

I laughed into my cocktail. *I know exactly what you mean.*

One morning Daria followed my Instagram and liked all my pictures, every single one. Her account was private, but I recognized her smooshed little face. I told Dino at breakfast.

That's weird, he muttered, absentmindedly munching. *Why would she do that? She doesn't know who you are.*

What? I stood up, heart pounding. The kitchen went sideways. *We've been dating for almost two years and your ex doesn't know who I am?*

He looked caught. *Well*, he stammered, *I'd hardly call her an ex. Also, we rarely talk. And whenever we do, we just talk about her. She's having a tough time. She needs me to listen. You know, as a friend.*

Oh! I said. *How sad for her. Why don't you call her right now and be a good friend? Don't let me stop you.*

I stormed out of the kitchen and into my room. I stayed there all day long.

In truth, I didn't think he was trying to string Daria along, nor did I think he was cheating on me. The logic behind his secrecy was far stranger, more damning. In some ways it was worse than an infidelity because I didn't know how to process it. What hurt me, really, was the idea that he hadn't wanted to show me off, brag a bit, tell his so-called friend that he was happy. It was one thing to keep his past affairs hush-hush, the flings with hard-drinking chicks that had no effect on his life. But for him to keep me, his present-day girlfriend, a secret? The woman he loved, who kissed his mouth daily? It made no sense. It hurt me more than anything he'd said or done before. It hurt worse than his disappearance; at least that was in character for him and the men I had known.

We made up, of course, but I never really forgave him. I still loved him, ferociously, but the bruise remained. I felt it on the apex of my heart, the betrayal. He didn't need me like I needed him. I could believe his soft-voiced explanations— *She never asks about my love life, Ruth, we only speak about her family, she's insecure, it slipped my mind*—but I couldn't un-know what I now knew: What I thought I owed him was different from what he thought he owed me. I'd been ready to give him everything; meanwhile, all he had to give was love.

Stupid puny love. It followed me around like a stray dog, this knowledge of his heartlessness. Not that he was a heartless person, but that his heart had not been with mine that night or morning when they FaceTimed, when Daria dished out her soggy woes, when she crawled to him for guidance. Perhaps I sound like the heartless one. I just wish that he had thought of me, that I'd been on his mind. He'd never not been on my mind since the day we first met. That was the difference between us. He was my deity; I was his girl.

That was the beginning of the end. I began to pull away, go cold. Though I believed he'd been faithful, I couldn't move on. Some deeply held suspicion had now been confirmed: our love was unequal, impermanent. I'd been a fool to think otherwise. Now I looked stupid for loving this man so wholly. Moreover, I wasn't cut out for love. It wore me out, the paranoia and shame, the butterflies in my pussy. Loneliness was my number, my go-to karaoke song. I'd known this all along but got caught up in the game. We broke up maybe three months later. I tried to follow Daria on Instagram; she blocked me instantly.

Sometimes when I went on my walks I fantasized about bumping into Nobody. They seemed like the type to wander at night. I imagined a meet-cute, a cinematic coincidence. They would be dressed in a trench coat, tall and thin. Not hotter than me, but not hideous either. We would recognize each other from across the street. We would approach, hug, then laugh nervously. *Fancy meeting you here*, they'd mutter. They would be somehow familiar. They'd have Simon's sad eyes but Dino's elegant bearing. Their voice would be mellow; perhaps they'd be smoking a cigarette.

Can I get a drag of that? I would ask, just for something to say.

I didn't know you smoked.

I don't.

They would laugh, a real laugh from their diaphragm. *Me neither.*

Then what do you call that? I'd point to their lit cigarette.

This? They would take a long drag, then step closer and blow smoke in my face. *This is a death wish.* The smell of jasmine would thicken the air.

Wow, I would say like a girl in a movie, *you totally get me.*

The fantasy would fade before any contact was made. I didn't think I wanted to fuck Nobody. If it happened, that would be fine, but the contact I craved was deeper. I already knew their darkest secret, something they hid from their lovers and friends. I was in so fucking deep now. My scanty desires had grafted to theirs; now we dreamed of similar motifs. Father figures, dying flowers . . . I was a kiss away from total ownership. But who or what did I own? Had I been bamboozled? I wanted to touch them and seal the deal. I wanted to smoosh our chests together and feel their heart beating, proof that they were, for the moment, with me.

The Monday after my thwarted sleepover with Emeline, I had a session at Dream House with someone named Albert. Or at least he was Albert when he first walked in. As soon as we were upstairs in the Red Room and the door was closed, she was Allie. Albert was a family man; Allie was a mouthy skank. She wore a microscopic fishnet dress and brought a gym bag stuffed with platform heels.

I'm kinda addicted, she said, giggling. *To shoes. It's a problem. Will you model some for me?*

Her face lit up. *Sure!*

First she put on a gnarled ass-length wig, eggplant-purple with glittery streaks. Then she showed off her Pleasers, pair after pair. Some had never been worn before, still in their boxes, an archive of smut. There was at least $4,000 worth of stripper shoes in that bag. She catwalked down the middle of the room, hands on her hips, lips studiously puckered.

Allie, I asked, *how do you afford all these shoes?*

She twirled in a pair of white patent over-knee boots. *Well*, she said, *I have a sugar daddy.*

Hot! What's his name?

She blinked at me. *Albert.*

She minced over to the bed and sat down beside me, suddenly pensive. *Sometimes Albert gets pissed at me because of my, uh, addiction.* She sighed, twining her fingers in her wig. It drooped around her like a space blanket. *Every few months, I go through a purge.*

A purge?

He makes me throw them all away.

ALL your shoes?

She nodded. *Uh-huh. I usually throw them off a bridge.*

But why?

It's complicated. She bit her raspberry-pink lip. *Albert's wife is a snoopy bitch. Sometimes she gets suspicious of us. He makes me destroy all the evidence.*

I took her hand and squeezed it. *That bitch.*

She's OK, I guess. Allie rolled her eyes. *It's not her fault she's jealous of me.*

Well, I said, *can you blame her?*

Allie smiled. *Not really.* She sprang up from the bed. *Can I show you my other collection?*

Of course.

She changed into a pair of rhinestone-encrusted stilettos. *For comfort*, she explained. Then she turned her duffel bag inside out and shook out a series of dildos. They alternated in length from shot glass to corncob to forearm, a few in the shape of octopus tentacles. One was designed to look exactly like an Oscar statuette. She squatted over a waterproof sheet and lowered herself onto a pineapple-sized biggie. I watched in amazement as she bounced up and down, her wig in her face. *Damn*, I cried. *You're a pro.*

You should see me when I'm warmed up! she shouted. *I'm just getting started!*

As she bounced, the straps from her heels dug into the flesh of her ankles, leaving thin lines. When she finally plunked down beside me on the bed, I pulled her legs across mine and massaged her ankles. The skin there was leaf-thin and lightly speckled.

We don't want Albert's wife to suspect anything, I said, rubbing the marks until they faded. *You know?*

She nodded, suddenly winded. *True*, she murmured. *She's very perceptive.* Her sparkle was dimming as the hour came to a close. *She's very smart.*

I patted her thigh. *We'll keep this between us.*

She smiled, extracting strands of her wig from her lip gloss. *OK,* she said. She stuck out her finger. *Pinkie-promise?*

I hooked mine with hers. *Pinkie-promise.*

I helped her fit her dildos and heels back into the gym bag. If you saw her on the train, you'd think she was headed to CrossFit. She put on her Patagonia fleece over the fishnet dress. The last thing to go was the tatty wig, which she bunched up like paperwork and stuffed, miraculously, into her jacket pocket. She blew me a kiss and said, *I know the way out.* She walked out wearing loafers.

As I was cleaning the room, I found some stray purple hairs on the carpet, coiled into question marks. Thinking about Allie made my heart hurt. She had what my mom liked to call a million-dollar smile. I thought of the money she'd spent on high heels, her brand-new Pleasers drowned like kittens. What a shame. I fantasized about bringing her with me to the strip club. She could buy a new wig, bust out her sluttiest platforms. If someone were to ask how we knew each other, I'd pull her close. *Isn't it obvious?* I'd purr. *She's my twin.* By the rules of the night, it would have to be true. All men present were my daddies and all women were my sisters. We kissed on the lips and drank from the same glass, we shared the same look—starry, vague—in our eyes. We just wanted to feel good.

Sometimes, when everything got a bit much, I closed my eyes and thought of Charlie. If a dude was rude to me at the club or Hugo scolded me for not recharging the vibrators, I locked myself in the bathroom and thought, Fuck Charlie.

Intellectually, of course, I knew these grievances had nothing to do with him. Our stop-and-start arrangement was forever ago. Should he cross paths with a place like Dream House, I was sure he would find it sordid and sad. When we were together, I was gifted access to his innermost sexual world. It was as tidy and muted as his wife's walk-in closet. He sometimes joked about paying another girl to join us in bed (*How about a spicy Latina?*), but he never did. He was too insecure to introduce another pair of eyes into the mix. He knew that I tolerated, even enjoyed, what he had, and this was enough for him.

You're easygoing, he'd say, petting my hair. *Men like that. They say they want a smoke show, but easygoing is better.*

For all his insomniac wandering, he was a fundamentally conservative dude who valued status and norms. His deepest desire, as far as I knew, was a cabin in Lake Tahoe to offset the house in Santa Barbara. He already had the beach; now he wanted the snow. Who knows, maybe in the intervening years he'd bought it. The nicest thing he could say about something was that it was high quality. I can sift through my cookie tin of memories for all the times he held out a glass of Merlot or a Swiss watch and declared, *Such high quality!* He even said it about a woman he worked with. We were lying in bed, indulging in the mildest form of postcoital gossip, i.e., talking about work. He was describing the intern, a willowy twenty-something who'd just transferred in from the New York office.

She's got a really good head on her shoulders, he'd said. *The quality of her ideas is surprisingly high. If she wanted, she could probably model.* I remember feeling jealous and changing the subject.

The libidinal underworld to which I belonged was as foreign to Charlie as gay bars or food banks. Still, he was my first foray into what you'd call sex work. He would claim he gave me money as a favor, but at the end of the day, he gave me money for sex. People saw us in restaurants and thought he was my father. We had sex and then he paid me, or sometimes he paid me and then we had sex. It was like waitressing but supercharged. And sometimes it was fun. Sometimes I felt like I was hacking the system, using my just-OK body to plunder the rich and help the meek to inherit. I made the mangy dreams of mild men come true. I wrote off manicures as business expenses, I sometimes grossed more than Charlie's hourly wage. I got paid to listen, to be told I was pretty, to wear sparkly things and dance to songs that I loved. Sometimes all of this really was true and my life was a bildungsroman.

Sometimes, though, things soured. I'd leave work feeling gunky, iffy, dotty, dazed, and though I stayed in the bath until long after dinnertime, I still couldn't get clean. This filth was not moral or social but intercellular. I'd been contaminated by male longing, operatic and shabby. I was paid to be a beam of light while dudes displayed their darkness. I carried their essences home with me, the secret stuff they'd never tell their wives or friends or therapists. *Don't repeat this to anyone*, they whispered, *or else.* How could I? Where would I even begin? Try as I might to have boundaries, shit still oozed in. I found myself hurting on their behalf, furious at someone named Sharon. On off days I was penetrated (by their bitterness, their grief, their BO) and I went home feeling, for lack of a better word, used.

Ophelia helped me cope. She put essential oils on my pressure points and guided me into hip-opening yoga poses. *The hips*, she said, *carry so much emotion.* After work we got cozy and dozy and didn't judge each other for our emptiness. It felt so good to zone out after hours of being zeroed in. Sitcoms put my mind at ease; I liked the levity with which sex and desire were discussed. The merry mess of one-night stands or sex with your boss was tidily resolved in twenty minutes or less. I preferred one-dimensional characters; they were trustworthy. You were either the nerd or the sexpot, funny or hot, Miranda or Samantha, no secret selves or second names allowed.

Ophelia understood what I needed. I hated talking about the bad days, especially with people not in our world. I didn't want to field their pity, their gentle suggestion that I "phase out of this lifestyle" or however they'd word it. *Show me a lifestyle that feels good all the time*, I wanted to shout. *Prove to me that your lifestyle is insured against longing. Show me a pie chart, a breakdown of breakdowns, the data on anguish.* Maybe then I'd consider going back to school. Maybe then I'd throw my Pleasers away (off a bridge, maybe?) and become a nurse or accountant, but only if someone could promise I'd never feel dirty. Until then, I had TV and blankets and rosemary oil to help with the bad days. I had good days when I felt divine and men cried in my arms. I had a duffel bag of singles hidden under the bed, an amount I couldn't fathom. For however I felt about Charlie and the nature of our relationship, it was too late now. I was in it. Baby was born.

The very first night that I danced at the club, Dino stayed up to greet me when I came home around dawn. He didn't ask me how it went. Instead, we sat together on the sofa and he rubbed my feet, unrecognizably mangled by my brand-new shoes. I'd failed to break them in. My blisters bled and my body ached and I felt happy and afraid. In a soft, rough voice he sang to me the only song he knew by heart: *Do you belieeeeve in life after love* . . .

He sang until I fell asleep, my feet still in his hands.

This time around, he and I met at the bus stop.

It was a Saturday afternoon and I woke up before noon with the sudden strange urge to go shopping. Ophelia was out and I had nothing better to do. I took the 1 to the boutiques on Fillmore Street and bought Ethiopian coffee beans, hand-dipped candles with names like Vespers and Death Drive, a face wash made from volcanic ash, $30 lip liner the color of dried blood. Really, I think, I just wanted an excuse to enter the world. I wore my hair down and had a warm farro salad with a glass of prosecco for lunch. I ate outside and smiled at the men smiling at me. They didn't notice me paying in fistfuls of ones. I was cosplaying as a normal girl, someone happy, clean, and healthy. I was some of those things, usually at least one of them, but never all at the same time.

Around 4:30 p.m. I headed back home. I was planning to get to the club early that night, to debut my new lip liner. I got off at California and Hyde, and there he was, sitting at the bus stop. He was wearing old Wranglers and reading a paperback. I could tell from the colorful, slightly raised cover that it was a drugstore romance novel. His nose looked monumental. I stared at him until he noticed me. He glanced up from his book, eyes glassy with tears.

Hi, he said.

Hi. I answered without thinking.

He swiped at his eyes. *Sorry.* He waved the book in the air. *I didn't see that one coming.*

I felt like I was in a dream, the words floating from my lips. *That's OK.*

He smiled and the world contracted. All the hills of San Francisco were leveled by that smile. *You live around here?*

Not really. What game was he was playing now? At first it was hide-and-seek, now it was charades. Of course, I'd play along too, pretend not to know every inch of him. I felt like I was a waitress and he was a very rich patron. *And you?*

He shook his head. *I just got off work and I'm trying to get into trouble.*

You're in luck, I said, lapsing into stripper mode. Flirtation came easily. *Trouble is my middle name.*

He smirked. *And what about your first?*

My what?

Your first name. He rose and held out one hand. *I'm Dino.*

Dino, I said carefully, taking his hand. It filled me with warmth, exactly as if I'd put my hand on a radiator. I studied his face for a clue, but he gave nothing away. His expression was cheerful, his body relaxed. He looked like a man whom luck generally favored, the type you would ask to blow on your dice. He didn't look like a man who was fucking with me. *I'm Baby.*

Baby, he said, hands on his hips. He savored the word. *I like that.*

Thanks.

Would you mind if I called you babe?

I kept waiting for him to break character. *Be my guest.*

I'd like to be. He winked. *Your guest.*

Are you asking to come home with me?

He smiled, faux-bashful. *Hang on, missy. Don't get ahead of yourself. How about a drink? We'll get a drink at a bar and then I'll come home with you.* He set his book on the bench and began walking uphill. I could make out the title: *Dream Angel, Forever.* I hastened to keep up.

Hey, I called. *What about your book?*

He waved one hand. *Leave it*, he said. *I know how it ends.*

We walked up the street to a bar I'd always passed and never been to, a dank neighborhood dive called the Hyde Out. We sat upstairs and drank IPAs, speaking like strangers. What's your favorite color? Do you like scary movies? There was a little dish of peanuts on the table. We compulsively cracked them as we spoke, sweeping the shells to one side. We didn't eat the peanuts, we just broke them open for something to do. When we left, the floor around our table was covered with husks. They crunched underfoot as he helped me into my coat. My mouth tasted like the circus; the beer went to my head. Dino held my elbow as we walked into the street.

Whoa now, he said, like I was a skittish horse. *Easy there.*

I'm easy, I said. I looked up at him imploringly, begging him to drop the act. *That's what they all say.*

He put his hands on his hips, not taking the bait. *Who's they?*

Oh, I said. *Wouldn't you like to know?*

I would, he said. *I would like to know.*

He buttoned my coat for me. Unlike during our first first date in Chinatown, I didn't look awful. This time around I was wearing a black leather skirt and a long-sleeved black leotard of Ophelia's. She was out with Lorenzo's parents at a fancy hotel with a view of the city. They were visiting from Sicily, which meant that Lorenzo would play the part of devoted boyfriend for the entirety of their two-week stay. I'd never seen Ophelia happier, touching up her cheeks with something called fairy dust as she got ready to meet them for aperitivo. She wouldn't be home until Monday. I'd planned to work that night, but now I knew I wouldn't. I looked at Dino and he looked at me. From where we stood on the corner, you could see both edges of the city. To the east, the civic mishmash of the piers, donuts and crabs and burnt coffee; to the west, the hills squiggling pinkly all the way out to the sea. There the fog lay in wait, a thick band on the horizon. In no time we'd be whited out.

You want to come home with me, I said, too loud. The longer we played this game, the more I liked it. It was fun to be strangers, shiny and new.

He nodded. *I want to come home with you.*

All right, I said, shrugging. *Come home.*

He stuck out his hand to hail a taxi, something no one did anymore. It was moments like these when he revealed his age, his thirty-seven years on earth. I liked dating older men because they were well acquainted with loss. They'd seen the rise and fall of rock and roll, good drugs, cheap rent. Their favorite bars had closed, their friends had died, the city had papered over their youth. Having weathered more shit, they were patient with me. They liked to solve my little dramas because it made them feel powerful. They couldn't bring their friends back from the dead, but they could fix my radiator, hang my curtains, hold me until I fell asleep. *Do you believe in life after love* . . . Sure, they were less ravishing now, their bodies ragged and libidos blunted; their lady-killing ways had paled and now they valued things like Costco cards and narrative tension. I didn't mind. San Francisco would forget them, but I would remember. Miraculously, a taxi appeared. Dino held the door for me and smiled like a millionaire. *I thought you'd never ask.*

That was how we ended up sleeping together for the first time again.

The very first time, I was jittery and unprepared. At twenty-five I was so filled with lust it made me klutzy, tripping over my tongue. I shook too much for buttons or zippers. While undoing my bra, one lover had to literally say, *Hold still a second.* It's hard to remember my very first time with Dino; I see it in fragments. A patchwork of body parts, lamplight, and lines poached from porn. *You like that, baby? Oh yeah, oh yeah.* We hadn't yet uncovered our mutual love for getting high, how it made our bodies blameless. The sex was passable. "Avalon" by Roxy Music played in the background. Without saying anything, he'd tried to finger my ass. I swatted him away and mumbled something like, *Not today.* He was graceful about moving on. I wanted to kiss him all night, practicing my vowels. *Ahh eee ooo uuu* . . . But then he took off my pants. He was efficient and gentlemanly, not rough but not gentle. He came into a little yellow washrag embroidered with ducks. Shortly thereafter, I pretended to come too.

The morning after our very first time, he brought me coffee on a silver tray with a separate dish for cream. This gesture touched me more deeply than our hurried, dim sex. I watched his movements, how carefully he watered his plants and opened his blinds. How intimate, to see him cup his spider fern and pluck the dead leaves from its stem. I wanted to be touched like that, like I was something precious that he owned, whose health relied on him.

The second first time we slept together, everything was different. He was still the last person to come inside me. I had a buzz from the beer and my leotard smelled like Ophelia. Moreover, we were protected by our little game. He wasn't him and I wasn't me, there was no history to wrangle, no past to undo. We forgot the strain and betrayal, the shared decay. Tonight I could be The One and he could be A Stud and nobody would call our bluff. I wasn't afraid because I wasn't myself; I was someone me-shaped from a dream, with bigger tits and longer hair, with more courage and less hang-ups. When I led him into his house, he looked around and whistled. *Nice place.*

I'll say. I threw my keys in the bowl. *Hungry?*

He walked behind me, arms crossed. *In a way.*

When I took him upstairs to his bedroom, he gave nothing away. He was such a good actor. He sat on the bed, running his hands over the mustard-colored bedspread. *Pretty color,* he said. The dogs swirled around him, eyes wet with joy. Naomi clambered onto his lap and touched her nose to his. *They like me,* he said, chuckling, pretending to be surprised. He picked each dog up and kissed her in between the eyes. *I'm good with animals.*

I stood in front of him, his nose level with my belly button. *So what does that make me?*

He smiled, undoing his coat. *A lucky duck.*

We fucked with no music. We kept most of our clothes on, forming slits where we needed them. We moved in slow motion, like cats feeling things in the dark. It was a staring contest with impossible stakes. He told me to do things and then watched as I tried. If I didn't do it right, he had me do it again. *Focus,* he chided, cool as a king. *Tsk, tsk.* The sheets turned to orange juice. I felt funny and flayed. I was his crucifix, fingered in times of distress; I could fit in his pocket, on a chain around his neck. He squeezed my middle until I saw stars. I found his eyes in the dark room and begged for more, please. He laughed, so meanly, in my mouth. He was a bully and I loved it. *Don't get ahead of yourself.*

The dogs lay in a line on the floor the whole time. They were quiet, watching, waiting. Who knows what they thought we were doing? Grooving or grieving . . . When we were finally done, they jumped on the bed. Old Dino would have shooed them off. This Dino gathered them up in his arms, pretend-biting their ears. *Silly little geese,* he said. *What are your names? I love you, I love you.*

I love you too.

We fell asleep all jumbled together like shirts in the wash. When I awoke around 3:00 a.m., he was still there. He was asleep, with Naomi tucked into his armpit. Relief flooded my body, better than orgasm. Whatever this was, it was real, or real enough. I was delusional, yes, but no more so than any other girl with a crush. I touched his cheek. It felt like the rubber ball he used to throw for the dogs; where had that gone? Another thing lost. Naomi whined in her sleep, her front legs moving uselessly. Someone told me, long ago, that when a dog did this, it meant she was running in her dreams. I placed a hand on her rump until she quieted down. Then I slipped out of bed and stood in the yard. I wanted to make a deal with the devil: *Please don't let this night end.* I wanted to stay in this moment forever, chilly and worshipful, cum streaked on my thighs. In the moonlight the grass looked like teeth. The air smelled of rosemary. I would sell my firstborn child, I would chop off my long hair, whatever fairy-tale currency was asked of me. Anything to stay here and watch the moon blanch the weeds, suspended in disbelief.

The next morning I awoke to find Dino beside me, thoroughly knocked out. He slept on his belly with his face in his arms, just like I remembered. I suppose I had expected him to disappear in the night. Watching him now in the weak morning light, his thick bare arms and cheeks made greasy by Vaseline, I felt an old fear—primal and senseless, an amoebic rush. It was not the same fear I felt when he first went away but a fear that had been with me far longer. It was the quick terror I used to feel whenever he used his shoehorn or cuddled the dogs, when he bit his lip while doing math, this debilitating rush of tenderness that made me want to scream. *Watch out!* I wanted to bellow. *I can't bear if you get hurt!* But we were alone in a warmly lit house, the doors and windows latched; the only person for him to watch out for was me. I was the monster under the bed, trembling at the splendor of the back of his head. It was this sort of fear that I felt that Sunday morning, Dino finally home again, snoozing in the nude.

What did I do? I got up and went to church. Only God could quell my ache. Dino didn't stir as I dressed in a hurry, turning my soaked-through panties inside out and hiding my body in a cardigan. I took the express bus to Valencia Street and sat in the very last pew. The church ladies smiled at me, undeterred by my sex stink. The pastor spoke of selflessness, of service. *Make your body into a house for the Lord*, he intoned. *You need to let God in. When the time is right, the Lord will come home and turn on ALL the lights.* He thumped his heart. *He knows where you keep the spare key.*

After church I bought a baguette and walked home. It was a week before Christmas and you could feel it in the air: a muted zing, both humble and festive, strings of light on the lampposts, the gigantic tree in Union Square. No matter how old I got, I still felt a tingle when I saw that damn tree.

When I got home around noon, Dino was still there. He was sitting on the couch, fully dressed, drinking coffee from the I ♥ DADDY mug I'd gifted him. I entered the room slowly; his back was to me. He was facing the TV, though nothing was on. The dogs were splayed around him, snoozing. I felt betrayed by their insouciance, as if the sorrow we'd weathered was nothing to them. What about our lonely nights, our wailing at the moon? Like bad friends, they forgot everything in the presence of a big hunky man. I couldn't blame them; I did it too. I stood a few feet away, just watching him breathe.

Howdy, he said when he saw me. He set his mug down on a coaster. *You're back.*

I'm back. I held up the baguette. *Have you eaten?*

I just made a coffee. I hope that's OK.

Of course, I said. *Make yourself at home.*

He chuckled in a way that confused me. Was he giving up the shtick? Would he finally come home to me? But then he stood up and pulled me to him, hands encircling my waist. *You're a very good host*, he whispered into my neck.

I try, I said.

He bumped his pelvis against mine. *You're trying very, very hard.*

We had sex on the living room floor, then again in the kitchen with the screen door ajar. By the time we sat down to eat, the baguette had gone stale.

Don't worry, he said. *I got this.* He started cooking plantains, eggs, tomatoes. He cut the baguette into pieces, buttered them generously, and fried them in fat. I noticed that he seemed to know exactly where everything was in the kitchen, the cast-iron and coconut oil and good silverware, though he did stop to ask if I ate cheese.

I eat everything, I said.

Good girl.

He plated our feast and refilled our coffees. He'd used an

entire carton of eggs. *Wow*, I said, pretending to be shocked. *Where'd you learn to cook so good?*

He shrugged. *I picked things up here and there.* He pointed to my plate. *You better eat while it's hot.*

I held my fork in the air. *Yes, sir.*

As we ate I was reacquainted with that glorious postcoital hunger. It was one of the things I'd loved most about sleeping around: the private bliss of settling into my bed, still leaking a stranger's juices, and eating the snacks I'd accrued on the long journey home. Gummy worms, Oreos, seltzer, saltines. Out with my date earlier in the night I would purposefully eat very little, so as to (A) compound my drunkenness, (B) minimize my bloat, and (C) save myself for this ritual. As I feasted in bed, I would think of an expression I'd heard my mom use to describe girls on *The Bachelor* when we watched it together: *She's a bottomless pit.* It felt true. Post-pounding, I was at home in my role as a hole. I felt both queenly and gross, indulging what felt like an innate need to be filled.

Now, in the sunlit kitchen, I piled my plate. When at last we were finished, he leaned back in his chair.

Phew, he said. *I feel great.*

Me too.

He looked at the digital clock on the oven and I felt my heart sink. *Looks like I better get going*, he said.

Really?

Yeah. He reached across the table for my hand. *I don't wanna wear out my welcome.*

I tried to keep my voice level. *You won't.*

He smiled. *That's what they all say.*

I wouldn't let go of his hand. *When will I see you again?* It was the question that had dogged me for the entirety of our date. What I wanted to ask was: *When will this game end?*

He pretended to think. *How about Thursday?*

That felt unbearably far away. I forced myself to smile. *I don't know, I work at eight that night.*

What do you do?

I'm an exotic dancer. I surprised myself by using this term. I usually just said stripper.

Dino raised his eyebrows. *For real?*

For real.

He sat still, digesting this information. His surprise seemed so genuine. Then he stood up and seized me in a hug. He bit down on my shoulder, making little chewing sounds. *Maybe I'll come by and see you then.*

On Thursday? At the club?

Uh-huh.

I tried to look up at him, but his grip was too tight. *Why?*

I like the idea of it, he said. *I want to watch men fall in love with you. I want to watch them want you, knowing that you're mine.* He chomped down on my neck. *All mine.*

OK, I whispered. It was all I could say. I had a bad feeling about this plan, but I wanted more than anything to please him. In love, I was obeisant. I was so low-maintenance as to scarcely exist. I was a mattress designed for his weight—squishy and giving. Test me out, break me in. I conformed to his body and lived in the bedroom, begging to be crushed.

That Wednesday, at Dream House, I had a session with Michelangelo, 9/12/97. He was younger than me, which was rare at the dungeon. He had long frizzy hair that partially shielded his face. He looked like someone who would work at Guitar Center. When we entered the Red Room, he took off his shoes.

You don't have to do that, I said.

Oh. He made no move to put them back on.

Well. I stood with my hands on my hips. He'd booked an hour-long session with me over the phone and given no details besides wanting someone "nice, not too mean, a little mean, but not too much." Everyone else was booked but me. *What did you have in mind?*

He looked down. *Do you happen to do, um, role-play?*

Of course.

His face lit up. *Excellent!* He reached for his backpack and pulled out two spiral-bound scripts, each an inch thick. In typewriter font on the cover, it read: *McBeth.* He handed me one. *This one's yours. I highlighted your lines in yellow.*

Oh.

I've been working on this for the last few months. When he stepped closer, I could smell peach schnapps on his breath. *It's an erotic adaptation of* Macbeth. *You know, by Shakespeare.*

I nodded. *I'm familiar.*

I took some liberties in modernizing it. Lady McBeth is the Mistress of a brothel just outside Vegas. The three witches are Midwestern tourists. And McBeth himself is an Elvis impersonator, determined to be the best one on the Strip. Ambition drives him mad.

I see. I flipped through the script and spied a line of dialogue: *O, curse this hellish corset! I long to free my marbled flesh . . .*

Michelangelo started to swing his arms in wide circles,

vibrating his lips like a horse. *Red leather, yellow leather, red leather, yellow leather.* He turned to me. *Shall we start with a cold read?*

I sat down on the bed. *Sure.*

We were a few pages in when he motioned for me to stop. *I'm sorry*, he said, *but could we start again?*

Is something wrong?

No . . . But could you try it again with a little more sex appeal?

I felt a wave of indignation. *More sex appeal?*

If possible, yes.

I pursed my lips. *I don't know if that suits my character. Lady McBeth seems rather reserved to me.*

You think? Michelangelo furrowed his brows. *I see her as more extroverted. More vixeny, you know? Channel your inner goddess, if you can.*

I took a deep breath. *All right*, I said. *I'll try.*

He smiled and tapped the crown of his head. *From the top!*

It wasn't long before he asked me to stop again. *What's wrong?* I asked. *Not sexy enough?*

Not quite, he said. *It's just . . .*

Just what?

You look so sad.

I put down my script. *Sad?*

Or something like that. He studied my face. *Are you sure you're OK?*

I took a deep breath. *I'm fine.*

He smiled in a way that was supposed to be reassuring. *The theater can bring up a lot of emotions.*

I forced myself to smile back. *No*, I said, *I'm fine.*

It was a long and grueling hour. I'd never ended a session

feeling so unsexy. Still, when I walked him downstairs, his
spirits were high.

We'll keep at it, he said. *This was a good run. Characters take
time to develop. Keep at your craft, K?*

K. I tried to hand him my script, but he jolted backward.

That's for you, he said. *To practice.*

Ah. I held the door open for him. *Gotcha.*

As soon as he left, I threw his script in the trash. I grabbed
a Diet Coke and locked myself in the upstairs bathroom. I
stared at my reflection, a pale, sleepy girl. Her eyes were
bagged and her mouth curved down. I saw my mother when
I smiled, that misty squinty look. I could be a lot of things,
but not a sexy girl. It was something I'd known for a long
time, though Michelangelo was the first to state it so plainly.
On sexy girls like Emeline or Ophelia, sadness was alluring.
It was mysterious and sensitive, inviting love songs and free
drinks. *Hey there honey, why so blue?* On me, sadness was
grimy and rumpled, see-through in all the wrong places.
Sometimes a hole is just a hole.

I turned on the faucet and washed my hands. My birthday
was coming up, though I hadn't told anyone. Would getting
older make sadness look better on me? More seasoned, more
ripe? I chugged my Diet Coke and went downstairs. I lost
myself in folding laundry, avoiding Hugo's eye. She was a
woman who wore her sadness like bracelets. It didn't look
especially good or bad, just natural, akin to crow's-feet and
low breasts. I didn't feel like talking; fortunately, neither did
she. She sat at the kitchen table, reading a magazine for rubber fetishists. She didn't seem particularly moved by it. She
read with a furrowed brow, humming to herself. Every so

often, she'd tap her fingers on the tabletop, her nails ringed with garden dirt, and mutter, *Damn.*

I left the dungeon that day while the sun was still out. I'd parked a few blocks away, in front of a shaggy yellow house with dandelions in the yard. There was parchment paper on the windows, wind chimes on the porch. It soothed me to imagine the granny who lived there, drifting about in old slippers, doing a puzzle or making egg salad, with no idea of what happened in the pea-green house just three blocks down. Perhaps she noticed the girls coming and going and assumed it was a tutoring center. A modeling school, perhaps, for the wayward and tattooed.

When I reached the yellow house, I found a man sitting on the sidewalk in front of it. He was old, with white hair and a snappy suit; it was clearly a possession he prized. He held a sign that said GOD'S BLESSINGS ARE MANY. He smiled when he saw me.

Hey, baby, he said. His voice was fluid and warm, like a radio announcer's. *Can you help me out, baby?*

Of course, I said. My pocket was fat with cash from the afternoon's session. I pulled out a twenty-dollar bill and handed it to him. *Be safe.*

Thank you. He looked into my eyes and squeezed my hand. *I love you, baby girl.*

I love you too, I whispered, then ran to my car. I got inside and sped away. I didn't want him to see me crying. I drove across the Bay Bridge to my favorite strip mall in the Excelsior, where I sat in the parking lot and continued to bawl. It had felt so good to hear those words. I wanted so badly to be somebody's baby. A part of me wanted to masturbate, to augment this good feeling. But mostly I wanted to just sit still and cry, replaying his words in my mind.

When I got home that evening, I could tell something was off. There were dishes in the kitchen sink, a weird human funk in the air. It smelled like the bathroom of a punk show, booze and sweat and vague distress. All the downstairs lights were off. I put my bags on the counter and tossed my keys in the bowl.

Ophelia? I called. *You there?*

I found her sitting in the upstairs bathtub, totally naked but for the charm bracelet Lorenzo had given her for her twenty-eighth birthday. It was adorned with the animals of the Chinese zodiac. From what I could tell, she'd drained the water from the tub but failed to get out. She looked like a mermaid plucked from the sea, beautifully withered, hair trailing on the floor. A half-empty bottle of natural wine was wedged in the shower caddy. Two lit candles flickered on the floor, filling the room with a licorice smell. Her eyes were pink from crying.

O, I said, kneeling beside her. I placed a hand on her head, which felt ice-creamy. She'd forgotten to wash the conditioner from her hair. *What's wrong?*

I can't do this anymore. She addressed the wall in front of her. Her voice was soft and thin. *This time it's too much for me.*

What is? I said, though of course I knew.

She stared into space as she spoke. *He'll never stop treating me like this. It's my fault, really, for letting it happen. I've made it so easy.* She started to cry again. *This doesn't feel good, Ruth. Isn't love supposed to, like, feel fucking good?*

I think so, I said, stroking her long, sticky hair. *I'm not sure.*

He used to make me feel good, she moaned. *I know you don't believe me, but it's true. Lorenzo loves me.*

I know.

She turned her face toward me, as if suddenly recognizing me. *You do?*

No one's all bad, I said, choosing my words carefully. *I'm sure he has good qualities.*

You think I'm stupid, don't you? She buried her face in her hands. *I don't blame you.* She looked up, alarmed. *Do I like him cuz he's mean to me?*

No, I said. *That's not it.*

He's so mean, she whispered. *I've never met someone so mean.* Her shoulders started to shake. *He hurts me. He hurts me. And what do I do? I just let it happen.* She started to pull at her hair. *In the beginning I really did think he was The One. I wanted to give him everything. Do you understand? Everything.* She placed one hand on her heart, her eyes moonish and mournful. *It really, really hurts.*

Come on, I said. *Let's get into bed and watch* Sex and the City.

She looked at me, frozen. *Are you gonna tell your little pen pal all about this? How stupid I am?*

My heart started to pound. *We don't talk about you.*

Of course not, she said. *Why would you mention me? You have more important matters to discuss.*

Ophelia, I said. *I'm worried about you.*

Oh, sure, she snapped, *of course you are. I know what you really think, Ruth. I can see it in your eyes.*

See what?

She pointed one long finger at me. *You hate him, don't you?*

Lorenzo? I tried not to stammer. *I can't say I like him.*

See! She stabbed the air. *I knew it. You never even gave him a chance. You wanted to hate him. It's easier that way.*

I took a deep breath. *It's hard when I see how he hurts you.*

She crossed her arms like a child. *That's my business.*

I know, I said, *but it's painful for me.*

Oh please, she sighed. *What do you know about pain?*

I felt myself shrinking. *I know that he shouldn't be treating you like shit.*

She raised her eyebrows, her voice suddenly honeyed. *Oh, is that so? Is that Love According to Ruth? And who are you, Ruth? Who are you, really?*

I forced myself to meet her eye. *What do you mean?*

She smiled, suddenly calm. *You're a scared little girl.* I'd seen this version of her during sessions at Dream House. Her brand of cruelty was quiet, precise, almost surgical. *Have you ever even been in love?* She held up one hand. *With someone REAL. A real, live man who can actually fuck you.*

Yes, I said, or thought I said. I could barely hear myself. *I have.*

And where is he now?

I opened and closed my mouth. *I don't know.*

She raised both arms in the air, still smiling. *There you go.* She staggered to her feet and stood naked in front of the mirror. *Don't take it out on me, darling. I'm not the reason you're alone.*

I know, I murmured. *You're the reason I'm not.*

She didn't say anything, kept her eyes on the mirror. The small room filled with steam.

I let myself out, the dogs on a leash. It was freezing and I didn't have a coat, but I kept walking. I walked and walked with no clear aim; it was the only thing I knew how to do. I couldn't see the ocean from here, but I could feel it in my gums, my pits. Ophelia had been my tie to the world and now I felt adrift, forlorn. I looked up: the sky was marbled, leaking light. O had taught me the name for this time of day—the blue hour. I said it aloud, tasting the melodrama. *Blue hour.*

I passed a man asleep on a stoop, his head resting on a suitcase. Without waking him, I emptied my wallet into his Styrofoam cup. I stuffed it with twenty-dollar bills, parking receipts, heart-shaped drink tokens from the club. As I was walking away, I noticed his sign. On the back of a pizza box, in familiar loopy red scrawl, someone had written: *take care.*

The sidewalk bottomed out. I dropped the dogs' leash and they stood in the middle of the street, watching me. Before I knew what was happening, I had my phone in my hand. My mind was black as it dialed, teeth chattering. He picked up on the fourth ring.

Hello?

Hi! I tried to sound normal. *It's Baby.*

I know. His voice was neither friendly nor unfriendly. *I have your number saved.*

I swallowed, an audible gulp. *Are you busy?*

Right now? Not particularly.

Oh. The dogs exchanged looks. *Can we meet?* I backpedaled. *You know, if you're free and you want . . . company.*

There was a treacherously long pause. I heard a car skid in the distance, the slam of a screen door. A bus announced its final stop. *Sure*, Simon said. *Why not?* He gave me his address. *Top floor*, he said. *Buzz when you're here.*

OK! I bellowed. I didn't know how to end the call. *Want anything? You know, from the store?*

No. He either chuckled or coughed. *I'm good. See you soon.* With that, he hung up.

I looked down at the girls, their leashes in a tangle on the sidewalk. Naomi blinked warily. She could see and smell my mania, the imminent breakdown. Her whiskers sensed rash decisions.

Don't worry, I murmured, freeing the leashes. *Everything's gonna be A-OK. I know this guy.* We began our walk home, where I would tuck the girls into Dino's bed before careening back into the night. I left the TV on for them. *He's a friend of mine.*

It took me forever to find parking in Simon's neck of the woods.

He lived in a stately brick building on Powell overlooking the Bay, not far from the tiki bar where Dino and I had our very first date, lifetimes ago, before everything melted. It was an interesting part of the city to live in. To the south was the faded grandeur of Nob Hill, the cable cars whizzing downhill, the ivy-thick manors swollen with light now converted to studios for finance bros and Frisco diehards who'd lived there since the AIDS crisis. It was the site of tourists agog and mannered ghosts. I wondered if Simon worked downtown; I'd always assumed he made his money in finance or tech. To the east was the splashy commotion of Chinatown, the underground restaurants and markets packed with spry elders buying jackfruit and live crabs. I used to see a doctor in Chinatown who would put stones on my back and twist my limbs, impassive and ruthless.

At your job you talk a lot, he muttered, touching my belly. *I can tell. Right here, and here, and here.*

After much circling I finally found a parking spot on the border of North Beach. I unearthed an emergency poncho from the trunk of my car and began to walk through Chinatown. It was a mild, moody evening, the last of the shoppers draining the shops. The sky was a valentine, purple and pink, strings of paper lanterns swaying in the breeze. I always felt humbled when walking through Chinatown. It was a world unto itself, a self-sufficient microcosm with its own sense of gravity. Elders hustled past me, their bodies made silent by multiple coats. Someone had wedged sticks of incense between the cracks in the curb; they filled the night sky with a secret perfume, plaintive and somnolent, the smoke making S's in the thickening air. Beneath this was the smell of rotten vegetables, car exhaust, BBQ beef, human shit, herbs that could heal a broken heart or slow spleen, plus the soft tang of the sea.

By the time I reached Simon's address, it was 8:30 p.m. The building's awning read THE ANTONIA. Good dancer name, I thought. He buzzed me in immediately. The lobby was striking, all scarlet and gold, the high ceiling painted with a mural of heaven: fat pink clouds and baby angels. A fainting couch was piled with Amazon Prime packages. A little sign by the

door read PLEASE DO NOT LET STRANGERS INSIDE, INCLUD-
ING DELIVERY DRIVERS! It looked like it had been written
with a calligraphy pen.

door read PLEASE DO NOT LET STRANGERS INSIDE, INCLUD-
ING DELIVERY DRIVERS! It looked like it had been written
with a calligraphy pen.

I rode the elevator to the seventh floor. The hallway here
was hushed and dim, a bag of trash slumped outside someone's closed door. I drifted along as if in a hospital. I found
Simon's unit, 702, and knocked kitty-soft, my heart skittering. I felt floaty and expectant, like he had something major
to tell me or I to tell him. Whether this news was good or
bad, I didn't know.

Coming! he called, then opened the door.

The first thing that struck me about Simon's apartment,
before I'd even stepped inside, was the smell. It hit me immediately, solid as a handshake. It was both alarming and
familiar, patently human. It had the saltiness of flesh and the
sweetness of rot, recalling the pubic under-scent of jasmine
and the burly musk of a crowded bus. It smelled like a kiss
you didn't see coming. Simon, standing in the doorway with
his hands on his hips, seemed not to notice. Perhaps he was
immune to it. He smiled at me, long hair in his eyes.

Baby, he said. He'd grown out his beard, grocery bag–
brown flecked with gray. I wondered if his neighbors ever
mistook him for a DoorDash driver and refused to hold the
door for him. *What a pleasant surprise.*

Indeed, I said, then made as if to hug him. He flinched,
stumbled backward, before acquiescing. His body was pleasantly squishy, thickened by leisurewear. The soapy smell of
his neck almost counteracted the apartment's dark funk.

Thirsty? he asked, pulling away. The bad smell swooped in.
Sure.

Come on in.

He led me into the high-ceilinged living room, shuffling slightly in his old-man slippers. He wore cheap gray sweatpants and a San Francisco hoodie I'd seen for sale in every Chinatown junk shop. I stayed close to him lest I touch something I shouldn't. He was saying something about the history of the Antonia, but I found it hard to focus because of the dollhouses. His apartment was full of them. They lined the walls, his secret neighborhood. There was a ranch house with a Lincoln Log corral and felt horse; there was a Hollywood mansion overlooking a glitter-glue pool. Doll-sized objects from every era lay around the apartment. I saw baby carriages, tea sets, rabbit-eared televisions, shag rugs the size of cocktail napkins, beanbags no bigger than a tangerine, loaves of Wonder Bread and Christmas hams that could feed a family of ants, ashtrays filled with gray litter, the world's smallest martini glass.

Wow, I said, nodding to the closest dollhouse. It was pink with white gingerbread trim. The lampposts out front were the size and width of tampons. It even had a mailbox with a teeny newspaper in it. *You have quite the collection.*

Oh, thanks. He smiled as if I'd said he looked thinner. *It helps pass the time.*

He popped into the kitchen, then emerged with two cups. *Here*, he said. He sat down on a saggy white sofa, indicating that I should sit too. Looking around the room, I couldn't help but notice that his doll furniture outnumbered his human-sized pieces. Amid the dollhouses there was a twin bed in one corner with a nylon sleeping bag on it, the sofa we sat on, and not much else. The apartment had once been

beautiful, and in a way it still was. The parquet floors were
well swept, the windows enormous and set toward the Bay.
The place wasn't messy or dirty but it had a morbid feeling, a
free-floating hopelessness, as if he rarely went out. The only
decoration I could see was a postcard taped to the wall. It
showed a picture of a palm tree and the squiggly orange
words *HI FROM HAWAII!* Below that was a child's cross
necklace, hung on a nail over the bed.

So, Simon said. He was drinking what I guessed was
Ovaltine from a paper take-out cup. The bottom had started
to rot. *You're looking well.*

I am? My eyes were pinwheeling and I couldn't stop shaking. I had mascara checkering my cheeks, my hair in a ratty
clump. I was wearing the same clothes I'd worn to the dungeon, a white cotton camisole that was meant to be slept in
and makeup-stained jeans, plus the poncho I'd found in my
car. I looked, if anything, unwell. *You're sweet.*

How've you been?

Oh, you know. I put my cup on the floor. *Can't complain.* I
settled into the couch and felt a prick in my thigh. *Ow.* Feeling around, I extracted a tiny frying pan from deep within
the couch cushions. It was real cast iron, just like Dino's at
home. *Is this . . . yours?*

Yes! he exclaimed. *I was looking for that. The Tuscan villa
has had to do without.* He slipped it in his sweatpants pocket.
Thanks for that.

No worries. I looked at my hands. Now that I was here,
bumping knees with my host, I couldn't remember why I'd
come. What did I need from this sad, soft man? How could
he, of all people in the Antonia, help me? Perhaps I'd come to

the wrong apartment. Perhaps I should've trick-or-treated down the hall until I found the perfect widower to fix me up, to make me his pet, to help me forget.

Simon seemed to register my vague distress. *Are you still getting my payments?*

I nodded. *Yes, thank you. Every month on the first.*

Excellent. He cleared his throat. *And how're things at the club?*

Same as usual, I said. *You know how it goes.*

Making money?

Uh-huh.

How's Sadie and the others?

We're good, I said. *We miss you.* The words burst from my lips like a cuss.

Oh, Simon said. *I'm sure that's not true.*

It is, I said. *It's true for me.*

His voice was soft. *That's nice of you.*

I scooched closer, suddenly emboldened. I remembered what I'd come for. *Do you miss me?*

Oh, sure.

I mean . . . do you think of me?

Think of you in what way?

I flapped my hands. *Any. Like, do I ever cross your mind? Not always, of course. Just . . . sometimes?*

He smiled, the lines around his eyes fanning out into Vs. *Of course.*

Good, I said. My heart unscrunched; my blood went warm. *That makes me feel good.* I began to play with my hair, something I only did when flirting or nervous. I suppose I was both. *Do you mind if I ask you another question?*

Go ahead. He chuckled. *There's no secrets between us. You already know all the, shall we say, unseemly things about me.*

That's true. I forced myself to unhand my hair, turning to face him with my purse in my lap. *We had a connection.*

Simon nodded gravely. *We did.*

We got each other.

He half smiled, bashful. *I'd like to think so.*

So why did it end? You know, our . . . arrangement?

He sighed, gazing over the top of my head. He interlaced his fingers like a doctor with bad news. *Well, Baby.* He was looking at his postcard of Hawaii. *Everything ends.*

This answer didn't satisfy me. *I know that.*

He sighed again, studying the postcard. It seemed to have a calming effect on him. I watched his eyes go glassy, his shoulders slump. His voice got low and moony, like he was describing a dream over breakfast. *Sometimes it's better to stop while you're ahead. Before things get dodgy, while everything's gravy. Why kid yourself? The end is nigh.*

I nodded, feeling my pulse jump. This was a song I knew the lyrics to. *Uh-huh.*

He smoothed out his pants, over and over, fretting the shabby gray cotton. *Sometimes it feels good to want something SO much. It hurts in a good way. Let's say I acquire that something. Now I can't keep desiring it. Now I have to keep it. That's a lot of work. Sometimes it's sexier to just . . . let it go. You follow?*

I nodded like a dog. *I think so.*

You know what's always there for me, no matter what happens? He paused for a moment, his eyes like TVs seen from the street. *That feeling. That longing. That bad-but-good want. That won't ever go away. That will never leave me. Capisce?*

I studied his soft, slack mouth. His lips were like orange wedges, white in the corners. *Capisce.*

That's my advice for the youth of today. Become a hungry hungry hippo, at home in hell. He laughed to himself, a weird, rusty sound. *My kinks are my superpower. My kinks keep me company.*

Simon, I said, bending toward him. I felt so close to something important, to finally naming what bound us. *Did something bad happen? To make you . . . this way?*

He smiled, snapping back to reality. *Oh, honey,* he said, turning from the postcard to me. His voice was normal again, as if we'd just met. *It's not that simple.*

Oh. I forced a laugh. *Of course. You're right. It's just . . .* I looked down at my lap, squeezing my purse. *Something bad happened to me.*

He didn't flinch; his face was kind. *I'm sorry to hear that.*

It's OK. I'm OK. I studied the floor, blond hardwood. I fantasized, for a moment, that I was alone here; I was a long-time resident of the Antonia. This apartment was mine, I bought wine and biscotti at the upscale bodega on the corner of Powell, I stood at my window and watched the fog eat Marin every evening. I was stable and whole and had never been left. *I guess I thought, maybe, that was why we are the way we are.*

He smiled patiently. *The way we are?*

Like . . . I scrounged for the words. What I wanted to say was, *We wear loss like a lover's T-shirt,* or, *We're saving ourselves for Death, a.k.a. The One Who'll Never Get Away,* but I didn't know if that made sense. It's like Simon said: We didn't kid ourselves. We'd locked lips with loss, we left the door ajar for her. We knew the white-hot secret of the world, which was that nothing lasts forever. Except, of course, longing. We pros could long forever, our arms linked in a chain. Looking back, that's what all of my hobbies have courted: the day-long K-holes on Dino's furred couch, the whoring around, even my doomed little romance with Charlie—I did it all to long, to get a passing glimpse of my chilly amour. Simon knew this about me because he was the same, he felt it too, that rapport with The End. I cleared my throat and tried to stay still, though I felt like I might float away.

I've always had this feeling I'll end up alone. I squeezed my hands between my thighs to keep them from shaking. *And I'm OK with that, really.*

But you're still so young, Simon exclaimed. He furrowed his eyebrows.

I had expected a warmer reaction. *That doesn't matter.*

It does, he said, his voice rising. *It does. Don't be stupid.*

I stared at him, taken aback. *I'm not stupid,* I whispered, though I really didn't know.

His expression was stormy. *What you're saying is bullshit. Are you serious?*

Dead serious. He took my hand; his was soft as brioche. His eyes were lava lamps, hot and restless. *You have so much going for you, Baby. You really, really do.*

I looked at him, this ruined acquaintance, feeling my eyes prick. *I do?*

You do. He squeezed my hand. *You do.*

Simon, I murmured. I'd never noticed the specks of yellow in his irises before. I'd always thought his eyes were brown, brown like coffee, brown like dirt. For the first time I found myself wondering about his age. He was old enough to be my father. *Do you ever think of really doing it?*

Doing what?

Doing S.

He blinked at me. *Pardon?*

You know. Suicide.

What? he yelped. He dropped my hands as if burned, then picked them up again. He clasped my hands to his chest. *No! Not at all. Oh, Baby, no way. I still believe in love, you know.*

Now it was my turn to feel shocked. *You do?*

Of course! He nodded to the window. *How can you not, in a city like this?*

I smiled, just a little, betraying myself. I felt happy and angry and naked and bereft. *Simon,* I said, *are you Nobody?*

He cocked his head. *In the grand scheme of things, sure.*

I let out a laugh, a bright, crass squawk, causing us both to jump. I couldn't get my thoughts in order. They swirled around me like panties in the wash. *So you haven't been emailing me?* It was partially a question, partially a statement. I was testing out this reality.

Emailing you? Simon frowned. *As you may remember, I'm strictly a phone guy.*

I do remember that, yes. I rubbed my eyes with the heels of my hands until I saw stars. *I'm sorry,* I muttered. *Someone's been emailing me, and I thought . . . maybe it was you.*

Nope. He bonked my knee with his knee. *I'm not the only lonely man in San Francisco, you know.*

I know. I smiled like a puppet. *Believe me, I know.* I felt suddenly, unbearably, biblically tired. Every muscle in my body shimmered. My hair felt heavy as a rained-on towel. It was an effort to even open my mouth. *I think I better get going*, I managed.

Sure thing, Simon said, springing up off the couch. *It's getting late. I have work in the morning.*

Downtown?

He nodded. *The Starbucks on Market. I open on Thursdays.*

Before I could reply, he picked up our cups and trotted into the kitchen. I was glad that he couldn't see my shocked expression. I stood up and peeked into one of the dollhouses. It looked like something from a 1950s suburb, sunny yellow with cream trim. Inside the house, everything was perfect. There was a Mr. Coffee on the Formica counter, microscopic bits of kibble in the thimble-sized doggy bowl, a gingham tablecloth. The only thing missing was the family. I looked in every room of the house, but they were all empty. The matchbox beds were tightly made, doll-blouses and doll-nighties arranged in armoires. There were doll-stockings hung to dry over the pencil-thick shower rod. I could've slid them on my pinkie finger. The butter was in the middle of melting. The more that I studied the house, the more it came to look like a crime scene. Either that or the family had fled of their own accord. The emptiness bespoke emergency, a plague or tsunami warning. I had to wonder if anyone had left a note, written on a rose petal or a scrap of confetti, tacked to the icebox.

When Simon reentered the living room, I lurched away, feeling guilty. *Thanks again for having me over*, I said, grabbing my purse. *Your place is lovely.*

Isn't it? he said. *I've lived here for so long, I'll never leave. How could I? I pay a third of what the new kids pay. We call that the golden handcuffs. Plus*—he waved at the dollhouses—*I need lots of space.* He shrugged, burying his hands in his pockets. *It's not a bad place to be trapped.*

I moved toward the door. *Well,* I said gently, *I'm off.*

Get home safe, he murmured. He took his hands from his pockets and held the tiny frying pan out like a compass. *Sweet dreams, Baby. Be well.*

You too.

The city was chilly and hushed on my walk back to the car. It was 10:00 p.m. on a Wednesday. The shops of Chinatown were shuttered, the restaurants half-empty, the dishwashers and bartenders chatting while they worked. Hot white steam pumped out of a grate. I walked through it, letting it touch my face and neck. It felt good, like a mother checking for a fever. The sticks of incense in the sidewalk had gone out. Ash collected on the curb in wan piles. An old man in a rubber apron appeared in a doorway across the street, emptying a bucket of water into the gutter. He smoked a cigarette without the use of his hands. We watched the water swirl and stall in the gutter. He seemed not to see me. With expert precision he spat the butt in the water, which had pooled at his feet. Then he turned and disappeared inside, his rubber apron squelching.

I arrived at the club at 9:30 p.m. the next night.

I'd spent the entire day sleeping, waking only to tend to the dogs. I felt craggy and worn out, an actor hired to play myself. Had I really seen Simon last night? Was it already Thursday? A part of me wanted to stay home from work, tell Dino not to come tonight and keep sleeping forever, but before I knew what was happening, I was shaving my legs. I had concealer, lashes, bronzer on—I couldn't stop now. I swung by a gas station en route to the club to buy Red Bull, though I was already late. I needed the pick-me-up; the higher door fee was worth it to not look so frayed. I chugged the Red Bull as I drove and threw the can out the window, blaring Pet Shop Boys to get in the zone.

You're sexy, I chanted. *You're sexy, you're hot. Tonight's the fucking night.*

As I entered the club, I resisted the urge to look at my phone. I still hadn't seen or heard from Ophelia since our fight. When I'd peeked into the guest bedroom that evening, the bed was made and the windows closed. She never closed the windows. *I'm a slut for a breeze*, she would laugh. Her hyaluronic acid and botanica candles were gone. She'd even plumped the pillows, like a fancy hotel maid.

Most girls were already out on the floor, so I had the locker room to myself. Emeline's long suede coat hung on the back of her chair, a reusable water bottle and plastic container of supermarket sushi on the counter next to her purse. I helped myself to a fat slab of yellowtail and wiped my soy-saucy hands on her coat sleeve. I was choosing which shoes to wear (over-knee boots or Lucite stilettos?) when I heard my phone ping. My heart rose and fell. It was not a text from Ophelia but an email from Nobody. The subject line read: *They say S rates spike during the holiday season . . .*

Something about seeing their name turned my stomach.

I could hear Ophelia's mocking tone: *Does your little friend want attention? Don't keep him waiting!* I threw my phone in my locker and took a deep breath. I needed to focus. It was finally Thursday, and Dino was a man of his word. I felt sure that he'd show, if only for a drink or two. It was like they said at church: I had to be ready. I had to fashion my body, ragged and sleepy, into a vessel for Him. I had to prepare myself to receive His light in any capacity He saw fit. In other words, I had to look irresistible.

I'd brought a new outfit from Candyland, a slinky pink gown with a pussy-height slit and matching satin choker, still in its bag. I didn't normally wear gowns, but this one made me feel sexy. I painted two circles on my cheeks in a color called Fever Dream and doused myself in Soft Core. As I was digging through my locker, I touched something slippery and pulled out the wig Emeline had given me. It was glossy, butter-blond, still unworn. Smiling to myself, I secured it to my scalp with beige bobby pins. Now he'd have no choice but to notice me.

As I was zipping my gown, Gigi limped into the locker room. She let out a yelp. *Holy shit, Baby!* she cried. *You look like a movie star.*

Thank you, I said. She looked like someone's weary mom, holding her shoes in one hand and nursing a blue Gatorade. I always forgot how tiny she was without heels.

It's good tonight, she said. *Dudes with real money. I think there's some sort of biotech conference.*

That's great.

You'd think so, right? My left knee is killing me. I need a smoke. She stood on tiptoe to punch my shoulder. *Go kill them dead.*

I'll try.

The night unfolded quickly. It was a busy Thursday full of corporate drones. I typically had good luck with men in suits; they liked to tower over me. They drank expensive whiskey and teased me in a daddish way, coming up with nicknames. I giggled at them all.

Wow, I would cry, *that's sooo me!*

I danced for an Army vet who called me Suzanne, then for a man who insinuated that he worked with Elon Musk and kept trying to bite me. *No!* I'd snap, like he was a bad dog. *No! I'll give you one more chance, OK?*

I was cruising for my next mark when I felt a tap on my shoulder, soft as snow. I turned and, of course, it was Emeline.

Hey, girl! she said, breathless. *Oh my god, your fucking hair!* Her face was lit up as if from within. She looked like a nine-ties supermodel, her hair ironed to the waist, a touch of glitter on her nose. She wore espresso-brown satin, her belly ring twinkling. She'd never looked more like a Sophia than to-night. *How's it going?*

It goes.

I just did an hour and a half with the lead singer of Judith Butplug. He was totally cool, kinda cute too. Have you heard of that band?

Before I could reply, I saw Dino. He was loitering by the stage, holding a beer. Veronique was performing, snaking up the pole to Madonna. His eyes ping-ponged all over her body, though he made no move to tip her. He would stare, then look down, as if afraid of offending her. He looked like the new kid at a high school dance. His lack of ease surprised me;

the Dino I knew was breezy and blessed. He could compliment a woman on her square-toed Bottega Veneta boots and really mean it. He was also wearing clothes I'd never seen before: a gray suit in a shimmery material that bagged around the shoulders, a white button-down open at the collar, a bunch of chunky gold rings. He looked like a Bible salesman and also a pimp. His bared chest was the color of grilled cheese, his dark hair slicked back with what looked like Crisco. But when he turned in profile to gaze up at Veronique, it could only be my Dino. There was that nose, that heavenly schnoz. I could hang my delicates to dry on that monster, I could put up wind chimes or a white flag (*I surrender!*). Just like that my heart filled with affection, a dozy tenderness shot with lust. How I missed that holy honker, rooting through my muumuus, infringing on my me-time. *Gimme that*, I used to say, pretending to unscrew it from his face. *I might need it for later.*

He turned and saw me. I waved him over, feeling both giddy and shy. He abandoned his beer on a table and began to walk toward me; it took me a moment to realize he walked with a limp.

Well, well, well, he said when he reached us. His voice was higher than I remembered it being. *What do we have here?*

Hi, simpered Emeline. Her voice was bunny-soft. *I'm Emeline.*

Of course you are.

She hooked arms with me. *And this is my best friend, Baby. We're really more like sisters.*

He knows me, I said, ignoring the sister thing. Did she say that to everyone? I locked eyes with Dino and smiled in a conspiratorial way. He smiled back, his thumbs hooked through his belt loops.

Sisters, huh? he purred. *I shoulda known. Emeline and Baby.* He affected a crooner's molten voice. *Oh, baby, baby, baby.*

That's me.

That's you. He ran a hand through his hair, shiny and hard like lemon meringue pie. *Well, now that we've all been acquainted*, he said, *how about a dance?*

Before I could reply, Emeline clapped her hands. *Good idea!* she cried. *How fun. I'm in.*

Good girl. They both turned to look at me. *And you, little Baby?*

I forced a smile. *Let's go.*

Emeline squealed and hugged me, her blond hair wrapping around us like a shower curtain. She looked at Dino over my shoulder and cooed, *Follow me.*

We entered the VIP room. Emeline first, then Dino, then me. He sat down, knees spread and feet planted. Music played, I didn't know what, swirly hip-hop. We both approached him, picking sides. I was on his right, closer to the door. I suppose, in semidarkness, we might have looked like real sisters, our long blond hair shielding our faces, the smell of Soft Core suffusing the room. We moved in choppy unison. He'd paid for thirty minutes, though Emeline had pushed for more. *Patience*, he'd told her. *Let's see how things go.*

Now, without looking at each other, we started to dance.

At first he watched both of us. He smiled and said encouraging things. *Very sexy. Just like that. Oh, that's nice.* Then his eyes started to slide. They slid up and down Emeline's perfect body. I tried not to look too, though I wanted to. It was like trying to ignore a TV in a tiny hotel room. Soon he wasn't even pretending to notice me. He was wholly focused on Emeline, literally licking his lips. Everything he said was addressed to her. *God, you're so hot. God, you're so perfect. God, I want you so bad.* Emeline smiled and blinked as if he'd asked for directions. Her neutrality encouraged him. I undid my halter to zero fanfare. No one noticed my nipples, pricked in the ruthless AC.

You want me too, he was saying. *I can tell. I know when a chick is interested. I can smell when she's turned on.* I was straddling one of his thighs, yet had to lean in to hear him. *Your pussy smells like candy. Like those gross little valentine hearts.*

I scanned Emeline's face for a reaction, but it was blank. She might as well have been on a man-shaped treadmill. At this point I stopped dancing. My body was bare, G-string panties on the floor. I exhaled and let my tummy relax. Neither he nor she noticed. I stood with my hands on my hips, watching Emeline grind. Fury filled me: Why did she get everything, all the world's love? Was it because she was beautiful? Or, worse yet, was she beautiful *because* of the love she'd received, the kind words and kisses, the rooms with a view? Everyone wanted a piece of her light, and she didn't even care. She was bored by her luck. Men queued up to touch her cheek, to be her keeper. Would men pick me if I'd been loved in this fashion? My heart was perforated; hers was plump and rose-gold. The injustice of it made me sick, but I also couldn't blame them. She'd turned away from Dino now, giving him a view of her heart-shaped ass. He moaned when she made it jiggle.

That's it. He buried his face in her bright blond hair,

speaking into her ear. *I wanna eat you up. Every little bit of you. I'll have you for breakfast, lunch, and dinner. I wanna chew you up and spit you out and chew you up again. If that's what you want, just tell me.*

She spun around to face him, cupping her breasts. *You're right*, she said flatly. She squeezed her breasts so hard they turned blue. I began to feel nervous, like I should pry her hands off them. Beautiful things should be handled with care. Didn't she know that? I could see little grooves where her nails dug into the flesh. *You read my mind, Daddy.*

I know, he said. *I fucking know.* He placed his hands on her throat. I watched in mute shock as he started to squeeze. Where was security? Who was this man? *Hey*, I said, or thought I said. *This isn't supposed to be happening.* Her eyes widened as he applied more pressure, her throat like a squeaky toy. Her body started to quake, though she didn't resist.

Hey, I cried, *this isn't right.*

They froze. Time stood still. Then, like paid actors, they burst into laughter. *Gotcha!* he bellowed. He threw his hands in the air and stamped his feet. *I gotcha so good!*

Emeline laughed so hard her whole body shook. Her breasts slammed around like big white balloons. They whacked him in the face, causing the pair to laugh harder. She had to cling to his shoulders for support, hanging half-naked off his thigh. They were suddenly unrecognizable to me, two strangers playing nasty games. His nose shriveled up before my eyes. *God*, she cried, tapping his forehead, *I love you!*

No, he said, grinning like a jack-o'-lantern. He was breathless. *I love YOU.*

No, you!

No, you!

No, you!

NO, YOU!

It was then that I picked up my G-string and left. I ran with my gown bunched around my waist, out of the VIP room, past the stage, and into the locker room. I grabbed my keys but left the rest of my shit in my locker, including my street clothes and full money bag. Noticing my bare breasts, I grabbed Emeline's coat off her chair and wrapped it around me. It was soft and warm, the suede like thigh skin, the color of a good tan. It smelled so strongly of her, Soft Core and honeysuckle and something acidic. Instead of going out the front, I left through the back to the alley where girls took their smoke breaks. The alley was empty, the concrete dotted with cigarette butts. They stuck to my Pleasers as I cut across the lot and jumped in my car.

I started driving before I knew where I was going. I needed speed, motion. I was on the freeway when I realized I was still clutching my panties, driving with them balled up in one hand. I let out a chortle, then rolled down my window and threw them into the night. *Good riddance*, I howled, though of what, I didn't know. My gown was still bunched around my hips, my bare ass gummed to the driver's seat. It felt good to drive with the windows rolled down, my pussy mashed into faux leather. The city smelled of trash and flowers, unwashed hair. I had strands of my wig in my mouth, unruly blond tentacles stuck to my lip gloss. I drove according to memory. My body knew where to go, as it hadn't been long. As the houses got bigger and the darkness darker, the streetlamps making big orange circles on black driveways and lawns, it became obvious where I was headed. I glanced at the dashboard clock: 1:15 a.m. He'd be awake for at least two more hours.

I parked right in front of the house: black wrought-iron gate, shuttered windows, a little flagstone path leading through the rose garden, the trampoline like a Gothic castle in the dark. I walked easily through the gate, my body at home. I could remember hopping from flagstone to flagstone on one foot, Charlie laughing and saying, *Quit it!* but not really meaning it. We were drunk or maybe high. He couldn't find his keys, so he used the spare set. They were hidden in a ceramic frog with a hole in the bottom.

Jesus, I'd said, laughing, *is that the best you can do? Don't you have, like, a retina scanner?*

He'd touched his forehead to mine and stared into my eyes. *What're you doing?* I'd giggled, feeling nervous in a sexy way.

Scanning your retinas, duh.

Now all the windows were dark but for one on the ground floor. Its shutters were closed but the edges seethed yellow. The clay frog was still there, under the third apple tree, as was the spare key. Standing in the garden, I finger-combed my long blond hair and buttoned my coat to the top. I could see my reflection in the darkened windows; I looked lean and important, a girl from a dream with a life-or-death message. When taking Emeline home from the bar, I'd chickened out; this time, I wouldn't falter. Stepping lightly in my heels, I used the spare key to let myself in.

The smell of the foyer hit me hard. I remembered that smell, of cleaning product and dead roses. I was twenty-three all over again, knock-kneed and shivery, I'd been sleeping around for a handful of months but felt certain that Charlie was different. He saw me. Though I playacted at coolness, I was skittish around him. I wanted him to think I was smart even more than I wanted him to think I was pretty. He was my friend, but one with the power to break me. He was a mean girl and I was his slave.

As I looked around the dim foyer, everything was the same: pink marble floors I could see my reflection in, end tables frothing with flowers, the chandelier overhead. I knew that he paid someone to replace the flowers each Friday.

That seems excessive, I'd told him. *Don't they last longer than that?*

He'd shrugged. *Happy wife, happy life.* It was rare that he spoke of his wife, about whom I knew almost nothing. She was a surgeon and ate very little, she cut her food into tiny pieces. For some reason he made sure I knew these two things, though I was never once told her name.

I was still wearing my Pleasers, which clicked on the marble as I crossed the foyer into the living room. There Charlie sat, slumped in an armchair with all the lights off. In the darkness he looked like a piece of the furniture. His back was to me as I edged along the wall, watching him. He still wore his suit and tie. His shoes were kicked off, flung across the hardwood floor; I could see the thick white padded socks on his feet and it made me pity him. For all his bravado, he was an old man getting older. A glass of Angel's Envy was sweating on the coffee table, next to a propped-up iPad emitting a white V of light. Judging by the way the light flickered, he was watching a video with the sound turned low. There was a body-shaped mass in one corner that turned out to be a Christmas tree, not yet strung with twinkle lights.

Everything else in the room was bloated by darkness; I had to wait for my eyes to adjust to make out his expression. He was staring at the iPad with his head in his hands. His face was slack, neither distressed nor engaged. He had the look of a swimming pool that had just been drained. His hair was thick and dark the way I remembered it; his eyes made me think of a shitty ghost costume, a white bedsheet with two slits.

He didn't see me cross the room, nor hear my heels on the floor. I started to wonder if he was asleep. For one split second, I thought about leaving, letting sleeping dogs lie. I could drive to Jollibee and practice deep breathing. I could lose myself in FetLife messages or suck dick in a Costco parking lot. Then I pictured Emeline on Dino's lap, his lovesick eyes, her bobbing breasts, and knew I'd see this through. She had taken something from me; it was only fair for me now to take something from her. It was a wife swap, a revenge plot, erotic tic-tac-toe. She'd set something in motion that couldn't be stopped.

As I got closer to Charlie, I was surprised to see an open bottle of Ambien on the coffee table next to his drink. When we'd partied together he'd only liked coke. I'd never seen him mix liquor and pills before, though it was quite possible he did it when I wasn't looking. He wouldn't have wanted me to fret or think of him as weak, though who was I to judge? I'd always preferred downers, that velvety free fall. I understood that type of edge, the opposite of adventure. Downers weren't fun; they were holy, dour, pesky little metaphors inviting self-sacrifice. I crept up behind him, heart in my throat.

Hi, I whispered. I stood beside his chair, arms crossed.

He started, just a bit. *Sophia?* he mumbled. He glanced around with a misty expression. It was gentle and expectant, like a bodega cat looking for scratches. It was clear that he was wasted. *Honey? Is that you?*

Yes, I said. I towered over him in my high heels. *It's me.*

Hiya, sweetie, he said. His words ran together. He smiled, and I could count every tooth in the dark. He was drunker than I'd ever seen him, his mouth hanging open in a Labrador's grin. *You're home early. Fun night?*

Not really.

He squinted at me. The light from the iPad made my blond hair look white. Everything else was bathed in shadow. *Is everything OK? I thought you were seeing your, um, boyfriend tonight.* He sounded bashful, like he didn't know the right word.

That was the plan. I played with my hair. *But it changed.*

How come?

I looked down. *We got in a fight.*

Aw, honey! Charlie flicked his eyes between the iPad and me. I could see what he'd been watching, a YouTube video titled *COMPILATION OF WORLD'S BEST KARAOKE SINGERS, WATCH THIS AND TRY NOT TO CRY!*

That's no fun, he added.

No, I said softly. I pictured Dino's hands on Emeline's throat, their jubilant laughter, her zigzagging flesh. *It isn't.*

Come here. He spread his arms wide. I stared at him, not understanding. He patted his leg, which looked thinner up close. His slacks were saggy in the thighs. *I'm sorry, sweetie.* He blinked up at me and looked genuinely sorry, his eyes round and fretful, his eyebrows knitted. *Come here.*

Trying not to shake, I lowered myself onto his lap. He immediately wrapped his arms around me, holding my head to his chest. He smelled like whiskey and shaving cream, the old-man funk far outweighing the odor of Christmas trees I associated with him. He kissed the top of my head, rocking me slightly. *It's OK, sweetie,* he whispered. *My baby. Don't cry.* I hadn't noticed my tears. They made straight lines down my cheeks and jaw, searing through my makeup. Realizing I was crying only made me cry harder. A sob wracked my body and he held me tight. My chest felt like an open window, shutters banging in the breeze.

Don't cry, he repeated, his voice thick with hurt. *Please don't cry. Daddy's here.* I buried my face in his neck and let my tears soak his collar. I was safe so long as I kept holding on, hiding my face in his thick dark hair. I squeezed and squeezed, using all my strength, and he squeezed back. *Boys aren't worth crying over,* he muttered. *You'll find someone new.*

He stroked my hair, and I wondered if he could feel the difference in texture, if my wig still smelled of plastic bags. Feeling his hands on my neck, I remembered what I'd come for with a hot burst of purpose. I tried to locate his cock beneath my legs, to ascertain its stiffness. I wriggled around but felt nothing. This angered me. Was I so easy to dismiss? I pressed my breasts against his chest and parted my legs. *Daddy,* I whispered. I tried to make my voice low and lusty.

I trickled my fingers against the back of his neck, playing with the scraps of hair there. *Mmm.* I brought my lips to his ear, that soft, droopy seashell. I enunciated every syllable, my lips snagging on his stubble. *Dad-dy.*

Yes, honey? He was neutral, patient, awaiting my question. He continued to hug me as though I were his teddy. *What is it, my love?*

I opened my mouth, but nothing came out. My mind went blank. I was pretending to be someone, but I didn't know who. He thought I was his sweet Sophia, but I'd only ever met Emeline, a name that meant nothing to him. Could I be either of those visions, leggy and heady and lighthouse-blond, unrepentant Daddy's girls? I was suddenly unsure. I knew nothing of their sleepy grace, the languor that love breeds. Was I Baby Blue, hard yet soft in six-inch shoes, who loved to laugh and shake her ass, or could I even be Ruthie, the version of me he swore he once knew? That Ruthie was so far from me now, that dumb dewy girl in thrifted panties and bra. I had to be someone, but I couldn't choose who. Every possible name felt so foreign; they bounced around in my brain like bingo balls in a cage. The longer I thought about it, the more helpless I felt. All the while Charlie sat there rocking me. At last I squeaked, *I'm sad.*

I know, honey, he said. *I know. Don't be sad. None of this will matter tomorrow, OK?*

OK. I took a deep breath, pressing my lips to his neck. It was textured like hamburger. I was struck, then, with a sudden weariness. I stopped arching my back and let myself slump in his lap. He blanketed me with his body, humming sexlessly, and I gave in to his embrace. I let myself believe in the words he was saying, as if they were meant for me alone. I closed my eyes and saw maroon.

You'll find someone who loves you, he was saying. *I know it, you will.*

Really?

Absolutely tutti-frutti. We giggled together, an inside joke. When I opened my mouth, threads of drool stuck to his neck. My voice was ragged, thin, no longer sexy. *Do you love me?*

More than anything. He spoke clearly and calmly. For a moment he seemed sober. *More than anything in this rotten world. God must have been happy with me, the day he gave you to me. You're the only thing that matters.* I felt a shift in his body, an internal hardening, a despair that he couldn't metabolize. It came out in his sweat, made his fingertips spiky. It was swift as a curtain being drawn, this dip in his mood. His grief wrapped around us like fog. He freed his right hand to pick up his drink.

Ahh, he said without realizing, as if his lukewarm bourbon were delicious. He closed his eyes to savor the taste and I saw my window for escape. Swinging my hair across my face, I sprang off his lap and stood behind the armchair. I placed my hands on his shoulders, anchoring him in his seat. I could feel his bones through his jacket.

Daddy, I said, breathless.

Yes, angel? His voice was distant. He looked as if he'd shrunk an inch, collapsed into his chair.

I'm a whore.

He smiled, staring out the window, though the shutters were closed. *Come again?*

I'm bored. I squeezed his shoulders. *I'm going to bed now.*

His face was soft, unperturbed. He wasn't listening anymore. *Good idea, baby. I'll hit the sack soon. I just need a minute.* He took my hand, flipped it over, and brought my palm to his lips. They were hot and creased. For one moment I thought: baby's ears. *Love you.* He spoke the phrase into my cupped palm, gifting it to me like allowance.

The words came so easily. *I love you too.* But I didn't pull my hand away. It hurt me to see him like this, crinkled and grim. This was not a man who windsurfed at dawn; this was a man who could barely dog-paddle. Had he always been this pathetic? Maybe that was why he chased such young girls— they were easier to fool. He could siphon their optimism, their dopey hope. The name of the website we met on was Seeking.com, and I could still feel him seeking, like a cat in the dark. He wanted it all; he wanted out. He wore his disappointments like a rank corsage. He wanted to be sleek and bright, baptized by his nightly high. I glanced down at the coffee table, feeling my extremities tingle. I knew how to help him, to take the edge off. *Did you take your pills, Daddy?*

Huh? Oh, sure.

Don't forget to take your medicine. I know how hard it is for you to sleep.

I crouched next to the coffee table and poured the rest of the Ambiens into my hand. Nowhere near enough to kill him, I knew, but enough to take him far away for a while. Emeline would have quite the scare trying to wake him when she came home from the club—her first brush, however fleeting, with loss. I didn't feel bad as I counted the pills; I felt gentle, benevolent, as if the little orange bottle were full of birdseed. It would make him feel better and teach her a lesson. Not everything was haveable, not everything was pure. This man, who lived to love her, was awash in sorrows I doubted she recognized. I recognized them, I knew them by heart. There was a time when he paid me to distract him from these sorrows with a body I didn't yet have a handle on. He'd told me what he wanted, and that was reprieve, to get as close as he could to death without actually committing. I thought of something Nobody had written to me in an email once: *Few people want to go through with S. It's so final, so severe, so unyielding. Absolutes aren't sexy in practice. But if we were offered the chance to try it out for an hour, to die and come back—who among us wouldn't say yes? Just to know. To give in. What could be more arousing than a little death?*

Here, I whispered, gripping his armrest. *Let me help you.*

Charlie smiled vaguely. *Thanks, Soph.*

I brought my hand to his mouth and he opened up automatically, good boy. I handed him his tumbler and watched him wash the pills down with the rest of his bourbon, by now mostly water. *Oof*, he shivered. *There we go.* He settled meatily into his chair.

Sweet dreams, I murmured. *See you soon.*

I left the room, walking gingerly in my heels so as not to disturb him. I walked across the foyer, up the stairs. I felt floaty and calm; this was my house. I'd walked this path a thousand times, on a thousand uneventful school nights. I was tired from rehearsal, wearing fuzzy pink leg warmers, my toes bloodied and sore. Mother was sulking at the dining room table, cutting her food into bits; Daddy was getting dressed for what he claimed was a work dinner, though we'd all already eaten.

I entered the bedroom. A few things were different—Susan Sontag on the bedside table, Charlotte Tilbury on her vanity—but the overall vibe remained unchanged. It was dreamy and pristine, the carpet like snow. The big lilac bed beckoned. Its bounty of bunnies called out, *All aboard!* Suddenly winded, I unbuttoned my coat and fell back on the bed. God, it felt good. I unspooled my limbs, let my blond hair drag on the floor. The satin bedspread was so shiny it almost felt lubricated. I wriggled my arms, made a snow angel. She still had the glow-in-the-dark stars on her ceiling, their light thin and queasy. I wondered what it felt like to get fucked in this bed, nudging the bunnies aside.

Come here often? I said.

I sat up. On the bedside table, next to her journals and jade roller and reusable water bottle, was a mirror-backed brush. It was exactly where she'd left it four years prior, still clotted with blond. I picked it up and examined it. Before I knew what was happening, I was prying the tangle of hair from the bristles. I freed it and held the blond wad in both hands. It was the size of a softball or a delicate sea creature. I placed it, gentle as a surgeon, at the foot of the bed. Then, reaching under my wig, I began to claw at my own hair. I bit my lips to keep from howling as I ripped out a comparable clump. When I was satisfied with its size, I placed my hair ball next to hers on the bed. Beside hers, mine looked ugly. It was a mud pie, a dust bunny. It looked like something you'd find under a bed, someone's dirty little secret.

I picked up her golden pouf of hair and surveyed the pile
of bunnies. They gazed back at me, merry and unassuming.
How many nights had they watched her sleep, kept her safe?
She had all the world's love, yet she still needed more. I
selected a big pink bunny with floppy ears and a bow tie. You
could tell by the way her fur was worn down that she'd been
hugged quite a lot. I placed her in the center of the bed, on
top of a pillow, and used one of my bobby pins to affix the
blond clump to her head. It fit perfectly between her two ears.

Gorgeous, I thought, examining my handiwork. Fabulous.
Just like that, she'd become someone else. She stood out from
the other bunnies with her prom-night updo. Sometimes that
was all it took to become a new girl: different hair, borrowed
lipstick, a trompe l'œil, stockings or the lack thereof, the
right combination of liquor and pills, a weird dream or fitting
rumor. No one wanted to admit it, but that's how easy it
was to let yourself go, that's how little it took to become
someone new.

Smiling to myself, I slid off the bed. I picked up the remaining hair ball, the one from my own head, the color of
pennies and dirt, and put it in my coat pocket. Then I adjusted my wig, smoothed out the bedspread, and hurried
downstairs. I didn't stop to check in on Charlie. I knew he
was far away, unreachable in his sludgy slumber, exactly
where I'd left him. He'd be there for a while.

My feet were on fire, but I had to keep moving. I put the
spare key back inside the frog and clipped down the little
stone path to my car. The night air smelled ambrosial, fattened by the sea. There was no use trying to savor it; I had too
much adrenaline in my system to stay still. I jumped in my

car and sped down the street, deserted at this hour. I went ninety, a hundred miles per hour. That was the weird thing about rich neighborhoods: you never saw anyone there. No one went for a walk. The houses looked empty, their windows like black eyes. I'd mentioned it to Charlie, the very first time we went back to his place.

God, I'd remarked as we stood in the driveway, *it's so quiet out here.*

Good. He'd stood behind me and clapped a hand to my mouth. His skin tasted bitter, secret cigarettes and hotel soap. He pressed his cock against my ass and inched us toward the garage. *Nobody will hear you scream.*

Charlie, I'd giggled. He pressed my forehead against the closed garage door. I felt scared and aroused, an animal in a net. *Oh, please.* I started to shiver; it was December and I wore a dress, a silly little slip that I would never see again. The words sounded different when I said them again. *Oh please.*

He noticed me shaking and gave me his coat. Just like that, he was normal again. He slung an arm around my shoulders. *Let's get you inside, kiddo.* He pinched the fat of my thigh and scrounged for his keys. *You're looking a little maroon.*

I made it back to the club with forty-five minutes until close.

Ignoring the bouncers, I made a beeline for the locker rooms. They were mostly empty at this hour; the remaining girls were out on the floor, hustling the last of the patrons. There were nights when I'd made the brunt of my money in that lawless last hour, when men's need was at its peak. Just one girl sat in the locker room with her shoes kicked off, taking zoomed-in pictures of her feet. She wore a bikini printed with hundred-dollar bills and had a tramp stamp that read: ASHES 2 ASHES.

My and Emeline's corner was empty, as I'd expected. She stayed busy all night. Maybe she was still in the VIP room with Pool Shark Dino, playing Uno or slow-dancing to the Carpenters. Her sushi remained untouched on the counter, the tuna having lost its sheen. I took off her coat and draped it back over her chair. I did my best not to look in the mirror; I was sure I looked crazed, my wig mussed up, my dress askew. I opened my locker, dug around in the mess, and pulled out my Ziploc bag of notes. It had the weight and feel of a Christmas present. Bracing myself, I walked over to Cookie, who was drinking hot chocolate and reading her Kindle.

What's up, buttercup? she asked, eyes on the screen. She sat on her rubber exercise ball, bouncing slightly as she read.

Cookie. I did my best to sound calm, though my belly was full of birds. I felt higher than I'd ever been. *I have something to show you.*

Right now?

Right now.

She glanced up, and I presented her with the Ziploc baggie of notes. She crab-walked her ball to the makeup counter, then dumped out the notes and leafed through them, eyebrows scrunched. *I don't get it,* she said, preemptively smiling. *What's the joke?*

It's not a joke, I said. I made fists to stop my hands from shaking. *It's notes. Th-threatening notes. From Emeline. I found them in my purse, my locker. Even in my car. She's, like, totally obsessed with me. It's getting out of hand.*

Cookie looked baffled. *These are from Emeline?*

I nodded, forcing myself to look in her eyes. *Don't you think they smell like her?*

She brought one of the scraps to her nose. *I couldn't say.*

I know it's her, I said, raising my voice. *I'm certain of it. I'm the only one who's nice to her. She must have gotten . . . too attached.* I held out my fingers. *First she starts stealing from people. Then she starts stalking me.*

Cookie raised an eyebrow. *Stalking you?*

Yes. She stole my used panties, right out of my bag. I waved my hand in the air. *What's next?*

Hmm. Cookie rubbed her jaw, brows furrowed.

Look, I said. *Look.* I led her to our corner and pointed to Emeline's coat, the bulging right pocket. We gathered around her chair, hunched like detectives.

What the fuck am I looking at? Cookie asked, squinting. The hair ball looked like a mouse.

That's my hair, I said. I lifted my wig and held out a chunk for comparison, the same bread crust–brown. I waved it in Cookie's face. *Don't you think that's pretty weird? Like, fucking stalker voodoo shit?*

Cookie leaned forward, examining the hair ball. It frothed over Emeline's coat pocket, looking friendly and alive. She made a move as if to touch it, then, at the last minute, jerked her hand back. *Yes,* she said. *That's pretty weird.* She straightened up, sighing heavily. *OK,* she said, massaging her temples. *OK, OK. Let me get this shit straight.*

I nodded. *Please.*

Are you telling me that you feel afraid?

Yes, I said. *I feel afraid.*

She looked into my eyes, almost imploring me. *And you're sure this is Emeline's doing?*

I didn't blink. *I'm sure.*

There was a long pause in which Cookie studied my face. I tried to keep it as blank as possible. She looked suddenly so much like my mother, sleepy and confused, that I wanted to hug her and ask for a cup of tea, something I'd never asked anyone for. Finally she broke, dusting her hands off. *All right*, she sighed. She avoided my eye. *I'll handle this.*

Thank you, I cried. *Thank you so much.*

Her voice was cold. *Don't mention it.*

I watched her walk away, the Ziploc baggie in hand. I'd never see those notes again; I was told later that management had to keep them on file for "safety reasons." As soon as she was gone, I ripped off my wig, sending bobby pins flying, and stuffed it in my locker. Then I took off my gown, touched up my makeup, and went back on the floor in a sequined bikini. It was the color of pistachio ice cream, the bottoms barely bigger than a postage stamp. I hadn't cashed out for the night, so I figured I might as well work; I was lit up with adrenaline. I felt hyper and profound and couldn't stay still. I cornered a very drunk businessman and perched on his knee. He gave me his cell phone and I wired myself $600 while he watched, smiling dopily.

What a good sport you are, I breathed in his ear. Ruthlessness suited me.

When I returned to the locker room at close, my corner was empty. Emeline's bags were gone, as was her coat. It was as if she had spontaneously combusted. There wasn't even a feather on the floor to mark her departure. I peeked inside her locker to confirm what I knew: it was cleaned out. There was just a touch of glitter on the metal wall. When I shut it, I saw that the name tag on the door had been peeled off to reveal the name of the girl who'd used it before her: Diana.

On my way out, I bumped into Sadie. She looked tired and serious in her wire-frame reading glasses. She wore a baggy black T-shirt that said THIS IS IT. She was sitting cross-legged on the bar, counting the drawer.

Hey, I said. *Emeline is gone.*

Who?

Exactly.

She squinted at me as I walked away. *Who's gone?*

I flashed her a thumbs-up. *Good night.*

Emeline saw me before I saw her. She was sitting on the hood of my car in the parking lot. She hid her face in her hands, shoulders shaking. Her bags were piled on the ground. She made a cartoonishly sad sound as she cried, a literal *boo-hoo-hoo*. When she saw me approaching, she sprang upright.

Baby! she howled. Her face was blotchy, swollen. Her concealer had been wept off and I could see little brown acne scars on her cheekbones and chin.

I instinctively stepped backward. *Hi*, I said, eyeing her. I spoke calmly; she seemed volatile.

She threw her arms in the air. *Hi!* Her suede coat flapped open to reveal a white tank and no bra, her nipples like spurs in the cold; she'd clearly gotten dressed and packed up in a rush. I'd never seen her so sloppy. I wondered if the coat still smelled of me, of Charlie's boozy sweat.

Did you hear the news? she stammered, wringing her hands. *I got f-f-fired.*

I relaxed a bit. *Yes,* I said, *I heard.*

They said someone reported me for harassment. She bit her lip. *But they wouldn't say who.*

Oh.

She raked my face with her eyes. *What am I gonna do now?* She tugged at her earrings as she spoke, little tasteful gold hoops. It was making me anxious; I didn't want her to rip them out. *What the fuck am I gonna do now?*

Emeline, I sighed, feeling my patience fray. This sordid little scene, this vivacious melodrama, it didn't make me pity her; it only pissed me off. I wasn't some dude who would bundle her up and dry her tears with the hem of my sweater. How dare she act like she knew pain. I pictured her driving home to Pac Heights, blasting T-Swift, finding her unconscious daddy doubled up on the floor. Drool on cashmere, stink of bile. Slapping his prickly cheeks until at last he woke up, grumbling, *Honey?*

Maybe then, I thought, you'll really know pain. Maybe then you can lose it, cause a scene, call for help. Save the fireworks for later.

Emeline, I said, trying to keep my voice level, *you're rich. You have nothing to worry about. You're gonna be fine. No matter what you say or do, you're gonna be fine.*

What? She looked puzzled, betrayed. *That's not what I'm talking about. I'm . . .* She choked on her words, her face crinkling with emotion. *I'm lonely.* She clawed at her hair, which looked gray in the dark. *I like it here. Everything else is so boring.* Her voice cracked; she looked down at her feet. *This is something I'm good at.*

I took a deep breath. *You'll find something else.*

She sniffled, trying to compose herself. *I will?*

You will. I studied the lines on her face. Her smeared lipstick looked bloody. *Nothing lasts forever.*

She filled her lungs up with air. *I guess so.* She reached for my wrist, her eyes wide and babyish. *I'll miss you.*

I felt myself recoil. *Why the fuck would you say that?* My voice echoed out across the lot, louder than I realized. The bouncers glanced over, then returned to their reveries. *You don't even know me.*

She dropped my wrist, took a small step back. *I know y-you,* she stammered. There was fear in her eyes.

No, you don't, I snapped. *You really don't. You don't know anything.* I pushed past her to open my car door. I slid in, slammed it, rolled down my window. *OK?*

B-but . . . She looked around in astonishment. *I thought we were friends.* She stood at my window like a beggar, arms crossed, with her hands in her armpits. It was hard to believe, in this moment, that men paid her to blaze. Her shoulders were concave, her face hammy and bloated, her body an afterthought in her misbuttoned coat.

We were never friends, I said. I looked at her and saw Charlie, a snappable heart, someone fragile beneath the bluster and charm. *Friends don't get friends fired.* I don't know why I said this; I guess I wanted to see her reaction, to watch her implode. I wanted to dish out the death blow. Now, this, I thought, is something to cry over.

She was still as she digested my words. She opened and closed her mouth. *It was you?*

I held her gaze, unblinking. *What do you think?*

I waited for her to freak out, to throw her Pleasers at me, to call me a heartless heathen cunt, to threaten to sue. Instead, she just looked at me. Her eyes filled with tears, but this time she was quiet. Even when they started to roll down her face and dampen her collar, she was quiet. I hadn't expected this. There was no venom, only grief. *Why?* she finally managed to squeak.

I shrugged.

She looked so small. *Baby—*

That's not my name. I put my keys in the ignition. I wanted to go now. I was over this scene, this spectacular chick. I wanted her out of my hair. *Take care.*

I backed out of the parking lot. Last that I saw her, she was sitting crisscross on the concrete, hands in her hair, softly weeping. The bouncers had noticed and were hurrying toward her, calling out her name.

I was halfway to Dino's when I noticed the note. It was tucked in the vents of my car's AC, a scrap of pink-lined notebook paper. It looked like it had been there for a while, possibly overnight. Spandau Ballet played on the radio. It was nearly dawn, the sky like forgotten sorbet. Taking both hands off the wheel, I grabbed the note and uncrinkled it. In that same loopy handwriting in faint pencil, it said:

good game

I have no more memory of the night after that. I have no idea how I got home.

I awoke the next day at 2:30 p.m. My mouth tasted like cigarettes, though I couldn't remember smoking any. I'd fallen asleep in my bikini and tights. The sequins left indents all over my thighs; my legs looked like the ridged edge of a butter knife. They reminded me of the summer Mazzy thought she was being abducted by aliens. She would wake up every morning to find little bruises and bumps all over her body.

Do you think they're trying to impregnate me? she'd asked. *Should I be flattered or scared?*

I told her to stop sleeping naked, but it was a hard habit to break. Eventually we uncovered the problem: she was allergic to dust mites. She threw out her down comforter and all was well. I envied Mazzy's problems; they always seemed to go away by dint of will, by the power of positive thinking and free shots. She was the star of her own paperback. The world was her oyster, one big aphrodisiac. I can hear her raspy laughter now.

The boys say I'm real good at shucking, she says. *I sure know how to shuck.*

I got up and walked to the window, shivering. Of course I'd forgotten to plug in my space heater. After the frenzy of last night, my room felt eerie and still. My adrenaline had fizzled out, as had my fury. I felt small and confused, like a kid on the street after the parade has gone by, glitter in the drains. The house was quiet, the dogs nowhere in sight. I wanted something big to happen, if only to distract myself from feeling alone. I threw on a sweatshirt over my bikini, went downstairs, and found Dino sitting at the kitchen table.

Hi, he said. The dogs were asleep at his feet. *I let myself in. The kitchen door was unlocked.*

Oh. I crossed my arms and walked toward the stove. *Want coffee?*

No. He stood up. *I've been trying to reach you all morning.*

Really? I fumbled with the kettle. *My phone's dead.* This wasn't technically true; it was buried at the bottom of my bag.

I bet. He came toward me and put his hands on my shoulders, turning me around. *I'm sorry about last night.*

I took my hand off the kettle, remembering the gnarly swirl of the last twenty-four hours. *Oh.*

He squeezed my shoulders. *I should have called to say I wasn't coming.*

Oh...

I know we had plans, but I got caught up in work stuff. I can't tell you what. By the time I was finished, it was too late to go out. I went home and crashed. He audibly swallowed. *I missed you.*

Uh-huh. I leaned against the kitchen counter, studying his face. He looked tired and old. His skin was the color I remembered, no longer orange. I tried to picture the man Emeline and I had danced for last night, but his face was suddenly grainy.

Baby, he said. *I want you to know that I wanted to come last night. I wanted to see you.*

I've heard that before, I murmured, looking down.

I know, he said. *I fucked up. I didn't mean to ghost you. I'm really not that type of guy.* He swallowed, brows furrowed. He looked like he was asking me for money. *Do you believe me?*

I looked at his seasick eyes, the lines in his forehead I'd always found sexy. His hair was dirty, dark with grease. He wore the same thing he'd worn on Saturday, the blue jeans and white eyelet blouse that he'd folded over the back of a chair before fucking me. *I do*, I said. *I do.*

Oh, good. He wrapped his arms around me and crushed me to his chest. God, he smelled good. He smelled like amber and daddy. He smelled like a Reno casino and a neighborhood dive. I wanted to live here, smooshed in his arms. I would give up this big house with its weird sounds and good light just to sublet the space between his belt buckle and throat. Here, nothing could hurt me. He buried his nose in my neck. *Baby*, he said. *God is good.*

Yes, I said, though I'd never once heard him talk about God before. Was that what he was doing in the weeks he went away? Did he leave me for God? That was way worse than a younger woman. How could I possibly measure up? I was puny and flawed, I had zits and poor impulse control. I ate candy for dinner. *Yes, yes, yes.*

He stroked my hair. *I'm sorry.*

I squeezed harder to confirm what I already knew: He was real. He was here in the kitchen we'd dirtied together, filled with our laughter, the kitchen that had always smelled of smashed plantains and Bustelo espresso. Now it smelled like the lavender cleaning products Ophelia used. *It's OK.*

He pulled away, smiling. *Wanna go to the beach?*

I looked at the sky, already leaking light. *Now?*

Why not? I can drive us.

But won't it be cold?

He waved one hand. *I'll keep you warm.*

Well . . . I couldn't think of any other excuses. *Give me five minutes, OK?*

He was already walking out the door, the dogs trotting behind him. *Five minutes starts now,* he called. *I'll be in the car.*

So we went to the beach. It was achingly cold, the wind bladelike and cruel. The ocean was the color of concrete. We hooked arms and walked up and down the length of the shore, hunched into our coats. He wore a yellow silk scarf tied babushka-style under his chin and leather motorcycle gloves. I wore my puffer jacket and a baseball hat I'd stolen from Dream House, embroidered with the words SEX SYMBOL. Sand got in our teeth. We talked as we strolled, keeping the conversation light. He told me things I pretended not to know: he was the oldest of seven, he was a self-taught cook. There were some things that were new to me. As a teen he'd wanted to be a rock star, as a kid he ate nothing but Filet-O-Fish. I hoarded these tidbits, privately hurt that they hadn't come up in our first go at love. What else had he hidden from me?

When we couldn't stand the cold any longer, we ran to the car. I noticed his limp. *Last one there's a rotten egg!* he called. I ran as fast as I could, but I knew he would beat me. When I asked whose car it was, he shrugged. *My colleague's. She lets me use it sometimes.* I felt irrationally furious that he worked with a woman. *Who is she?* I wanted to snap. I didn't dare to inquire about the nature of their arrangement or where they both worked. I just smiled and said, *How sweet.*

We drove aimlessly through the city, the heater on high. We drove for an excuse to keep talking. We spoke of the things that are only of interest to the newly in-love, our quirks and firsts and horoscopes. *This month I'm supposed to reconnect with old flames . . .* It was suddenly dark out; despite the rolled-up windows, we could feel the fog in our throats. We drove through Golden Gate Park, Bernal Heights, Russian Hill. We had nowhere to be, and instead of feeling sad, it felt lucky. We drove through the Tenderloin and saw an old man walking down the street. Every few steps, he would pull a bullwhip from his coat and crack it in the air. The sound of it shone in the night like a gunshot. *Damn!* someone yelled from a doorway. *You almost blew my pussy off!* We laughed so hard Dino had to pull over.

Jesus fucking Christ, he said. *This city is cursed.*

No, I said. *It's magical.*

He looked out the window at the tent cities and street queens, human-shaped bundles of blankets, junkies cuddled on doorsteps. *Then it's a dark sort of magic.*

While we were cruising down California, I felt my phone buzz: another email from Nobody. For the first time I had no real desire to read it. I was busy. I looked up at Dino, absent-mindedly touching his nose as he drove, and turned off my phone.

Who was that? he asked. *Jealous boyfriend?*

You wish. I put my hand on his thigh. *It's Nobody.*

When at last we got hungry, we went to a dumpling spot deep in the Avenues, where the air tasted salty at all times of day. The restaurant looked like someone's shabby living room. All the old ladies there knew Dino. They gave us free dumplings to go with our soup, chive-and-lamb packages leaky with juice. They were so good I saw God, just like that, strolling past. We drank tea that tasted like paper and ate gigantic bowls of broth thick with noodles. *It's actually one long noodle*, Dino said. He insisted on paying and left a grandiose tip. *Byebye, Daniel!* the ladies called as we walked out the door, into the night. The fog hit us like a fist.

Daniel? I asked.

He smiled, suddenly sheepish. *It's easier than Dino. Someone heard Daniel and it just sorta stuck.*

Gotcha, I said. *Can I call you Daniel?*

He leaned down to kiss me, our full bellies bumping. *Absolutely fucking not.*

It was 9:30 p.m. when he finally drove me home. He went slow down my street, as if he didn't know which house was mine—at one time, ours. Then he idled out front, heater still on. At night, the powder-blue paint looked black.

Well, I said. I didn't move from my seat. *This is me.*

This is you.

I had a lot of fun today. Everything I said sounded stupid. *Thanks for the ride.*

Anytime. He turned and took my face in both hands. He stared into my eyes, his expression suddenly dark. It was a look I scarcely recognized, this mix of uncertainty and male shyness. On his face, it looked strange, like a uniform he'd been forced to wear. *Are you ready now?*

For what?

Instead of answering, he kissed me. He kissed me so hard

and so long that my lips started to hurt. Butterflies mutinied in my belly. They picketed, they unionized, they moved away and started families. When at last he pulled back, he was smiling. It relieved me to see him at ease. My kiss was the cure, the skeleton key. He was the Casanova I knew, the man who got lucky. He had no pores, tight pants, and a bounty of light. As he aged, he got sexier. How could such a man exist? Why wasn't he in Los Angeles, getting paid to tan, or in New York, cutting deals? Why was he wasting his light on a girl like me in the smutty streets of San Francisco? I'd never know.

Jeez, he said, dragging his thumb over his bottom lip. It was fat like a plum. *Are you real?*

I think so.

He sighed and placed a hand on my belly, full of soup. *I guess I'd better go now.*

Where? Now it was my turn to feel fearful.

I've got some business to attend to.

What sort of business?

He just smiled. *I'll call you. OK?*

OK. I gathered my things and slid onto the sidewalk. I carried my leftover soup in a plastic bag that had a red rose printed on it with the words THANK YOU VERY MUCH. *Wait*, I said. I ran around to his side of the car. *Can I have one more kiss?*

Baby, he said, laughing. *Of course.* He rolled down his window and leaned toward me, steadying himself with one hand on the steering wheel. We kissed like movie stars, like castaways. We kissed like the economy depended on it. My pussy felt like a neon beer sign buzzing on the corner. I pulled away first, feeling dizzy. I picked up my soup, looking at the words on the bag. *Thank you very much*, I murmured. Were those the magic words?

He rubbed his jaw and smiled like a dope, looking me up and down. *God*, he said, more to himself than to me. *I'm a goner.* Then he straightened up and gripped the wheel. *See ya soon, OK?*

I stood on the sidewalk and watched his car drive away. I stayed there even after his taillights had faded into the night. I truly didn't know if I would see him again. If you had asked me right then, standing out in the cold, I could've gone either way. I could've picked the petals off a daisy like we did in elementary school: *He loves me, he loves me not . . . He's coming back, he's gone for good . . .* I wanted to believe him. His kiss felt so sincere. It was different from our first attempt at romance. This time around, we were savagely present. We were carnal and thoughtful. We didn't try to mask our fear; we kissed around it like a canker sore. I felt like there was nothing I wouldn't do for this man. At the same time I felt afraid of him, his bulk, his secrecy.

Standing there, still tasting him, I felt a gladness edged in sorrow, plus a tremulous anxiety. I knew this was the price I had to pay for falling in love again. I got to do what everyone wanted but no one could. I got to go back to the very beginning, to the melted days of yore. I was Bambi-legged and pie-eyed again in the face of his want, the Eden of his jeans. It was blotto nights and tender mornings, pointless walks and pineapple juice, our lips sore to touch from 24/7 kisses. It was everything good and nothing boring, the world busting with light. It was all the clichés rinsed and wrung out for use: *I want you so bad, this is a dream come true, you are the one, baby baby.*

Would I do better this time? I hoped so. The first time around I hadn't been ready; I'd let love go to waste, like seltzer gone flat. This time around I knew better. I was hungry in a novel way. My heart was a pie left to cool on the windowsill—have some no please I insist. It was meant to be cut into. This time around, I'd be humble and hopeful, though surely just as dumb. I wouldn't go into our romance with the expectation of wholeness; I would accept the self-shattering as the fair tax of love. I'd bring a basket to collect all the pieces and if one or two got lost in the shuffle, oh well. We lost things every single day. I was ready to be broken.

I picked up my soup and walked down the little concrete path into the yard. God, the lawn was scrubby, all dandelions and weeds. I wondered if I could find a sub with a green thumb to bring it back to life. I paused on the stoop, looking into the windows. I could tell that Ophelia was home. The lights were on and music was playing, Roy Orbison, Prince. I could smell something garlicky cooking, full of vitamins and minerals. I saw it all before it happened, a happy prophecy: Ophelia dancing in the kitchen, barefoot. Her hair soft and clean in one long braid down the middle of her back. The dogs content under the table, gnawing the bones she had given them. She would throw herself on me as soon as I entered. *I'm sorry, I'm so sorry, God, I'm a bitch. Can you ever forgive me? I'm a wreck, I'm a mess.* I would say I'm sorry too. We would hug and talk over each other.

Love, she'd say bashfully, *it just makes me crazy.*

I know, I'd say. *I know I know.*

Then we would sit down to eat the meal she'd prepared. The dogs would sit with us, each with her own chair and place setting. I would touch each of my friends on the forehead and smile. *God*, I'd say, *is good.* Then we'd dig in, eating our dinner with our hands tied behind our backs. It was a game to see who could finish first. You had to lick your plate clean to be considered a winner. This was what I saw as I loitered in the garden, my soup congealing in the nighttime air, my little piggies turning blue. Most or all of it would come true, depending on your perspective.

The next morning I awoke to three different voicemails from unknown numbers.

It was early, not just for strippers but for everyone else too. The sky was still pink, Ophelia sleeping beside me in Dino's big bed. I put on her coat and went to get my coffee and donuts from 7-Eleven. I played the voicemails as I walked.

The first one was recorded at 2:07 a.m. The speaker's voice was frail, anodyne, winded. It reminded me of Truman Capote. The speaker took long pauses between most every word. In retrospect I realize they may have been drunk.

Good morning, Miss. Or evening. Please forgive me for calling. I'm trying . . . to gather my thoughts. I pictured this literally, the speaker scooping them up like rubber duckies in a bathtub. *You haven't answered my most recent emails. Of course I can't blame you. I always knew you'd . . . move on. You have no more use for me now and I understand why. But I must say . . . something has been eating at me. It's a question I'm, well, dying to ask. I apologize in advance if you find it, um, crass . . . but . . . if you really were to do S, what would you miss most?* There was a burst of static, like they'd dropped their phone. *For myself, I'd have to say reading. Also, the beach. I really would miss that. Or maybe—*

The voicemail cut off. They'd reached their time limit.

The second message was four seconds long. *I almost forgot to say happy birthday*, the same frail voice said, a little louder this time. It was as if they'd taken a shot between voicemails, gaining some gusto. *Happy birthday, Mistress.*

The third message was from a number with a Los Angeles area code. *Howdy, Ruthie!* There was music and laughter in the background, the sound of glasses clinking. *It's Mazzy! Sorry if it's loud in here. My phone's dead, so I'm borrowing some dude's.* A male voice squawked, causing Mazzy to giggle. I found myself smiling too, picturing her in a merciless tube dress. *Sorry, not SOME dude, my GOOD FRIEND, is that better? Jesus Christ. Anyways, I know it's late, I just wanted to say happy birthday. I love you forever and hope you—stop! I'm almost done!—have a fabulous day. I think of you often. Remember: you're powerful and wanted and deserving of love and—oh my fucking god, I'm done! Happy now? Jesus. Anyway, I miss you, Ruthie. Call me, OK? Buh-bye.*

I saved Mazzy's message and deleted the other two. Then I put my phone in my pocket and kept walking, arms crossed against the morning chill. An odd brew of emotions bloomed in my chest: I felt happy but sad, woozy and blushing. It occurred to me that although I told Dino he was my first love, it was actually Mazzy. She'd come along first, in that diehard way of girlhood friends, and he'd come along after. She'd been with me since I was sixteen, crying over boys who didn't know my name. We practiced kissing on grapefruits, we showered together like children. I still had the number to her family's landline memorized.

I hadn't told Ophelia that my birthday was today. I was turning twenty-eight. Was that old or young? I didn't know. When I was twenty-three, I wore heart-shaped stickers on my face. When I was twenty-five, I fell in love. I only drank tequila and pineapple juice, as if that said something important about me. At twenty-seven, I grieved and made bank. I felt tired when I pictured it, twenty-eight years contained in my body, an overstuffed carry-on. At the same time, it seemed like a sexy number, rounded and lush. Young for a writer, old for a gymnast, the perfect age for a bartender or anonymous fuck. I would throw away my flavored condoms and start reading about Bitcoin. I would buy satin sheets and retinol creams and carbonated water. I'd be sleek but fun, poised but game. I would dance with my eyes closed alone in a bar. All my shirts would be see-through, chopsticks in my hair. I couldn't ever be embarrassed. From now on, I'd sleep naked with the windows ajar; that felt very twenty-eight. I took comfort in remembering what Simon had said, his eyes wet with meaning: *You're still so young!*

As I walked, I thought about my answer to Nobody's question. What would I miss most about being alive? It felt like bad luck to say what aloud. Instead I kept my answer close to my heart, like a locket containing my lover's hair. It felt good to hold it there. It was both a secret and not, both hush-hush and public. I tried to imagine what my loved ones would say. Ophelia would miss sudoku, Dino would miss lingerie, Mazzy would miss Aperol. Or maybe Ophelia would miss yoga, Dino would miss ice cream, Mazzy would miss trashy paperback novels. The things we loved most were both elemental and petty. You squeezed them while you slept, these scraps. They made your body look beautiful, like the perfect accessory. Dog's kisses, blue jeans. No one was dumb enough to say justice or family. No, we lived for Halloween and yard sales and driving at dusk with the windows rolled down. We lived for honeymoons and midnight snacks, blow jobs in chain hotels. We lived for paper valentines. It was garbage, but beloved. *The devil's in the details*, my mom used to say as she stared at the TV. So too, it seemed, was heaven, or something just as good.

I was doing a load of laundry when I found the last note.

It was later that evening. I'd spent the day at the pool, a birthday treat to myself. I'd showered at home and my hair was wet, making lines down the back of my shirt. Dino still hadn't called me, but I wasn't worried. I knew he would call when the time was right. I felt this truth like a bellyache; I carried my faith like a pencil behind one ear, like a diaphragm in my purse. Ophelia was out to dinner with the feeding-fetish client and the dogs were in the doorway, napping. The note came tumbling out of my puffer jacket, along with a fortune cookie wrapper and handful of sand. On the back of a receipt, in loopy red ink, it read:

love u

I studied the other side of the receipt: $36 at Happy Family Gourmet, plus a $20 tip, dated last night at 8:30 p.m. That was the name of the dumpling spot out in the Avenues. Dino must have slipped the receipt in my pocket when I wasn't looking. I stared at the note, feeling the back of my neck prick. Different thoughts flew at me: Dino's sketchy friendship with the managers of the strip club, the spare car keys I'd given him early on in our relationship, the love letters he used to write for me on junk mail and take-out menus. I still had his grocery list, tucked into a drawer, but at this point I didn't feel the need to compare the two artifacts. The truth of their authorship hit me like a sneeze.

I smoothed out the receipt, then folded it, origami-style, into a little paper crane. I went upstairs to the room that used to be Dino's and put it on the dresser, next to his Fabergé egg. I thought of my Ziploc baggie of notes, locked away in the manager's desk. I wished, in that moment, that I could comb through them. Maybe I'd shake them out over my head like so many dollar bills. A sense of lightness spread through my body. I'd been wrong all along: He hadn't gone away, not really. He hadn't left me high and dry. He'd been with me, obliquely, like fluff on my sweater or a bruise on my thigh. It was like they said at church: There were hints of Him everywhere, in green lights and blue hours, in the cherry blossoms (so early!) shed across the concrete. You were never alone. You just had to know where to look. Once you knew, you could see that the world was made up of secrets, hidden rooms and second names. The secret truth of the notes had been clear all along, like a phone number written on a bathroom wall (*Call Diana for a Good Time . . .*). All those nights I'd spent waiting, he'd been waiting too.

Thinking of the notes, I felt happy. I felt so happy I could die. I pictured them filling my locker, spilling onto the floor, roses on a hotel bed. I didn't feel scared. At the end of the day, obsession was not so different from love. They both gave boning to our flouncy lives. They were twins in a porno; why settle for one when you could have both? It felt good to be the object of someone's obsession. This way, he couldn't forget me. This way, I couldn't leave him, no matter how hard I tried. I was in him and he was in me, despite the long lonely nights. Be still and know that I am with you, oh, baby baby baby. Mazzy would laugh if she could see me now, this tremulous romantic.

This is not the Ruth I know, she'd say. *Ruthie, have you gone soft?*

Maybe so. I was soft now, easeful, prepped for love. Of course, I was still scared.

I went downstairs to the laundry room and put in a new load of clothes, all my dirty lingerie, stockings and teddies and garters and thongs. I used the rest of Dino's Italian soap, the kind that smelled like strawberries. The dogs trailed behind me, out of the laundry room and into the yard. They chased each other through the flower beds until they got tired and dropped down in the doorway. I hung the first load on the clothesline, but the fog came too quick. The dogs ran into the kitchen, looking back to see if I'd follow. Instead I stood in the garden, bare-shouldered, O-mouthed. I felt tiny and holy. The night air smelled of jasmine and gasoline. The fog draped around my body like a boa, like a hug from a man. It was heavy and wet. I wanted to see how long I could stand there, how much I could bear. The girls whined softly from the kitchen, watching me disappear.

ACKNOWLEDGMENTS

Thank you to the incomparable Annie DeWitt and Mary Alice Stewart for shepherding this book into the world and believing in me. Thank you to Milo Walls for their fierce vision and for dealing with me so gracefully; thank you to everyone at FSG for embracing this scrappy rat and taking a chance. FSG is truly my dream publishing home. Thank you to Kishani Widyaratna and the rest of the Fourth Estate team. Thank you to Kerry Cullen and Jim Rutman for being the very first to believe in me. Thank you to Jenkin van Zyl, Cyrus Dunham, Emily Clancy, Jo Livingstone, Kyle De-Medio, Harriet Clark, Vivvyanne Forevermore, Lara Prior-Palmer, Arlen Levy, Franke Leasing, Marissa Leitman, Jelle Hardison, Myles Cooper, Wren Farrell, Tom and Lupe Eichelberger, Anya Prisk, Izaak Schlossman, Adam Schorin, and Lisa Borst, whose words of kindness and encouragement brought me out of my darkness. Thank you to Fantasy Makers, a strange and dreamlike place that lives on forever in my mind. Thank you to Aunt Charlie's Lounge, my swirly pink home. Thank you to my parents, my very favorite and most caring rats. Thank you to CC for teaching me about love and piggies; this book could not exist without you and our love. The years spent writing this next to you in North Beach were some of my happiest ever. I think of them daily. Thank you to Petunia Tutu, Annette, Harriet, and Momo, for the kisses. Thank you always to Maria Silk, my forever wife. I love you so much it renders me speechless.

A Note About the Author

Brittany Newell is a writer and performer. The author of the novel *Oola*, she has had work published in *Granta*, *n+1*, *The New York Times*, *Joyland*, *Dazed*, and *Playgirl*. She lives in San Francisco.